IN REAL LIFE

Published by Tuttle Publishing, an imprint of Periplus Editions (HK) Ltd.

www.tuttlepublishing.com

Copyright © 2014 Lawrence Tabak

Library of Congress Cataloging-in-Publication Data in Process

ISBN 978-0-8048-4478-9 hc
ISBN 978-0-8048-4521-2 pb

Distributed by

North America, Latin America & Europe
Tuttle Publishing
364 Innovation Drive
North Clarendon, VT 05759-9436 U.S.A.
Tel: 1 (802) 773-8930
Fax: 1 (802) 773-6993
info@tuttlepublishing.com
www.tuttlepublishing.com

Asia Pacific
Berkeley Books Pte. Ltd.
61 Tai Seng Avenue #02-12
Singapore 534167
Tel: (65) 6280-1330
Fax: (65) 6280-6290
inquiries@periplus.com.sg
www.periplus.com

First edition
17 16 15 14   10 9 8 7 6 5 4 3 2 1   1407RP

Printed in China

TUTTLE PUBLISHING® is a registered trademark of Tuttle Publishing, a division of Periplus Editions (HK) Ltd.

IN REAL LIFE

LAWRENCE TABAK

TUTTLE Publishing

Tokyo | Rutland, Vermont | Singapore

Dedication

To my gamers, Josh and Zach

Acknowledgments

This book was inspired and informed by my two gaming sons, Josh and Zach. The story was wisely tightened and the writing consistently improved by the careful editorial work of my agent, Kate Epstein. For help with cultural details and transliterations, as well as mathematical insights, I'm indebted to Professor Ki-Suk Lee, Department of Mathematics Education, Korea National University of Education. Careful and helpful readings were provided by a number of kind souls, including my wife Diane, Josh Tabak, and Stephanie Carmichael. Last, but far from least, to the editorial team at Tuttle, led by Terri Jadick, who guided this project with care, sensitivity and enthusiasm.

Part I
KANSAS

1.

School called. Again. Unexcused absence, blah, blah, blah. My interception rate on these calls is eighty-four percent (This is Seth's father, how can I help you?), but they had called Dad while I was at Mom's. So Dad calls Mom and pretty soon I can hear the screaming right through my headset even though I'm in my bedroom with the door closed. And I have a good headset. She's getting so worked up that DTerra, my best friend, picks it up over my mic and says, "What the hell is that?"

"Nothing," I mutter and then hit mute. I love the feeling before a game starts. The buzz of adrenaline, the little turning in the stomach. I'm determined not to let a little parental meltdown break the mood. "I HAVE talked to him! I've talked to him until I'm blue in the face! YOU talk to him!"

"Sounded like an orc attack."

Despite the screaming I laugh. DTerra's real name is Donald Terrance but I usually just call him DT. He lives five hundred miles away in Moorhead, Minnesota, which he says to think of as a twin city of Fargo, if the twins were deformed dwarfs.

"Don't you yell at *me*," my mom is yelling into the phone. "Friday was your day. It was *your* responsibility to see that he went to school."

Actually, I did go to school. I just left at lunch. All I had that afternoon was a study hall, gym and a review session in AP physics, which I already understood. I hadn't really missed anything.

"OK," DTerra says. "You ready to make our move?"

I say, "One minute." I actually like to draw out the pre-game excitement. And making the other team wait a couple minutes. It sets the stage. Shows them who's in control.

Plus I haven't looked at Brit Leigh's Facebook page for maybe twenty minutes. She changes her picture about that often, so it's always worth checking. If she knew how many times a week I visited her homepage I bet she'd have me arrested for stalking. Last time I looked she had 149 friends, which includes just about our entire sophomore class. It's easy to remember because 149 happens to be the 35th largest prime number, and we have 35 kids in our English class. Anyway, the point is if I had any balls at all I would at least be one of those 149. But I don't, and I'm not.

"Seth! Let's take these guys now!"

We're scheduled to play a two-man game against a team from Germany with a rating a little higher than ours. We've been waiting to play these guys for weeks. If we win, we'll move up into the top ten on our server.

"One second," I say.

Brit has added a picture of her, a friend and two senior guys goofing around. The four of them are draped all over each other and leaning into the camera and acting high or drunk. Which is possible. Even goofy she looks pretty amazing. Brit and I have been in the same school since middle school. I think we took geometry together. But I never really noticed her until this year.

It started near the beginning of the year. Our history teacher, Mr. Hobson, has this way of talking to the girls in the class. At least certain girls. I'm not sure if it would be more or less creepy if he was younger or more handsome, but he's an old guy, at least as old as my dad, and when you get up close to him you can see craters in his cheeks and his breath is pretty awful. Anyway, he'll call on girls in class and say stuff like, "Brit. I bet you know who the Continental Congress assigned to write the first draft of the Constitution. Because I'm sure you weren't out carousing like half the girls in this school, dolled up like streetwalkers, doing God-knows-what on a school night."

And Brit, instead of blushing or putting on that "OMG" face and looking at her friends in disbelief, she just stared him in the eye and said, "Mr. Hobson, are you asking me about James Madison or are you asking me about my social life?"

Everyone started laughing and now it was Mr. Hobson who was blushing. Brit and I have American History and English together and if it weren't for her presence, I'd probably have missed so many classes I'd be flunked out by now.

Actually she knows who I am, I'm pretty sure. She said hello to me once at the mall food court. She was with a bunch of girls and I was with my mother. So I was walking as fast as I could and looking at the ground. The thing is, you have to be someone, do something, before the girls pay attention. So my brother, for years he spends three hours a day shooting hoops in the front drive. It looked like some kind of boredom torture to me, standing in the corner with a rack of balls, shooting the same damn shot over and over. Of course, Garrett would probably say the same about playing twelve hours of Starfare a day. But then he got to be a famous star on the basketball team with every girl in school worshipping him.

I pick up the morning paper and there it is on page one.

LOCAL BOY WINS WORLD STARFARE TOURNAMENT, $30K

Brit is waiting for me outside of homeroom. Everyone is high-fiving me and patting me on the back. She says, "Seth! That was so cool. I hear you're going to buy a Porsche."

I don't care if everyone is watching or not. I step in close and wrap my arms around her and pull her towards me. Then our lips are meeting and she's kissing me back and sighing.

"Seth! What the hell?"

DT is always a little wired. It's not like they're going to start the match without us. So I tell him that I've got to check my broadband speed, even though it's fine.

I wish I knew exactly what it is about Brit. It's not like she's the school goddess or something. She's got normal, brown hair. Cut shoulder length like most of the girls. Wears the same sorts of nice clothes. But she's different too. She has this sort of confidence. When she's standing up in front of the class, like she did last week, giving a report on some old poem…it's like those moments in a movie where the music wells up and everyone's leaning forward. She shakes her hair and then brushes a strand back behind her right ear. And my pulse doubles and I can feel something electric glowing inside of me and spreading through my body….

Just before I tell DTerra I'm ready, my mom starts pounding

on my door so hard my Starfare Horizons poster starts shaking like a fan is blowing. Luckily I have a lock, but it's one of those you can pop with a little metal stick, if you work it around a couple minutes. At least it gives me plenty of warning.

"Not now!" I shout.

"Your father is on the phone and you'd better talk to him. And I mean now! Anyway you know I HATE talking through a locked door. Why do you have to lock it anyway?"

Well, that's pretty obvious, I'm thinking.

"Seth!"

"I'll call him back on my cell," I shout. The game is about to start and DTerra is telling me what he's going to be doing and it takes total concentration. I tell my parents it's like when my older brother was starting on the basketball team, dribbling down the floor. Would they stand up and scream, "Garrett! You forgot to pick up your dirty socks like you promised" or "Garrett! Have you finished your English essay?" But no matter how many times I explain it, they just don't get it.

Mom mutters something but I can tell she's giving up, so now I just have to get my head back into the game. That's why I dream about getting away from all this school and family crap and just focusing on what I need to do to make it to the top. And making it to the top means making it to Korea. E-sports are huge in Korea, with twenty-four-hour TV broadcasts and teams that train like madmen. The top guys are pulling in six-figure money. I don't talk about it, because people would think I'm crazy, but someday, if I can cut through all the crap that's holding me back, that's going to be me.

Then my room and my mom and school disappear and the game starts. My hand is dancing over the keyboard, my mouse is clicking like a Geiger counter. Every extraneous thought is gone and I'm deep inside the glowing screen, mining resources and figuring out how to counter the German team's troop development. As I'm clicking I'm shouting out orders to DT and marching across a landscape of spiked mountains and fire-glowing valleys. A skirmish starts and the screen lights up with explosions as we trade cannon blasts. I yell for DT to finish them off while I check the spybots I've sent to the western quadrant. My whole being is now tunneled into the world on the screen, every neuron in my brain is firing for one purpose. Another hard-fought, glorious victory.

2.

Thank God, back at Dad's. He's on the road; I'm on the Starfare warpath. For once pumping in decent hours, really getting into the groove. I'm taking four AP courses, two are a breeze, two are a pain, but I've got sixth period study hall, which means early release. I scamper across the parking lot, between all the hand-me-down Acuras and BMWs, cut through two rows of McMansions on a bike path and I'm plugging in at Dad's condo. For dinner I take a fifteen-minute break, scoot around the corner and I'm at KenTacoHut—my favorite restaurant. American, Mexican and Italian under one roof.

For months all I've been thinking about is this online tournament that gives away seats at Nationals. At my age, the top Korean kids are already challenging the pros. If I can't even make U.S. Nationals then I'm worse than awful. Rather than dream about becoming a pro-gamer, I might as well plan on winning *American Idol*. And most dogs sing better than me.

As the day approaches, my classes get longer and longer while all I can think about is getting back to the computer. It seems like a year before we get to the Friday of the weekend tournament. The teacher is blabbering on, something about World War I. As soon as he says the word "battle" Starfare games start echoing in my head like pop music worms. I close my eyes and I can see the flashes of a Starfare firefight, and feel a glimmer of the excitement of battle. When the last bell sounds I'm out of there like there's a fire and jog all the way home. The computer takes what feels like an hour to boot up and the game queue is endless. I run to the fridge, grab a Pepper, and then, at last, my game is up and I'm back where I belong.

Saturday, 10 a.m. and I'm finally sitting down in my bedroom at Dad's, waiting for the first round draws to be announced. I'm so wired I can't sit still. I get up, walk around the room, check to see if the draw has been posted yet, get up, walk around. All I can think about is winning the seat at Nationals in San Diego and getting the free entry and hotel room that goes with it.

Once I get into the first round, I'm actually calmer than I was when I was waiting.

I get lucky and they pick one of my favorite maps, Horizons, and I'm quickly in the zone, coasting by a half-dozen decent players. My sixth qualie match goes fast so I'm a bit ahead of the rest of the draw, queued up, waiting for my next opponent my right leg bouncing up and down like it has a muscle spasm. I'm getting so close, just three more wins. I'm all nerves and Starfare buzz, trying to calm down by scanning one of the Starfare message boards when I'm startled by an IM on my personal account in all caps:

Stompazer: HEY NOOB READY TO GET STOMPED

I don't even bother replying. This guy Stompazer has been stalking me for over a year. Ever since I got written up in this computer magazine. They did a story on whether the next generation of American players could produce a Starfarer who could compete with the Koreans. I talked to a reporter on the phone for a few minutes and the story itself was pretty lame. But this guy Stompazer thinks he's going to be the LeBron James of Starfare and is pissed off that they didn't mention him in the story. He's a couple of years older than me and I have no problem saying he's a decent player. But he has way too much time on his hands. Just about every day he's IMing or emailing me a challenge, saying how he's going to knock my butt around or grind me into little pieces or stomp my ass. And that's the clean stuff. I've changed my handle a couple of times but someone must be feeding him info because he just pops up and laughs at me for trying to avoid him.

Stompazer: BETTER PUT ON A HELMET ASSWIPE CUZ IM GOING TO KICK YOUR HEAD IN

When I pop up the tournament screen I mutter a few choice swear words, because there it is. I've drawn him in the round of eight, game to start in three minutes.

Stompazer: THE GREAT AMERICAN HOPE IS GOING DWN

I try to ignore this guy because I'm pretty sure he's seriously deranged. And he's spent all this time researching me and tracking me online. I'm pretty sure he knows where I live. All I know about him, besides he's nuts, is that he lives somewhere in California and is a senior in high school. He's had a few good wins, but so far I wouldn't say he's done anything to make people think he was going to take the Starfare world by storm. I decide if I'm going to play him, I'm going to have to acknowledge him.

ActionSeth: Hey
Stompazer: THAT ALL U GOT TO SAY...U R SUCH A PUSSY

I'd bet anything that Stomp is a complete loser IRL. Not that my real life is all wins. But at least I'm not spending all my free time harassing people online. I shut down the IM and concentrate on the tournament clock. We've played one-on-one ten times and he lets me know every day that he's up 6-4. What I've never told him is he's so obnoxious that in half those games I just tanked to get rid of him.

But this one counts. A lot. I try not to think about how painful it would be to get this close and go down. To Stomp. But as soon as the start screen lights up, my nerves are gone. As always, the action is frantic. For about twenty minutes it looks like a draw to me. But Mr. Stomp doesn't know a couple of things. First, I've been training harder than I ever have in my life. And I know this Horizon map like the way my tongue knows the back of my teeth. As we get into the midgame it's pretty clear that I've got the upper hand when it comes to knowing the little quirks, taking the shortcuts, squeezing all those extra resources. My material advantage just grows and grows and the more I relax, the more I'm able to press him. I take special pleasure in a furious battle outside his home base, knowing that I've got superior numbers. I'm shooting fireballs so fast the screen looks like a strobe light, generating a rumble of sound effects like a Kansas thunderstorm. Normally you're way too busy to message your opponent but Stomp starts throwing up little IMs on the game screen, stuff like I'm a lucky suck. I just smile to myself and concentrate on finishing him off. It doesn't take long.

I know Stomp will do everything in his power to stalk me if I stay online, so I shut down the computer and soak it in. Next weekend, it's the final four. I'm really happy with that, because I'm not getting in the kind of hours I think I need to really take it up a notch. During my best week, I'm getting around thirty-five hours. The Koreans pros, who absolutely dominate, they're training twelve to fourteen hours a day, six days a week. And they're working these maps as a team, a dozen of them just pounding on it hour after hour, sharing every little quirk and advantage they stumble on. Even if I had fourteen hours a day I couldn't compete with that.

Somehow I get through another week of school while all I can think about is the upcoming final rounds. The way I took out Stomp has my confidence level up a notch, but the waiting on Saturday is still excruciating. I'm getting a bunch of IMs from my online friends, wishing me luck. It's a good thing I have a heavy-duty office chair, because I'm rocking it back and forth like I'm on horseback. Then the clock is ticking down to zero and from the first mouse click I just fall into this incredible groove. It's hard to explain. I watched my brother hit seven three-pointers one night and I asked him how it felt and he just shrugged and said, "Sometimes you just know everything you throw up is going down the hole."

I'm in the same zone. Everything just flows. In the battles my mouse is clicking so fast that it's almost a solid noise and I'm gliding over the map like a marble on glass. I dominate the semis and in the finals I don't think I miss a single shot and squeak out a really close match against a well-known player, AceMaxer. Just like that, I've got a free seat at Nationals right after school gets out. The winner of the individual event at Nationals gets $30,000.

All my online friends, like DTerra, they're IMing me, screaming stuff like, "AWESOME DUDE!" and "NEXT STOP NATIONAL CHAMP!"

When things settle down it's just me and DTerra.

```
DTerra: man 1d give anything to b there
ActionSeth: so come
DTerra: no way im going to qualify
ActionSeth: come a day early and play the qualies and
    grind in
DTerra: u think I got a chance
ActionSeth: sure... u said your old man travels a lot
ActionSeth: so get some frequent flier points...u can
    crash at my hotel, cheap trip
DTerra: OK will work on it...gtg...cu
```

I shut down the IM and sit there in a bit of a daze. Thinking about what I need to do to win that $30,000 and, of course, what I do with the money. First thing would be the ultimate gaming platform. I waste at least an hour a week browsing for a new rig I couldn't possible afford. Until I win Nationals. That will leave about $27,000. Which I'll need to cover my expenses while I train for the pro circuit. I can finish high school doing an online program, which costs a couple grand. I've checked it out completely and it's totally legit. If you're a famous teen actor or sports star, it's pretty much automatic. If I'm going to be the first American to break into the pro game in a big way, it just makes sense that I'm going to have to train harder than any American ever has. Especially when you know how hard the Korean pros are working and how the best of them peak at age nineteen or twenty.

Then I plan what I'm going to say when I'm interviewed for Computer Gaming World after I win Nationals. When they ask me what's the most important source of my success. I picture myself standing on a stage holding an oversized check for $30,000. I have the answer all planned out: "My parents' divorce."

That was back in ninth grade and, for one thing, they were spending so much time screaming at each other that it was getting really hard to concentrate on anything. Mom kept the house. Dad started renting a condo in this new development out on 124th street, just down the street from the high school.

Back then Dad and me, we had pretty good times. We'd go to all of Garrett's junior AAU games and sit in the stands eating popcorn and cheering. Back then I was still in pee-wee ball and he thought I'd be just like Garrett. Except that I was terrible at basketball. And soccer. And baseball. Still, Dad came to all my games and stood on the sidelines and yelled and afterwards we'd go get hamburgers and a milkshake. Tell me that I'd grow into it. To stick with it. Ever since I dropped out of sports he's been on my case. Telling me that I'm wasting my life staring into a little glowing screen. It's gotten even worse since Garrett left for college.

That's probably not all of it. I sort of pieced together that he got passed over for some sort of sales director job. When I think about it, he's been pissed off about everything since then. But the good news for me is that he took a different position and he's on the road half the time. And of course I've got a key to the condo. It's almost like having my own place. Plus it's only a five-minute walk from school, so when I ditch classes, I'm there in no time. Starfare paradise.

I should have known it was too sweet a deal to last.

3.

I think it's funny when my dad and I have a "serious" conversation in his "study." First of all, he's the only person in the world who would call it a study. Like he was a professor or something. True, there is a desk in the corner. Of course, there's no chair, just a mini-refrigerator stocked with beer where your legs would go. And the big cabinet against the wall isn't filled with technical manuals or legal books—it opens to a forty-two-inch flatscreen TV. The bookshelves are stuffed with Garrett's trophies and autographed sports junk. He can spend almost the entire weekend in there, in this big brown recliner, watching football or basketball and drinking beer.

Somehow I've got to break through the clutter and get him on board with Nationals. Problem is, even with free hotel and entry fee I still need an airplane ticket, and although I've got a couple hundred in a savings account at the bank, I can't touch it without Dad's permission. So I've got to hit him up for the money. I knock on the door. He insists that I knock before entering. God knows why.

"Yes?"

It's amazing how much meaning my dad can pack into one word. When he says "yessss?" in that tone, he's saying, "Now what? Can't you see I'm busy (watching something incredibly boring and meaningless on TV, like a golf tournament without Tiger Woods)? I'd rather not deal with it at all, but if it's absolutely necessary, then make it quick."

So I say through the door, "It will just take a sec."

Then he says OK and I open the door. I have to stand there, in the doorway, until some no-name golfer finishes hitting a putt from about twelve inches, possibly the most boring televised sporting activity in the world. He putts, the ball barely rotates, excruciatingly slow across the screen. The ball hovers on the edge and then, finally, drops in. Polite applause. My dad turns and says it again.

"Yessss?"

"I've got this great opportunity," I begin, trying to set up the pitch. My dad once gave me this lecture about the secret of sales. He travels around the Midwest selling some obscure service to small companies that can't afford the really good service that the big companies buy from his competitor.

He arches his eyebrows, and I see I've actually, for a nanosecond, got his attention.

"Yeah, I won this big online tournament and I qualified for the

Nationals in San Diego. I'll have to fly in on June twenty-sixth and fly back on the thirtieth. I won the entry fee and I get a free hotel room. That's worth around $600, about half the cost of going."

Dad gets this puzzled look on his face and he runs his fingers through his hair. He's pretty vain about his hair, which is still thick on top, a little gray above the ears. He keeps it fairly long and combed straight back, sometimes with this gel or grease.

"You telling me they have *Nationals* for all the dweebs who play computer games? What kind of title is that? King of the nerds?"

"OK," I say, biting my tongue. "But seriously. It's really hard to get the invite, and it's a great opportunity. They've got $150,000 in prize money."

I let this sink in for a few seconds, while he continues to stare at the TV, as if he's worried about missing some amazing chip shot or hole in one, which is nuts, because every time there's a really great shot they replay it at least a dozen times.

But he turns towards me and for at least a second I've got his attention. "Did you say 150 Gs?"

I nod my head.

"So how much you asking for?"

"I can a get a flight for around $400 and then a little something for food…"

"Bottom line, please," he says, like he's some big-shot CEO.

"I'll need about $600, I figure."

Now I've really got his attention.

"Six hundred. That's a lot of money, Seth."

"I know." Knowing it is, and it isn't. He and a girlfriend once spent that much on bar bills at Vegas in a weekend. Then again, I have to work at a fast food joint every weekend for six months to save that much.

"Six hundred bucks, huh."

"Six hundred bucks." It's possible to have an entire conversation with my dad where every other line is a repetition of the previous one.

"OK. Let me get this straight. You need $600 to go play computer games with a bunch of geeks from across the country. You fly to San Diego, go sit down at a computer and pay to play for three straight days. What I want to know is, how is this different from what you do every day here, for free?"

"Well, for one," I reply. "No one is putting up $150k in prize money."

"And you've got a legitimate shot at this $150k?"

"Well, not all of it. No one wins it all. It gets divvied up into different events. Different specialties, it's hard to explain. But I feel like I've got a shot at a piece of it."

After the last online win, my rating jumped up twenty points, and that makes me fifth in the country.

My dad screws up his face in this way he does when he really thinking. Like it takes an awful lot of effort.

"OK," he says. "I'll make a deal with you."

"A deal?" So typical. My dad thinks he's this great wheeler dealer sales expert.

"I'm going to give you the money for this trip. Not lend it to you. Give it to you. On one condition." He arches his eyebrows, waiting for me to ask him what the condition is.

"What condition?"

"You can go to California. Play with your nerd buddies into the wee hours. But when you come back empty-handed, that's it. We forget this whole idea of playing the computer for money. In the meantime, you buckle down, get off that God-forsaken computer long enough to do your homework, stop skipping classes, get your GPA up, and maybe, just maybe, you'll be lucky enough to get into a fine university like your brother."

So then we shake on it, just like two businessmen. And I get back to my computer and start working on my moves, because I'm going to have to play flawless. Or, as Mrs. Lawson, my English teacher would insist, flawlessly.

4.

The rest of the semester I worry about screwing up and having Dad take back my ticket to San Diego. So I go to all my classes (mostly) and do my homework (as fast as possible, mostly in other classes) and concentrate on getting a seat in English and history behind Brit so I can stare at her the entire class without being too obvious. Even if it's just the back of her soft, shiny hair, I watch the way the light plays off as if it were some hypnotic kaleidoscope. And for at least that moment, the Starfare game playing in the back of my mind goes on pause.

A couple of weeks after Dad agreed to give me the cash I get an IM from my brother.

3-PointShooter: Hey
ActionSeth: Hey
3-PointShooter: Good going
ActionSeth: ?
3-PointShooter: Heard u got the old man to cough up the dough to send u to some tourney
ActionSeth: Yeah pretty amazing

Garrett, he's not into gaming like I am, but at least he understands. When I was about nine a friend of his lent us his Nintendo 64 and we started playing Mario Kart. At first Garrett, who was fourteen, killed me, but I spent every waking hour working on it and after a couple of weeks I started winning. It was the first time I had beaten him at anything and he just shook his head and laughed and claimed it was unfair, that I was practicing too much. I think it bothered him a bit until I showed him the times I was posting online—I was in the top hundred in the country on a couple of courses.

We IM a little bit more about nothing much and then he wishes me luck at the tournament.

I'm spending every extra hour I can online, trying to get it together for Nationals. It's a Wednesday night and I'm at Mom's.

I've drawn a game against this kid from Korea. No one famous—they would never mess around playing against crap Americans, but he's got a really high rating and I'm just barely hanging on. I'm not even sure why I'm struggling. I've won at least twenty games in a row and feeling like I'm on my way to a really good showing at Nationals. And then this. The action is incredibly fast and I'm pounding on the keyboard, wheeling the mouse and trying to keep track of three fronts at once.

In an intense game like this, you're in so deep the room around you just disappears. When you're in the middle of a battle, and your fingers are flying across the keyboard, you're not looking *at* the screen, you're not playing *at* a game, you're IN the game. Like those science fiction movies where someone gets sucked up in a wormhole or drops through a hole in time. It's sort of like that. You get that same sense of being pulled into this other world. It's not as though you believe your body has gone anywhere, but your mind, your consciousness is actually sucked through the screen. And you're not alone.

Not by a long shot. Sure it's a world with all of these strange creatures and complicated rules, but it has dimensions and textures and players who become friends and geography you have to learn the way you know your neighborhood and the way to and from school. And if you're good, like I am, then you move through this world with the kind of confidence that Kobe Bryant shows when he cuts to the basket, or when Payton Manning goes back to pass from his five-yard-line with ten seconds on the clock. That's why it's simply not acceptable for someone to start knocking on my bedroom door when I'm into a tough game, any more than you'd expect Kobe or Payton to stop, right at that critical moment, and chat up a couple of spectators. I know it might sound conceited, when I talk about these sports superstars, but that's the way it is.

So naturally Mom pounds on my door at the worst possible time.

"Seth! Seth!"

Out of the corner of my eye I see something unexpected on

the northeast corner of the map. Crap, crap crap! Somehow he's got three cruisers completely armed and moving in formation and that just seems impossible. I had a spybot up there just minutes ago. Unless he had them cloaked. But how?

"Seth! Why didn't you pick up the phone?"

This comes at me like a voice shouted from a distant mountain across miles of canyons on a foggy morning.

Then I see movement on the opposite corner and OMG it's another three cruisers that come out of nowhere and I'm thinking, maybe this is one of the Korean pros slumming on an American server. Playing under a pseudonym just to yank someone's chain. Like mine, because I've never, ever seen anyone develop that much firepower that quickly and I realize I am totally screwed.

"Seth, it's someone from your school."

Maybe I could distract him with a direct attack right at his home base, but that would be suicidal.

"It's a girl."

It's like the screen blinks and when I look at it for a second it's not a 3D world but just a flat screen with a dozen blinking blips. I suddenly hear the game's sounds, which are usually lost in the background, like the computer's fan. First the crunching sound when one of my land fighters gets crushed. Then the clattering of an army marching on pavement, sounding like hail on a roof.

"What did you say?" I shout.

"Seth, open the door. You know I hate talking through a closed door! It's a girl from your school. Her name is Bret or Brit, I couldn't really tell."

I was going to lose the game anyway.

5.

The only reason Mom isn't freaking over a call from a girl is my older brother Garrett. I once did a count of his Facebook friends:

298 girls and 87 boys. Garrett Gordon, high school jock exemplar. Minor: tennis doubles, third round state. Major: shooting guard, 19.6 point average. Hobby: going steady with beautiful girls.

Garrett's been hanging out with a series of girls since eighth grade. So many I gave up trying to keep them straight years ago and just call them all Kimberly. That makes me right about half the time. Kimberly is always pretty and perky and active in school—she's got the lead in the school play, or is a varsity cheerleader, or has a room full of tennis trophies. And naturally, my brother is always there to give me advice about how to hook up with a Kimberly of my own. And to say I have no interest in the Kimberlys would be a lie. Kimberly looks amazing, I can vouch for this, even when she's flat on her back on my dad's sofa, with her hair and makeup mussed, popping up with a gasp when I burst through the door and turn on the light at 2 a.m. back from a night of gaming over at Eric's.

"Crap," I said simultaneously with my brother, who was cursing me, and I'm fast enough on the light switch to be unsure if what I saw was a naked torso or a near-naked torso or a semi-naked torso. The image was stuck on my eyes like when you shoot a flash photo in a dark room, and I was happy to have it there, because I would want to examine it carefully, as soon as I got through the living room and into my bedroom.

"Sorry," I muttered, as I shuffled through the now darkened room, knowing the way by feel.

"Jesus," I heard Kimberly sigh. "Garrett, I really, really have to go. I had no idea it was this late and if I get caught sneaking in I'm going to be in so much trouble."

By then I was down the hallway to my bedroom door and I could hear my brother in the background as I locked it, making the kind of soothing sounds people make to calm a fidgeting horse. I just slipped out of my clothes and into bed and closed my eyes really tight, making that picture come back, the shock of blond hair flying into the air and Kimberly's arms pushing Garrett away. She looked just awesome and I'd give just about anything to be

Garrett for just that minute, or better yet, the minute before I burst in, as long as I didn't have to stay Garrett forever. The last thing I want to be is Dad's favorite sports star.

So to put it mildly, I don't have the kind of practice Garrett does at these sorts of things, and when I pick up the phone I'm kind of stuttering so that Brit has to say, "Seth? Is that you?"

"Yah, no nah," is what I actually spit out.

"Seth?

Finally I manage to say yeah.

"Oh great. Hey, the reason I'm calling your house is that I don't have your cell and if you check Facebook I've friended you. Anyway, you know that final group project thing that we have to do for history?"

Brit Leigh's Facebook friend? After an entire year of trying to get up the nerve. Just like that? As far as a history project, I'm thinking, but blanking.

"Anyway, Ben and Katie and I wanted to know if you'd be in our group?"

Something about this project thing is in the back of my mind. Maybe a handout we got a few weeks ago?

"We're going to meet at the library tomorrow afternoon at four, you know the branch over by Panera?"

"Yeah?"

"Well, will you?"

"What?" I muttered.

"You know, be in our group…"

"Ha, yah," I mutter, thinking, what a moron.

"Seth?"

Finally I managed to say, "Yeah, sure, I guess…" and then, before I can stop it from actually being uttered I add, inanely, "but why…"

There was a pause, and she said, "Seth, you're kidding right?"

I shake my head before I realize that she can't see me and say "no." And I'm not kidding.

"Seth, everyone knows you're like the smartest kid in class. Like when Mr. Hobson asked about that strategy thing during the Battle of Gettysburg and no one knew a thing about it and you finally raised your hand and explained it like you had just spent a week preparing a report on it?"

"Oh, that thing." Mr. Hobson asked if anyone could give an example of a critical tactical maneuver in the Battle of Gettysburg. There was a long silence. Since I knew a little bit about the Twentieth Maine's famous bayonet charge on Little Round Top I finally raised my hand and blabbered on about it for a while.

A couple summer back my mom had decided it would be good for Garrett and me and her to have one last vacation together before he left for college. Since money is always an issue, she got my Uncle Andy to lend her his lake house in Northern Wisconsin. So it takes us almost two days to drive there, which is pretty awful to contemplate in itself, and then we're stuck in this little house without any Internet connection and a TV that gets three stations.

Uncle Andy has a job with some big corporation in Minneapolis, but his hobby is the Civil War. So I'm stuck up in the middle of nowhere and he's got about five-hundred books, all on the Civil War. With nothing better to do I read though a couple of them. And what's sad is that I was actually getting interested, especially in the whole battle strategy thing. I mean, it's not all that different than the strategies I use in Starfare. So I had read a couple accounts of the Twentieth Maine's wheeled bayonet charge, which is one of the more famous battle maneuvers in the whole war. That's why I could answer Mr. Hobson's question. I got so into it that I went up to the board and drew a diagram, which I can scarcely bear to think about, it's so embarrassing.

So just like that I'm in the Brit Leigh History Group. I say this out loud about ten times. Like pinching yourself to see if you're in a dream. All because Mom tortured me with that vacation to Uncle Andy's lake house. The world works in weird ways.

I immediately get on Facebook and sure enough, there's a message from Brit. Of course, now I have to worry about what Brit saw. I glance through my friends list and realize that it's not as bad as I thought. Not all geeky gamer guys. There's a couple of girls who used to play Magic with us at the local card shop. Becca, who's my friend Eric's girlfriend. And some of Becca's friends. And a bunch of girls from school I don't know that well who probably friended the entire class. And Mercedes, this girl from middle school who told me she was not named after the car. We had this lame unit on ballroom dancing in eighth grade and we sort of became regular partners. I'm not even sure how it happened. After the unit was over she was always sending me dumb little emails and asking if I was going to the football game that night or the mall over the weekend or if I wanted to get together to study. Which at the time was no, no, no because I wasn't wasting prime gaming time at football games or hanging around the mall and I never studied. Thinking about it now, I just sort of shake my head because she was pretty and nice and I was just clueless.

Then I look more closely at the picture I've got posted. It's awful. And that's what Brit saw. It's a picture Mom took of me when we were on vacation. I was sitting on the side of the dock, just sort of staring at the little fish that poke around the slimy poles that hold it up and didn't even know she took it until we got back home. It was near the end of the vacation and my hair was lighter than it usually is. It's not as though I liked the picture. It's just that I hate having my picture taken and that was the only one I could find.

People always say I take after Mom, mostly because my hair is light and wavy like hers, while Garrett has my father's straight, dark hair. I also got my mom's height gene, because last time we stood next to each other I was about a half-foot shorter than Garrett, although Mom tells me that all the boys on her side of the family were late bloomers. Come to think of it, my pants aren't dragging on the ground like they used to, so maybe I am still growing. Anyway, Garrett's no giant himself. Dad says the only reason he wasn't recruited by any of the big D1 basketball schools was because he's not even six foot, although that's what the high school programs said.

At least it's an interesting picture, the way the sun was playing off the water behind me. Maybe, I thought, someone would like the way I looked, like I was contemplating the meaning of life or quantum mechanics. Like I was one of those brooding, sensitive boys who get the girls in bad teen movies, when everyone knows in real life they don't. Anyway, I was probably thinking about some Starfare battle of the past, trying to figure out a more efficient way to harvest lifesource points.

6.

Mom has this big guilt trip over taking her current boyfriend Martin to a week at this yoga or meditation or some other drink-the-Kool-Aid institute in California. She gets all wound up about me staying alone and eating sugary cereal and fast food, but I tell her after all these years of taking care of us, she deserves it. After managing to avoid a teary goodbye scene with them I'm getting really comfortable over at Dad's. I'm finishing up my third Starfare win in a row when I glance at the computer clock and realize I'm going to be late to Brit's history group. Especially since I have no choice but to bike. I'm still gasping as I ditch my bike on the library rack.

The group has a table in the back and Brit sees me first and waves. So naturally that reduces me to a state of total imbecility. Rather than have to talk I squirm down into the open chair and pick up a copy of the assignment that's on the table. I'm pretty sure everyone is staring at me because I'm still breathing hard and my forehead is damp and I wonder if I smell too.

I skim over the assignment and figure out that we have to pick a topic and do a group presentation on the Great Depression. On the plus side, presentations are usually no-brainers. Then again, you have to sit through all the others, which can be excruciating.

"Black Monday and the stock market collapse, WPA and federal job creation, Conservation Corps…" Each one sounding as bad as the previous.

I glance over at Brit and she's concentrating on the topics, resting her chin on her hand. She's wearing a T-shirt with these shiny things that make star patterns, including one centered perfectly on her right breast. When she looks my way I jerk my eyes back at the paper.

In the end we choose the Dust Bowl topic, even though one of the girls didn't even know what it was. And when you think about it, it is sort of goofy name. Sounds like where Kansas U goes to play football in December when they're 8-6. Meanwhile, I'm trying to figure out how to game this so that I can either end up doing some part of the project one-on-one with Brit or do something that only takes fifteen minutes. I end up taking on the computer stuff—setting up the PowerPoint with pictures and maybe getting some old songs to play at the beginning and the end.

When I mention I saw a whole photo exhibit on the Dust Bowl at a museum, taken by some photographer paid by the government, Brit reaches across the table and puts her hand on my arm. I'm stunned to discover just how many nerves a human has in the forearm.

"I just knew you'd be a big help," she says. I find the courage to meet her eyes and the look she's giving me seems pleasant enough, but it's missing anything special. And believe me, I'm open to the smallest, subtlest sign.

7.

There's great news one week into Mom's trip. She wants to stay another two weeks at her "Institute."

"I really feel like I'm close to a breakthrough," she says when she breaks the news by phone. I have to answer a dozen questions about what I'm eating, but I lie cheerfully, thinking only how much of a win it will be for my Starfare game.

"You deserve it, Mom," I tell her, and mean it. "It's great that you can take time for yourself."

Then she wishes me good luck at the tournament and I tell her I love her, which I know is kind of corny to say, but it's true, and I know it means a lot to her.

"I love you too honey," she says, and then we hang up.

With Mom out of the picture and Dad on the road I'm getting tons of online time. Stomp badgers me every night for a rematch, but I just ignore him. Block him from my IM, but he seems to always reappear with a different screen name. I can tell it's him, because he's always screaming in all-caps and calling me a putz, whatever that is.

At about midnight the day before Brit's group meets again I spend my twenty minutes putting up some titles and pasting in photos. At our second and final meeting Brit acts like I should be nominated for a genius fellowship.

"I would have never found that music!" she gushes. "It's perfect." I file shared a couple of Depression era songs. "Brother Can You Spare a Dime," opens the show and this Woody Guthrie song about hobos ends it. I'm such a dork that now that I'm Brit's Facebook friend it's like my life is complete. I still can't bring myself to even say hi to her in the hall.

We take the AP exam for Calc two weeks before finals week, which is a breeze, and so it's pretty much goofing off there. History is just presentations and our group is almost last. I think my PowerPoint kills and Mr. Hobson actually says "nice job," which is, for him, excessive praise. I love finals week—only an hour or two at school a day.

My gaming is going great. I'm playing straight through to one or two in the morning. Grab a bowl of cereal for dinner, or call in a pizza, and I'm good to go.

Two days before I'm booked to leave I get into a game with a really annoying player who is just awful. He keeps sending me idiotic messages about how lucky I am and how he's just setting me up for a late game surprise. He's so bad I decide to humiliate him by taking over his base with miners—which would be like winning a tank battle with Toyota pickups. One good thing about miners is that you can stack them up like Legos and I decide to try to build a bridge over his fortifications. It's almost working when I realize that I'm giving him time to catch up. So I send some warriors after the miners and I'm amazed that they just cruise up the back of the miners and breach his fortress, destroying him in seconds. There's no way that warriors are supposed to be able to get through these walls—it's like the scene in *The Lord of the Rings* where Saruman uses gunpowder to blast a hole in the walls of Helm's Deep.

After the game I stop and think about what I've just discovered. If players were unaware of this move, they'd never try to defend it and I could turn any game around in just a few minutes. It was like when the U.S. was the only country with the atomic bomb— I could rule at will.

The only person I even mention it to is DTerra, and I don't go into the details. He's talked his dad into letting him fly out for Nationals, getting in the night before I do to play the grinder. It will be nice to have someone to hang out with—and rooting for me.

When I finally get to bed the night before my trip I'm still wired from the frantic practice games. I stare at the ceiling, where a break in my curtains produces a little bar of light from a street lamp. It looks like an arrow, pointing towards my door, the hallway, the future.

"Hey Brit," I whisper. She turns around in the chair in front of me, her hair spinning across her face.

"Maybe you heard—I just won this big tournament and $30,000 and need to celebrate. I'm thinking of dinner at The American Club, maybe scalp some front row seats for Lady GaGa."

Her jaw drops and now it's her who's stuttering.

"I'm going to rent a stretch limo—should we get the Escalade or the Hummer?"

8.

Dad dropped me off at the airport. The whole way he was on his cell, some heated business discussion about the proper way to allocate costs to projects or something. While I'm getting my bag out of the trunk he pulls the phone from his ear and shouts, "Call me when your plane lands."

While I'm waiting for the boarding call my cell rings. It's Mom. She says she can't believe I'm old enough to be jetting across the country by myself. That it was just yesterday that we were sitting at the kitchen table, playing board games.

"You remember Chutes & Ladders?" she asks. I say I do.

"I should have known, even back then, about you and games. Every day you'd beg me to get out a board game or a deck of cards. And you weren't even in school yet. In kindergarten you could read every Monopoly Chance card. And I'd have to explain what a 'bank error' or 'beauty contest' was."

"And then there was the time at the pediatrician's? You're four years old, sitting on the floor with one of those really complex wooden 3D puzzles that you have to make into a ball? So we're sitting there, and the doctor keeps losing his place, distracted by you down on the floor, where you're working with all the wooden shapes. So finally I say, 'He really likes puzzles.' And the doctor nods and says, 'I see that, but honestly I've never seen anyone solve it before.' And sure enough I glance down and you're putting the final piece into the ball."

Then they call my boarding group. Mom says she'll call me later, to make sure I got in OK.

I've got a bunch of saved games on my laptop and I spend the flight going over these. Surprise bonus: they hand out warm chocolate chip cookies and the flight attendant, who looks a lot like that actress from *CSI*, gives me extras.

The hotel turns out to be really nice, right down the street from the convention center where the tournament is being held. I have a room on the eleventh floor which looks out across the city and part of the ocean, where I can see the front end of an aircraft carrier. My room number is 1123, which is easy to remember—the first two digits add up to the third and the middle two digits add up to the fourth. I try to call DTerra on his cell but get voice mail. That's a good sign. Probably still in the qualies.

He got a room for one night and then is moving into mine to save money. I'm so anxious to find him and so nervous about the tournament that I don't really think about how cool the view is, or how blue and sparkly the ocean looks. I throw my bag on the bed, pop my iPod earbuds in and head over to the tournament site to find out a little more about that $30,000.

They really didn't need to put up all the huge "STARFARE" banners at the entrance to the convention center. All you have to do is follow the flow of black T-shirts, computer backpacks and bad complexions. They're coming from all directions and funneling through a set of giant glass doors in the side of a white concrete building that is so long and tall it looks like it could have been built to keep out the barbarians on the other side. As I get closer to the doors and pick up my pace I feel taller and lighter.

As I climb the final steps into the center I'm behind a group of three guys and a girl, all in T-shirts with their Starfare screen names on their backs. I catch "Gforce22," "HelterSkelter" and "GamerzG!rl." I don't recognize any of their gamer names. But then only about half of the people there are actually playing in Nationals. On top of the last chance grinder there are at least twenty sidebar tournaments and a lot of people show up just to play in the side events and watch their heroes. The thing is, if they knew who I was they'd probably all stop and stare and start whispering. This realization has a strange effect on me. Back home, at school, I'm lost in the crowd. Here, when people start connecting me to my screen name, I'll be like one of North High's celebrities. Like Garrett.

9.

The convention hall is actually a cool place. They keep it kind of dark, so that floor is lit with the glow from the hundreds of monitors set up on row after row of tables. Up front they have four feature tables facing a huge area of seating with giant projection screens above the players so the crowd can watch the matches in real time. Around the perimeter of the room are about fifty different vendors selling everything from gaming mouses to comic books based on Starfare.

One corner of the computer area is roped off and about twenty players are pounding on their keyboards, working to take one of the eight spots open for grinders. I wander over but can't tell if DTerra is still there. It's kind of dark and I've only seen a couple of pictures of him.

So I check in at the desk for "Players A–G" and get a bag of stuff and a card with my real name and screen name which hangs over my head on a red cord. My screen name is printed in big bold letters and I get stopped a half dozen times as I wander back to the qualie area. I'm hanging around the roped area, looking at all the players when I hear someone behind me saying, "Holy shit, there goes ActionSeth!" I resist the urge to turn and stare back.

I'm leaning over the ropes, trying to get a better look at a guy who might be DTerra when someone pokes me on the shoulder.

"Hey champ."

I turn and recognize him right away from his Facebook pictures.

"Jeez," I say. "Why didn't you tell me you were a giant?" He's at least six-five.

"Same reason you didn't say you were a midget."

"If my brother was as tall as you, he'd be in the NBA."

Then we're talking a mile a minute and I find out that he got knocked out one round earlier.

"You'd laughed if you'd seen it," DT says. "I played it like a real noob."

We decide to wander outside and try to find a decent pizza place. As I squint into the sunlight DT stops and says in a serious voice, "You run into you-know-who yet?"

"Who?"

"Guess. He's obnoxious. Hates your guts. And weighs about three-hundred pounds."

"Stompazer weighs three-hundred pounds?"

"At least. He stomps you, you're dead. Of course, he'd have to catch you. So don't worry. The guy can hardly get up a flight of stairs."

I laugh, picturing him. Because I had pictured him as this jocky, muscular guy.

"And catch this. His real name is Morris."

"Morris?"

"No joke. He makes the nerds here look like Greek gods. On the other hand, his old man is supposed to be some high-tech billionaire. Maybe he can get him on *Biggest Loser*."

We're both laughing when DT coughs out one more piece of information. "And he just qualified for the main event."

10.

The hotel has this big meeting room set up for gaming and it's open all night. DT drags me down to where there must be a hundred players hanging, most of them drinking energy drinks and eating fast food. He nods towards a far corner where a tall girl with long blond hair is standing, watching the action on a laptop. "I'm trying to get a game with her later," he says. "She said she played you in last year's online qualifying."

"Yeah? What's her name?"

"Morgan, but she plays under RaiderRadar."

I immediately recognize the name but would have never matched the two. Sometimes I try to imagine a face behind a screen name I'm playing. But "hot tall blond girl" just isn't the first image that comes to mind.

DT wants me to go over and meet her but it's already late and I tell DT I have to head up to the room and get some sleep. In bed, I'm a little too nervous to fall straight asleep. Thinking about the tournament and the prize money and how Dad will react. When he sort of reluctantly and absentmindedly asks, "How'd it go?" and I pull out a check for $30,000.

I don't know what time DT came in because I was dead asleep and I barely hear my cell phone alarm at seven-thirty. The sunlight is painful when I step outside and I'm still groggy when I get to the convention center. They've got a big table with stale bagels and dry muffins and I try a bite of each before tossing them. The first round pairings are up on boards around the room and when they say "take your seats" I head to the one numbered 112. I quickly pull out my keyboard and mouse, plug in, and make sure they're working and right where I want them. They call out five minutes, then count down and suddenly my computer screen lights up and I'm in the Gondwanaland map. But no opponent. After about ten minutes a ref comes by, writes something on his clipboard and tells me that I've won by default.

Later I hear that four guys rooming together stayed up most of the night gaming in the hotel and all of them slept through the first round. I shake my head when I hear that. Imagining traveling all the way to San Diego for the biggest tournament of the year and sleeping through it. Actually, one loss doesn't eliminate you because it's a mixer. Each round players are paired against others with similar records. After ten rounds, the top eight fight it out in single elimination. Final eighters all get some decent money, but the prize pool is really top heavy. The big money goes to first and second.

I win my second round pretty easily and during the break DT wanders into the hall and finds me working though some moves on my laptop. About a minute later so does the one person I've been hoping to avoid.

"Would you look at this," comes this booming voice from

behind my head. "No wonder I couldn't find you. You're such a puny wuss."

When I turn my head there is a wall of human flesh behind my head. Before I can do anything DT jumps up and says, "Well fatso, I'm not."

Stompazer laughs, this big theatrical laugh like a movie ogre.

"I don't deal with noobs or stickmen," he says. "And you're both."

Just then the tournament director announces that the pairings for round three are posted.

"I'm just waiting for my chance," Stomp says, "I'm going to take you down."

"Sure," I say. "Just like last time."

"Last time was a fluke!" He's all red in the face and almost screaming. "Never happen again. Never!"

I stand up and head off to one of the pairing boards, trying to act like he's not there. But truth is, he's a truly creepy presence. Big and obnoxious like one of those giant trolls in a massive multiplayer RPG that require a team of forty gamers to bring down.

11.

I start nervously, but sweep my next round and rack up another routine win in my fourth. I'm keeping my secret weapon under wraps until I need it. After lunch break we sit back down and I know I'm going to be paired against someone who is 4-0 or 3-1 at the least. The tournament director gets us all in our seats and I see I'm up against an older guy who is 4-0. He's got a scraggly beard and stringy hair and looks like he hasn't slept or bathed since the beginning of the year. Most guys, they'll say something when they sit down across from you before ducking behind the monitors. This guy, who plays under the handle MilesBlue, says nothing.

"Round five will begin in three minutes," the announcer says.

Miles comes out smoking and it's a toss-up through midgame when I decide I can't wait any longer and begin to sneak some miners up against the back of his main fortress. Then I suddenly stack them up and send a couple warriors over the top. A couple of minutes later the game is over. As we stand up the guy gives me a weird look.

"Sure would like to know how you pulled that off," he says.

"Practice, practice, practice," I say and offer him my hand. He declines the offer.

That makes me 5-0. For the final round of the day I'm surprised to get assigned one of the feature tables, even though I should have guessed. Only ten people are 5-0. It's pretty exciting, playing in front of a crowd, your every move showing up on a twenty-foot screen. I know there'll be no easy matches the rest of the way, and I recognize most of the guys at the top of the results list.

I used to watch Garrett and his teammates before high school games. Running the drills and slapping each other and just before the lineup was called, making this circle with their hands around each other's shoulders. I realize I have my own rituals before a match, just like they did. I play with my mouse, moving it to the right, then left, than back again. My right leg gets the bouncies, and I like to rock in my chair. I go through all of this stuff, and do it again, because being on the feature table, it's just that much more nerve wracking. I stop rocking my chair and focus on the screen as the game clock ticks down.

As the match gets underway I forget about the crowd and the projection of my game and just concentrate on trying to get the upper hand. Only when I pull my new maneuver and hear the combined gasp from the crowd do I remember where I am. The game winds down fast after that.

DT runs over to the roped area and gives me a huge high five.

"Man, you are hot!" he says.

I notice that a whole bunch of judges are congregating around a laptop at the judge's table. I don't think much about it. There's always at least one player who appeals a game or complains that it was the equipment's fault.

We hang out until they post the final results of day one. Only five of us are still undefeated. But I groan when I see that Stompazer is 5-1.

I figure if I go 2-2 or better on day two I'm guaranteed to make the final eight. That would put me just three matches from $30k.

DT and I head out to the same pizza place we found the night before. Despite being the first week of June, it's surprising cool outside and the air smells of the ocean and grilled food from nearby restaurants. We talk Starfare nonstop. DT keeps telling me that I'm going to sweep the whole tourney undefeated. That there's no defense for my new move. I try to be modest, but I'm not arguing. By the time we get back to the lobby I'm so beat I just want to collapse back in bed. DT says he's going to see if Morgan is hanging in the gaming room before heading up. I'm asleep within seconds of hitting the stack of oversized hotel pillows.

12.

It doesn't take long, next morning, to figure something is up. Before the assignments come out they have all of the competitors gather in a big scrum in front of the judge's table. The head referee clears his throat over the mike. Then he taps it and says, "Is this working?" We all shout for him to get on it with and he does.

"After due consideration of yesterday's match play the judges and Starfare's software team have decided that a minor patch will be in effect for today's matches. This will be transparent to most of you, affecting only an anomaly in an unintended use of miners."

I feel something falling from my chest toward my shoes.

"However, we have determined that nothing illegal or unethical was involved in the use of this bug and all matches from yesterday will stand."

I feel like everyone is staring at me.

As we disperse and wait for first round pairings I keep telling myself that it's no big deal, that I can still match up even with anyone in the field. And that I don't have to win every match to make the final eight.

But I never quite get back my equilibrium and sleepwalk through my first two matches, losing both of them. DT shows up around then and sits me down and gives me a real cussing out. I guess it helps because I win a close match in round three. With one match left, DT and I run through the possibilities and after doing the math about ten times conclude that a win gets me in for sure and that a draw would put me into a tiebreaker with two or three other players. The tiebreak goes to minutes played which would be a give-me, with all the quick games I played on day one.

Final round I get paired with another 7-2 player and as we get set up to play I explain to him that we can both make the final eight if we agree to a draw. But if we play, only the winner will make it. Actually, I don't tell my opponent that it will go to a tiebreak and it all depends on how fast he won his matches. I guess he's a little afraid to play me because he quickly agrees to a draw. We call a judge over and then get to sit down and relax and wait for the final eight announcement. I never know what to do, waiting. Luckily DT is there to distract me and we watch a bunch of goofy videos he's got bookmarked on his laptop.

When they announce the final eight I'm actually relieved that my last opponent is there with me. He would have been so pissed off if he had lost the tiebreak.

Within a few minutes the eight of us take our places at the featured tables. I look out over the convention floor. Every seat is taken. Across the table I'm surprised to see the same bearded guy I beat in round five.

"This time, straight up," he says.

"OK with me," I respond.

But it's not OK. Maybe it's nerves, maybe it's the look the guy gave me before the game. Like when he wasn't playing Starfare he might have a hobby dismembering smart-ass teenagers.

I start slow and although he can't quite put me away, he keeps his edge right up until the clock runs out. Just like that, I'm out. I can't even stand waiting around to see who does win. I pick up my $2,000 check from the judge's table during the break before the final four. I stare at it for a while, thinking that it's a lot of money. And that it's not. I mean, I couldn't exactly whip it out and show it to Brit.

"And what's that?" she asks.

"It's money I won playing a computer game."

"Oh," she says, nodding with understanding. "Nerd money. That's very nice, Seth. Thanks for sharing. Got to go—I'm supposed to meet this hunky guy from the football team after school. We're going to go make out for a couple hours."

Besides, final eight. So weak. That's not what I came here for.

I fold it into my pocket and head back the table where DT is watching our stuff. We're about to head out when a moving mountain steps in front of us.

"Heading home, putz?" Stompazer says. "Are you crying? Looks like you're crying."

DT and I split up, to head around him. But it's not a small detour.

"Maybe I'll spend some of my $30k to come out to Kansas and kick your butt in person."

We continue to head for the door, to the sound of his big, deep, infuriating laugh.

DT and I get an early flight, check out of the hotel and take a cab to the airport where we've both got to wait hours for our flights.

I'm just sitting there, leaning over, staring at the floor and moping when my cell rings. I check and see it's my brother.

"Hey," I say.

"So how are you doing?"

I tell him I lost. And he says something about Dad wanting to bet him that I'd come home empty-handed.

"Not exactly empty," I say. "I won $2,000."

"Holy crap, that's great! I should have taken that bet…and how come you haven't been taking Mom's calls? She's called me three times, wondering if I've heard from you."

It's true that I got her voice mails, but I had to keep the phone off during the tournament and she was calling from some sort of public phone and didn't leave a callback number.

"I might as well warn you," Garrett says. "I think Mom's really off the deep end with this Institute she's attending. I've done a little Internet searching and I'm not sure what to make of them. I mean, they don't seem like a cult. Not like the really nutty ones, who are waiting for visitors from space or the end of the world on a certain date. They've actually got an accredited university where they seem to be studying a lot of mystical crap. Like trying to figure out how these Indian holy men can slow down their heart rates to like fifteen beats a minute. Anyway, she's pretty nuts about it. If she calls, you'll get an earful."

I ask him when he'll be back home and he sort of sighs and says that he already told me that he was staying for the summer to work the school's basketball camps.

"I'll be back for a couple of weeks before practice starts." Then he tells me to pay attention at school—that I'd like college and I should stop screwing around and get some decent grades. "You might even think about coming here," he adds. "Three girls for every two guys. Even a computer nerd might have a shot of hooking up."

Yeah, I might as well accept it, shoot for being just another anonymous college kid. DT and I head over to an airport sandwich place and we do a replay of the tournament. He tells me that it was a great show, even if I didn't win. But it's not true. If I want to make it as a pro, I have to be able to dominate crappy Americans like the guys at Nationals.

13.

Before the divorce, if Garrett's sixteen-and-under AAU basketball team had gotten deep into one of the big national tournaments you can bet the whole family would be there to cheer and greet him. Instead I pick up a voicemail when I get off the plane from Dad telling me to grab a cab.

Naturally, I have no idea where you go to pick up a taxi and end up wandering all the way down to the wrong end of the terminal. I reverse course and in the meantime a jumbo jet full of Japanese tourists has landed and picked up their luggage and I have to wait in line an hour to get a cab. There's a couple of Japanese teenage girls in front of me with their parents and they keep looking at me and whispering and giggling, covering their mouths when they laugh. I'm thinking I got some sort of goober hanging from my nose or unzipped pants. I can't say I'm sorry when they get stuffed into the back of a Lincoln.

I almost choke when I have to pay $65 to the cab driver. That leaves me about two bucks. Inside the condo is dark and smells of cigarette smoke with a hint of overripe garbage. Dad's left a note on the kitchen table next to a $20 bill telling me to order something to eat if I'm hungry. "Stick around," he writes at the end. "We need to talk."

Naturally I'm thinking something about school, but my midterm grades had arrived a long time ago and I was passing everything and it's too early for final grades.

It must be close to midnight when I hear the garage door. I know I should be working on my game, but I couldn't resist looking at the results from Nationals. Stompazer got all the way to finals, spilt the first two games and lost a close one in the decider to the guy who beat me, MilesBlue. Stomp took home $12,000. I'm too depressed by that news to do anything but just veg out. So I'm watching the *Seinfeld* where George gets a job with the Yankees and orders wool uniforms which naturally drive the players crazy.

"Seth," Dad says as he throws himself onto the couch next to me. To tell the truth, he doesn't look great. Hasn't shaved, hair mussed, oozing the smell of smoke and booze.

"Mom sold the house."

"What?"

"Yeah, I didn't believe it at first either. Apparently she and that goofball with the ponytail—what's his name?"

"Martin."

"Yeah, Martin. Anyway, they've decided to move into this Institute in California she's gotten involved with. So she's sold the goddamn house. Put it up for sale about $20k below market, took the first offer a week later."

"She can do that? I mean, you don't have anything to say?"

"Nah, that's not even the problem. She can have the frickin' money from the house. She was the one who needed to have a kitchen as big as this apartment. Counter space for the take-out, I suppose."

"But what about my stuff?" I had a whole closet full of clothes that I didn't wear and boxes of stuff that I hadn't looked at in years. But I bet those Magic cards were worth a small fortune.

"Seth, I promised I wouldn't say anything until she talked to you, so I would appreciate it if you kind of played along when she calls. You'll have plenty of time to clear out your stuff."

It was late and I was pretty burned out from the tournament. Maybe I was missing something.

"And, Seth, there is a bit of a bonus in this."

"Yeah?"

"Mom wants us to keep the van. Since we have a two-car garage. I'll need you to help me get rid of some of the junk down there. To make room. She says she's not sure what she wants to do with it yet. So the way I see it, no reason you shouldn't be able to drive it, after you get your license. When you're around."

I shake my head, like maybe I had heard that wrong.

"I get to drive it?"

"I told her that we were spoiling you, but she insisted."

That sounded like a really good trade to me. I get to live in one place instead of two. And get a car. Who cares if it's a dorky looking mini-van? It has a radio, a CD player and air conditioning. I could even drive it to school. Get home faster and practice more.

"Nice."

"That's it?" Dad says. "Nice?"

"Extremely nice," I add with a big grin that says it all. But hadn't he said something odd? About when I was around? I mean, when am I not around?

"Seth." Dad was looking at the floor now, not at me. "This is where it gets a little more complicated. Mom thinks that living here, full time, it wouldn't be the best thing for you. You know how much I'm gone, and your mother thinks it would be better for you to make the move with them to California."

"California? Are you kidding? Living with Mom and that, that guy? Why can't I just stay here with you? I've been spending most of my time here anyway."

Dad shakes his head. "I know, I know. That's exactly what I told your mother. But you know how she is…"

"I know I'd go crazy living in some yoga institute. I can't even touch my toes."

Dad looks up at me, chuckles.

"I'm pretty sure it's not like that, Seth."

"OK, then *you* move there."

"I know," he mumbles. "I know."

In the background I hear the TV. A professional voice from an ad for a local used car dealer saying, "No credit? No problem!"

"Listen," Dad says. "Mom is going to talk to you. She thinks that it would be good for you to go with her. That you could, and I quote, 'develop spiritually.' And one thing I agree with—it would at least get you away from that goddamned computer."

I had heard Mom talk about the Institute and I pictured a bunch of cabins stuck into a side of a mountain and people walking around in white robes and sitting in circles, meditating for hours.

"Dad, you can't let her do that to me. I'd go nuts."

"That's exactly what I told her. But you're going to have to make the case yourself. You know she doesn't agree with a damn thing I say. She wants you to at least make a trip out there and see it for yourself. She tells me they've got an excellent high school right on the premises."

I can only imagine what kind of high school that would be. The curriculum would probably be all yoga, Zen meditation and mantra memorization, with breaks for tofu and organic greens. I'm sure there wouldn't be a computer within miles.

So when Mom calls later that night we have an hour shout fest. She and her boyfriend are living in some sort of apartment at the Institute and they want me to move in. They've got this sort of porch room that I'd have all to myself. I manage to get her to admit that not only is there no broadband at her place, there's not even a TV.

"Honey, it will be so good for you," she says. "Think of it as a fresh start. I've toured the high school and the teachers are just amazing. It's nothing like what you're used to. They've got an integrated curriculum that focuses on developing the entire spiritual being of each of their students. Their arts program is wonderful. You could start drawing again!"

I groan. When I was about five I got into drawing dragons and Mom thought I was some sort of artistic genius. She even got me a private art tutor for a few months until he tried to get me to draw something besides dragons.

Finally I can see that I have no choice but to agree to visit. Just one more trip to California. Like father, like son. On the road again.

14.

The three days in California at Mom's Institute feels like a month. At first, she's telling me that there's no computers. I don't see even one TV. Instead I have to go to a bunch of these group meetings and I don't know why, but they have a million questions for me about computer gaming. Then we go for endless walks and waste at least an hour at each meal, sitting around and talking. But then, out of the blue, they invite me do this experiment and take me behind locked doors where, to my amazement, there's a computer and a broadband connection. They wire my head with a dozen plugs and have me play a game, while all these machines are clicking and tracking my Starfare brain waves.

When I finally get home from the airport it's close to midnight. Even though I'm exhausted I check my email and see a couple from DT. I log onto Starfare, slip on my headset, and catch him between games to tell him about the trip. How weird it was out there. Especially the brain wave thing.

"You won't believe this," I say. "This guy who runs the place and this scientist. They think playing Starfare is like Zen meditation."

"It's got to be at least as good as sitting cross legged and humming 'om,'" DT says.

I tell him I've got to get some sleep and sign off. I'm out for fourteen straight hours and must miss a long and heated phone conversation. Because Dad comes out of his study while I'm eating my second bowl of Lucky Charms.

"Seth, you know how stubborn your mom can be, right?"

I nod.

"Well we've been on the phone—more than once—and she's been scheming again. She's got you lined up to work at his summer camp they run. She wants you to fly back out in a week."

I start to stutter in protest but Dad lifts up his hand and silences me.

"Now here's the deal," he says, pulling up a chair and getting right to the point. "I think you're going to like what I ended up negotiating for you."

"Yeah?" That Dad, he's a terrific negotiator. That's why Mom got the house and the van and he got to rent a condo.

"You can stay here for the summer and next school year. On a couple of conditions."

He's got my attention. Because I was just thinking, I get forced to move in with Mom, it could be months before I'd ever see another one of those amazing little blue and yellow marshmallows that swell up after a few minutes in milk.

"You've got to get off that damn computer and hit the books. B average, or you're out of here."

"But Dad," I begin, thinking that I've got some pretty tough courses coming up next year. When I was in grade school I got hooked up with this aggressive Gifted Education program they have in Kansas. It's called GE, which is totally confusing, because it sounds like a brand of light bulbs.

The way it works is the more kids they identify as "gifted" the more money the school gets. So the day I turned eight, which is the minimum age, I took a bunch of tests and, just like that, I was in the club. Which meant I got to start taking all these accelerated math and science courses, so that when I got to middle school I was taking half of my classes at the high school and when I got to high school I was ready to start with APs. Next year I've got two AP courses first semester and I have to commute down to U of Missouri-Kansas City to take math in the afternoon, since I've already taken every math course at high school. I've already got about fifteen hours of college credit.

"But nothing. B average, or you're out of here. And this summer—no staying up until four in the morning and sleeping all day. Your mother and I are in agreement—you get a job, or you can ship out. After all, your mother has that job all lined up for you with the summer camp they run out there."

"But what kind of job?"

Dad gives me one of those looks, like he's dealing with some sort of moron. I'm pretty sure I'm about to hear about how he started a paper route when he was twelve and worked every week of his life since. But he just shakes his head again and says, "Give me a break. I don't give a crap whether you flip burgers or shovel horse manure. Just get a frickin' job before your mother drives me crazy."

15.

The next morning, a Saturday, while unpacking my jeans I hear something crunching and I pull out my Starfare check. Everything had been so messed that I forgot to even show it to Dad. I smooth it out and take it into the kitchen. He's standing by the sink with the newspaper and a steaming mug of coffee.

"Not bad," he says, holding it up to the light like it might be counterfeit. "One month's rent and utilities. Endorse it on the back and I'll drop it in your savings account at the bank. I've got a bunch of errands to run. By the way, I'm out of here bright and early tomorrow—up to Des Moines, then Milwaukee and Chicago."

On the way out the door he turns and says, "I left the paper open to the want ads. Why don't you start by checking them out?"

Instead I plug in my laptop and punch up DT, who's online, like usual.

We chat back and forth about some of his latest games and then I tell him that if I don't get a job I have to move.

> **DTerra:** OMG, a job?
>
> **ActionSeth:** I know. What can I do IRL?
>
> **DTerra:** my older sister worked at the movies and mom thinks I should apply there except you have to wear this costume with a black coat and a little tie
>
> **ActionSeth:** they have movies in Fargo?
>
> **DTerra:** stfu they even have a movie named Fargo and its pretty good 2
>
> **ActionSeth:** I don't know about working at the movies any other ideas?
>
> **DTerra:** I saw this guy from my English class working at the ice cream store and I asked him if they get freebies
>
> **ActionSeth:** yeah?
>
> **DTerra:** what?
>
> **ActionSeth:** do they get freebies?
>
> **DTerra:** I don't know...he wouldn't answer me. I don't think he recognized me. I sit in the back, besides you'd get pretty sick of ice cream.

DT, he's always really positive about my gaming. Sometimes I think he just likes being the cheerleader. Because we both watch a lot of pro matches and we both know that I'm not even close to that level. The difference is that DT, he thinks it's just a matter of time and opportunity. Sometimes I feel absolutely certain I can do it, but most of the time, I'm worried I'm just another day dreaming kid. Just like every eight year old with a baseball mitt who says he going to be a Major Leaguer when he grows up.

When D'Terra signs off I look through the want ads that Dad left but they're all weird jobs that I don't even recognize like comptroller and asset manager. Garrett had summer jobs, but they were always working with his high school coach at basketball camps. Too bad they don't have computer gaming camps.

But then I remember the last time Dad and I picked up pizza at Saviano's, this place in the strip mall a few blocks away. There might have been a sign on the door, something about help wanted. And I'm thinking, if I'm going to get freebies, I might as well get freebie pizza.

So I get out my bike and head over to Saviano's.

16.

Sure enough, the handwritten "help wanted" sign on the door is still there, next to an old Jayhawk basketball poster. I step inside. The service counter is in the back of the store, past a dozen or so round tables with checkered black-and-white tablecloths.

Behind the counter a girl is standing with her back to me, folding take-out boxes. I make my way through the restaurant and stand by the cash register for a few minutes, watching her. She picks up a flat sheet of cardboard, does something with her hands which is just a blur, flips it over, tucks in two tabs simultaneously and throws in onto a stack.

I try making some noise with my feet, but she's already onto another one. She's wearing a baseball-style hat with an auburn ponytail hanging down. When I look closer I see the iPod cords. Her ponytail does a little circular dance every time she flips a box. She's singing along softly with whatever she's playing.

I wonder if I should make some louder noise. And how loud that might have to be to get past her current iTune. And it's not like I'm buying something. If I clear my throat, that will be really lame, and I can't just yell something at her. Maybe I should go back to the door and try to open it really loudly. I'm frozen with indecision when she turns, as if I had actually done one of these things.

"OMG," she says, with a startled jump, staring at me like I had a hand inside the cash register. With a quick wave of both hands she pulls out the ear buds. "How long have you been standing there? I'm so sorry!"

I had already told myself not to look at the menu up on the wall, because then I would look like an actual customer. No problem there, because I'm staring at her, like an idiot. She looks amazing. I'm thinking I had seen her before because there is something familiar about her. Maybe she just reminds me of someone, maybe that girl who should have won *American Idol*.

As she takes a step towards me, wiping her hands on her sides like she had been tossing pizzas instead of cardboard, she gives me a nervous smile. I'm just frozen staring at her hazel eyes, looking like they know something special, something slightly amusing and private. She's just my height, so as she steps closer we're exactly eye to eye and for me it's like trying to keep your eyes on the road at night when someone is driving at you with high-powered brights.

"You know, you could've said something…"

I look down at my feet and nod dumbly.

"Well, can I get you something? The ovens should be hot by now."

I shake my head and look back up. She's still smiling, hesitantly. Perfect teeth.

"Well, something to drink maybe?" Now the amusement seems

to be transitioning to worry. Like maybe I was retarded or a criminal and had wandered in off the street, having just escaped from some sort of halfway house.

"The sign," I finally say.

"The sign?" She mulls this over, like it was some sort of insider message, perhaps from someone outside the Matrix.

"Oh, that," she finally says, pointing to the door. "Did I forget to turn on the neon again? I'm always forgetting that. Because I almost never open. Usually I work the late shift."

She steps around the counter and then comes back, looking more puzzled than ever.

"It's on," she says.

I shake my head and stutter, "Not that sign."

"Oh," she says. "So this is some sort of guessing game? Do I get twenty questions?"

I'm completely flushed now and close to just racing out of the restaurant. "No, no. The other sign. About the job."

"Oh," she says with a sigh. "You want to apply for a job?"

I nod. She reaches under the counter and pulls out a sheet of paper and a pen. "Here you go. Fill this out, but the owner does all the interviews. He'll be in after four. You can bring it back then. Best to come early before we get busy."

I reach for the paper she's holding. I really want to ask her if she goes to North, because maybe that's where I've seen her.

As I take hold of it she points at my chest with her other hand.

"You go to Dakota State?"

I have to actually look down at my chest to realize I'm wearing one of the shirts Garrett brought back from school.

"That's my brother's," I say.

"The shirt?" she says, her face lighting up again with that knowing smile.

"No, the school. Maybe both. I don't know. I just grab whatever's in the drawer."

"Yeah?" She seems to getting more information out of this statement than I intended. "Well, good luck with the job thing.

We could use some more help. Gets pretty crazy here Friday, Saturday nights."

"Thanks," I say, and make a beeline for the door, not looking back.

17.

I fill out the application when I get home. The rest of the afternoon I worry about going back to Saviano's after making a fool of myself. I actually thumb through the North yearbook Mom bought over my protests. Looking at every picture until I'm not even sure what she looked like. So now I'm hoping she's still there, so I can see her again.

When I get to the strip mall I look through the window before I go inside and see a guy I recognize from high school standing at the counter. I walk up and he sees the application in my hand.

"Hang on," he says. "I'll see if the old man is in the mood."

I stand at the counter, taking in the smell of pizzas and glancing over at the only table occupied—a young family with a little girl in a high chair, another girl standing on her chair while her mom pulls at her shirt, telling her to sit.

"You're in luck!"

I turn, startled.

"Follow me," the guy says. As I walk around the corner he says, "You go to North, right?"

"Yeah."

"I think you took Calc BC with a friend of mine. We saw you in the hall last year and he's like, 'Hey, there's that little freshman who's in my calc class.' And I'm like, 'Whoa, he's not even Asian!'"

We walk down a little corridor lined with metal shelves filled with cans of tomato sauce and other ingredients. "I'll introduce you to the old man."

At the end of the hall is a metal door that looks like it leads outside. Halfway down we stop and my guide knocks on a battered door to the side.

"Yeah?" I hear someone call.

"It's Kurt. Got the applicant for you."

"Hang on."

Kurt rolls his eyes and whispers to me, "Be patient." He heads back to the front of the restaurant. It's at least three minutes before the door opens. The man standing there is short and round and is wearing a worn-out and stained Kansas City Royals baseball hat. He's not really that old, maybe my dad's age. Behind him a small desk is stuck in a cluttered room no bigger than a closet.

He just stares at me like he has no idea why I'm there.

"Mr. Saviano?"

"Shit no," he says. "Name's O'Neill. Charlie O'Neill. But who the hell is going to buy a pizza from O'Neill's? Would you?"

I don't know whether I should say the obvious or if that would be an insult.

So I just shrug.

"Sit down and fill out this government shit storm of paper. Then copy your driver's license and social security card on that Xerox machine to make sure you ain't no undocumented alien."

I'm guessing my driver's permit will work. It looks pretty much like a license.

O'Neill shuffles through a pile of papers on his desk, like he's lost something. Then he stops and looks up at me, staring right into my eyes.

"You ever work a cash register?" he asks.

I shake my head, then add, "But I'm good at math."

"Oh yeah? Well, I've got one for you. Steve can make a pizza in four minutes. Tom can make a pizza in six minutes. How long does it take them to do a pizza together?"

The formula just pops up in my head, the way a mental picture appears when someone says "elephant" or "tornado." It's 1/4 pizza/minute + 1/6 pizza/minute or $(3/12 + 2/12) = 5/12$ of a pizza in one minute, or 12/5 for one pizza, which equals 2.4 minutes.

"Well," I say. "Assuming they don't get in each other's way, it would take two minutes and twenty-four seconds."

O'Neill gives me a hard look. "You heard that one before, right?"

"Not really," I say. He gives me a harder look, like he might have missed something, first glance.

"Either way, I like your moxie. You can start on Monday, come in at four. Hannah will show you the ropes. We start you at minimum wage, work hard and we'll talk about a raise after a couple of months."

"Hannah?"

"Yeah—she's only been here a few weeks. But she's real sharp. Worth twice the average kid I've had in here over the years. And I've had plenty."

It takes me about ten minutes to fill everything out, and I copy my driver's permit on an antique Xerox machine in the corner and leave it all on the top layer of the desk. I have no idea where my social security card is. I can ask Dad, but I bet Mom is the one who would know.

18.

When I get home I IM DTerra and tell him I got a job making pizzas. He tells me that's awesome and asks if I can eat as much as I want for free. I just ignore him because the main thing is that I don't have to go live at the Institute with Mom, now that I've got a job. Because I feel like I'm close to something with Starfare. I realize having that shortcut move at Nationals, that wasn't about my real skills. I might have even done better without it, because I wouldn't have got flustered against the guy who won it, MilesBlue.

Even though Nationals turned into an epic fail, lately when I play I get the feeling I'm on the edge of a breakthrough. If I can just climb up that one last rung everything is going to seem simpler and slower and I will be able to move through the game the way Keanu Reeves moves through the Matrix once he discovers he's The One.

I play a one-on-one game of Starfare while DTerra finishes up his game and then we get in a queue to play some two-on-twos. We're deep into our third game when, somewhere in the back of my mind, I hear Dad slamming the door. After we win I tell DT I've got to go and I head downstairs to tell Dad about my job.

I find him in his study, watching a golf tournament.

"Hey," he says, as I step through the open door. "Catch this."

I walk around and stand next to him while we watch a replay of a chip shot from some guy in checkered pants that bounces on the green and works its way to within a few inches of the hole.

"Jesus, I could die and go to heaven happy if I hit just one shot like that in my life."

As far as I could figure, Dad only plays golf about once a month. I have no idea how he thinks he could get any good at it, playing that much. If I played Starfare once a month I'd be a total noob in no time, and that's starting out good.

"Dad," I say, "I got a job."

He looks away from the TV, at me, looking surprised.

"That was quick work."

"Yeah, I'm starting over at Saviano's on Monday."

"Saviano's? Think you'll be able to get us some free pizza?"

I tell him I don't know. Then he fires off about a dozen questions, about how much I'm making, how many hours I got guaranteed, whether I get overtime. Each one I answer by saying I don't know yet, that I haven't even started. Each time I say that he looks more disgusted.

"Sounds a little shaky to me," he finally says. "But don't worry. I'll pump it up when I talk to your mom. You at least bought yourself some time."

Before I go to bed I send out an email to Mom and Garrett telling them about my new career in the food services industry. Mom says she checks her email a couple of times a week, so I don't expect any immediate response. But Garrett is right on top of it and IMs me.

> **3-PointShooter:** Hey nice job with the job...bet dad is in shock
>
> **ActionSeth:** not really
>
> **3-PointShooter:** man I miss those Saviano pies. Tell Saviano he opens a store up here he'd make a killing
>
> **ActionSeth:** there's no Saviano—guy's name is O'Neill
>
> **3-PointShooter:** who cares as long as it tastes good
>
> **ActionSeth:** exactly
>
> **3-PointShooter:** how many hours?
>
> **ActionSeth:** not sure yet, maybe 20 or so
>
> **3-PointShooter:** cool u get free pizza right?

I'm not sure if I should say anything but I figure if anyone has good advice in this department it's Garrett.

> **ActionSeth:** 1 10-inch with every shift. And there's this girl who works there
>
> **3-PointShooter:** alright little bro! Now you're talking, hot right?
>
> **ActionSeth:** well, yeah, but it's more than that
>
> **3-PointShooter:** better yet. if you look in the back of dad's bottom dresser drawer he has about 10 boxes of condoms...
>
> **ActionSeth:** I know. But I've hardly talked 2 her yet...
>
> **3-PointShooter:** Just show that ur interested in whatever she's interested in man. Good things will happen. I promise.

I sign off with a sigh. Maybe it's that easy for Garrett.

19.

On Monday I wake up late, get some Lucky Charms and spend some time watching some new Korean tournament Starfare games that have just been posted. Every time I think I've stepped up my game I watch these guys play and realize that I'm slipping further behind.

It's just seems that they're able to make every move faster and with fewer steps, like when you solve a math problem in nine steps and then the teacher shows you how to do it in five. But then again, once the teacher shows the shortcuts they're immediately obvious. I'm thinking that if I were training with other pros and we were all trading shortcuts and strategies, it would probably be the same.

In the back of my mind I'm trying to figure out whether I should get to Saviano's early, to show how eager I am, or right on time, to show that I can follow directions. I finally decide that it would be best to be a little early so I head over to the store, but when I get to the door I change my mind and just hang outside, checking my cell phone until it says 3:59.

Once inside I see the girl who gave me the application standing behind the register. When I get near I start to tell her that I'm here to work but she shushes me and I see she's counting change. She's got her hair tied back again, green Saviano's Pizza baseball hat on. Her lips are moving with the count, and I can't take my eyes off of them. I'm trying to read what number she's on, but I can't read lips and in my mind she's whispering, "Seth, Seth, Seth." This makes my face feel hot so I decide to memorize the menu. I figure that will come in handy.

I'm all the way to the subs when she startles me and says, "The old man docks us if we're short." She's wiping her hands on her apron, like the money was filthy, which is what my mom is always saying. "So I always count it out, start of my shift. Supposed to be $50, and about half the time it's off. About a hundred percent of that time it's short."

I nod.

"Anyway," she says. "It's right today. Hey, I saw you waiting outside. If the place is open you can come in."

I'm thinking of how stupid I looked standing out there, not knowing she could see me the whole time. Just kind of walking around, looking at my phone every so often.

"You're Hannah, right?" I ask.

"Oh yeah. You're Seth."

Mr. O'Neill must have told her.

"I read your application, Mr. Seth Gordon." She gives me a grin, like she'd actually been looking through a family photo album, with pictures of naked babies. "What can I say. It was sitting on the counter and I got here early. Sounds like you're some sort of math brain."

You had to put down the courses you had taken the previous year.

"Not really."

"Well you are compared to me. My goal is to take as little as possible."

She waves me around the counter. "Come on, I'll show you what you're going to be doing."

I follow her into the back room, watching the way the two pale, faded spots on the back of her jeans move with each step, like the worn denim was alive and an extension of her skin and I can't help imagining what that might feel like if I just reached out…

As we walk through how to use the ovens, how to work the assembly area, she tells me a little bit about herself. Like how much it sucks when your parents make you move halfway across the country the summer before your senior year. Hannah had lived most of her life in New Jersey. But she didn't really have an accent, like those kids on the *Jersey Shore* show.

When I ask she says, "Where I lived people don't have Jersey accents. It's not a plus when you interview at Ivies."

At around five a couple of more guys show up for work, and for the next couple of hours I just sort of follow them around and watch. Hannah is working the front of the store and when it slows down at around ten I punch out. Before I head out the back door I pick up Hannah's time card and check out her last name. When I get home I light up my monitor. It takes about two minutes to find her Facebook page.

She's got hundreds of friends, but the only one I recognize is a guy from my school, Steve, who works with us at Saviano's. Probably the rest are from New Jersey.

But I find out all kinds of stuff about her. Like one of her favorite quotes: "You have to fling yourself at what you're doing, you have to point yourself, forget yourself, aim, dive." Which comes from someone named Annie Dillard. So now I have to wiki Annie Dillard and Google the quote. It comes from *An American Life* and I make a mental note to grab a copy from the library.

And then I stare at her picture. It's a weird photo of Hannah— at first I didn't even recognize her. She's done something with her eyebrows to make them huge and dark. They look the way painters draw seagulls from a distance—black wings. And there's a stuffed monkey over her right shoulder, palm leaves behind her and a shell necklace around her neck. Her hair is parted down the middle and pulled back, tight. I spend a long time trying to figure it out.

And then her photo gallery. She's got a couple dozen photos that she's taken and they're really interesting. Not a bunch of goofy snapshots or anything like that. They're really complicated photos. Some of the color ones, you can't even tell what she was taking a picture of, because it's all sort of blurry and abstract like a painting. I stare at these for a long time too.

Then as long as I'm on Facebook I check out Brit's page. She's got a new photo up mugging with the same senior guy I used to see her with in the halls. Some guys, like Garrett, they must just be born with a gift. They just understand girls the way I understand numbers. Flipping back and forth between Hannah's and Brit's pictures, I'm thinking I got screwed in the gift department.

But all of these distractions, plus work. It's killing my training time. And in the back of my mind, the clock is always ticking, ticking down.

20.

Next night, I just go to work like I've been doing it for years. And actually, after a couple of hours, I could do it without thinking.

So I end up standing there elbow to elbow with Steve or one of the other guys, and you'd get to talking. Maybe that's what Mom was saying when she said work would be good for me, because usually I'm not much of a talker. But I can listen.

My third shift I get lucky and it's just me and Hannah working on the pizza assembly line. At first it's really busy and we just are working and talking about the orders and how it would be nice to get a break.

Then around eight o'clock the orders slow down. We're straightening things up, getting the pepperonis out of the olives, wiping down the stainless steel when suddenly Hannah stops and looks right at me.

"If you could do anything you wanted with your life, what would it be?"

Of course, the answer is obvious. But I can't just blurt out that I want to play computer games for a living without revealing myself as a mega-nerd. So I just sort of shrug and grunt which Hannah takes as a cue to answer her own question.

"I want to do something that makes a difference, you know?" An order flashes up on the monitor and I pull a large tin off the rack, the ones with the crusts already on.

"Back when we lived in New Jersey, Mom and Dad would drag me and my brother to New York on weekends. Usually to a museum. Which I hated, for no other reason than I had no choice and I'd rather hang out with my friends. Anyway, one day, about a year ago, we go to this big art museum downtown. And I'm grumping about it in the car and my little brother is being a total pain in the ass, poking me and pulling my hair and whatever. So when we get to the museum I tell them that I'm going to go check out the fourth floor and I'll meet them in the lobby in an hour. You know, just to get away from them."

While she's talking another order comes up and Hannah stops to grab an extra-large tin. I finish my mushrooms and see that she's starting to work on hers, spreading out the sauce, but in slow motion, like she's painting a picture with the ladle.

"So anyway, I'm just wandering around aimlessly and I find myself standing in front of this huge painting. It's what they call surreal. Everything is painted realistically in detail, but the stuff doesn't make any sense. Like a dream. There's this giant plaza like area in the foreground, kind of like a chessboard, and these ugly decomposing animal-like creatures are standing around, like chess pieces, I guess. But one side of the plaza is eroded away, like the way the coastline is after a big storm, when chunks fall into the ocean…"

She glances over to see if I'm following her and I look up and nod. She's got a strange, intense look on her face and I just want to stare at her, but I start on the green peppers instead.

"Anyway, your eyes follow the lines of this plaza and there, on the edge, there's a young girl, painted perfectly, like a photograph. And she's hanging onto the edge of the plaza and dangling there by her hands, naked above this bottomless canyon. And there's no one there to help her, just these creatures who look like wax statutes of weird mythical creatures who have been half melted. And I just stared at that painting for like an hour and it seemed to me that it was speaking right to me, that I was that girl, or that I was supposed to save that girl. I'm not sure…"

She seems lost in that thought and I finish my pizza, slide it down the line and take over on hers, rearranging the pepperonis so that they meet O'Neill's specs—not quite touching, but covering the whole pizza.

I want to ask her what that has to do with what she wants to do with her life. Save people maybe?

Then she starts talking again. "Something about that painting, the way it reached out and touched me. That's what I want to do. I want to touch people that way."

"So are you good at it?" I sometimes say the first thing that comes to my mind and as soon as I do I realize that I sound like an idiot. I get what Hannah is saying, about doing something great. When I was about eight or nine I got into reading these little biographies of famous people, written for kids. Each one of them starts out with the famous person's birth and then has about a hundred pages on their growing up. Then in the last chapter they become president or invent the light bulb or whatever. I think what I liked about these books was trying to figure what happened when they were kids to make them do great things. And then to wonder if I had any of these things working for me.

So even though the first thing that comes to mind is Hannah painting, I know she could mean a hundred other things.

"What?" Hannah says. Looking at me now like I've broken some rich and delicious trance.

"Well," I mumble. "I was just wondering, you know, about painting. Do you paint?"

She looks up at the tag in front of her and sees that her pizza is gone. I point at the one in front of me as I put the finishing touches on it.

"I got it," I say.

"Oh thanks," she says. "Guess I got carried away. What did you ask?"

"Painting."

"Oh yeah, sure. I paint. But I suck." I wonder if it's true or it's like me and Starfare. Like I know I suck, but I'm still really good compared to almost anyone else.

"You know, I saw some of your photos. They're sort of like that."

Hannah actually jumps. "You saw my photos?"

Now I'm wondering if I should have said anything at all. Like she'll think I was spying on her or something.

"They're up on your Facebook page." And before she can say anything about it I just start rambling. "You know, those color ones. I think they're flowers. They remind me of this exhibit my mother took me to at the Art Institute. They were by this famous woman painter…"

"Georgia O'Keefe?" Hannah asks.

"Yeah, that's it. I mean they reminded me a lot of her flower paintings, which when you look at them, they're not just about flowers…"

"Exactly," Hannah is saying, looking at me with a sort of shocked expression, as if I were a superhero whose mild-mannered secret identity had just been inadvertently revealed.

Then she picks up another crust and begins to work the sauce. After a minute she asks, "What would you do if your parents told you you'd have to move halfway across the country your senior year of high school?"

So I tell her about my mom moving to California and how close I was to having to move out there. Hannah has about a hundred questions about that and I get the feeling that she might actually like living in a place like the Institute.

"Anyway, at least you didn't have to do it. Move, that is. Leave all your friends. I mean, it's not like you can't stay in touch. But I get a text from one of my old friends, and it's all about some party some guy I don't even know threw the night before with a bunch of new people I never met and after a while, what's the point? And then some people you'd most expect to stay in touch with, they have no interest. Like it's not as if you moved. It's like you died."

I say, "Yeah," wondering if she's thinking about some guy, back in New Jersey. And then thinking about how weird it would seem to Hannah to find out that my best friends, like DT, are online. True, I do still see Eric sometimes, but last semester he started hanging out with Becca, who is actually really into gaming. She was in our World of Warcraft guild for a while and now the two of them are inseparable. So mostly I'm online with DT and other guys. Not many people seem to understand how that works.

But that night, when I'm back at home, lying in bed, my mind still firing like a Starfare screen, I keep hearing Hannah's voice, talking about seeing that painting and the passion for something special.

Back when I was in grade school Mom seemed to worry a lot about my gifted program. She was always saying that everyone is special in their own way and has their own talents and that I shouldn't think I was better than anyone just because I could do more math than them. Not that that was a problem, because no one gave a crap that you could do long division in first grade. They were more interested in how far you could throw a football or who could run the fastest.

But when I think about it now, I'm thinking Mom was wrong. Not everyone can shoot a basketball into a tiny hoop from thirty feet, over and over like Garrett. Not everyone can paint a picture so great that it can stop a beautiful girl in her tracks. Not everyone can have the mental and physical skills it takes to absorb an entire Starfare map, assess your opponent's strategy while tapping out commands on the keyboard faster than the hardest song ever on Guitar Hero.

No, very few people have what it takes to be great at any particular thing. And if you find that thing and don't go for it, that would be the ultimate fail. I try to imagine what it would be like living with that. And all I can come up with is Dad.

21.

The next day I get up relatively early, at least for me, with a fresh determination to make some progress. But one of the hardest things for me is to figure out what I need to do to get better. It's not like I can simply ask someone. I'm already the best player in Kansas City. Probably by far.

Sometimes I think about how much coaching Garrett got. From school coaches. From older players. From college coaches at sports camps. I once looked it up online. Garrett's college basketball coach gets paid $350,000 a year. He damn well better know a thing or two about the game.

So I never really know if I should be spending more time watching pro gamers, or reading the strategy message boards, or just playing the best competition I can find. Which is also a problem, because when you get to my level, you can't just click on a server and expect to pick up a really good game at random. Chances are you'll be playing someone you can beat without any real effort. And how is that supposed to make you better?

So I do what I normally do, a little bit of everything, and then before I know it it's time for my evening shift at Saviano's.

22.

Two good things about work: Hannah, and for every four hours you work you get one ten-inch pizza. Of course there are down-sides. Shifts without Hannah. Getting sent home after three hours when things are slow and not getting your ten-inch. And of course, those countless hours of lost training time.

But to be honest, walking from my place to Saviano's, I'm not thinking about Starfare skills or lost practice opportunity or improving my national ranking. I'm thinking about Hannah.

Even though it's only a few blocks and the sun is low, I can't believe how hot it is. It's not just that's it hot and still. But the air is so thick and heavy you'd think that it wasn't normal air at all, but something thicker and murkier, like a winter dream when you have twenty pounds of blankets weighing down your legs and you're trying to run away from that monster from *Alien*. After half a block I can already feel the moisture beading on my forehead. It sucks to get all sweated out before you go to work. The air smells of cut grass and tilled gardens and every few seconds a cicada will scream from one of the trees above, quickly joined by dozens of others, wailing like a tornado warning.

The tornado sirens don't penetrate to the depths of the restaurant, through the piped in music and the rattling of plates in the dish-washer, where Hannah and I are busily assembling pizzas. I don't know what makes me step away from the counter and down the hall. Only as I approach the back door do I hear a faint whine. When I push the door open to the back parking lot the sirens aren't nearly as troubling as the sky. A line of dark clouds with a yellow-green hue, oddly humped, are almost straight overhead. A roar from the right turns my head. I can see the massive dark funnel, like a black hand of the devil, spewing debris as it snakes ominously across the ground. Directly towards me. Not more than a mile down the road.

I slam the door and race inside. I scream Hannah's name and she turns from the counter. Her expression is surprise and concern. I run to her and grab her hand and pull.

"We've got to get the cooler!" I yell. And because we don't have time I half drag her towards the metal door of the walk-in refrigerator.

"Tornado!" I yell and then we are inside and I slam the door shut and pull Hannah down. Just as I lay myself on top of her the world explodes and we can hear what it must sound like to be in the midst of a bomb attack. We can feel the entire room rotating, as if we were on a carousel and not solid ground, and then, as fast as it began, it's completely quiet. I realize I'm still on top of Hannah and as she stirs, my head on the nape of her neck, I smell her hair and feel her from the tip of my chin all the way to my ankles.

I roll to the side and say, "Sorry."

"What the hell?" Hannah says as we stand up. She's brushing the front of her clothes with her hands, as if I had thrown her onto a dirt pile instead of a shiny, stainless steel floor. I try to open the door, and can only move it a few inches.

"Let me help," Hannah says, and together we push, the sound of something against the door grating. We finally get it open a few feet and step outside. We stare, stunned, at the still-dark sky which some-how glows directly overhead, tornado and emergency vehicle sirens the only sound. Nothing but broken boards and twisted roofing and mounds of debris at our feet and for hundreds of feet around us. The restaurant and the other shops are just gone.

"Oh my God," Hannah says as she throws her arms around me. "You saved my life!"

The spray of an evening sprinkler hits my face and I step away from the stuttering arcing spray. The restaurant is just a half block ahead.

Stepping into the cool restaurant is like jumping into a pool. I look down at my shirt, a few wet spots of perspiration on my chest. Hopefully not enough to raise a stink.

Hannah and I had worked assembly the previous shift and it had been great. Sometimes she seems like she's in a bad mood. Won't talk, does her work robotically. She'll ask me or Steve or one of the others if they'll close for her. Then you turn around and she's gone, disappeared. I figure it has to do with being so far away from all her friends and stuff.

But on Thursday it was just the opposite. The night before she'd seen this Netflix movie called *Fur* and all she could do was go on and on about it. It was apparently about some famous photographer named Diane something.

All evening it was like, "And then she did this just amazing series of photos of these circus performers who were like deformed and tattooed and grotesque, but not in her photos. It was as if she could see past all that ugliness and find their souls. Seth, you just have to see her work." She says she'll text me the link and pulls out her phone and I give her my number.

I didn't really follow a lot of what she was saying, but it was impossible not to get caught up in her enthusiasm. So that night when I got home I looked at trailers of the movie and read a little about Diane Arbus, the photographer, and looked at some of her pictures.

So after a quick stop in the restroom to mop up a bit I'm ready to pick up where we left off. Because I think Hannah's going to be impressed that I did all this research and I've even got some questions for her, because some of the photos were pretty weird.

So as soon as I get to the back room, Jake, this college guy who is one of the night managers, he tells me to get an apron and start making pizzas. I barely have time to acknowledge Hannah, who's working up front. We get really busy and I don't even see her for most of the night. Instead I'm shoulder to shoulder with this new guy who is working to buy mods for his Honda. So all night it's a monologue about whether a Borla exhaust system is better than a Bosch, whether twenty-inch rims are worth it and whether I think the black ones would look too dark on his black car and how much money he needs to save to lower the suspension. He has absolutely no clue that I couldn't give a damn.

So as we clean up, I'm thinking that an entire evening is an awful thing to waste. I'm bent over the counter, trying to wipe down the stainless so it doesn't streak, which is impossible, when someone grabs me from behind.

Hannah has wrapped her arms around me and has a chin on my shoulder. She's whispering something into my ear.

I can't hear her, because my blood is pounding like Niagara Falls. I don't care, as long as she doesn't let go. But she does.

"Well," she says, "can you?"

I turn around and shake my head and try to indicate that I don't know what she's talking about without appearing to be an idiot.

"Couldn't hear you," I say.

"Oh," Hannah says. "Steve and me and a couple of friends are going downtown to watch a midnight showing of *The Rocky Horror Picture Show* at UMKC. I've got the rice."

She's sort of bouncing up and down, singing something about a time warp dance. I have no idea what she's talking about.

"Rice?" I say.

Hannah yells out to Steve and he comes over, a mop in his hand.

"Looks like we got a Rocky Horror virgin! Seth, you've got to go with us!"

I say sure. Dad's out of town and I'm going to be up for another four or five hours anyway.

After we wrap up the cleaning we follow Steve out to his car, a little Nissan. The night air is still hot and heavy, but not as unbearable as it had been on the way to work. Hannah insists I ride up front but when we stop to pick up Steve's friends she says, "Hop back here—back seat for the short-legged."

I come around the back and slide in. When a guy and a girl come running out the guy jumps in the front and the girl hops into the back, so that I'm in the middle of this tiny back seat, thigh to thigh with Hannah and the new girl, who has long dark hair and looks, in the thin light, like she might be at least part Asian or Hispanic.

Steve twists around and says, "That's Steph." He nods towards the front seat and says, "And this is Gunda Din."

The guy in the front seat, dark bangs almost over his eyes, looks back and says, "You can just call me Gunnar."

Steve cranks the car and shouts back, "Everyone got their seatbelts on?"

I don't. I watch Hannah grab a belt and clip it in and hear another click from Steph's side.

I realize my belt must be stuck under us somewhere.

"I think it's under us," I say stupidly to Hannah.

She just grins and says, "So get it!"

My first try, directly behind me is fruitless so I have to start digging in the area between us.

"Oh," Hannah says, with mock drama, "That was *so* not the seatbelt you just grabbed."

Everyone is laughing except me. She makes me keep hunting and if we weren't in a crowded car with strangers I would have been having the best time of my life. My hand is directly under her ass and she's wiggling like she likes it. Even in the crowd, I'm getting plenty worked up.

Finally Hannah has pity on me, lifts herself up and grabs the wayward belt for me. As I drag it across my lap I'm not only in heaven, being crushed on both sides by two hot girls, one of whom is, beyond my dreams, Hannah, but incredibly relieved to be able to strap everything down in place.

Just like in the car, I get to sit between the two girls at the theater. If I sit kind of bowlegged my knee rests against Hannah's. She doesn't seem to mind. Mostly I'm thinking about that point of electric contact, and my arm on the armrest. Which Hannah sometimes shares. So my movie review is a little thin: Weird costumes, press my knee a little against Hannah's, listen to people yell out the lines, weird songs, listen to Hannah sing along, something about a guy dressed up like a girl, wedding, throw the rice all over the theater, hope that Hannah puts her arm back on the armrest. movie over, lights go up.

"So what did you think?" Hannah asks.

"Amazing," I say. Especially the part where you put your hand on my arm. But not as good as the drive back. We stop at my place first and before Hannah lets me out she puts a hand on my thigh and squeezes. I just about pass out from happiness.

"Thanks for coming along," Hannah says as she jumps out. I mumble thanks for inviting me and then she's back inside, the car door slams and I'm standing alone.

When I get inside I check a few things on the computer and then go to bed, still buzzing from the evening, the car ride, my hand underneath Hannah, her hand on my arm during the movie and best of all, that squeeze of my thigh. So my mind is about as far from Starfare as it could be, as I imagine what it would be like, if she were here, lying there, right next to me.

23.

You know those suspense movies and TV shows, where a bomb is set to go off and the timer keeps ticking down and there's always something getting between the hero and the bomb? That's my life. I read a few years ago online about a study done on Korean gaming pros. They're usually world class when they are fifteen or sixteen and join a pro team as soon as they get out of high school. They peak at nineteen or twenty. By twenty-four or twenty-five most of them are out of the game, burned out or forced out by hotter, younger players.

That means kids younger than me are already making a dent on the pro circuit. And every day they get better and better. Summer is my big chance to make up ground. Normally, I could game all day. But this work thing is really cutting into my training time and not only that, but sometimes, instead of getting inside a game I find myself drifting, thinking about something Hannah said to me at work. Or the way she had her hair loose that night, instead of tied back, her hand brushing a strand back behind her ear.

So Tuesday I've got the night off at Saviano's and I'm resolved to avoid distractions. No work. No Hannah obsessing. I'm catching up on some forum chat about a new map that's scheduled to be released in a few weeks when I get an IM from DT.

DTerra: Hey, check this out.

He's attached a URL from GamerNews.com. I cut and paste it into my browser window and open up the website.

U.S Corporation Announces Plans to Break Korean Pro-Gaming Stranglehold

Mountain View, CA., July 2; Xerus Systems, one of the world leaders in connectivity technology has announced plans to form the first non-Korean-based Professional Starfare Team. The world's most popular computer strategy game, with over six million active players worldwide, is the backbone of the pro-gaming culture centered in South Korea.

"We have some terrific players based in the U.S., where Starfare was invented," announced Kai Butan, the team's new captain and manager. "Plus we're looking at talent in Europe and Southeast Asia as well."

The team will be solely sponsored by Xerus Systems. Andrew Gold, the founder and chairman of Xerus, was cited in the corporate press release as saying, "We see this as a golden—pardon the pun— opportunity to showcase our brand, which has, for twenty years, been at the forefront of one of the most challenging and competitive technology businesses in the world."

The team is planning to have a complete roster in place and be in Seoul, Korea, in time for the upcoming Starfare season, which begins in earnest in September.

ActionSeth: Holy crap

DTerra: No shit

ActionSeth: Who are they going to get to play?

DTerra: Kai Butan, he's that German guy that got to the final eight at world's a couple of years ago.

ActionSeth: Heard he burned out

DTerra: Well, u know one guy on the team for sure

ActionSeth: Yeah, who

DTerra: You're punking me, right?

ActionSeth: Just tell me

DTerra: Xerus—doesn't ring a bell?

ActionSeth: STFU and tell me

DTerra: OK Andrew Gold, the guy who founded Xerus? He's got this kid who plays

ActionSeth: Oh no

DTerra: U got it—Morris aka Stompazer

So I spend the next two hours trying to find out more about this new team and how they're going to put it together. The forums have a bunch of threads going but they're all speculation and rumor.

I'm about to give up and just get some gaming in when an IM pops up.

STOMPAZER: HEY NOOB HEARD THE NEWS?

I really don't want to get into it with him, but my curiosity overcomes my revulsion.

ActionSeth: Yeah congrats, I guess.

STOMPAZER: We already got the number one European signed, Mutant007. We invented the damn game and now we're going to shove it up those stuck-up Korean's asses

ActionSeth: So why u telling me

STOMPAZER: Because now you've got something to work for. Maybe if u bring your game up a couple of notches we'd consider u

ActionSeth: If ur playing I should b playing

STOMPAZER: LOLing...like at Nationals, you noob. If u can't even make it to the finals there how u going to keep up with these Korean superstars?

The next message I send him is pretty straightforward. And crude.

STOMPAZER: Be nice little man or ur never getting that try out

I shut down the IM platform and simmer for a while. Thinking my entire life is just some big setup to see how much humiliation one person can take. I'm so pissed off I'm in absolutely no shape to try to play and that means another day with my game sliding. Another day with the clock ticking. Another day closer to that moment when I find out I've been living in a dream world. When all my plans prove to be just other case of a kid who thinks he's setting himself up for glory, when the only thing he's lining up is a series of one disappointment after another.

24.

Next morning I sleep really late and when I finally drag myself into the kitchen Dad has left and there's a letter open on the table. It's from Mom. I read it while I eat some Crispix. Mom was always insisting that I eat non-sugared cereal, so I guess seeing her letter inspires me.

It's a long letter. She has lots of details about how the programs are going and her job working with a summer camp they run at the Institute. I'm really glad I didn't get hooked into working there. I have no idea what I could possibly have done.

After I fold up the letter and put it back in the envelope I see a note from Dad. He wants me to clean up my room and vacuum the whole place before he gets back in two days. So that gives me plenty of time to procrastinate.

I look online for more information about the Xerus team, but there's nothing. I send an email to Garrett telling him that we got a long letter from Mom. That she seems to be doing great. I ask him when he's coming back to town, because even though he told me once, I forget that sort of thing immediately.

Then I IM DT but he's not at his computer.

When I run out of stuff to look at online I put myself into the queue for a Starfare game, even though I don't have my normal, blood-pumping anticipation. The first game is a joke, but at least it takes my mind off of Stomp and his new team. By the second game I'm in the zone and time just evaporates as I win three straight. When I glance at the time on the computer I realize I have to get ready for Saviano's. If my memory is right, Hannah is on duty too. Just that thought sends a wave of adrenaline through my body, a sinking sensation and heavy heartbeat—the same sort of delicious anxiety I get before a big Starfare tournament.

I shower up and head outside. As I step out the front door it feels like I just put my face a foot too close to a campfire. It must be at least 100 degrees. It makes me think how nice it would be if I were pulling out of the garage in an air-conditioned car.

So I'm pretty pitted out by the time I get to the restaurant. Which sucks because I just took a shower. The first thing I do is check the schedule. And Hannah's not on. Which turns the whole shift into slow motion. What makes it worse is I get stuck working again with ricer boy, who keeps bugging me to come out on break and look at his new wing. So I go to humor him and resist the urge to tell him it looks like he just welded an ironing board to the back of his car. Because I have to admit, as stupid as it looks, at least he *has* a license and a car.

25.

Friday night, I'm off work. Around seven I hear the garage door opening and I realize Dad's back. Luckily I'm between games so I race downstairs and pull out the vacuum while he's unloading his car and I've got it humming by the time he steps through the kitchen and into the living room.

He rolls his eyes when he sees me vacuuming, but at least he can't start right off yelling at me. By the time I'm winding the cord back up he's got the door shut in his study and I figure he's lying back in his favorite chair, sipping some sort of martini or bourbon or whatever he's drinking these days.

When I get back to the computer I check my IMs and see that I missed one from DT. He wants to know if I have time to play some two-on-twos. I'm about ready to say sure when I hear a text coming in on my cell. My heart skips as I begin to read. *Hey can't believe we both got Friday off…I'm going crazy around here. Let me know if u want to do something H*

Hannah. I love texting because no one can hear you stuttering. I write *sure*, thinking that I'm lucky that she's new in town and doesn't know many people yet. Because I'm not getting a whole lot of offers like this. I mean, this past semester I'd have been in heaven for a week if Brit had just stopped in the hall and chatted with me.

While I'm waiting for her answer I send DT a message saying I can't play. Of course he wants to know why not, since I never say no. I tell him I'll talk to him later and sign off.

Hannah says we could go to Westport and hang for a while. Which is fine with me because I'm starving and there's this place there with really good pizza. She writes that she's got the car for the evening and I give her directions to my place and have just enough time to jump in the shower. I actually worry about which T-shirt to wear. Which is not like me at all.

I wait for her outside and after about five minutes a blue minivan slows down and then I see Hannah waving. I jump in. She's got her hair tied back so I can see at least three golden studs in her ear and she's wearing this white frilly blouse with some sort of needlework design. I've never seen her behind the wheel and she looks out of place to me. Which is the way I still feel when I practice driving.

"Sorry about the car," she says as we pull out. "They won't let me drive the sports car."

"Hey, this is great," I say. And I mean it. She could have picked me up in a semi and I would have been happy.

"You can help navigate," Hannah says. "I still get lost every time I go anywhere."

I get a wave of hot anxiety because I'm the worst at finding places. I've been trying to pay more attention about how to get around, knowing that I'm going to get my license before long. But for years I've just spaced out between departure and destination.

But between the two of us we find our way to Westport and get lucky with a parking place behind the pizza place. As we step through the double doors we get hit with a wave of pizza smell which is somehow totally different than Saviano's.

"I'm pretty sick of pizza," Hannah says.

"Me too," I say, although I'm not. Even though I should be.

"Don't worry," I add. "They have a lot of different stuff. I saw they got a 'Best of Kansas City' for their subs."

"Oh great," Hannah says. "Where did you see that?"

I point to a framed poster on the wall across from us and Hannah laughs. "Yeah, I saw that too."

We have to wait for a table in the front of the restaurant next to this long deli counter filled with all sorts of salads that I wouldn't eat if I were starving. Standing there I want to stare at Hannah but I know that would be really lame so I just glance over at her and try to think of things to say. It's noisy and they're playing some sort of old rock music.

"I bet this place reminds you of home," I say.

She nods and as she looks around she lights up with a smile.

"This is just like Conte's. This place we used to go to downtown in Princeton. When I was little I used to go to the pool with Iris, my best friend back then. The pool was just across the street. And Mom and Dad would pick us up at the pool and we'd all just walk across the street. Our suits would still be wet and we'd be starved. You know how hungry you get after an afternoon at the pool? Like you haven't eaten in a week. We'd sit on our towels and order these giant pizzas and start shivering from the air conditioning. The wait was just excruciating. It would feel like hours."

A waitress is calling out a name and at first I think it's ours but she calls again and she's saying "Smith," not "Seth."

I'm just standing there fidgeting when someone taps me on the left shoulder. Surprised, I glance to see that it's not Hannah, who is looking the other way. I turn around the other way and there is the broad, pock-marked, sporadically hairy face of Big John Dauber. He's an older guy I've known for years. We used to play Magic together at the local card shop, Netherland. Next to him is his buddy Mark, aka Murk, who has shoulder-length hair held back by a red bandanna. Both are wearing some sort of goth-style black T-shirts.

"Hey," says John.

"Hey, man," Murk chimes in.

I glance towards Hannah who has turned around, so we're all facing each other.

"Man, nice job at Nationals," John says.

"You should hear the guys at Netherland," Marks chimes in. "It's like you're some sort of celebrity or something."

"Yeah, and not just the average dork we know you are!" John adds.

Hannah takes a step closer to me and both of the guys look at her simultaneously.

"Holy shit," Murk says and he's actually blushing.

"I take it back," John says.

There's a moment of awkward silence and it's Hannah who speaks up.

"Aren't you going to introduce me to your friends?"

"These two?" I blurt out. Like I might still have a chance to disown them. Both of whom are momentarily mute.

Hannah rolls her eyes.

"OK, sure. I mean this is Mark. Although we usually call him Murk. Which is too complicated to explain. And this is Big John."

They're both staring at Hannah.

"And this is my friend Hannah."

"Nice to meet you," Hannah says. And then, as if my prayers have been answered, the waitress is calling "Seth, party of two." I tell the guys we got to go and before another embarrassing word can be exchanged I've grabbed Hannah's hand and we're following the waitress into the back of the restaurant.

But I can manage to hear Big John say, "Holy shit, how the hell did he manage that?"

26.

As soon as we get seated it starts.

"OK, Mr. Seth Gordon, what is this about your secret life?" I can't tell if she's seriously angry or fake angry. But she's leaning towards me, across our little booth. She's got a scowl and she's drilling me with her eyes. All I know is it feels intense.

"It's no secret," I say. Which is true. If it's on the net, then it's public knowledge.

"Well, it's a secret to me. You got some sort of Bruce Wayne thing going here or what?"

"Talk about secrets," I say. "I had no idea you were into Batman."

"Don't try to turn this into a conversation about me. What are you, some sort of king of the Goths?"

"Not a king," I mumble lamely.

"A prince? Come on. Just come clean. What makes you famous among whatever *Dungeons & Dragons* underworld those guys live in?"

The waitress steps up and saves me for a moment. We order drinks and subs even though I'm thinking pizza. When the waitress steps away Hannah is right back on it.

"Nationals? Didn't I hear those guys say 'nationals'? What's that all about?"

I see no way out now so I just tell her. As quickly and as simply as possible. Hannah has both elbows on the table, cradling her chin and she seems completely absorbed as I tell her about my sordid life as a competitive gamer.

When I finish Hannah seems satisfied. She brushes a strand of hair behind her ear and says, "So this gaming thing, exactly how good are you?"

I tell her that I'm pretty good, compared to most people. But that I suck when compared to the pro-gamers.

"Pro-gamers?" Hannah says. "You mean someone actually pays people to play those games my little brother is always begging me to play with him?"

I explain that it's not every game and that the pro game is mostly a Korean thing. She has another dozen questions before the food comes. I try to steer the conversation elsewhere, so I ask her about school.

I must have hit a hot button with the school topic because as we eat our subs she has a bunch of questions about North. I can tell she's matching it up against her old school.

"You know," she finally says after I do my best to describe North to her. "Back in New Jersey I was really into that whole high school social thing. Had a bunch of friends I'd hung out with forever. And we'd do stuff with these guys. And I thought they were all the best friends ever and that I wouldn't get into that boyfriend, going steady thing…"

She's looking through me now, thinking about that world. Then she blinks hard and she's looking at me again.

"But you're not interested in all that. What do you know about your yearbook?"

She tells me about working on the yearbook staff at her old school and how she was all set to be photo editor. How she is never going to forgive her parents for moving the summer before her senior year.

"Not that I have any real interest in that sort of hack work," she says. "But I got access to a lot of equipment. Lighting and stuff. Plus the darkroom and printers."

Unfortunately I don't know anything about North's yearbook

or photographers or equipment.

"The only good thing about moving is we have a lot more room. So Mom and Dad let me take this attic space and make it into my studio. It's actually worked out really great. I need a large format printer and I'm hoping the school has one…"

"Your stuff is so far ahead of what they're doing they'll be begging you to work with them."

"You really like my photos?" She's rolling and unrolling a paper napkin.

"Yeah, I do. It's not like the other crap people put up. You know, fuzzy stuff taken with a cell phone that's probably funny to the five people who where there when it was taken."

The waitress comes over and asks if we'd like something for dessert. We both say no and she says she'll bring our check.

As she walks away I say, "But one thing I didn't really get…"

Hannah is waiting.

"That portrait of you. With the weird eyebrows. And the shell necklace and the little stuffed monkey…"

Hannah laughs, nervously, I think. "Oh God, that was something I worked on last year. It's probably totally lame. It's based on a famous self-portrait by this Mexican painter. Frida Kahlo?"

I shake my head. Mom has taken me to lots of art museums and exhibits, but if I've seen her paintings, I can't remember.

"I know, who is going to get that? As if my friends are art historians or something. I should take that down. I think I will as soon as I get home."

"You shouldn't," I say with surprising conviction. "It's interesting. It made me stop and think. You know how hard that is to do on a Facebook page?"

Then we talk about the courses we're taking and find we have a couple of classes in common even though I'm technically a year behind her. But then we compare birthdays and we're only like two months apart, because of the way the kindergarten start days work. So that makes me feel a little better, because it seems like girls don't want to go out with younger guys. Anyway, all my classes are junior and senior stuff. Plus the math class that I'm signed up to take at UMKC, because I've run out of math at North.

When the check comes Hannah grabs it and insists on paying. "You can get the next one," she says when I protest. And I'm so psyched there will be a next one that I don't utter another word.

As we head back to the car I'm thinking she's forgotten about the gaming stuff and still thinks I'm a fairly normal guy. But as she cranks the engine she turns and grins and says, "OK gamer boy. Let's head to your place. I want to see you in action."

27.

On the drive back I try to figure out how to tell her this is a bad idea. Because I've spent years trying to keep these things—school and gaming—in separate compartments. Virtually no one at North is onto my gaming life. And the local guys I game with— they're mostly out of high school or go to different schools.

But when I think about it, I really don't know how to explain why I've kept these things separate. I guess because if girls like Brit thought I was a gaming nerd they'd never be seen with me. The guys I've seen her with, they're the regular, popular guys you'd expect. They play sports, they've got dozens of friends, they walk the halls like they own the place. They're all Garretts.

So I direct Hannah to Dad's place and when we pull up I say, "I guess you should know that my dad is out of town. I think he'll be back tonight, but really late."

"And your mom is living in California, right?"

"Right."

"So you're telling me we'll be all alone in your dad's cozy little bachelor pad?"

"Well, that's not exactly what I meant."

"No?" Hannah cuts the engines and the lights so now when I look at her I can just see her silhouette. The streetlight down the block casts just enough light so that I can see a little glint from her eyes and the perfect curvature of her cheekbone and nose.

"You weren't planning on trying anything, were you?" she says, turning to look directly at me. Luckily it's too dark for her to see me blush. I hope.

"No, no, nothing like that."

Hannah pops the door and says, "No, I didn't think so." But the way she says it makes me pretty sure she's just punking me. And at the same time, the blood is rushing, thinking about being inside my place with her, just the two of us.

As we walk up the front stoop I say, "Are you sure…"

"Just open the stupid door," Hannah says.

So of course I fumble with the keys and drop them and when I finally get the door open and pop on the light Hannah steps through in front of me.

She does a full take of the living room and says, "Well, I can tell your father is man of exquisite taste."

"Yeah?" I say, looking around at the velour couch, the big screen TV, the painting of the seascape as if I had never seen them before.

"That painting is a nice touch—starving artists I bet. And that throw rug. It's like the Dude's rug in *The Big Lebowski*. It really ties the room together."

"Yeah," I say. "I've often thought so myself." Thinking, she can quote *The Big Lebowksi*. She's even more awesome than I thought. And Mom, she would say the same thing about Dad's sense of style. Back at our old house he had a whole room in the basement that was just for his sports stuff. The rest of the house was hers.

"OK," Hannah says. "Let's see where you destroy the hopes of every little gamer boy in America."

Crap—my room. Which is completely covered with dirty clothes. And my computer desk looks like I'm some sort of world class Dr Pepper can collector.

"Just give me a minute," I say, and I run upstairs. Stuff all of the laundry under the bed, throw my bedspread over the messed covers and realize I'm just going to have to live with the cans.

I'm breathing hard when I run back downstairs. I find Hannah in Dad's study.

"Nice room," she says. She's checking out the rows of Garrett's basketball trophies, the framed pictures of his teams, the Chiefs memorabilia.

"Well my dad thinks so."

She walks over and opens the refrigerator and glances at the rows of beers.

She looks back up at me as she shuts the door and says, "My dad has his own getaway room too. It's not beer and football. He's more into classic rock and crime novels. But I get it."

Being in Dad's room kind of creeps me out so I say, "Come on, you can be the first person to see my bat cave."

It is one of the dizziest, most exciting moments of my life. Leading Hannah into my bedroom. The scene of 1,001 fantasies, many of which have recently begun with, well, leading Hannah into my room.

Hannah heads straight for my desk and begins looking over my computer equipment. I feel like giving her a hug just for not mentioning the general disarray and the expanse of Dr Pepper cans. When she touches the mouse it lights up and her hand jumps back as if it had shocked her.

"That's a weird-looking mouse."

I've got one of the better gaming mouses, a Logitech G6. When you touch it, it glows with a spiderweb of blue decorations. It has a couple more buttons than a normal mouse. My gaming keyboard glows red.

"Serious gamers can get really particular about their equipment," I say. "It's like, I suppose, a musician. A couple of years ago my mom took me to see these old rock and rollers downtown, Elton John and Billy Joel. And Elton John, he just starts ranting about the problems with this grand piano he's being forced to play, as if it's a piece of junk and not a Steinway."

I put my hand on the keys. "I like this keyboard too. Here— type something."

Hannah leans over and pushes a couple keys that audibly click. "Weird," she says.

"It's a mechanical keyboard. Most modern keyboards work with electrical contacts; this is more like the old style. But with a mechanical keyboard you get better feedback—you can tell if you've missed a stroke."

When I glance over at Hannah she seems interested. I sit down and start up the computer, then get up and grab an extra chair from Dad's bedroom and set it next to mine. As the screen begins to glow a block of text appears.

I'm anxious to boot up the Internet but as I reach for the keyboard Hannah's leaning in tight.

"Just a second," she says. "What is this?"

"Oh that doesn't have anything to do with gaming. It's not important."

"I'll be the judge of that."

Hannah reads the first line out loud.

> Below is a report on the Woltman Mersenne work you have queued and any expected completion dates. M9481531. Lucas-Lehmer test, 29 20:0909
>
> The chance that the exponent you are testing will yield a Mersenne prime is about 1 in 85843.

After this box is another with a bunch of lines of code and numbers. "What the hell is that all about?" she asks.

It's bad enough that I'm giving myself up as a gaming nerd. But a math nerd too? I see no way out so I sigh and say, "OK, I signed up to participate in this international effort to find the largest prime number. There are about ten thousand computers all working on the problem and I have the software installed that runs in the background. Basically it takes an insanely large number and divides it by every possible number. If none of them come out as a whole number, then I may have found it."

Hannah shakes her head. "And you just signed up for this, for what? Fun?"

"Well, yeah. First of all it's pretty cool, being part of that. And if the number I'm working on turns out to be the first prime number over twenty million digits I get my name attached to it and win a cash prize of $50,000."

I let Hannah soak that up while I click through Mozilla and start to boot up the Starfare server.

"So what games have you played?" I ask Hannah.

"I don't know. A bunch of stuff. My brother is always begging me to play with him. He's got a couple of those car racing games. I'm terrible at those. And Wii stuff like tennis and bowling. I'm actually pretty decent at Wii tennis. Back in New Jersey when we were in grade school we were into the Sims for a while. And last year some of my friends back there wanted me to get into Farmville but it never really took."

"You ever play any multiplayer strategy games?" I say as the Starfare screen pops up.

"Not really, but I knew this guy back home. He got into one of those, I think it was called World of Warcraft. He just disappeared for a year."

I laugh as the IM screen lights up. "That happens a lot."

I punch through a series of pages to check on the latest ratings and see where I'm standing on the national list. Still number five.

"What's this? Hannah asks.

I point to ActionSeth on the list. "National rankings. That's me."

I click back onto the home page and get into the queue for an advanced one-on-one.

Within a minute I've got a couple instant messages from players I know, throwing insults and asking me where the hell I've been.

Hannah wants to know who all these people are and I tell her about a few of them. For instance, Grrr2 is a college guy. Real name, Saahil Bhupati. Computer science major at Carnegie Mellon. He's always getting on these rants and is just generally hilarious. He played a lot more before he started college, but we still do some two-on-twos. Then a message from that girl who was at Nationals, RaiderRadar. Wanting to know if I could play a quick game.

"Her real name is Morgan," I say. "She's probably the top-ranked girl in the country. I think my friend DT has a thing for her."

"And you?"

"When we play, it's all business," I say. "If I don't play my best, she'll show no mercy."

"Why don't you play her then," Hannah says and I say fine.

So I IM RaiderRadar and we get in the queue.

Hannah is leaning over the monitor, trying to keep up with the banter when a message, all caps comes across.

HEY PUSSY HEAR UR GAME IS STILL SHIT. U ALWAYS WERE A NOOB.

It's Stompazer. I shut down the IM window.

"Well," says Hannah. "I guess this gaming stuff is no different from the rest of the Internet. Hang out long enough and creeps will find you. "

"Yeah, that guy is a real jerk. He's been on my case for a long time. Thinks he's going to be world champ. And he would be too if you could just buy it. His old man is on every one of those 'world's richest guys' lists."

Hannah is nodding. "Oh I know. We had a guy like that back in Jersey. Came to school in this million-dollar Porsche and expected everyone to kiss his shoes. His father hired Mellon Collie to play for his sixteenth birthday. Can you believe that?"

Then my game comes up and after a twenty-second countdown I'm in. I can usually tell within three or four minutes if I'm going to have an edge, but Raider has always given me tough games. Naturally, I'm a bit distracted, thinking about what Hannah is thinking, but my hands seem to know what to do on their own.

The first ten minutes can be extremely intense and I've got a lot of stuff going on at once, which means I'm all over the map, getting my munitions factories up and running while coordinating three different spybots which keep me posted of my opponents developments. If you were watching my hands, the way Hannah was, it wouldn't make any sense at all. It would be like watching a little kid trying to pretend he was a piano virtuoso, my left hand a blur of action, the mouse clicking and weaving like it was alive and trying to escape my grasp.

It's over in about twenty minutes. As usual my endgame is just a little stronger.

"Good game," Raider IMs. "My honor, let's do it again soon." Then she signs off.

"My honor?" Hannah says looking at the now-quiet screen. "What the hell was that anyway? I couldn't make any sense of it, other than you seem to be really good at whatever it is."

I rock my chair back.

"That, my dear, was a short display of some pretty damn high-level Starfare."

I click through to a site on the pro game. The title is "100,000 Fans Gather to Watch Starfare Finals."

Hannah leans in closer to the monitor. "A hundred thousand people to watch a video game?"

"Only in Korea. That's where the action—and money—is."

Then I show her the page which lists the pros' year-to-date earnings. And when I tell Hannah my plans to get on that list, she doesn't laugh or act like I'm nuts. So I just keep talking, telling her how it works, and how the American players haven't really broken through, yet.

And then, I almost faint because she asks if she can watch me play again. "I want to see that look on your face," she said. "I don't think I've ever seen anyone that intense."

She doesn't have to ask twice.

28.

When I've won the second game Hannah starts asking one question after another. "How do you learn this stuff?" "How many people play?" "Who are all the people messaging you?"

Normally I don't talk much, but once I start there's no stopping me.

"When did I start? Man, that's like trying to remember when you had your first ice cream cone or the first time you saw the Simpsons. My mom says I was on the computer when I could hardly talk. Then my mom and dad started buying these stupid little computer games. If you looked at one of those now it would be like, I don't know, seeing a horse and buggy. As I got older the games kept getting better and better and I just grew up with them."

For some of her questions I jump around the Web.

For my online friends I show her a few profiles, which are actually pretty hilarious. We are looking at this photoshopped picture DTerra made of his head on a World of Warcraft ogre's body then I hear a muffled ring tone so naturally we both pull our cells out. Hannah pulls out her cell and says hi.

After a couple of "OKs" Hannah flips her phone shut. She's sitting a little behind me and to my left. When I turn my head she's right there. I'm not sure if the warmth is from my reddening cheeks or from her. I'm holding my breath, but with that last inhalation I smell her breath, sweet as vanilla.

"You might be shocked to hear this," she whispers. "But I actually had a really good time tonight. You know, this gaming thing is a pretty strange world. But I don't mean bad strange. I mean most of the artists I like are pretty strange."

This is the time, I'm thinking, where I lean in and she closes her eyes and I kiss her. And I really want to. But it's not like in the movies where everybody is placed just right and the background music is there and the director is saying to the actress, "Now close your eyes and lean in..." Because when I start to lean I can't even reach her. And then she's standing up.

"I was supposed to be home ten minutes ago," she says. "But there's something..."

I stand up. Now we're close to being in the right position. But she's turning, heading towards my bedroom door. She stops in the doorway. "I've got something I want to show you."

"Now?"

She steps back into the room and reaches out. I'm about to grab her hand when she says, "Give me your phone."

I dig it out of my pocket and hand it over. She punches though the menus and fills out her whole profile. I'm trying not to be too obvious, peering over her busy fingers. When she puts in her actual address I'm pretty sure something like a gasp escapes my throat. She pretends she doesn't notice.

"Now I have to get home. Tomorrow. Call me."

I walk her to the front door. After she's gone I head back to my room and flop onto my bed and look around. I've got a Starfare poster from one of their new release campaigns. A bunch of crappy little trophies on my dresser which you get for showing up for games from back when I was doing soccer and basketball. A bookshelf, mostly science fiction and fantasy. I'm thinking something's different. It was like when my mom would come in and straighten things up. Or when I went to summer camp one year and she painted it. When I got home she took me into the room and said, "So what do you think?" And I couldn't figure out what she was talking about, even though I could sense it. It was the same feeling. Something had changed, but I wasn't sure what.

29.

I don't hear Dad get in but when I wake up late I know he's home. I can smell coffee. But by the time I get downstairs he's gone. I'm into my second bowl of Frosted Flakes when I notice the note on the kitchen table.

"Seth, call this number. Some Chinese guy."

I stuff the note into my pocket and head upstairs to check out some stuff on the Internet. After a while I get into a Starfare game and then another. I've just mopped up the second game when the landline rings. Usually I let it ring through to the answering machine but for some reason I go into Dad's bedroom and pick it up.

"This is Seth Gordon?"

The accent is really heavy and the connection is fuzzy but I say yes. He tells me his name which sounds to me like Young Come Hill.

"I'm coach for Team Anaconda. Perhaps you've heard?"

That I hear perfectly well. It's the name of one of the top four professional teams in Korea. Main sponsor ANC Computers.

"Of course," I say, and I quickly name the top two players on his squad, both of them famous. Everyone on that team is an amazing player.

"Very good. Impressed. We also very impressed. I was at your Nationals in June and saw you play."

He does this weird laugh and adds, "Our whole team enjoy your creative use of miners. Very funny for us!" He laughs again and then clears his throat. "Anyway, after some many considerations we have decided that you are maybe most promising young American player."

"Yeah?" I'm pretty much too stunned to actually speak a sentence.

"We believe that with the proper application of our proven training methods that you could become very successful. Yes, very successful."

There is a bit of pause and I hear him talking to someone else, away from the phone, talking what I guess is Korean.

"Mr. Seth Gordon?"

"Still here," I say, as if I was going to hang up on him or something.

"I am calling because Team Anaconda is doing promotional tour across U.S. Chicago August fifteen and sixteen. We hope you to come and meet our players and maybe practice. Then we talk about your future. We pay for airplane ticket. Pick you up at airport. All very easy for you."

My heart is racing like I just ran a gym class mile.

"Mr. Seth Gordon?"

"Yeah, still here." I say.

"So you think this could be a yes? That you meet us in Chicago?"

For some reason I think of Stomp. Could he be capable of punking me like this? How did I know if this guy was real? I could just imagine Stomp and a couple of his buddies putting something like this on. Sitting around the phone, holding back their laughter.

So I'm a little cool when I say, "Absolutely. You just send me the tickets and details." That way, if nothing shows up, I can always tell Stomp I was on to him. And if the tickets show up? Hell, this could be start of my new life.

Yeong, or whoever it might be, rattles off my address and says that a FedEx package should be there in a day. Then he gives me a number which I jot down on a scrap of paper.

"You have question, you call."

"I will," I say, and as soon as I hang up I race back to my computer and look up Team Anaconda. Sure enough, there is a picture of Sun Kwon Yeong. But then again, if I can look up his name, then so can Stomp.

I IM DT but he's not online. I text him that I've got some big news. I've got to figure out how I'm possibly going to be ready. I've got two weeks to get my game into shape before I mix it up with some of the best pros in the world.

Then I collapse on my bed. Just lying there, dying to talk to someone so I dial Garrett.

"Hey kid brother," he answers. "I thought you'd lost your phone again or something, it's been so long since you called."

"Yeah, sorry about that, but you know how it is."

"Oh yeah. Dad says you got a girlfriend? What kind of miracle is that?"

"Up yours. And she's not really my girlfriend. Not like a Kimberly."

"A what?"

"Nevermind. It's just that she's new in town. Doesn't know many people. We've done a couple things together, is all."

"It only takes a couple of things."

"STFU, it's not like that."

"Not yet. Anyway, what's up? Usually you only call on my birthday or if you need to borrow something I left at home."

So I tell him about the call from the Korean team and he can tell from my voice that I'm pretty worked up.

"OK," he says. "OK, calm down. It sounds good. Sounds like a good opportunity, but there's no need to go nuts."

"Are you kidding?" I'm almost shouting. "The Chicago Bulls call you up and say they want you to come down and scrimmage. You're going to be what? Calm?"

"Have you told Mom or Dad?"

"Not yet."

"Well. I'd get on that. You're still a minor. I'm not sure you're allowed to blow your nose without permission. Let alone fly off to Chicago and get picked up by some stranger."

I want to argue with him, but know he's right. So I promise to call Mom and Dad and fill them in.

"So how's your summer?" I ask.

"It's fine. Got one more camp and then I'm going to come down and make your life hell for a couple of weeks. In fact, I'm flying in on the fourteenth so I should see you before you go on this Chicago thing. That is, if Mom and Dad let you."

30.

Mom made me enter a number at the Institute into my cell and that's the first number I call after hanging up with Garrett. I get an answering machine and even though I hate to leave messages I leave one, asking that Sunny Gordon call me.

Dad is on the road again, but he does most of his business over his cell and he picks up immediately. I start to explain it to him when I hear an announcement in the background.

"Say again," Dad says. "And make it quick. We're starting to board."

For some reason my dad always has to be the first on board every flight he takes. He gets something like a million miles a year and so gets all these perks. So when they announce they're boarding babies and cripples and triple-platinum members, you can bet that Dad will be pushing past the strollers and elbowing the cripples to be the first to stow his bag in the best spot above his seat.

I start explaining again.

I'm halfway through when he says, "Look, Seth, I've got to run. This sounds a little fishy to me. You text me the number of these guys and the name of their outfit and I'll check 'em out."

Like he has access to the National Security database or something.

So I say OK and go back to my computer and look up some info on Team Anaconda. I text him the basics and sit there staring at the computer screen. I just can't believe I'm going to have a chance to audition for one of the greatest teams in the world.

As I'm spacing out staring at the screen DT's IM pops up and asks what's up.

I tell him to sign onto the Starfare platform so we can talk. I slip on my headset and we're both on so I just let it all out in one manic burst.

"Holy shit," DT says. "You think this has anything to do with Stomp's team?"

"Maybe. You think they're worried about them?"

"Who knows? The main thing is they're interested in you. I've been telling you for years, you got some mad skills, dude. They know what they're doing."

I asked DT if he thought it could be a practical joke. That Stomp was just setting me up.

He pauses for a second and then says no, that it was way beyond Stomp.

"All he can do is scream and swear. No way. This has got to be real. And you had better get your game in shape."

I agree and we get in the queue for some advanced two-on-two action.

31.

That night I get a call back from Dad. He says he called and talked to the Yeong guy and did a little research and that it sounds OK to him. But he wants me to clear it with Mom.

I call and leave another message at the Institute.

I do a short shift that night, no Hannah. Totally boring and slow and I'm happy when they send me home after about two hours. There was a pepperoni pizza sitting in the take-out warmer for most of my shift. Sometimes people order and never show up. Who knows why. When I ask the manager he says I can have it.

So I walk home with an extra-large pizza. As I'm walking I call up Eric, who lives just a few blocks away and asks if he wants to come over and help me eat it. He says sure, but that he and Becca are just finishing up a World of Warcraft raid. Would it be all right if she came along?

They must be hungry because the pizza is still warm when they show up at my door. We eat it while watching a reality show about these people trying to be the next great American artist. In this episode they root through a big pile of garbage and try to turn the stuff into great art. They come up with some really weird displays. I wouldn't want to live with any of them, but the judges seem to like a couple.

I tell Eric and Becca about my tryout and they're pretty blown away. Eric used to play a little Starfare but never got very good. But he knows I've been doing really well with it.

After we knock off the pizza they decide to hang out awhile. So after the show is over we head upstairs to my room. They pull up chairs and watch me play a game. Eric's saying stuff like, "Damn, I never knew you could double your gamma cannons like that," and yelling encouragement when I get into a really big fight. And Becca, I can tell she's pretty impressed that I have a chance to go pro. She keeps asking stuff like how much a Starfare pro makes and whether there are any girls on the Korean teams. I tell her six figures is common for the good ones. I'm not sure about the girls because I see the names online but I don't know Korean names that well. So I just say probably.

It's kinda nice having live encouragement. I'm almost through with a second game when my phone rings. It's Mom. When I pick up and say "Hi, Mom," Becca and Eric exchange glances. I cover the receiver and tell them to take off if they want. After they leave I let Mom tell me all about her latest advances at the Institute while I'm blasting my way through the final stages of the game. I grunt and throw in some one-word comments.

"Seth," Mom says after about ten minutes. "Are you there. All there? Or are you gaming?"

"Here, Mom," I say, after a little pause, because I've got to get into the melee, toss out some carbide bombs and get out before they detonate.

"Sounds like you're gaming."

"No, Mom, really." Just a couple more blasts and I'll be done.

"So, Seth," Mom says. "I just got off the phone with your father and he said something about you wanting to fly to Chicago to play computer games with some Korean people? I don't know, Seth. You're only fifteen."

"Almost sixteen," I say automatically. Almost done.

"Neither your father or I know who these people are, Seth. They might have good intentions, but they might not. I'm not sure this is a good idea. You need to keep your mind focused on your studies. You'll be taking college courses next year and you have such a wonderful future, with your math abilities."

Done. I shut down the screen so I can focus.

"So I would say no to this thing," Mom is saying.

"No?" I can't believe this. "But Mom. I'd have a chance to meet some of the greatest players in the world. Play with them. It's going to be awesome."

"No, Seth. It's not going to be 'awesome.' It's going to be 'thanks, but no.'"

This is so typically Mom. She still thinks I'm just a kid. But she can be really stubborn.

"Mom, I've got to do this. Think of the most amazing thing that you could get to do. Like the world's greatest yoga guru calls you up and says come on over and be my private student. What would you do?"

"Seth, there is no such thing as the world's greatest yoga guru."

"You know what I mean."

"And you know what I mean. The answer is no."

I can see this is going nowhere. Out of the blue this comes to me.

"So what if Garrett comes with? He's free that week. I'm sure he'd come along. And Dad, he's got a ton of frequent flier mileage. He's always saying that he wishes he had the energy to travel for fun. It wouldn't really cost anything."

I can tell Mom is mulling this over. Even though Garrett is just a few years older than me, Mom and Dad consider him completely mature.

"You've talked to Garrett about this?"

"Not yet. But I was talking to him and he said he wanted to do some stuff together. This would be the perfect stuff. It would be like the old days, when he was living here and we'd hang out together."

I can tell from the pause that I've hit the right button.

"Mom, I'll talk to Garrett tonight. Call me tomorrow and I'll give you the details."

She says OK and hangs up. Now I just have to get Garrett on board. But when I call it goes straight to voice mail and after the third time I leave a message.

I'm just sitting there, buzzed from all the excitement. Wishing I had someone to talk to when I think of Hannah. I check my watch at it's almost eleven. Shit.

I call her cell and she picks up immediately. Before I can get a word out she's saying, "So you're really pushing it, aren't you. I mean, I ask you to call me today, and it's still today. Barely."

I stammer a bit and finally say, "Well, something happened today. Something sort of…I don't know, important."

"Yeah, me too."

"You first," I say.

"Well, I was going to show this boy something. Something that I've never shown anyone."

Now I'm really flustered because what I'm thinking probably isn't what Hannah is thinking. Or even more probably, she wants me to think what I'm thinking even though it isn't right.

"But now I'm not so sure that's a good idea."

"No?"

"No. Now your thing."

I tell her about the call from the Korean team and as much of the details of the conversation I can remember.

She keeps saying, "Wow."

"Well, that's my thing," I conclude.

"That was quite a thing," Hannah says.

"Yeah."

"So you are going to have to learn Korean?"

"I suppose a few words wouldn't hurt. And the really good news is that my mom, every time we got takeout Chinese, she made me eat it with chopsticks."

Hannah laughs and says, "OK, I forgive you. But I still have something to show you."

"OK."

"How about tomorrow afternoon?"

"Sure," I say. "Where?"

"I'll pick you up at one, OK? Got to go now."

It takes me a long time to get to sleep that night. But I'm fine with that because everything that's racing through my head, it's all good.

32.

When the phone rings it's the middle of the night. Or my night, at least. Naturally I can't find the thing, because I can't remember, in the fog of sleepiness, which shorts I wore the day before. And despite Dad's nagging, I haven't picked up my room and my entire wardrobe is spread across the carpet. I manage to find the right pocket just before it rolls to voice mail.

"Woke you up, didn't I?" Garrett sounds pleased with himself. "You know some of us have to go to work every day."

"I work nights, in case you forgot."

"Oh, my bad," he says in a way that makes it clear he isn't sorry. "You left me some sort of frantic message, dude, in case *you* forgot."

"Just me give me a sec," I say, to clear my head. I was dreaming about playing Starfare in front of a huge crowd and every time I scored a kill there was thunderous applause. I really would have liked to finish that game.

"OK, here's the deal," I start. I give it to him as simply as I can. How Mom doesn't want to me go to play with the Korean team. But that I was sure she would if he would come along. I even tell him I've got enough money saved up to pay his airfare if I had to.

I let him digest all of this and then he says, "Let me get this straight. You want me to tag along on a trip to Chicago where you are probably going to play Starfare for twelve hours a day. While I, what, sit and watch?"

"No, no," I'm actually shaking my head, as if he could see. "You can duck out as soon as we get to wherever. I'm supposed to get a package later today, with all the info. I bet you know lots of people in Chicago. You can go visit one of your old girlfriends. You should have one in every city in the country by now…"

"Hey, STFU. I cherish every one of those relationships. And as a matter of fact, we've got a guy on our team from Chicago who's been bugging me for a year to come and see the big city."

"See? Perfect solution. We tell Mom that you're chaperoning me. You call what's his name and hit the town. Details to follow."

So after hemming and hawing and trying to get a rise out of me he says that if that's the only way this thing is going to work that I could count him in.

"Thanks, bro!" I almost shout and cut the call before he has a chance to reconsider.

Then I go back to sleep.

33.

When I wake up, again, I immediately think of two things. First, the FedEx package from the Korean coach. If it's a real deal and not Stomp punking me. And then, almost simultaneously, the thing that Hannah is going to show me that she's never shown anyone before. I try not to think too much about the second thing. That leaves the package.

Dad is off on another road trip, so the kitchen is sort of a mess. I make a mental note to load the dishwasher and scoot past to the front door. As I open it the heat is like a pressurized cloud smothering our place, waiting for an opening to push inside. I step onto the stoop, ignore the papers that are lying, yellowing in the driveway. Only when I turn to go inside do I find the package leaning against the house just next to the door. I grab it and slam the door against the heat. Rip it open on the way to the kitchen table.

I lay the contents out on the table. A letter signed "Coach Yeong" which I set aside. A folder with a bunch of clippings on Team Anaconda, as if I hadn't heard of them before. And an airline envelope. Inside are e-tickets from Kansas City to Chicago. Behind the letter is a hotel reservation confirmation for a night at a Hyatt Hotel on Wacker Drive. I read the street name twice and shake my head, thinking, nice name. Then I grab everything and take it up to the computer. When I Google the Hyatt I see that it's a huge hotel right on Lake Michigan. It looks great.

I write it all up in an email and send it to Garrett and Dad, asking Dad if he could use his airline miles to get Garrett a ticket. I'm pretty sure he will, because he'll do anything for Garrett.

Then I sit back and read the letter and the rest of the stuff in the package. It's all there in writing. Team Anaconda is looking to add the best American talent to their team. It doesn't make it clear how many people are trying out, but you can tell it's not just me. Even though it's weeks away I'm getting the kind of nerves you get just before a big match. Heart racing, face flushing.

I send a note to DT telling him that he was right. That it's the real deal.

Then I check the message boards to see if there's any buzz from anyone else getting the invite. I find a bunch of stuff about Team Anaconda's promo tour—they're going to be in Los Angeles and Seattle before going to Chicago. Then New York and Atlanta and Las Vegas. But no one is talking about tryouts. I understand, because I'm not tempted to post anything. Why encourage more competition?

I'm still sitting there in my night shirt and the first pair of old shorts I could find when the doorbell rings. I look at the computer clock and swear when I see it's a little after one.

I run into my room, grab a fresh T-shirt throw it on and run down the stairs and open the door. Hannah. Smiling through the screen door. Hair glowing in the sunshine. Giant round sunglasses.

"You going to invite me in?" she finally says. "I'm going to melt in about thirty more seconds."

"Yeah, of course," I stammer and open the screen door and hold it as she brushes past me, smelling of something sweet and flowery.

"Hey," she says. "You forgot to put away your breakfast dishes."

From yesterday, I think. I actually haven't eaten anything yet today.

"Oh yeah. Behind schedule. I was just about to jump into the shower." And then I blush. Because this is not an image that I really want to project. "We got time? Only take me five minutes."

Hannah gives me a serious look. "Must be nice to have short hair," she says. "I've been giving it serious thought."

I could imagine two girls spinning this into an hour conversation, but all I can think of is that Hannah would look great, hair short, long whatever.

"So did you hear anything more about your thing?" Hannah asks.

"Oh yeah. Got a package. Tickets to Chicago. It's all upstairs by the computer. You can look it over while I…"

Hannah seems puzzled by this pause but then she seems to get it and grins and shakes her head.

"Don't worry," she says. "I'm not going to try to sneak in and satisfy any of your sick fantasies."

My first instinct is to defend them as not sick at all, but I'm a little tongue-tied so I just wave her to follow me upstairs. I leave her with the computer, grab some fresh clothes out of my room and duck into the bathroom. Cold water, I'm thinking. I've heard that works.

34.

We head south in Hannah's van, the heat drying my hair faster than a blow dryer. I play with the vents, trying to get a thin stream of cool air to keep me from sweating out my clean T-shirt. We head down Metcalf away from town and turn right onto a road that I don't recognize and then a mile down, turn left onto an even smaller road. The street sign says Sherman Court. One jog to the left and we're onto a small cul-de-sac.

"The big white one is ours," Hannah says. "It used to be a farmhouse. The developer left it here and put in all these other lots around it. I love it—it makes all these new houses look tacky." The other homes are all three-car garages with a house stuck on the side. Hannah's has to be the one at the end of the street with the longer driveway that curves around to what looks like a separate garage off behind the house. It has an old-fashioned porch across the front and appears much thinner and taller than the neighbors. We pull into the driveway, next to an older two-seater Mercedes.

"That's my dad's pride and joy," Hannah says. "I'm pretty sure he'd trade my brother or me for it if it came down to it."

As we climb the broad steps to the porch I can hear the deep barking of a large dog and then the skittering of dog nails on the door. Then I hear a voice yelling "shut up, Barkley." And the door swings open. A boy, about twelve, is holding a panting golden retriever by the collar with his right hand, staring at me with puzzlement. I can see in his face the resemblance to Hannah, especially in and around the eyes.

He turns to the dog and yells, "Quiet! It's just Hannah and another boy."

Hannah brushes past me and bends over and begins rubbing the dog's face vigorously. He sits and then rolls over, letting Hannah rub his stomach.

"Hannah!" says the boy, using the same voice he used when he was trying to quiet the dog. "You know you're not supposed to bring boys over when Mom and Dad are gone. I don't know who he is. He could be an ax murderer or a serial rapist."

"Jeez, Zeb, what kind of way is that to talk? You got to stop watching all those damn crime shows. It's Seth and he's a friend of mine." She tells me to come in, holding onto to Barkley by the collar. The dog is desperately trying to get his nose onto me, his back half rotating in unison with his tail like a fish's fin against a stiff current. We shut the door against the heat and I glance around. A wide staircase with a fancy banister. Flanked by glass cases filled with some sort of little porcelains and decorated plates.

"Barkley a sweetheart," Hannah says. "You like dogs, don't you?"

I watch her caressing the dog with obvious affection. We never had pets and I'm a little leery around dogs.

"He'll just try to lick you to death."

Then she turns to her brother and says, "Zeb, say hello to Seth."

"You're not supposed to have boys over when Mom and Dad are out," he says again, looking defiantly at Hannah, ignoring me.

"And you and your friends aren't supposed to be throwing a football around the house. You could break one of Mom's favorite antique vases."

"Hey," Zeb says. "You promised."

"Right. Now why don't you get back to your stupid Wii."

As he slinks away, pulling the dog along, Hannah smiles at me and whispers. "We pinned that one on Barkley."

As we walk through the hallway I can see that this is not a house built for indoor football. I step closer to one of the glass-fronted cabinets to get a better view of the elaborately decorated plates and pottery.

Hannah sees me staring and says, "That's my mom's thing. She travels all over going to shops and auctions. God knows where we're going to stow the next pile of crap she brings home."

"Your Mom and Dad?" I ask, hoping that I'm not sounding either too defensive or too hopeful.

"They went shopping. You know the antique mall on the way to Lawrence?"

I shake my head.

"It's like a secret society of these hoarders. They've collected all the trashiest leftovers between the Rocky Mountains and the Appalachians, gathered it all together and piled it onto tables in this big barn-like building."

"Yeah? Pretty sure I missed that one."

"Did I mention you can buy hot dogs that have been boiling in pots for days?"

"OK, now I really want to go."

She leads me up the stairs and I feel my face flushing.

At the top of the stairs she points down the hall. "The last door," she says, smiling slyly. "That's my bedroom."

Then she turns and looks at me, flushed and wide-eyed. I feel perspiration beading on my forehead. Then she starts laughing.

"For God's sake, Seth. That's not where we're headed. Is that what you thought?"

But when I look into her eyes I can see that she's just goofing with me. "Come on," she says, and dances around the corner where there's another set of stairs, narrow, wooden and worn.

On either side of the stairwell are a half-dozen of her color photos, matted and framed. More flower pictures like she has on Facebook, so closely focused that they could have been something else entirely. A hot air balloon inflating or colorful flags in a stiff wind or some anatomical blow-up, fleshy and alive.

At the top of the stairs there's a plain, unfinished wooden door. Hannah takes out a large, black, old-fashioned key.

"To keep the brother at bay," she explains.

With the key in the door she turns and says, "Now this is my favorite part of this house."

She stops before the door is entirely open. "You know, when I started taking a different kind of photo, I thought I had someone who would understand. But then I put some of my earlier stuff on Facebook and when I asked him what he thought…"

She seems stuck with that thought and I don't know what to say.

"But that was another world," she finally says and we step into a dark room. I can feel her close to me and want to reach out and touch her, but resist. She locks the door behind her by feel and talks to me while we stand there in the dark. She must be able to hear my heart, which is echoing in my ears.

"But when you looked at my photos. You just seemed to get it. And then the way you're into those games. Even when some people don't understand, or think it's a waste. It's like when Mom and Dad try to get me to think about studying something practical in college and not just do art. And I'm like trying to tell them that it's not just fun and games. It's who I am. That's probably why I did that self-portrait. You know, the takeoff of Frida Kahlo. She has this famous quote, "I was born a bitch. I was born a painter."

Then she flicks a switch. Three bare bulbs hanging from the center beam light up the long, thin windowless room. The sides of the room go up straight for about four feet and then slant into the peak beam. At the far end of the room I see a large white backdrop and three large white umbrellas on stands, and a bunch of lights and a large camera on tripods.

"My studio," Hannah says, extending her arm and opening her hand as if welcoming royalty at a ball.

"Wow. That's a lot of equipment."

"Now you know why I have to work so many damn hours. I started with film, but that was just killing my budget. Now I'm mostly digital. Still, the printing can get expensive."

Halfway down the loft there's an old patterned couch.

"Sit down," Hannah commands. "I'll get my portfolio."

At the studio end of the room she reaches behind the backdrop and pulls out a large black case.

Drags it over to the couch and plops down, so close our legs are touching. Lays the folder across our knees and zips it halfway open before stopping.

"Now, I want you to promise something."

"Sure."

"You haven't heard what yet."

"True. But I'm sure…"

"Promise you won't laugh at me."

"Why would I laugh?"

"I don't know. Because I'm stupid. Or awful. Or crazy."

"Those aren't laughing matters," I say.

She pokes me with an elbow and unzips the portfolio the rest of the way and then pauses. "Just so you know," she says. "Some of this work. Well, it might have caused some problems if people saw it. Back in Princeton, the darkroom was in this sort of side building and when we were on deadline, well, we had keys. So I worked on this stuff at weird hours. On weekends, at night."

She flips over the first page. It's a large black-and-white photo of a blond angel surrounded by flowers and framed on either side by some sort of Greek-looking columns. At first it just looks like some sort of sappy old postcard photo but then my eyes are drawn to the angel's body, which is wrapped in sheer white fabric. You can see right through it. The dark auras of her breasts and a dark triangle in her lap.

"Holy shit," I say, as I look deeper at the angel's face and see behind the round rouged cheeks and long blond wig that it's Hannah.

"Just tell me what you're thinking. Now, honestly."

I stutter something.

"Just how it makes you feel."

"I don't know, Hannah. It's weird. First you see an angel, and then you look again, and, I don't know. It's like these two things are together when they're not supposed to be. It's, it's disturbing." I wanted to say more.

"Exactly, I knew you'd get it." She closed the portfolio and looked directly into eyes. "It's just what society expects of us. We should be some weird kind of erotic angels. Like when you listen to these pop divas, they sound like breathy little girls, like Shirley Temple, and then you watch their videos and they're doing some sort of pole dance in lingerie. It obviously sells, but where does that leave the rest of us? So you said it was disturbing. But does it kind of turn you on, too?"

I stutter again but manage a nod.

"Exactly," she says. "I've got a whole series like that one. Amazing what you can find in a school's drama closet. Thirty years of school plays produce one weird-ass collection of costumes and props. Here, let me show you something a little different."

She stands up and thumbs through the portfolio and drops it back in my lap. It's a color picture this time. In the fall, long grass the color of hay leading up a hill to a farmhouse, but that's not where my eyes go at first. There's a naked girl, lying sideways on the grass, propped up by her arms, looking towards the house. I'm thinking Hannah, but then I look closer and it's a mannequin, carefully coiffed with a head of long, black hair with a glimpse of a matching patch down below. I know I've seen that picture before, or something like it.

"Not going to make the yearbook," I declare.

Hannah laughs and takes the portfolio away and lays it gently on the floor. Then she sits down next to me and holds my face with both hands and we're kissing. First sitting up and then sliding slowly down on the couch. And in a flash I think of Garrett and his Kimberly but then all I can do is sigh and sink back into that old couch like it's a pillow pile, like the softest moment of consciousness before you fall into a deep sleep, like the billowing clouds that support a beautiful, naughty angel.

35.

The next morning I hear Dad in the kitchen. Must have gotten back late last night. I wander into the kitchen, just staring into nothingness, thinking of Hannah. I can close my eyes and picture her exactly, giving me that sly smile when she's said something particularly insulting.

I'm such an idiot about girls. I mean, I sort of know stuff, but last night—it was all kind of confusing and now I'm wondering if I just bungled it. It seemed like Hannah liked what I was doing, but maybe she was just being polite.

I'm sitting at the kitchen table when Dad comes in.

"Hey young man," he says. "How are things?"

"OK," I say.

"Just OK?"

"Maybe better than OK. If someone got me some breakfast."

Dad opens a cabinet and pulls out a bowl.

"You know, it would work out a lot better if you loaded the dishwasher after you ate. I had to spend a half-hour last night digging out the sink."

"Oh yeah, I meant to get to that…"

"Too busy?"

"Well, I do work late some nights."

"Corn flakes OK?"

"Sure."

Dad pours some milk into the bowl and sets it front of me.

"Thanks," I say as I lift the first spoonful.

"And it had nothing to do with the girl you had over the other day?"

Half the cereal in my spoon splashes onto the table.

"What?"

"Oh, I ran into our snoopy neighbor when I was getting the paper this morning. The old lady who lives two units down. She said she saw a very cute young girl come to our door day before yesterday."

"Oh that. That was nothing."

"No? Actually I would put that it the category of something quite a bit more than nothing. Like astonishing?"

"It's just this girl I work with. She gives me a lift sometimes. I guess she feels sorry for me. Not having my license yet."

"Look, Seth," Dad says, sitting down next to me. "I had this talk with your brother years ago and I would have had it with you before, but I just wasn't sure you were ready."

I'm thinking, anything but this. I stare into my cereal, carefully spooning the floating flakes.

"I know you kids today, you have access to all kinds of stuff we couldn't have dreamed of when I was a kid. So I don't have to tell you the old facts of life or anything. I just wanted you to know that in my dresser, in the bottom drawer, in the back…"

I'm nodding like I knew exactly what was there. Because I had scoped out his bulk supply of Trojans years ago.

"Well, that's it," Dad says. "I've got a couple of local calls to make today so I'll see you tonight, OK?"

"OK."

I'm still playing the spoon through the leftover milk.

"And, Seth?"

I look up and nod.

"I did a little checking today and booked the Chicago tickets for Garrett. Had to use double points, so I hope you appreciate it."

"Thanks Dad," I say. And I mean it.

36.

As Garrett and I walk out of the security area at O'Hare there's a guy with a goofy black hat and a sign with my name on it. Garrett has an NDS duffle and I just have my backpack but the guy insists on carrying them both.

Garrett looks at me as we walk away, arching his eyebrows. I can imagine him saying, "This is the life." At the end of the terminal the driver leads us outside into what smells like a cloud of heated car exhaust. Then he pops the back door of an idling, big black Lincoln and we settle back into the cool leather.

Garrett punches me on the shoulder as we pull away and whispers, "I like these Korean guys already."

On the drive to the airport and on the flight Garrett had asked about a thousand questions about pro-gaming and the Anacondas. Which made me feel pretty stupid, because I could only answer about one out of ten. But I figured I'd find out a lot more once we got to the hotel and I hooked up with the Koreans.

Just thinking about playing with these guys produced a nervous rush. I'd been digging up as many of their games as were archived, and there were plenty. Almost every major tournament had at least one of the Anacondas in the final four. Every one of their top guys looked awesome.

One of the things Garrett had peppered me on was what made these guys so good. I had a hard time putting my finger on it. I finally told Garrett that it was like the difference between a good high school basketball player and a good college player. It's not that they do one thing better. They do everything better.

As we drive out of the airport Garrett has his iPhone out and looks like he's got a few hours of texting to catch up on. So I stare out the window and watch the people in the cars that are stuck next to ours. I had thought Kansas City had crappy traffic but I couldn't believe how bad it was from the airport the entire way downtown. The only things moving faster than twenty-five miles an hour were the trains going by and the guys on motorcycles flashing past between lanes.

Garrett seems to know exactly what to do when we finally get to the hotel, leading us through a giant revolving door and up an escalator. This black-haired girl with a name tag that says "Katya" and an accent greets us at the front desk. In about thirty seconds Garrett is chatting with her like they're old friends. I have no idea how he does it. She says there's a package for a Mr. Seth Gordon and Garrett nods towards me.

"That's for my kid brother. He's the guest of honor here."

I can tell from her look that she thinks he's kidding. Just like everyone since I can remember. She just assumes it's all about Garrett.

When she leaves to get the package Garrett turns to me and says, "I'm getting happier by the minute that you talked me into this trip. I think I'm in love."

"Again?" I say. Garrett rolls his eyes.

Katya gives me a brown envelope and while I'm opening it Garrett leans over the counter and is saying something softly to her. I'm guessing he's getting her personal phone number.

I take out a letter and read the instructions. Basically they say, get unpacked and settled. (I'm thinking, throw my backpack on the bed.) Then call this number.

I pull Garrett away from the desk and we head to the elevators. On the way up to the twenty-second floor Garrett says "I may need the room later."

"You wish," I say.

"No you wish," he responds.

By the time I'm ready to dial the number Garrett is already sprawled on one of the beds. He's got a beer out of the little refrigerator under the flat screen TV and has a Cubs game on.

When I call the number it's picked up on the first ring.

"Coach Yeong."

I tell him I'm all checked in and he says, "Good, good. You come to lobby in thirty minutes. Meet players. Then come. We have exhibition at Game Emporium."

"Great."

I tell Garrett that I'm going to some sort of exhibition and he grunts and then shouts, "Holy crap, I can't believe he swung at that sucker pitch!"

I don't have any patience for baseball so I grab my backpack and head out the door. If I was with Mom, she'd be asking all these questions about where I was going and when I'd be back. She'd have to tell me to check in before I went anywhere else. And when we were going to dinner. And where. Because we'd need reservations.

Garrett just grunts and waves a beer bottle. So much better.

I find a spot to sit in the corner of the lobby, wondering if I would be able to recognize the Koreans from their web pics. And what I'd do if I miss them. And what I'm supposed to say if I don't.

Then I see them come out of the elevator banks. Four young Korean guys in bright green, shiny shirts with a dramatically drawn red snake curling around their chests. An older man, maybe thirty or so, leading the way.

I head in their direction.

"Mr. Seth Gordon!" the coach calls out to me when I'm halfway across the lobby. I feel like everyone in the hotel has stopped to stare at me. Watching him half run in my direction and grab my hand, shaking it aggressively.

"So happy to meet you. Come, you meet team!"

We all shake hands. I'm immediately confused about who is who. They all look sort of the same in their identical shirts, same haircuts. But I get the impression that none of them are as happy to meet me as their coach.

I follow them out to the front of the hotel. A stretch limo is waiting. The coach gets in the front and the five of us climb in back. There are two large seats facing each other. I end up at the far end of the one facing backwards.

They're all talking a mile-a-minute in Korean. Ignoring me, which is fine. I'm looking out the window at downtown Chicago. We go over a river, past what looks like a tourist boat. Head down a couple of blocks busy with pedestrians and then turn right. Soon we're on an expressway, Lake Michigan on the far side of the car.

After about ten minutes I feel someone tapping on my knee. I turn away from the window and all four of the Korean pros are looking at me. The one directly across from me says something that sounds like English, but I shake my head. He tries again.

"You," he is saying, then pointing at the other three. "You help?"

"Help," I say. "Sure. With what?"

"American girl," the guy says, and all of them laugh. "Very sexy. American girl."

I shake my head.

The four of them lean together and start talking again.

This time it's the guy next to me who talks. "You help, we meet, very sexy American girl?"

"You want me to help you meet American girls?" I say, thinking, hey, I've got enough trouble as it is. But they all nod and start jabbering again.

"Well," I say. "I really don't know any girls in Chicago."

This starts another conversation. The result must not be in my favor because they all dig out some new 3DS model that I don't recognize and ignore me the rest of the ride.

37.

It takes about twenty minutes to get to the Game Emporium. It's a huge box store, size of a Wal-Mart. About a hundred kids are gathered out front, jumping and cheering as we get out of the limo.

The Anaconda guys walk slowly through the crowd, bowing, shaking hands, signing autographs. No one pays me any attention. When we get inside the store a couple guys in red Game Emporium shirts run up and get all excited. More bowing and shaking hands. Then they lead us through the store to the back where they've set up hundreds of folding chairs in front of two giant projector screens. In front of the screens, on a raised platform, are four gaming stations, two facing two.

The kids from outside are streaming into the area, grabbing seats and waving for their parents to catch up and join them.

Coach Yeong says something in Korean and I follow him and the team back behind the screens. We gather around him in a sort of huddle as he holds out a plastic cup with little pieces of paper in it. Each of the players takes one from the cup. Yeong looks at me.

"You too Seth Gordon."

I take a number and look at it. It has the number four.

Yeong reaches over and takes it from my hand. The other four players show their numbers to him.

"Very good. Very good." He says, and then talks for a couple minutes in Korean. Then everyone bows and I watch three of the players step onto the podium and begin to get settled behind the waiting computer screens.

"Go, you go!"

I look at Yeong. Dreading the epic fail I see coming.

"You number four. You play Tae-Uk."

I shake my head.

"No thanks. I'll just watch this time," I mutter.

Coach Yeong scowls and shakes his head.

"We bring you all the way here. To Chicago. To play. You play!"

He takes a step towards me and for some reason I think he might be getting ready to hit me so I scramble up on the podium and take the empty seat. I can feel the sweat under my arms. I hate it when guys get those big dark sweat circles under their arms. I realize I'm about to be one of those guys.

As I sit down, adjust the mouse, I nod to Tae-Uk across from me. He sees me but makes no gesture. I try not to think about the hours I had spent reviewing his win in the finals of one of last year's pro events. He had absolutely owned Joon Hyeok Yim, who had once won six pro tournaments in a row and is considered a Starfare god. OMG, I think, I'm about to get royally owned. In front of an audience.

When I glance out across the murmuring crowd I see that almost all the seats are taken. Then the lights go dim and they roll a Starfare promo tape. Without warning the Starfare starter screen for Gondwanaland pops up on my screen and the audience is cheering and I glance up and see that my computer screen is now being projected above me. At least if I'm going to get owned, it will be on one of my favorite maps.

Coach Yeong steps out to a microphone and I'm too nervous to listen to all that he's saying but I start when I hear my name. I glance over and he's reading from a script.

"We are pleased to introduce one of America's most promising young players, playing out of Overland Park, Kansas. Among the top ten American players, and rising rapidly, Mr. Gordon had a deep run at this year's Nationals. Please give a round of applause to ActionSeth, Mr. Seth Gordon!"

Then the lights go down another notch and the cheers start again and with a flash the screen lights up and we're underway.

All I'm thinking is please, please don't let me be humiliated in something like five minutes. Then the action is immediate and frantic and I'm not thinking about the crowd or getting embarrassed. I'm just clicking and punching the keyboard as fast as I can. It's like back when Mom made me take piano lessons and I thought I'd learned my little piece. Then the teacher, this smiling, evil old woman with hair the color of ashes, would lean over and set the metronome to a pace about three times faster than I'd been practicing. I can't believe the speed that Tae-Uk is setting. At the same time, I can feel my own speed rising, the way a biker can be pulled along in the draft of a rider just in front. I'm not winning, but it sure feels like I'm playing the best of my life.

When Tae-Uk finally wraps up his victory I'm completely drained. Only then do I hear the cheers again. He stands up and seems to be waiting for me to do the same. When I rise, he bows, and I try to imitate the same move. When I glance at the other big screen I see the other two Korean pros are in the endgame, which makes me feel better. Because I couldn't judge how long my game had taken. But it must have been decent. The other game finishes just a few minutes later and the lights come up. Coach Yeong has us all stand in front of the crowd and bow. The fourth Korean player joins us and following directions from Yeong they sit back down in the player seats and with another cheer, the lights dim for a second round.

I follow Yeong behind the screens and he shakes my hand.

"Very good show," he say. "Very, very good for American."

I say thank you, although I'm not sure that wasn't partly an insult.

I slink away and stand to the side of the room, watching the games in progress. The action is simply amazing. It makes me wonder if Tae-Uk had been slumming a bit, just to keep me in the game. I'll probably never know, since it was clear that our communication was going to be limited to sound bites like "sexy American girls." Or maybe I'm better than I thought.

Afterwards we drive to a sandwich place where Yeong tries to include me in the conversation. And mostly fails. I don't eat much.

Then we drive about a half hour to another Game Emporium in some other suburb and do the whole thing again. This time I get to play a different pro in the second game and I'm pretty proud of the fight I put up. Of course, I lose.

The way back, the guys are more relaxed, laughing as they play their 3DSs, sharing little 3DS achievements. No one offers to share with me. I'm actually relieved. I like looking out at the cars next to us as people try to look through the limo's tinted glass, imagining we might be politicians or rock stars. Or, I imagine, if we were in Korea, pro gamers.

Back at the hotel Yeong tells me to meet him and the team in the lobby at seven o'clock for dinner. Garrett is out when I get to the room and I flop onto the bed and check the time. One hour to relax. I flip through the channels about a thousand times until it's almost seven.

I figure we'll probably go to some Korean restaurant, which is a worry. I have no idea what Korean food is like, but I probably would hate it. Yeong seems happy to see me, but the four guys, still wearing their bright green Anaconda shirts, ignore me. We head outside. It's still hot out, but not Kansas City hot. There's a breeze coming from the lake, where I can see dozens of sail boats, and off in the distance a peer, where a ferris wheel is already lit up for the night. We walk down the hill to Michigan Avenue and turn left. I've never been to Chicago before but there sure are a lot more people walking around than I'm used to. A lot of them staring at us as they walk by. I guess they're not used to seeing a bunch of Koreans in red and green snake shirts.

After about ten minutes I'm relieved when we walk into a place called Italian Kitchen. Because I'm starved. We get seated at two adjacent tables—the four players across from us, and the coach and me across from each other at a booth.

At first he doesn't say anything, head hidden behind the big menu. Just studying it like it was a puzzle. Finally he lowers the menu and says, "Italian restaurants, my favorite. You?"

"Oh yeah. I actually work in one."

"You work?" Yeong seems troubled by this information. "How is this possible with your training?"

"I know," I reply. "My parents make me. Otherwise I'm with you entirely."

"So, you go to school. You work. And still you play very good. Very interesting. Very interesting."

Then he's looking back at the menu and pointing.

"So Mr. Seth Gordon, Italian Restaurant worker. You can have this knowledge. What is this, this manicotti? We not have in Korea."

I've heard of it, but damned if I can remember what it looks like. So now I look like a complete idiot.

"Actually, Coach Yeong. The place I work, we specialize in pizza."

"Oh, pizza. Very delicious here in America. But maybe makes American large? I see so many large Americans."

So right there I decide I better go with pasta. Which turns out to be delicious.

As we eat Yeong asks me a bunch of questions. Hard to answer, when you're trying to lasso a giant string of spaghetti. And not get it all over your shirt.

I answer as best I can and after a few minutes Yeong starts telling me about his team and how hard they work to be the best in the world. They have the best training facilities, the pick of the top talent.

"Every little boy in Korea. He only wishes to someday be a Team Anaconda."

Sounds right to me. When we get back to the hotel Coach Yeong asks me to follow him into the elevator. On the twentieth floor the players head down past us as Yeong opens his door.

"Come, I want you to see."

Inside Yeong sits down at a table with a couple of laptops. He points to a chair next to him and I sit down. Watching him open a Starfare screen and tap out a few commands. A game starts playing. I blink a couple times, because it's a replay of the first game I played that afternoon at the Game Emporium.

We watch for about a minute and Yeong pauses.

"Here," he says pointing at a spot where my miners are working. "Here you make first problem. You start your mining here," and he points to the center of the deposit. "In Korea, we study very carefully. Five percent faster to start here." And he points to the edge. "You start here and move this way." His finger goes in a circle and then goes around again and again in smaller circles. "What you call this way?"

"Spiral?"

"Yes, yes. Spiral. Much better this way."

Then he starts the game up and after about thirty seconds he stops and shows me another mistake, and a minute later another one. Not really mistakes. But I can see that he knows better ways, ways to increase your power a bit faster, a bit more efficiently. I can see how this stuff adds up. And what gets me excited is that everything he says seems absolutely obvious once he points it out. Some of it I could do tomorrow. And some of it, like how many clicks I'm making per second with my left hand on the keyboard, well, that might take a lot of practice.

"Now," he says. "You try to do it better."

He points to the chair on the other side of the table and I step around, light up the laptop and follow his directions to get to a one-on-one with Yeong on the Gondwanaland map.

I try to remember everything he told me, but each game in Starfare is like chess. The openings are similar, but they quickly diverge into an infinite number of possible moves. Maybe I'm a little self-conscious about not making the same mistakes, because I don't quite get into that zone where it's all flow and no effort. Yeong is clearly very good, although I don't think he's as flawlessly fast as the guys on the team that I played earlier. Because the game is close right until the end, when we trade forces down until he's up by just a few troops for the win.

Yeong stands up and bows and says, "Good game."

I stand and try to bow like he did.

"We have early airplane in morning. So now it is good night." Then he walks me to the door and as I stand in the doorway I can't resist asking.

"So, like, when will I hear back from you?"

"In time, Mr. Seth Gordon. We call in time."

And then I'm out in the hall and wondering what the hell had just happened. If I had blown it completely. Or not. As I take the elevator down to my floor I go round and round with the possibilities.

To top it off, my key won't open the door. I try about ten times, but my swipe just lights up the red button. I'm about to go get help when the door opens a crack.

"Seth?" In a whisper.

Garrrett's nose in the doorway, the security chain pulled taut. "Expecting someone else?"

"Look," Garrett still whispering. "I'm going to need a few more minutes here. So how about you just wait in the lobby. I'll be down in a bit."

"Fine."

More like an hour. I see the girl from the front desk, the one with the accent, bouncing across the lobby in a tight skirt and black heels like some sort of runway model. And a few minutes later Garrett is waving me over from the elevator banks.

"Thanks," he says.

"No problem. You have a nice date?"

Garrett looks at me, eyebrows arched. "The best," he says with a giant grin. "Anytime you need a chaperone in Chicago, I'm your man."

"You are the man," I mumble. "Like always."

"What?"

"Nothing."

"So give me the dope. How'd you do with your tryouts? You going to be the first Gordon in the family to turn pro?"

I tell him I doubt it, that I lost all three games I played.

"But you're, like, playing the best guys in the world, right?

"I guess."

"So you're not supposed to win. Not yet. It's all about potential. They like your potential?"

"Maybe." I say. "But maybe not."

38.

The next morning, when we land in Kansas City I turn on my cell and there's a text from DT wanting to know every detail and one from Hannah. Saying that she hoped I had a good tryout and that I should call her when I get back.

So I'm in a much better mood immediately. Even though I've only got a couple more weeks of summer vacation, which means my practice time will soon take a steep dive. On the bright side, I've got my driver's test scheduled for the day after I turn sixteen, in ten days.

About twenty times a day I'm checking my email, expecting to hear something from Coach Yeong. Then I'm flipping open my phone compulsively, looking for a text from the Koreans or Hannah. I text Hannah on the way home and over the next couple days we trade messages a couple of times. But for the first few days I'm back she's always got something going. She's just heading out with her mother shopping for school clothes or babysitting her brother or getting ready for work. Our shifts don't overlap at Saviano's and even though we're texting a lot I wonder if she's still interested. The way she was, that afternoon up in her studio.

Plus I almost screw up and miss this mandatory orientation for high school students at UMKC. If Mom was around, she would have been all over it. Half of me says, blow it off, you're going to be training with Team Anaconda, while the other half is saying, quit dreaming, you idiot, and don't screw this up. Because taking a college course, you get double high school credit, which means I cut my time at school pretty drastically.

Luckily they send out an email reminder the day before and I'm panicking about how to get there. It's a two hour meeting in the afternoon. Dad is on the road. I can't find Garrett but I text him and he says he's going to be doing an all-day basketball clinic at UK with his old high school coach. At first I try to figure out the bus routes on the Internet, but it looks like it's going to take me all day to get there, if I don't screw up the transfer. So I text Hannah and ask for a big favor. And I'm so desperate I actually tell her it will be interesting. Sort of like a preview of going to college.

She says she has to check. A few minutes later she texts me back saying that she can get the car, and what time should she pick me up.

This time I'm standing at the window, waiting a half hour. I'm out the door before the van is even stopped.

"Hey," I say, climbing in.

"Hey to you," Hannah says, and it's like she's uttered some magic invocation that sends something like a shiver straight through me. I try not to stare. She's got her hair tied back into some sort of pile in the back, forehead bare, a few strands across her cheek. The big sunglasses.

I wonder if you're supposed to lean across the seat and do that little cheek kiss that I see couples do. Not like we're a couple. But I haven't seen her for almost a week and it feels like we should be celebrating some sort of reunion. So of course I just sit there and click the seatbelt on. We sit like that for a moment until Hannah reaches out. Touches me on the thigh and says, "I'm really glad you asked me to come along." My leg feels like it's connected to an electrical outlet.

"Look," she says, lifting her hand off of me and pointing at the dash. "I thought this would, like, keep us from ending up in the wrong state."

It's a GPS mounted on the front dash.

"Excellent," I say. "Although we are in the wrong state."

"Exactly," Hannah says as she reaches over, grabs the GPS and hands it to me.

"You're Mr. Tech Smarts," she says. "How 'bout you program it for wherever we're going?"

"Right. I know we have to get on the Interstate so you can head that way."

"Which way?"

"OK, hang on," I say, because I get confused about which ramp is best. "Just have to…" I click through the menus, find places of interest, colleges and punch it up. As I snap it back into the holder the GPS is telling us to drive two hundred feet and turn right.

As we head out, Hannah says, "So how does it feel to be starting college?"

"I don't know. Weird. I mean, it's not like I'm really going to college."

"Well, when I told my parents about it, they were pretty impressed."

"I don't know. A lot of people at North take college courses."

Hannah seems to be mulling this over. "I wonder what they have in photography."

"You should check it out. For next semester. If you run out of courses in high school, they actually pay your tuition. It's a pretty sweet deal."

The GPS gets us to campus and we drive around a bit until we find a visitor's lot.

The orientation turns out to be really boring. We sit in the last row and after about five minutes Hannah pulls out her phone, reads some texts, and starts typing. She's at it for about half an hour when I lean over and peek.

"Just some people back in New Jersey," she whispers. "No one you know."

On the way back home I mention that I'm going to have a mini-van of my own, if I pass the test.

"When was the last time you failed a test? Like, never?"

"It's not the written part, it's the driving part."

"Just don't run into anyone."

"But I'm worried about the parallel parking. I suck at parallel parking."

Hannah laughs. "You know how many times I've had to parallel park since I got my license?"

I guess zero. And am right.

When we get back to my place I ask Hannah if she wants to come in.

She takes off her sunglasses and arches her eyebrows. "Just what do you have in mind, young man?"

I stutter for a moment and then say that we've got some ice cream.

"And just what do you propose we do with that?"

I know she's just trying to get me flustered and the fact that it's working only makes it worse.

"Hey," Hannah finally says. "I'm just, like, kidding. I promised Mom I'd go straight home because she has to run some errands."

She pulls out her cell and dials. "Thanks for the reminder. She told me to call when I dropped you off."

"OK," I say. "No big deal." Although it was a big deal. It took me the whole ride back to get up the nerve to ask her in.

"But let's do something before school starts," Hannah says. "Because I know it's actually going to get crazy busy." Then she's talking to her Mom.

"OK," I say as I shut the car door and then watch her drive away. My heart sinking at the sight. While hanging onto the promise of seeing her soon. Then I race up the stairs to check my email and see if Team Anaconda has made its decision.

39.

The worst part of waiting is handling all the messages I'm getting from my online friends. It seems like every minute I'm online someone is asking if I've heard back yet. Finally I just start telling everyone to check my Facebook. That I'll post news as soon as I get any.

But a funny thing is happening with my games after just hanging around with the Koreans for a day and getting those pointers. Every person I play, even ones with really high ratings, now seems a couple of levels slower. I'm winning every game, and they're not even close. Like I've broken through to a higher stage, and maybe I have.

Hannah and I have a shift together the last Saturday night before school starts and the first thing she asks is if I'm packing for

Korea. It's still early and we're both working the front of the store. Folding take-out boxes.

I try to explain that it's still way up in the air.

"But you'll go if they ask, right?" She doesn't look up from her boxes.

And I realize that I've spent so much time worrying about getting asked that I haven't put any thought into what would happen if they did. What that would mean. Like not being able to see Hannah anymore.

So I say, "I don't know." I flip a box onto the pile and watch Hannah's hands fly through two boxes in the time it takes me to do one. "What would you do?"

Hannah stops and looks at me. With such intensity that I'm immediately nervous. She has the most amazing eyes. In the restaurant light, dark green. I can't hold the look and I reach out for another cardboard flat.

Hannah is talking now, and when I glance at her she's looking right through me, as if I was just the foreground in front of some awesome landscape, like the Grand Canyon or Yosemite Falls. "If I'd been dreaming of doing something, something special, for my whole life? And someone comes along and says, 'Here you go, we're going to give you every opportunity in the world. And pay you?' Are you kidding? Sign me up!"

"Yeah, I suppose." And I know she's right. I could be ready to go tomorrow. "But there's stuff I'd miss."

"Stuff?"

"Oh you know." And I pick up another square of cardboard because I want to say her name but for some reason I can't.

Then the phone rings and Hannah's taking an order and a family with two little kids comes in and I go over to the cash register and ask them if I can help.

After I take their order there's another little lull. I feel like I need to say something to Hannah. To tell her that the worst thing I can think of is having to say goodbye to her.

But she talks first. "A year ago, I thought I had it all laid out. I'd have a great senior year, hanging with the friends I'd had since first grade, taking every art class at Princeton High. Build a really amazing portfolio and get into one of the big art schools, Parsons or RISD. Maybe get discovered by some gallery. Or not. But it all seemed pretty clear. I had my friends and even this special one. At least I thought he was special…and then, bang, my parents drop the big one. And a couple of months later I'm in Kansas. Which as far as I know is just a flat, scary place from *The Wizard of Oz*. I know no one. I have no idea what kind of art department there is, if there are any cool teachers like we had back home. Just like that, my life is completely changed."

I'm trying to translate what she's saying. To me. And what she means by a special guy. I just get this picture in my mind of a really handsome jocky guy. Probably rich and sophisticated too, like those prep school kids in movies.

"So Seth. What I'm saying is, be ready. Ready to get the most out of what you have. And ready for whatever happens. Be ready to make the most of it all."

I nod, although I'm not catching everything.

"And when we get off work tonight? Let's go out and celebrate."

"Celebrate?"

"Yeah. We'll celebrate. The great unknown. You. Me. Korea. A new school where I don't know a person."

"Not true."

"OK, where I know one person."

"But not just any person."

Hannah smiles with a far-away look. "No, not just any person. Some person who I will never, ever…" Of course, I'm thinking the worst as she breaks into a big smile. "…take a math class with."

"OK," I say. "It's a date."

40.

By the time we get done putting everything away and mopping it's well after midnight and there's really no where to go. We sit outside in the van for a few minutes, complaining about how busy we were and what a mess it was.

"You still got some ice cream?" Hannah finally says.

"Probably not. Garrett eats everything in sight."

"Your older brother, right? You didn't say he was back home."

"Yeah, for another few days. He's got practices starting soon."

"Well, I say we go check the freezer," Hannah says. "Just in case."

The house is dark when we get there and we park out front. As we walk up the front door, I wonder if the old lady down the street is peering out her window, trying to make us out.

As the door closes I'm not sure who makes the first move. It just happens. I'm holding her and we're kissing. There in the dark. And I know why people prefer kissing lying down because something crazy in going on in my head and I can't really stand straight and when I stumble we almost both end up on the carpet. Hannah is laughing and I'm laughing. Hannah says we should go upstairs. I've actually been picking up the dirty clothes in my room, hoping that Hannah might, someday, make a reappearance. I lead her up the darkened stairs, the skylight shaping the outline of the steps.

Hannah holds my hand as I lead her to my door. My computer is on and the case casts a blue light across the room. Hannah and I sit on the bed and kiss again and it takes all my willpower to stop from falling backwards, down into the beckoning blankets and sheets.

"You know," Hannah says. "I'm not sure this is right."

"You mean being over here? Alone?"

"Not that. I don't care about that. It just feels like I've been here before."

"In my room? You have been here before."

Hannah laughs and shakes her head. "No. Not that. It's just

that when I was back in New Jersey. And I knew we were going to be leaving. This guy I mentioned?"

I really didn't want to talk about her old boyfriend.

"Everybody said he was great. My friends thought he was great. His coaches thought he was great. Even my parents liked him. OK, so he was great. But when he found out I was leaving, it was all of sudden we should get really serious. Like we had to make up for lost time. Like I was going off to war or something. And when I had second thoughts, he said fine. But it turns out it wasn't fine. Sure, there were all these promises about keeping in touch and visiting. That I'd be back East for college. But then we move and I hear nothing from him. Nothing. And then I hear he's going out with Allison, who I thought was a friend. And then my other friends, they let it slip that, actually, they started going out before I had even left. So I have a pretty good idea where long-distance relationships end up."

Hannah is staring at the floor, like there might be an answer there. Then she looks right into my eyes. "In the sewer."

No one says anything for a minute. Finally I say, "So you think I'm like that guy?"

It's dark in the room. But I can see Hannah's hand and I reach out and hold it with both of mine.

"It's not that you're like that jerk. My leaving, it was as traumatic to him as, well, watching some neighbor you never met pack a moving van. But, Seth, for me. Getting that close to someone and then having it disappear. And seeing all of your old friends just sort of drift away. No, it's not that you're like that guy. It's that you're like me."

I put my arm around her. I'm literally shaking. I don't know if it's from what she said or the fact that Hannah is here, next to me, in my room, on my bed.

Then without any warning Hannah flops back on the bed. "Nice mattress," she says.

"I like it."

Then I lie down next to her and as I put my arms around her add, "I like it even more now."

41.

Sunday is my birthday. If Mom was around she'd have baked a cake and made sure that I got some stupid presents. But I don't want a cake or presents. I want my driver's license. I want to see Hannah. I want to hear from Coach Yeong.

So I sleep late and I'm planning on getting up, really thinking seriously about it, when my cell rings. Naturally it's Mom.

As soon I say hello she starts singing "Happy Birthday." Which is so corny I actually kind of like it.

"Did you get the package?" she asks after the first chorus.

"Package?"

"Oh, no. They promised it would arrive on Saturday. You sure it didn't get there?"

"Pretty sure."

"Well, go check the front stoop. Between you and your father, a box could sit out there for weeks."

Which is true.

"Hang on," I mutter as I slip on a pair of shorts and my flip flops. "I'll check."

"So what do you have planned?" Mom is asking as I head downstairs. A box of pizza with two slices left, which I swear I had thrown out the night before, is sitting on the table.

"I don't know. Me and Garrett might go out for dinner."

"Your dad isn't going to be there?" I can hear her talking away from the phone, voice muffled. I picture her with a hand over the handset whispering something angrily to Martin. That was just so like her.

"I guess. I mean, we didn't talk about it or anything, but I think he told me he'd be back today."

I open the door and off to the side, behind a planter with dead flowers, I see a box that is about three feet tall and kind of thin.

"Mom, it's here! They hid it behind the flowers."

She tells me to open it and I take it inside and try to, although it's hard to do while holding a cell phone. Finally I walk it over to the kitchen and get out a steak knife, set down the phone and manage to cut through the tape.

I pull out a folded blue pad and a DVD that has a picture of a woman sitting on the ground, twisted into a weird position. It's called "Yoga AM and PM for Beginners." Gee, thanks Mom.

"Mom, thanks a lot," I say.

"Seth, you've just got to try it. I know you're not getting enough exercise and this would be just perfect for you. It would even help your, you know, computer thing."

"My computer thing?"

"Well, yes. Yoga has been proved to help with concentration and dealing with stress. Doesn't that sound useful?"

I grunt an affirmative. Then Mom asks about the trip to Chicago. She says that she is very supportive of my interests. But that I should know that she and Dad both agree that school always has to come first.

"Are you ready for school?" she asks. "Do you have your backpack all packed? Pencils and notebooks like we always do?"

"It's all set," I lie.

I answer another ten or fifteen questions. The final one, "Is Garrett there?"

I run upstairs and open his door and he groans and throws a pillow over his head. I have no idea what time he got in.

"Here," I say, cheerfully, tossing him my phone. "It's Mom!" And leave them to their conversation and head back downstairs.

In the spirit of Mom I eat a bowl of non-sugared cereal. The blue yoga mat and DVD are on the table, along with the box it came in and all the stuffing and yesterday's pizza.

42.

I've got a bunch of birthday greetings waiting on the computer. DT did this Photoshop card for me. My Facebook picture head cut out and stuck on top of a little wrestler who's been pasted jumping on top of this sprawled, giant sumo wrestler. The sumo guy has a headband that says "Stomp." The caption says, "ActionSeth stomps Stomp on his sixteenth birthday!" DT is really good with Photoshop. He could probably get a job doing it.

I'm reading through some other messages when I get a text. From Hannah. She wants to know if I'm free at two o'clock. She has a surprise. Hell yes, I say out loud, but I just text back, *sure*." Then she writes she'll be over.

I jump in the shower and find some clean clothes. I'm reading a news story about Team Anaconda's exhibition in Las Vegas when the doorbell rings. The computer clock says 1:55.

Hannah is standing with what looks like a large plate, wrapped in tissue paper with a red ribbon crisscrossing. Very professional.

She leans over and gives me a quick kiss and says, "Happy Birthday!"

Inside she looks askance at the mess on the table but then the mat and DVD catch her eye. She hops over and holds up the mat.

"Nice. Jade Yoga—I hear these are the best!"

Then she is looking over the DVD.

"Wow, I can't imagine my mom thinking of anything like this. I'm dying to meet your mom."

"Actually, if you're interested, you can borrow it. I'm pretty sure I'm not doing yoga any time soon."

"No? I started hot yoga before we moved. I'd love to find a place near here."

"Hot yoga?"

"It's great. Sort of like yoga in a sauna."

I get this picture of Hannah in a black leotard doing some amazing contortion, sweat dripping off her brow. This image is enough to trigger an immediate physical reaction so I sit down on the couch, the present in my lap and say, "OK if I unwrap it?"

"Sure."

I'm taking off the ribbon when I hear Garrett cough. He's standing at the bottom of the stairs, wearing nothing but his boxers.

"You must be Hannah," Garrett says. And then, as I watch in amazement, he walks over and shakes her hand, as if he were wearing a suit and tie.

"Sorry for the informality," Garrett says. "My inconsiderate brother failed to mention that we were having guests."

"Guest," says Hannah, still holding Garrett's hand, smiling. "And you must be Garrett. Seth didn't mention you were such a romantic."

Garrett looks down at his boxers, which have little hearts all over them.

"Oh that. These were a gift."

"I'll bet," Hannah says. Then she looks at me. "Seth was just opening his first gift."

I fumble it open and find a plate piled high with large, fragrant chocolate chip cookies.

"Very nice," Garrett says. "Breakfast." Then he takes a couple steps back, saying, "I think I'll slip into something more comfortable." He winks at me before heading up the stairs.

"Well," Hannah says when he's gone. "Your brother has some sort of knack for first impressions."

"His coach always said he was good under pressure. OK if I try a cookie?"

"Don't ask me, they're yours!"

I grab a first, soft bite and with my mouth full, "Delicious. Thanks!"

"Come on," Hannah says. "I want to show you your second present."

43.

When we get to Hannah's house we go straight up to her studio.

"Everyone's at my brother's soccer game," Hannah says as we climb the stairs.

"I thought you weren't supposed to have boys over when your parents are gone."

Hannah stops in front and turns around.

"You forgot the birthday exception."

Inside she motions me over to a computer monitor which she lights up with a touch of a hand. It's a black and white photo of a guy in a sailor uniform kissing a woman in white, wearing what I think is an old-fashioned nurse's uniform. In the middle of a crowded street, looks like New York. I've seen the photo somewhere before.

"You recognize this?" Hannah asks.

I nod. "End of WWII, right?"

"Yeah, it's one of the most famous photos ever."

I look at her questioningly.

"So hang on." She walks across the room and comes back holding two garment bags. She unzips the first and it's a sailor's uniform.

"We're going to redo that photo. I got these from a costume store downtown." She points to a green background at the end of the room, where the lights and camera are set up. "I can swap the backdrop later. Don't you think it will be hot?"

All I'm thinking about is that kiss in the photo. The girl is tipped back, balanced on one foot.

"You think you can handle that?"

"I don't know…"

"Here, try this on. I know the nurse's costume works." And just like that she starts taking off her jeans. She's got white pantyhose underneath.

So I change into the sailor suit while Hannah slips on the white

134

dress over her T-shirt. Mine seems a little big but Hannah is like, "Perfect. Perfect. Say 'ahoy' or something!"

"Ahoy," I say, as I try to figure out how to get the blue shirt adjusted. Hannah comes over and straightens out the collar from behind. I spin around and pull her close to me, but she wiggles away, giggling.

"Save it for the photo."

After she's satisfied with the angle of my sailor's hat she leads me over to the screen. She has some marks on the floor and tells me where to stand. She opens up her hand and shows me a small remote. Then puts my right hand on her waist. She wraps the hand with the remote behind me and then tells me to do something weird with my left arm, so my elbow is sort is sticking out.

"Perfect," she says. "Now kiss me."

I do, and barely hang on as she leans back. Then the flashes fire.

"Again!" Hannah commands. No arguments from me.

We try a few more and then Hannah runs around and checks the pictures which flash up on a laptop next to the camera.

"Pretty good," Hannah says. "Except this time I need to bend over more."

She checks the marks on the floor and then puts my hands back in place.

"OK," Hannah says. "Just don't let me fall."

I don't.

44.

Late Sunday afternoon Dad actually does get back and the three of us go for my birthday dinner to the Olive Garden. I love their breadsticks. While we wait for our food Dad gets out his cell and manages to reach the Institute office and a few minutes later Mom calls back.

So for a couple of minutes it's like we're all together. It feels a little weird since we haven't really been out together for a long time. Probably Garrett's high school graduation. But still, it's nice.

Monday I get my birthday present from Garrett. He drives me the DMV and hangs around a couple hours while I take the written and driver's test. It's a great birthday present. I get a perfect score on the written and when I do the parallel parking thing it's just a bunch of cones and although I don't get really close to the curb I don't run anything over. Just like that I've got my license.

When we get home I ask Garrett if I can use the van and he rolls his eyes. So I drive around the block a few times. It feels really weird driving alone, like the feeling you get when you're out for the night and you're in line at a food place, and have just patted all your pockets, realizing you've forgotten your wallet.

Then I drive over to Hannah's and park in front of her house, idling, AC pumping. Wondering if I can just show up like that. I have my phone out, texting her when I'm startled by something knocking on my window. It's Hannah's brother, on a skateboard.

"Hey," he says. "You stalking my sister?"

I roll down the window and mumble something. Embarrassed to be embarrassed by a smart-ass twelve year old.

"If you give me a dollar I'll tell her you're here. It's OK, she's doesn't have anyone over right now."

"Anyone over?"

The kid looks at me like I'm a real loser.

"Well, it's not like New Jersey. Always some guy or guys hanging out. But I didn't mind. I could usually get one of them to play Xbox or Wii. How about you? You play video games, right?"

"Sort of," I say.

"That's not what Hannah says. She says you're like a pro. Come on, we'll play some Mario Kart."

I shake my head as a text comes in. Hannah says she'll be right out.

"Maybe some other time," I say.

I see the front door swing open and Hannah pops open the

screen door to the porch and jogs down the stairs. Hair bouncing, smiling. She flips open the passenger door and jumps in. Leans towards me and says towards the open window, "Zeb, get lost, will you."

"Eat my shorts."

"OK, Bart Simpson. Just go work on some new knee scabs or something."

Zeb flips her off as I roll up the window.

"Wow, let's see it."

"See what?"

"Your license, stup."

I get out my wallet and give it to her. She flips it open and starts laughing.

"Worst picture ever!" she says. She looks even more amazing when she's laughing.

I grab it back and look at it. I didn't think it was that bad.

"Don't worry. I've been working on the other photo." She pauses, as if remembering the moment fondly. "I think it's going to come out pretty great. I might even add it to my portfolio."

"Look," she says. "Mom and I were just getting ready to drive down to the Plaza. She wants me to buy a few more 'outfits' before school starts. As if jeans and a top are an outfit."

She shakes her head. "She's like driving me nuts. But I have to humor her."

I must not be using my poker face because she notices my disappointment.

"If you've got a sec come on in. Mom's been asking to meet you."

"Yeah?" I'm wondering what Hannah has been saying about me.

So I turn off the car and follow Hannah up the stairs and into the family room.

"Hang on," she says. "I'll tell her you're here."

On the mantel there are a bunch of old photos of Hannah and her brother. I'm browsing them when I'm stopped by what looks like a recent picture of Hannah all dressed up for a formal. Hannah looks annoyed. She really does hate snapshots. It's a weird shaped photo, not quite square and then I notice what looks like part of someone's arm on the right side of the picture. And the border on the top and left doesn't match what is clearly a trim job. I'm staring at the picture when Hannah surprises me from behind.

"This is Seth!" she says.

I turn around. Hannah's mom is smiling and walking towards me with her arm out so I shake her hand. She just stands there grinning and I feel like I'm getting graded or something. She's a little taller, a little heavier than Hannah, but very nice looking in a sort of formal, ready-to-go-out way. Not like my mom who always looks slightly frazzled.

"Nice to meet you," I finally say and she lets go of my hand.

"Hannah has told me so much about you!" she says. I blush. I have no idea what sorts of transfer of information are normal between daughter and mother. I have the sinking feeling that it goes well beyond the nothing Garrett and I convey. "She says you're quite a young mathematician. Taking college courses already!"

This is just the sort of stuff adults are always saying to me. And there's never anything you can say in response.

"I like your collection," I say out of desperation. Nodding towards a glass cabinet in the corner with a bunch of ceramics.

"Oh that," she says. "I'm afraid Hannah wouldn't agree with you there. She thinks it's just clutter."

Hannah steps up next to us and says, "Mom, that's not true. I just think you overdo it sometimes."

"Well, I'm so glad Hannah has made friends. You should have heard her a few months ago. You would have thought we were dragging her to the North Pole or somewhere."

"Mom."

"Well, it's true. And it's so nice that you'll be in the same school. I'm sure you'll introduce her to lots of people."

I nod and glance at Hannah who is standing a bit behind her mother, rolling her eyes.

"Well we were just off to the Plaza," Hannah's mother says. "And we've got so much to do before school starts…"

"Me too," I say, idiotically. Then Hannah grabs my hand and leads me out of the door and down the steps.

"You see what I have to deal with every day?" she whispers. Honestly I didn't see anything that bad but I nod to be agreeable. When we get to my van she says, "Don't worry. You'll have a chance to show off your driving skills. Congrats on your license. And thanks for coming over!"

She leans over and gives me a peck on the lips. I climb in and shut the door. Look at her longingly through the open window.

"You look so cute behind the wheel," she says. "I'll text you when I'm free."

I watch her bound back up the steps. Thinking this thing that we somehow have, this amazing thing. It's as miraculous and fragile as one of those giant shimmering soap bubbles you can make with those large plastic rings. And I sit there for a minute, wondering if there's anything I can do, if there's any trick, to keep it from bursting.

45.

The days are ticking down for school starting and I get up early on Tuesday so I can have breakfast with Garrett before he heads back to school. We don't say much, but I'm glad he was able to come back. Help me with my license, meet Hannah.

As if he's reading my mind Garrett looks up from his cereal and says, "That girl of yours, Hannah?"

"Yeah?"

"You don't have to hear it from me, she is really something, and not just hot. I'm not kidding, if you weren't in the picture…"

"Thanks for the consideration," I say, sarcastically.

"She didn't bat an eye, the other morning."

"It was the afternoon."

"Whatever. Anyway, don't screw it up."

Just what I've been thinking. So I ask him, "How do I screw it up?"

This seems to snap something in Garrett. He pauses and shakes his head. "Jeez Seth. I don't have near enough time…"

I can see his mind spinning, tabulating all the lost Kimberlys. "Sometimes you never know. And sometimes," he smiles slowly, "Sometimes you can't forget."

I admire his honesty, but don't see much actionable advice here. So I scoop up another spoonful of Lucky Charms and just say, "Right. Don't worry. I won't get caught in bed with her sister."

"Shit," Garrett says, choking on his cereal. "You know about that? How the hell would you…"

And then we're both laughing so hard that I'm afraid milk is going to come out of my nose.

After breakfast I help Garrett load up his car. When he's behind the wheel and about to pull out he motions me over.

"One more thing," he says. "Not that I know squat about this gaming world. But I've been around sports a long time. Remember Mitch Hudson—played center for us last year?"

I nod, although I don't.

"Anyway, the guy is six-eleven. A real horse. Not much finesse, but come on, how many guys are there that size? So first he waits for the draft. Nothing. Then his agent, who must be a complete loser, keeps telling him that a call will be coming in any day, for a tryout. He waits and waits. Almost flunks out last semester, he's so stressed out. Nada. Nothing. He's playing in Greece this year, for peanuts. Anyway, what I'm saying is, the longer you don't hear from those Korean guys…"

I tell him I know. Then watch him as he drives away, faster than he should, as always. As I head upstairs to the computer the place seems somehow emptier than it has ever been before.

46.

Hannah and I have our last shift before school on a Wednesday, and I'm hoping we get assigned in the back together, but Jake, the night manager, he sticks me there with this new kid while Hannah runs the register. All the managers seem to like her up front. Either she's really good at balancing the register or she makes a good impression. Actually I think it's both.

So I'm halfway through the shift, resigned to dealing pepperonis for another couple of hours when Hannah sticks her head into the kitchen and calls for me.

I hop over to the door. Hoping she's going to say something personal or ask if she can come by my place after work. I glance down at my white apron, which has more than its share of tomato sauce.

"Hey," she says. I'm confused by her smile. I give her a questioning look.

"There's a girl out front asking for you."

"A girl?"

"Yeah. She's really pretty. Says that you two are pals from school."

I take off the apron, throw it onto the counter and step out of the double doors. Brit and some guy I recognize from North are standing at the register. She's waving at me.

When I get to the counter she says, "Hi Seth! I heard you were working here!" Then I realize Hannah is standing next to me.

"Yeah. Hi to you too. And..." I'm looking at the guy with her who is really familiar but I can't remember his name.

"Luke," he says.

"Yeah Luke. Yeah, it's good to see you guys." Then I look over at Hannah who is just standing there, taking it all in.

"Um, Brit. Luke, I'd like to you to meet my friend. Hannah."

They all say hi to each other. "She just moved here this summer and is going to be at North with us."

Brit asks her what year and when Hannah says senior she moans and says that it must be horrible having to move before senior year.

Hannah nods and then glances at me and says, "Well, it's not all horrible. I mean I've already met some really nice people."

Brit is looking right at me and I think she's got it all figured out. I'm always amazed at how quickly some kids can do this social processing. Like you have to just spell it out for me, but people like Brit, they can do social calculus the way I do regular math.

"You know you're working with the biggest brainiac at North," Brit says. "He personally salvaged my A in history last semester."

I'm shaking my head, blushing. "Not true," I protest. "Innocent on both charges."

Hannah seems to be enjoying this exchange immensely.

"If you get a break come sit with us for a minute," Brit says, looking at both me and Hannah. Then just at me. "You're making this pizza for us?"

"I could. Or I could delegate it to one of my many minions in the back."

Brit laughs and says that I should make it. That she likes the personal touch.

I go back and take her order off the screen and put on a lot more ingredients than Mr. O'Neill would be happy with. When I get it in the oven I stick my head out and see that it's slow out front and Hannah has snuck off, pulled up a chair to Brit and Luke's booth. They seem to be getting along famously.

I'm thinking about joining them when Jake picks up the phone and types in a five-pizza order. Then some women's softball team comes in. By the time we get all caught up Brit and Luke are gone.

That night, when we're cleaning up, Hannah says that it was nice to meet some more kids from North.

I tell her that she'll fit right in. That the key thing was getting involved. And then I realize that I'm just saying stuff my mother used to tell me all the time. The fact is, I'm not involved in anything at school other than spending as little time there as possible.

As I put away the mop I'm hoping that Hannah will want to do something after work. Maybe come over to my place. But as we help Jake lock up she says, "I promised I'd head straight back. Mom wants me to get into going to bed on time, to get on schedule for school."

That sounds like a mom. My van is in back, just next to Hannah's and I stand with her as she unlocks her car.

"By the way," Hannah says, standing with the door open. "Brit says you had this major crush on her last year. She thought it was so cute."

"She said *what*?" And I'm thinking how to deny it. But I'm pretty sure my jaw just dropped about a foot and that I must have looked, in that pose, like an embarrassed idiot. Which is just as good as saying, "Just because I browsed her Facebook page a hundred thousand times doesn't mean…" Hannah swings inside the van Just after shutting the door she rolls her window down.

"Come over here," she says. I do. She leans out of the window and I step in next to the van and we're kissing. Then she leans back into the van, looking completely happy.

"She doesn't know what she's missing," Hannah says. "That hunky guy she was with? Luke? Dumb as a doorpost."

And she leaves and I just stand there in the lot for minute, watching her tail lights. Wanting to jump in my van and chase her, like some romantic idiot in a Hollywood movie. Chase her down and make her stop and jump into her van and pull her to me and just hold her as tightly as I can.

That's what I think about as I drive home alone.

47.

My college course starts a few days before high school, so on Thursday morning I get drummed out of bed by my alarm about three hours before I'd prefer. I drive the van downtown, find commuter parking and throw my parking pass on the dash. I sit there for a few minutes, wondering how bad I'm going to stand out. Second year calc, probably mostly sophomores, who are what, twenty years old?'

I know where the math building is and it's not hard to find room 211. It's not like a high school classroom. More like a mini-theater. About twenty students are already there and I find a place in the back row, near the door, so no one really sees me. Once I sort of scrunch down in my seat I feel immediately better. More students wander in and take seats, but no one pays me any mind. Then the professor comes in. He's wearing a tie-dyed T-shirt stretched over a round stomach, and has wild black hair, sort of like a young Einstein.

He seems happy to get started, starts yammering in this thick accent while writing his name and phone number up on the board. I take out my cell and enter it—Otto Wacwalick. Polish, he says, in case anyone was curious.

And without any more small talk he's writing the first formula on the board. As the class goes on, I'm thinking it's a good thing he likes to write on the board, because I'm missing half of what he's saying. But the math is easy to follow—stuff we covered in my last AP class. So by the end of the class I'm feeling better about handling it. I want to test how long it takes to get back, to see if I can make my fifth period when high school starts. Plus, if I scoot fast the college kids won't get a good look at me.

So, Tuesdays and Thursdays I'll be going downtown for math. But that means I'll have a three-hour break from high school Monday, Wednesday and Friday. I can get home in like five minutes, get online and get some serious gaming in.

When I get back from my first math class I pull up Team Anaconda's site. I've been keeping an eye on the guys on Team Anaconda. They're not currently the top team in Korea, but they're close. I try to picture them in training, wondering how they work together. Starfare is about to introduce a new map and I can imagine how intense that must be, with a dozen or so people just plugging in and exploring every inch of it, looking for where the resources are buried and what sorts of obstacles are going to be generated and how they can be defeated.

I keep checking my phone, because Hannah said she'd let me know when she was free, and that was days ago. So now I'm worrying that she's lost interest. I drive over to her house three times but I end up just wheeling around the turnaround, hoping she doesn't see me. At least I don't see any other cars out front.

In the meantime, DT and I IM about how crappy it is that school starts in four days and then we play a couple two-on-twos. Just as we finish the second game the doorbell rings. I tell him I've gtg, but I'm thinking it's probably Mormons or the UPS guy. Maybe Mom sent me another package.

I open the door and it's Hannah. She's smiling and holding a wrapped package the size of a large book. It's hot outside, as usual. I feel like Hannah's dog, being held back by the leash of my consciousness. If I had a tail, it would be wagging uncontrollably.

"Come on in," I say.

"OK, but can't stay long." She holds the present out to me. "Go ahead and open it!"

I set it down on the table, happy that I had moved the dishes to the sink. Sit down and Hannah sits across from me. I'm fidgeting in anticipation. I take my time, trying to stretch out the moment. Me and Hannah, the excitement.

I slowly pull off the Happy Birthday wrapping paper, which is decorated with pictures of trains and balls and balloons. Hannah saying, "I know, it's awful paper but it's all we had at home. Stuff my mom got years ago for little boy birthdays."

Inside is a silver picture frame, which initially is backwards. I turn it around. It's the picture of me and Hannah, leaning backwards, kissing. Just like the original. Except the background. It looks like a New York street, but it's all messed up, full of dust and debris. It might even be the same street, but barren and wrecked and deserted, cars along the side coated in gray, and I recognize it as a photo taken on 9/11.

"Wow," I say. Because the effect is really something. There we are, all black and white and clean and neat while the rest of the world, in color, but barely, looks like a war zone.

The weird thing is, you can see my face perfectly, but you can't really see Hannah at all, just the back of her head, the back of her white-sheathed legs, her hair hanging down.

"Wow," I say again. "That's amazing."

"Thanks. Thanks for being, like, a good sport. And definitely, going into the portfolio."

"I do make a pretty good sailor," I say. "Maybe I should be thinking Naval Academy."

"Don't think you're the military type," Hannah says. "Although you'd be great at working those drones."

"Something to drink?" I ask. Wondering if we have anything in the fridge.

"Nah, got to go. Mom needs the car. But I see that we both have Friday off. How about doing something then?"

I'm nodding like a bobble head and then she's out the door.

I take my present and go back to the computer, try to get psyched up for a game. Somehow I'm just not in the mood. I keep looking over at the picture, which I've set next to the monitor. Thinking about what it felt like to be kissing Hannah.

After a while I give up and decide to get my math assignment out of the way. A bunch of problems from the back of the first chapter. Routine, although there's one towards the end that is kind of interesting, because I can see two ways to solve it. One way that uses the proofs in the chapter, but another way that relies on some stuff we touched on first semester in Calc BC. So I do it the alternative way and get it done in three steps instead of the five that I might have used. So at least I feel good about that.

48.

So all day Friday I'm wired about getting together with Hannah that night. I spend most of the afternoon playing some half-hearted Starfare against noobs and reading message boards. I really get into this two-hundred-page thread about a guy getting divorced because his wife is disgusted with his gaming. Everybody's got an opinion or another story about how gaming either screwed up a relationship or—a decided minority—brought a couple together.

So when my cell rings the first thing I think is that it's Hannah. I punch it on and say hello, trying to sound cool and not all breathless.

"Mr. Seth Gordon?"

Now I am breathless. I recognize the heavy accent immediately, Coach Yeong. Thinking, well, it's nice that they would call and personally tell me that they picked someone else.

"Yes?" I choke out.

"Mr. Gordon? This is Coach Yeong!" Then he pauses.

"Yes?"

"From Team Anaconda?"

"Of course." Then I worry that I've been rude. I've heard that you can insult people from other cultures in a thousand ways without even knowing. Saying "Of course," has got to be one of them. So then I add, idiotically, "And how are you?"

"Fine. Very fine. Thank you. Thank you very much." There is another long pause, so that I wonder if we've lost our connection. Then I hear Yeong clear his throat.

"I call with news." Count to ten. I'm thinking, is this like a two-way radio conversation? Where you have to say "ten-four" or something before you can talk?

"We have spent many hours talking about this decision. Very big decision for team. To have our first player from West. Many, how do you say, considerations?"

"Yes, I understand."

"And it is our opinion that you, Mr. Seth Gordon. You are the player with great potential. We agree, you could be great Starfare champion."

"Excuse me," I say. "Did I hear that right?"

"Oh yes. Of course, this is big decision for you also. To leave home. Family. To train so hard, like Korean pro. It is very big decision."

"You want me to join Team Anaconda?"

"Oh yes. We very much excited to have you come and join team."

"And you're wondering if I'm interested?"

"Yes. You. Family. Everyone."

"When do I start?"

"Excuse. I do not understand."

"When can I begin? I'm ready now."

I hear Coach Yeong laugh and then speaking Korean to someone, away from the phone.

"Very good. Mr. Seth Gordon. Very good. But we have much to talk first. You are very young…"

"Sixteen, sir."

"Yes, well, still very young. And much to do before. We have many papers to read. Parents must sign. And league rules."

"League rules?"

"Yes. Yes. We cannot make contract with player if there is no, how to do say, finish gymnasium?"

I have no idea what he is talking about. "Gym class?"

"No, no. School. Must finish school. Get paper from school."

"Diploma?"

"Yes, yes. Diploma. Very good. Must have this from what you call tall school."

"Tall school?"

"Yes, before university."

"Oh, high school."

"Yes, yes. High school. League says must have high school paper before or while you play first year of contract."

"But I won't graduate from school for, like, two more years!" My heart sinking.

"Understand. No hurry. Contract is for next season, not one playing now. We can extend. We wait. But we also do investigate. You hear of school over Internet?"

"Yes." I'd looked into it. Was ready to go that direction if I had won the $30k. "We do research. Many Americans get diploma studying over Internet. You talk to school. We send package. You will find many papers, contract. Then we talk again soon."

"OK," I mutter.

"Package coming. You, parents read carefully."

"OK," I say. "OK. Great."

And then I hear the connection drop.

I collapse into my desk chair. Heart racing like I've been biking up a steep, endless hill. I've got to get online and tell DTerra and my other friends. They're going to absolutely lose it when they hear.

And then I think about telling Hannah. And the excitement immediately turns cold as I realize what I'm telling her. That the most exciting news in my life, that the best news I've ever heard, is that I'm leaving. Someday, maybe someday soon if I'm lucky, leaving for another life halfway around the world.

49.

So I'm a wreck all day Friday, trying to figure out how to tell her, or if to tell her. Here I am, the only person in our entire high school that she really knows, and I'm trying to figure out how to take off. I know if I were in her shoes I'd dump me.

I text her at around five and ask if eight o'clock is OK.

She says sure. Movie?

I really need to be able to talk about this, so I write that when I was on campus I saw a bunch of posters. For a free concert at the student center. In this place they call The Cellar. Some folk rocker called Jesse Owen Olds. Heard of her?

Neither of us have, but she's starting at nine, so I say we can drive down, get there a bit early and get a good seat.

By the time I get to Hannah's the sun is setting, putting a yellow glow to her house as I head down the street. Hannah is out the porch door as I pull into the driveway.

"Thank God," she says. "I swear they get together every morning and have a conference on how to drive me crazy."

I glance over as she gets buckled in. Hair tied back, the earrings shining in the low sunlight. She glances over at me with a look that goes right to the heart. I feel like a hero, rescuing the princess from imprisonment in the evil lord's castle.

"You look great," I say.

"Oh, I'm a mess as usual. Zeb, like, locks himself in our bathroom a half hour before I'm supposed to leave. I know he does it on purpose, just to annoy me."

We hop on the freeway and head downtown. I'm getting really good at driving to campus. So at least I don't worry like I used to about what exit to take and all that.

Hannah has to give me all the details on the stuff her parents and little brother have been doing and I just sort of grunt and nod.

"So I Googled this singer," she says, as we get close to campus. "She sounds pretty interesting. She's opened for a lot of good acts. Toad the Wet Sprocket. Aimee Mann. Regina Specktor."

"Great," I say, even though I don't know any of them. I'm pretty lost when it comes to music.

When we get on campus we have to ask someone for directions to The Cellar. Turns out it's not really a cellar, but this dark room on the bottom level of the student center, an old building that looks like a church. It's just a big room with lots of pillars and little chandeliers covered with red shades. At one end of the room is a raised platform with a microphone and a couple of suitcase-sized amps. The platform is a mess of red and black wires, steel cases for electronic equipment, a velvet lined open guitar case.

The room is about half full. They serve beer and most of the people have little plastic pitchers on their wooden tables. Hannah and I pick a table near the middle of the room and I get her a latte and I get a Coke.

"So," says Hannah. "Recognize anyone from your class?"

I look around us.

"This crowd looks more like their parents," I say.

Hannah scans the crowd. "You think so?"

"Yeah," I say, lowering my voice. "Not that many bald sophomores with gray beards."

I keep meaning to change the subject, to tell her about the call from Korea. But I just put it off as the room fills and finally breaks into applause as the singer takes the stage and plugs in her guitar. She looks more like a college student than most of the audience. Dark glasses, brown hair to her shoulders, brown T-shirt and tight jeans. She's nice-looking, but not fancy, none of that glittered hair and raccoon eyes that you see in all the music videos.

As she hits the first chords the room positively rings with the sound and I realize that I won't be explaining things to Hannah. Not during the songs, at least. I notice two more sets of amps on the side of the stage, taller than me. The room echoes with each strum. Then she starts singing.

"I didn't mum yum wha diz me,

"I didn't sum hum wuzza a knee"

I look at Hannah, who seems to be really into it. I wonder if I'm supposed to be understanding the words.

"This wiz a wunna tum a bird,

"Wha izza tunna willa third."

When she gets done with the song, polite applause.

"Wow," Hannah says as she claps. "That was really great."

"It was?" I say. "I mean, it was!"

We listen to about five songs and then the singer stops and talks for a minute. She asks something about living in a dorm, which I can barely understand. Then she says that she has CDs for sale in the back, which is the first thing that I've heard through the mic that I completely understand.

Before she starts the next song I tell Hannah I have to hit the bathroom. When I get back the singer is off the stage and they're playing recorded music.

"Hey," I say as I sit down.

"Hey," Hannah says. "You like that set?"

"Sure." Play with the beads of water on my bottle. "Hannah," I finally say. "I got that call I was expecting. Yesterday. You know. From those Koreans." Now she perks up, and leans towards me across the table.

"You got it, didn't you!"

I nod.

"Omigod, you got it. That is so, so, terrific!"

I was thinking she was going to hate me for it.

"It's not a done thing," I add quickly. "Contracts, parents. Plus I have to get a diploma."

"You have to graduate first?"

"Something like that."

"Well, Jeez, it's not like you're not smart enough to get it. You're already taking college courses."

"I bet it's more complicated than that. I'm going to make an appointment with my counselor at school."

Hannah has about twenty more questions, which I can't answer. Then the singer comes back on stage and tunes her guitar and then hits a really loud chord and shouts something. A bunch of the people in the audience start whooping. When the song begins it's too loud to talk and I can't say I'm sorry.

When the song is finally over I say, "You know, I thought you might be, you know, upset over this Korean thing."

I glance over and Hannah reaches out and touches my arm.

"Seth, look, you're the thing I like best about Kansas…maybe the *only* thing I really like about Kansas. I get your texts and, sure, I think it would really be fun to drop everything and get together. But then I think about how it will end, maybe in just a couple of months and I, I don't know, I just sort of…"

The singer steps off the stage, unslings her guitar and grabs a water bottle. I wish I could have more time to think about what I want to say. Because I want to tell her I don't care about what might happen in a couple months. I care about now.

The singer slings her electric guitar over her shoulder and is preparing for another assault.

Hannah is working a strand of hair with her hand. She sighs. Takes my hand. "Look, Seth. I don't think I'm explaining things very well. But this Korea thing, if you can work out the details, and I bet you will…it's a great opportunity. I'm not saying, like, don't go because it's a huge risk or you might not like it or might not do as well as you think. I'm not saying don't go because of me, or us. In fact, I'm just trying to make sure that 'us' isn't a factor. Of course you have to go. It's what you've been dreaming about for years. But there are things that are in our control. Things we can do that will make it easier. For both of us."

Then the girl with the guitar bounces up on the stage and looks right at me and Hannah and smiles. Like she knows that the first chord will drown out the most important conversation I've ever had. And then she proceeds to do just that.

On the way home I glance over at Hannah, who's just staring straight ahead through the windshield. The passing headlights flash across her face. I want every one to be a camera flash, so I can have that image forever. She's thinking about who-knows-what. Probably about three steps ahead of me, like a Korean pro toying with me in Starfare. Maybe she's already thinking of life post-Seth. Plotting who she'll be driving around with on Friday nights, when I'm halfway around the world.

50.

I get a meeting with a counselor at North the day before school starts. Miss Gibbons at 8 a.m. She's got this fake-looking blond hair and a big mug of coffee and is so perky I want to run out of the room. She has my file in front of her, and I can see she's looking over my transcript as she pulls a calculator out of her desk drawer.

"My, you have an awful lot of credits for your year," she says.

And it's true. I've been taking high school courses since seventh grade.

"But these grades," she adds. "All over the map."

I've heard that tune before.

"Well, that's another story, I'm sure," she says with what I take to be a fake smile. Looks at the calculator and shuts my folder. "Here it is in a nutshell. By the end of the semester you're going to have plenty of credits to graduate. The only thing you're missing is PE and one semester of English requirement. But they just changed the rules for PE—it's only required for semesters in which you're enrolled as a full-time student. So all you really have to do is pick up a semester of English."

I'm stunned. I figured this was going to be the biggest hassle ever.

"So I just need one semester of English? And if I can't take it here…"

"No problem, really. That course is offered by the state's virtual classroom. We have a lot of kids around the state taking it via the Internet. So you can do that wherever you might be. Didn't you say China?"

"Korea."

"Oh yes. It sounds like a wonderful opportunity," and she pauses for a second as I see her eyes drop to the folder, "Seth."

"We can register you for the online class later this semester, and you'll get your diploma when you finish senior English."

So I head back home. In a daze. It's August. Thinking that I can call Coach Yeong up and say that I can start in December when the first semester is over. In four months. Wondering if I was sort of hoping the school would say no and I could just hang out for a year. Me and Hannah. Keep working on my game like I had been. Now I might have to be ready to go in just a few months. Knowing how far behind the Korean pros I am.

I really don't want to think about it. So I get home and go back to sleep for a few hours. Getting up. That's by far the hardest part of going back to school.

But when the day comes, I do it. Zombie my way around the first three periods, counting down the minutes to my long break for my UMKC class. Every year, school sort of sneaks up on you at the end of the summer and hits you over the head with the same old boring scene. Except this year, it's different. Because I'm the guy who knows all the ropes and Hannah is the new kid.

So I have this whole different thing going on. Instead of just laying low and being as invisible as possible, I have to pretend I know stuff. So that I can show Hannah around. Introduce her to people. Tell her which teachers are cool and which are jerks. And once school starts, it's not like Hannah is right there. It's a big school and the only class we have together is English, fifth period.

Plus I'm out for a big chunk of the day to get to my calc class. And on off days, I'm using that time to get some quality gaming in. So I'm not really around during the key moments, say lunch, when I figure Hannah is really feeling alone.

So second week, on Wednesday, when I don't have calc, I text Hannah and say that I'd like to meet her for lunch in the school cafeteria. She gets right back, says sure.

So I get there a few minutes after second lunch and wander around the cafeteria. It all comes back to me from years past: the unappetizing smell of the hot lunch line which reeks like a big pot of chicken soup being spread around with a dirty mop, the buzz of hundreds of conversations, the clank of trays hitting tables, and occasionally, cutting above it all the squeal of some girl saying "ewww," or "no way!"

Finally I see Hannah at a table at the far end of the cafeteria and I head over. I don't have any food, since I wasn't sure if Hannah brought her lunch or went through the line. I figured I'd play it by ear.

Halfway there I realize I'm going to pass a table with a bunch of kids from my class. Brit is in the middle of the table facing me.

As I walk by she says cheerily, "Hi, Seth!" And I say hi back, but maybe not loud enough for her to hear. She's probably just amused, thinking, there goes that guy who had that pathetic crush.

Then I'm at Hannah's table. She has a brown paper bag in front of her and is leaning forward, talking to a group of four girls who all seem entranced. While she's talking she's absentmindedly peeling an orange. I walk up and stand behind Hannah until one of the girls clears her throat and throws her eyes in my direction. Hannah turns.

"Oh, Seth!" she says. "Here, we'll make room!"

She scoots to the left and I climb over the bench and sit down. Not much room, so I'm pressed up against her shoulder and the sensation sort of throws me off stride, so I'm glad when she starts talking.

"I was just telling them how great you've been. You know everyone?" she says, her eyes indicating the four girls at the end of the table. Of course I don't, so I shake my head. Although I recognize them.

"Anyway," she says. "This is Maddy," and she points to a girl with large black glasses and red streaks in her hair. "Sunita," an Indian girl with dark skin who smiles at me. "Iris," a small Asian girl who says, "We had history together last year." I nod and am about to stutter something when Hannah continues, "And Caroline." Caroline is a tall girl with long, straight black hair who I remember from middle school, where she stood out in the hallways, towering above everyone.

"We're on yearbook together," Hannah says. "And we have tons of work to do. The photo files are a mess."

I say hello to everyone.

"You don't have anything to eat!" Hannah says. "Aren't you going to get something?"

"Maybe," I say. "Maybe later."

"So how's your college class?" Then she looks at the other girls and explains that I'm taking a math course at UMKC. So naturally I blush bright red and look down at the table.

Hannah sees that she's embarrassed me and says, "Anyway, I was just telling them about this idea I had for a sort of a photo collage to open the yearbook. Taking shots of the school and kids here and interlacing them with pictures from the major news stories of the year. You know, to like, show how we're connected to all of that, even though it sometimes feels like high school is a different world altogether."

This starts a buzz of conversation. I watch Hannah interacting with them and realize that in two weeks she's made more friends in high school than I did in two years.

I'm half listening to the buzz of their conversation, wondering if the line at the sub station will be short enough to give me time to grab one, when Hannah turns to me.

"We must be boring you to death," she says.

"Not at all," I say. "I love yearbooks. In fact, I have my own copy of National Lampoon's Yearbook. Which was formally owned by Larry Kreiger, the guy from *Animal House*."

Blank stares. Garrett gave it to me as a birthday present a few years ago. I'm guessing the typical high school girl is maybe a little behind on classic gross-out movies.

I catch the Indian girl giving the tall girl a look that I translate as "What is this guy talking about?"

Then I excuse myself, saying I needed to grab something to eat. When I get back everyone is packing up. I sit back down next to Hannah as they leave.

"You've got about two minutes to eat that sandwich," Hannah says. And in a softer voice, "And thanks for being nice to my yearbook friends. They're a little old-fashioned."

"No problem." I swallow a mouthful and add, "Have you submitted your angel picture yet?"

Hannah waits until I take another huge bite before she hits my shoulder. I choke a bit. My eyes watering. I can see she's not really upset.

"No," she says, "But look for a sailor boy on the cover."

51.

When I get home from school on Monday there's a good-sized FedEx box on the doorstep. I drop it in the entryway and get a knife from the kitchen. If Mom was around, she'd yell at me for using one of the good kitchen knives on a box. But of course, she isn't around, and I'm pretty sure Dad won't care one way or another. I go to work on the box right there, in front of the door.

Inside is a folder filled with a bunch of papers. I set that aside and pull out a couple of smaller boxes. One has a Team Anaconda branded mouse and the other a Team Anaconda heavy-weight mouse pad. The mouse pad is made out of some sort of laminated plastic. Inside is a three-dimensional snake team logo. Very cool. And I also find a soft package that has one of those shiny green and red Team Anaconda shirts and two T-shirts. I unfold the team shirt. On the back it says "ActionSeth." That really blows me away.

I sort of just collapse there in the doorway for a few minutes, taking it all in. I mean, it's one thing to imagine playing pro Starfare, it's another to have all this stuff that you can see and touch and wear.

On Tuesday I hem and haw in my room. Try on one of the new T-shirts, take it off. Finally, I say what the hell and decide to wear it to school, thinking that people will just stop and stare. Instead the only person who notices is Hannah, who I run into in the hall after second period, on my way to the parking lot to head to UMKC.

"Hey," she says, as we step to the side of the traffic. "What's that picture thing on your shirt. Something to do with *Star Wars*?"

"Well-known game for highly intelligent humans, it is," I say in a lame Yoda voice.

Hannah shakes her head. Doesn't get it.

"You're the one that brought up *Star Wars*."

"Yeah, but I get it mixed up with *Star Trek*." Which is like me telling Hannah I can't tell the difference between photo journalism and photosynthesis.

"I got a whole bunch of stuff from Korea," I say. "I'll show it all to you, but I'm going to be late for my math class."

"OK, college boy," Hannah says. "If you have to go, you have to go."

Then she leans in and gives me a peck on the lips, right there in the hallway. Which is not exactly going to cause a scene. I've seen stuff in the hallway that couldn't make it on primetime TV. But it's something of a hallmark for me. I mean, a year ago I could have put "kissing a hot girl in a hallway at North during school" as among the "ten least likely events in my high school career," probably right up there with scoring a touchdown and getting elected Homecoming King.

So I sort of float out the parking lot and think about it all the way to UMKC.

We get our first quiz back at the beginning of the period. I was pretty sure I got them all right, but I see I have a ninety-four. I got only partial credit for one question. Next to the problem is scrawled, "Right answer but show your work!"

I almost raise my hand to argue my case right there because I did show my work. True, I didn't use the stuff we were working on in the recent chapters—I attacked it with a different set of equations. The ones we had touched on the previous year.

So I can't concentrate at all and when the prof dismisses class I grab my backpack and run up to the podium. The prof looks at me for a second, but then seems to be staring at my shirt. I figure it's just typical nerdy professor behavior. Not being able to look someone in the eye.

I blabber on for a minute until he interrupts me.

"Come on," he says. "Another class is coming in here. But we can talk in my office."

Which turns out to be just one floor up and down a hallway.

He's got a bunch of cartoons on the door, which I don't have time to read. Inside he sits at his desk and I take a chair across from him. A wall of math books behind him. I slide my quiz over to him and start explaining.

"Hang on," he says. He pulls out a pencil, taps it on the desk as he looks over my paper.

"OK," he says. "Ok, I see what you're doing here." Taps his pencil again.

Then he looks up at me as if he hadn't seen me before. "My apologies," he says. "I think my TA just didn't follow it." I watch him cross out the ninety-four and write one hundred. Then he logs onto his desktop and I wait while he clicks through some screens. Updating my score, I assume.

When he finishes he looks up at me and says again, "I'm sorry my TA didn't catch that. It was actually quite elegant, the way you attacked that problem. Very neat. Where did you learn that technique?"

I explain that we just touched on something related in the AP course. And I had looked into it a bit more, I don't know, because it seemed interesting.

"So what other math have you taken here?"

I tell him it's my first college class. That I'm actually still in high school.

"So you're a senior?"

"Not exactly," I say. Because I'm not sure what I am.

"So you're what? Eighteen?"

"Well I just turned sixteen actually. Last week."

He sorts of snorts when he hears that, raises his eyebrows like I've caught his attention now.

"And not that it's any of my business," he continues. "But I've put a little time into Starfare. You play a lot?"

I admit I do.

"You play seriously?"

I nod.

He glances again at my quiz, which is still in front of him. "Seth?"

He pauses and I can see the wheels turning. "You're not, by any chance, ActionSeth?"

I say I am.

"Holy cow," he says. "I watched that entire game you played in the quarterfinals at Nationals. That was really something."

All I remember is that I lost.

"ActionSeth," he says. And then he mumbles it a couple more times. "I heard somewhere that you might be from around here.

"So, ActionSeth. Taking Calc 301 at UMKC," he says. "So what do you think you might do with this mathematical ability that you seem to be gifted with?"

I hem and haw and finally mumble that I might just play on Team Anaconda.

Now his eyes are really open. "No way," he says. "They've never had anyone from outside of Korea, have they?"

"Not yet," I say. "But it looks like I might be the first."

"Holy moley," he says again. "Well, I can say that I'm damned pleased to have you in my class, Mr. ActionSeth. And if you decide that maybe you'd prefer to pursue some advanced mathematics instead of a Starfare career, you just let me know. I might have some ideas for you."

I say OK and excuse myself and walk out, shutting his door. I look down at my shirt, thinking that I had no idea. I stop to read the cartoons. My favorite shows a math professor at the end of about thirty feet of blackboard equations. Another professor is pointing to some figures at the very beginning, saying, "And *here's* where you made your mistake."

52.

That night I spend some time going through the stuff that came from Korea. There's a long contract with a place for Mom and Dad to sign but the language is all screwed up and it's hard as hell to figure out what it means. I see a section that says I get the equivalent of $5,000 U.S. a month but the next section seems to be saying that I have to pay for housing and food and incidentals which has a list of about a hundred things. I have no idea whether I'd have anything left at the end of a month or whether I'd owe them.

Finally I bite the bullet and put a call into Dad who's on the road until Friday. After all, he's the all-star businessman. Of course I have to leave a message, but for once he gets back to me after just a half-hour. Turns out he's got an old frat brother who's an entertainment lawyer in Hollywood.

And for once, Dad actually comes through. This lawyer friend goes through the contract line by line. Sends it back with a bunch of edits and a letter saying he's made sure I'm getting a decent deal. That I'll be putting money in the bank from day one. A couple days later he actually calls me up and goes through some stuff. Makes it clear that I have an open-ended ticket back to KC. That I can leave anytime if it doesn't work out.

When I hang up I'm sort of dizzy. Because it's all coming together. It's really, really going to happen. I'm turning pro.

53.

As I get deeper into the semester I sort of get in a groove. High school is like a dream that I float in and out of. A series of boring classes punctuated with Hannah moments. College calculus is another kind of a dream—the material flows, I get what the professor is talking about, do the readings, do fine on the quizzes and tests. But behind it all, like a song you can't get out of your head, is Starfare and Team Anaconda. A buzz in the back of my brain, churning up a constant stream of anxiety.

But not everything is going faster. There's Hannah and me.

I mean, I know she said that stuff about not getting too close, making it easier. But I also thought she'd see the other side. That you couldn't just stop living because something bad might happen in the future.

But it's also true, when she says how busy she is. Because she's gotten involved in tons of stuff. She's got yearbook, and she's still working lots of hours at Saviano's. They call me to come in, but I only do it if Hannah's on too. Plus she started up a chapter of this environmental group she was in back in New Jersey.

And when we see each other at school, it all seems cool. But every time I suggest we do something together, it's always one thing or another. And just when I'm totally depressed she texts me. A special exhibit at the Nelson-Atkins Museum by a photographer named Ray something opening on Friday. Can I go? It's free! I can tell—even with nothing more than the text—that she is totally excited. I wait a couple minutes before texting back. To make it seem like I'm clearing my schedule.

We drive downtown after school and she gives me the whole story on this guy. Describes some of his famous shots so well I'm sure I could ID them by looks alone. When we finally park Hannah leaps out of the car and I have to almost jog to keep up with her.

Inside she is just as wired, skipping from one photo to the next like a little kid at a carnival. And I swear, as she dances in and out of the light around each photo the other people in the gallery can't help staring. Like she's glowing, like she's part of the exhibit. Then she's calling me over, pointing at the way the photographer uses the light to balance the composition of a street scene. And when I say that this other photo of a train station looks like an impressionist painting, she explains exactly what he did in the darkroom. Talking so animatedly that by the time she's done there's a half-dozen people circled around, as if she was an official guide or something. We stay until they announce closing and it doesn't seem that we've been there long at all, even though it's been almost two hours.

When we get back to my place she just follows me inside like she lives there. And then we're kissing. I kick the door shut. And although my brain is reeling, I can't help thinking. It would be great if the museum brought in a new photo exhibit every couple days. But then, after all that excitement, it's another week of nothing. Finally out of frustration I decide to get some expert advice.

"Hey," I say when Garrett picks up.

"Hey, bro, what's up?"

"Dad says you scored seventeen last Saturday in that exhibition game."

"Yeah, got a hot hand. But we lost by five, so who cares."

We talk about basketball for a bit and finally Garrett, who knows me better than I'd admit, says, "But I'm guessing you didn't call to chat about shooting percentage. Right?"

So I tell him about me and Hannah. He listens quietly and then says, "So let me get this straight. You're taking off overseas in, what, a couple of months, and you're surprised your gf is getting a little distant?"

I admit it sounds a little stupid, when he puts it like that.

"So what you doing about it?"

"Doing?"

"Yeah. Just sitting at home moping, I bet."

I mumble something and then ask him what I'm supposed to do.

"Well, what have you got her lately?"

"Got her?"

"Yeah, like presents. Tokens of your affection. Like those boxes you get at Christmas."

I mumble something, because the honest answer is, nothing, never.

"OK, I'm thinking like Valentine's or birthdays that sort of thing."

"I'm pretty sure Hannah's not into that stuff," I say.

"Trust me, she's into it. So what's the excuse. She got a birthday coming up? How about an anniversary?"

"Anniversary?"

"Yeah. Like one year since your first date. Gfs dig that shit."

"Well, no birthday soon. Let's see. I met her in June, so that's like six months."

"There you go. Six month anniversary. Get her something."

"Like what?"

I can hear him sigh, picture eyes rolling. "OK, here's the deal.

You go out to the mall, go to all the jewelry stores. Ask them what high school girls are shopping for. Then buy whatever that is."

"This is really going to work?"

"Trust me."

So on the weekend I go to the mall. Listen to all these older women in heavy makeup tell me what's hot. They can't wait to show me samples. In the end I pick out earrings, two Hs covered in tiny diamonds. Costs me just about everything I've saved from the pizza job.

So on Sunday afternoon I drive over to Hannah's. Ring the bell. Snow piled in the corners of the porch. Wind making the porch swing creak.

Hannah's mom answers and invites me in, where I battle the bounding Barkley. Hannah comes down the stairs, looking surprised, puzzled, beautiful.

I reach into my pocket, hand her the wrapped box. Mumble that it's been a great six months, knowing her. Then, looking at the ground, mumble something else about having to leave and then I'm out the door. Don't look back.

Although it's too depressing to actually keep count, it's been at least fifty hints and a dozen blunt invites without Hannah agreeing to get together. But the day after I drop the gift I text her and she says sure, dinner on Wednesday. We decide to go back at the deli in Westport where I was revealed as a closet gamer.

When I pull into the driveway she's out the door, down the stairs. Bundled in a red and black knit hat and matching scarf.

"OMG," she says, as she slides into the front of the van. "If anyone had told me how cold it gets in Kansas I would have just refused to come."

The van is warm and she swipes off the hat and leans over, pecks me on the lips. I can see from the glow of the dash the sparkling H in her right ear.

"Thanks for the earrings," she says.

"You don't have to keep them," I say. "I have the receipt…"

"Shut up," she says. "I love them."

It's easy to find a place to park in the middle of the week. I'm happy to find a close spot. It's really getting cold at night and I still haven't figured out where my coat is. I think it's in a box we packed from our old house.

"So," Hannah says as we take a seat in a worn, wooden booth in the back of the restaurant, near the welcome warmth and aroma from the pizza ovens. "Getting nervous about everything?"

What I'm really been stressing about how is hard it's been getting any one-on-one time with Hannah. I know what she said about not getting too close, but I'm not talking about make-out sessions. Just going out for a dinner or a movie or something. But I'm not about to blurt that out. So I tell her about my dreams.

"It's basically the same every time," I say. "I wake up in the middle of the night and my heart is pounding and I'm twisted around in bed."

"Dreaming about me again, I see," Hannah says, with her sly smile.

"No, those are the good dreams," I say, immediately embarrassed. So I just keep on blabbering. "These are always Starfare dreams. They're all basically the same. I'm playing in front of a big crowd. Kind of like those exhibitions I did in Chicago. Except something is always wrong. My mouse is only working once every ten clicks. Or the monitor is in slow motion. And the crowd is on their feet, yelling and jeering at me. But I can't understand anything they're saying."

The waitress comes over and I convince Hannah to try their pizza. They do this thin crust that droops as you pick it up. New York style. I'm anxious to try to get her to understand why I'm confused about the way she's been acting, but after we make our order Hannah says something about liking the waitress's charm bracelet and the waitress actually sits down next to her. Goes into this long explanation about what a bunch of them mean. When she finally leaves Hannah leans across the booth a bit and says, "So you *are* nervous. I would be too."

I'm facing the kitchen and I watch the guys behind the

counter rolling out the dough. Thinking how many hours I wasted over the past months doing the same.

"You know," Hannah is saying. "I get something like the same thing when I've been thinking too much about college. Going through the catalogs or looking at my portfolio. I have dreams where I see a bunch of art professors standing around, and they're all looking at something on the table and laughing. And then I realize it's my portfolio."

"But your stuff is terrific," I say.

Hannah shakes her head and says, "Sure. You can say that. You're not an art professor." And then she continues. "Plus, my parents. They think I should study something practical. Like pre-med. They're always saying, 'You can do the photography on the side.' I could just kill them sometimes."

This I can relate to.

"But I've got, like, plenty of time to worry about that stuff," Hannah says. "You've only got what? A month or so?"

I can't believe it's only a month, but when I think twice, she's right.

"Last time we talked your mom was still having doubts."

"She still thinks I've twelve," I say. "But get this. Dad, you know, the pro sales guy. He gives her the full pitch treatment and gets her to sign the contract."

"Yeah? How'd he do that?"

"Well, I promised I'd call or Skype her at least once a week. Starting now. Plus he told her I'd be making enough that I could pay for college."

"Is that true?"

"Sure. If I get to top ten in the world."

"So get to top ten in the world."

"Easy for you to say. It's like me saying to you, 'Just get a full-ride art scholarship.'"

"I know," she says. "We can only dream."

After we eat Hannah says she's got to get back to work on her English paper. Which makes me groan, because I haven't started mine either. It's an essay on *1984*. On the way home we talk about what to write about. I always try to go for the easiest topic. For me, it's a discussion of how much stuff in the book has come true. That's perfect, because truth be told, I haven't had a chance to finish it and I can pick up the missing ingredients in about five minutes on SparkNotes. I try to convince her that it's that easy. That she should come over for a little.

"It may take *you* fifteen minutes. It's going to take me a couple of hours."

So she insists I take her straight home. After I drop her off I go sit in front of the computer, trying to get motivated to do the English paper. Instead, staring at the kiss photo and feeling awful. I thought talking to her would fix everything, but it's actually worse. Because for years all I've been thinking about is making it as a pro-gamer. It's like in *The Wizard of Oz*, when Dorothy and her friends first see the Emerald City. All shiny and bright and all you have to do is follow the road. But then they get to the scene where the road is overgrown with poppies and it's not so clear anymore.

Thinking about Hannah is like those poppies. When I'm thinking about her the path gets foggy. This plan, which over the years has hardened clear and crystalline, like one of those trophies they give the winner of a Starfare Grand Prix, it drifts out of focus. And I have to blink my eyes, like windshield wipers in a fog, to get that image back.

After that night out, when we meet at school it's all good. But it's the same old story if I suggest we get together after school or do something on the weekend. The one plus is that without work and without Hannah I've got more time to try not to fall further behind with my gaming. As soon as I get the crap like the English paper out of the way. So I do. I'm still using the five-paragraph essay that they taught us in GE English in fifth grade. Lame intro, three things in the book that came true, a paragraph on each of those things, repeat the intro. It takes me exactly thirty-four minutes. I'm sure it will be at least a B.

Coach Yeong and I have been trading emails and he helps set

me up with games when he can, which is hard with the time difference. Sometimes he'll watch and send me notes afterwards, things that I can work on. So for the first time in my life I actually have some direction and feel like it's really helping. Who knows, maybe I will make a fortune yet.

Hey Hannah, it's me!

Who?

You know, Seth. Calling from Korea.

Oh yeah. Bad connection, could barely hear you. So how are you?

Great. In fact, I just won my first Grand Prix event. It comes out to close to $20k.

That's wonderful, Seth.

Yeah, well, the reason I'm calling. I know it's almost spring break, and I thought we could get together.

Get together?

Yeah—I've got tickets reserved for both of us. We can meet in Hawaii on April 6. Maui, actually. I've booked five nights at the best hotel on the best beach. I'll email you a link. They've got all these pools with waterfalls and stuff. It's amazing.

Oh, Seth. That sounds like a dream come true. I can't believe you would do that. I can hardly wait…

54.

As the semester comes close to an end, it's like the days are accelerating. I've got a ton of stuff to do and I want to see Hannah. When I'm sorting through my clothes, making piles of stuff I think I should take, I see the yoga pad and DVD in the corner. I pick up the pad, set it down on the floor, do a couple of dumb stretches. Then I text Hannah. Ask if I can stop by to give her something. She says she's doing some project for world history so she can't hang out. Fine.

She steps out onto the porch and I hold out the pad and DVD.

"I'm not taking this with," I say. "Thought you'd get some use out of it."

"I can't," she says, glancing back at the door like she's worried. That the dog would get out? That the guy from the environment club will pop up? "This was a gift from your mom."

"She'd want it to be used," I said. "Otherwise it's just gathering dust in the corner."

Hannah reaches out and takes them from me. Hugs the pad the way I'd like to be.

"God it's cold out here," she says. And then I notice she's just in stocking feet. Goosebumps on her arms. "Hey, we'll get together. At a better time."

"Right," I say, standing awkwardly, now that I have nothing to hold. "Well, good luck with the history project."

"Oh it sucks," she says. "I'm terrible at these big papers."

"No you're not," I say. "But too bad you can't do it with photos."

"No kidding." She's sort of jumping from foot to foot. From the cold. Or maybe she's just anxious for me to leave.

"OK, well, I've got to go too," I lie.

"Yeah, I know how crazy it is. When you're getting ready to move."

"OK, well I'll text you later."

"Great," she says. As she turns back to the door, she looks over her shoulder. Strand of hair across her right eye. Those hazel eyes. Watering a bit—from the cold? Click, I think, wishing I had this photo, forever. "And thanks for the yoga stuff. I'll use it, I promise."

"Great." The screen door slams. And then I'm just standing there, alone on the porch. It seems like a long drive back.

Part II
KOREA

1.

Looking out the window of my Korean Air jet out of Chicago, I see, through a break in the clouds, the checkerboard snow-spattered pattern of what might be Illinois. Or Iowa, maybe. I'm already lost.

The last few weeks are a blur. Getting through all my classes and getting everything ready for the trip. Worrying about the passport arriving, and then still worried when it does. And then there was that weird photo session. Coach Yeong arranged for me to go to a place downtown where they took about 200 photos of me in my green Team Anaconda shirt. I might have looked a little glum, since all I could think of was how much more fun it was having Hannah take my picture.

And Hannah. When I think back, she really was great. Even though she could see the dead end ahead. After I gave her the yoga stuff we had this great week. We'd either do something together after school or I'd come over to her house after dinner. Her dad was never around, but her mom always seemed happy to see me. Of course, it might have been only because she knew I was heading halfway around the world in a few days. When I asked how it was that we had so much time together all she said was, "I'm being selfish."

So Hannah and me. We're still something, I guess. At least, we were. I mean, I know I'm as crazy about her as always. And there were a couple times over the past few months, when we were finally alone. Wow—not healthy to spend too much time thinking about that. Not while sitting on a Korean Air flight going 700 mph just about as far from Hannah as possible.

Then there was the scene at the Kansas City airport. It was so weird that it already feels like it happened to someone else. In my mind, I wanted it to be just Hannah and me. One of those romantic goodbye scenes from the movies. Full of longing stares and pitiful embraces and promises.

But Dad insisted on coming with us, so it was the three of us.

I checked my giant bag with my entire wardrobe of hoodies and jeans. We were standing there awkwardly near where the security line begins. No one was really talking.

I was looking at Hannah, who was trying not to look at me, while Dad pretended to be looking somewhere else. She looked sad, but smiling. And tears. I'm sure I saw them, barely.

If I was the weeping sort I'd be right with her. It just felt awful. Awful to be leaving her, and home, and Dad and being so far from Mom and Garrett too, if truth be told. But awful to be excited about going too. Like I'm somehow a traitor.

So in the end, I gave Dad a hug, and he patted me on the back. And then Hannah, and I really want to kiss her goodbye, but it just felt wrong there in public with Dad watching. Now, as I watch the clouds rushing past below, I'm pretty sure I blew it. That she will never forgive me for wimping out. As soon as I can I'll write her and tell her that I really wanted it be different. Like the New York street photo we posed for. That's what it should have been like.

And when I'm not thinking about leaving Hannah and home, there's Starfare. Could I be nuts to think I could be one of the best in the world? What will they do if I can't measure up? Where would I go if they fire me? Go back to high school? After graduating? That seems impossible.

Instead of figuring it out, I dig through my backpack and get out the first book for my Internet class. I really hope I can knock off this class as easily as possible. The lectures are all online and you can work through at your own pace. My intent is to get it over with fast so I can concentrate entirely on getting my game up to speed.

I pull out my copy of *The Scarlet Letter* and start speed reading. I just want to get the flavor of it before I resort to SparkNotes. I get through a couple of chapters when my eyes get heavy.

I'm out for what must be about an hour when I'm wakened by a young Asian flight attendant. Korean or Western dinner? I'm a little flustered, because I've been wondering about Korean girls for a couple of months. And now here one is, leaning towards me and smiling, speaking perfect English.

I decide to go safe and get some sort of Western-style chicken dinner. Plenty of chance ahead to experiment with Korean food.

2.

Luckily I sleep for most of the flight but am groggy as hell when we land in Seoul. All I can see out the windows is blinding sun. I nod off again as we taxi and wake to the bustle of people gathering their things. I slip on my backpack and it's only by luck that I notice that my headset cord is lying on the seat, still plugged in. I can almost hear my dad's voice, telling me how bad I am at looking after my stuff. But I think I do a pretty good job of looking after my important stuff. It's not like I've ever lost a laptop.

I just stumble along with the passengers in front of me, trying to remember the dream I woke up from. I was playing a game of Starfare, in front of huge, cheering crowd. But instead of having a hand on my mouse it was a fork. And still, I was playing, and in the dream, the fork was working, but not very well, because my cruisers were moving in slow motion, no matter what I did with the fork. The crowd was booing and laughing and making fun of me and I was probably doing some weird things in my seat, because when I woke up I was curled in a strange position and my forehead was damp with sweat.

The passengers lead me down a long corridor. When we go by a food court I'm relieved to see signs in English as well as Korean. It's mid-afternoon but to me it's the middle of the night. Although I recognize some of the restaurants, there is something different about the food smells, something foreign and sour. The same with the overall scene: all the thousands of people pulling their little wheeled bags, dressed in regular clothes, but the buzz of conversation has a different tone, and as people walk by I hear what I only assume is Korean. I'm still groggy and I just follow the flow to baggage claim. I hope it's the right one. But after standing for a few minutes I see our flight number up on a display on top of the carousel. So at least I can relax about that. How I'm going to connect with Coach Yeong or whoever they send is still a mystery.

At the luggage carousel I stand back and wait for my bag. I read something online how Asian people think English sounds like dogs barking. Well, Korean has a sing-song sound to it, like it was being chanted, not just spoken. I wonder how long it will take before I can say a few things. Like, "Nice game, better luck next time."

When I get my bag I follow the flow of people to a large room with a couple dozen long lines. I'm used to grabbing my bags off the carousel and scooting out of the airport. Customs, I realize. I find a line with other American-looking people, dragging my bag along as if it were loaded with weights. There is an older couple in front of me, and a family behind me, talking in French or Italian. I've been in line for about ten minutes when I notice that everyone is holding little cards.

The woman in front of me sees that I'm trying to get a glance at her card. She just gives me a motherly look and starts talking. She's short, with hair so neatly streaked in blond that it has to be dyed.

"It's a customs card. Have you filled one out?"

I shake my head. She turns to her husband, who isn't paying a whit of attention to me or his wife. He's wearing a Nike baseball hat over graying hair, staring in the other direction, focused on the lines, as if trying to figure out which one is moving fastest.

"Honey," she says. "Honey—you have an extra customs card don't you?"

"What?" he says, turning, surprised and perhaps annoyed that I've become part of his scene.

"You're always grabbing extras. You have an extra card for this nice young man?"

"Oh, hang on." He starts patting his pockets and comes up with another card and holds it out. His wife offers me a pen.

I start filling out the form. Name, address, blah, blah, blah. Push my bag forward a few steps. Local address. I dig through my bag and find Team Anaconda's return and write that down.

"Are you doing a semester abroad?" the wife asks.

I really don't want to get into it so I say, "Well, yeah. Studying. Might be more than a semester."

"I bet you'll love it," she says. "Every time we come over to visit my daughter I think how much I missed by not traveling when I was in college. Of course, back then, it was a pretty exotic thing, to study overseas. Now everyone seems to do it."

"You got the passports?" the husband barks.

"Yes, dear." She smiles at me, as if excusing his rudeness.

"Our daughter did her junior year in Korea and now she's in her third year of teaching English in Seoul. Honey, is this our fourth or fifth visit?"

"Fifth," the husband says. The line moves and we all push our gear ahead.

"So, do you have friends in Korea? Other students traveling with you?"

I shake my head.

"Well, I'm going to give you Sarah's number. She's so well acclimated to the culture. Plus she's always taking people under her wings. Just her nature. Even when she was little. Always bringing home stray cats, lost dogs. She's just so nurturing."

She pulls out her pen and a pad of paper, scribbles something and hands it to me. I fold it and put it in my wallet.

She continues to chatter until we're up to the counter. I'm digging out my passport when a little guy in a uniform steps up to the counter and calls out, "Mr. Seth Gordon?" Like an idiot, I raise my hand, as if I'm in sixth grade.

He motions me to come with him and we walk past the counter a bit down the hall where he unlocks a door and takes me into a small room with another uniformed guy at a desk and two older Korean men standing. I'm thinking, maybe someone planted drugs in my bag. I'm probably going to go prison for thirty years and have to crack rocks with a sledgehammer as heavy as my luggage.

Then one of the men grins as big and bright as a neon sign

and lunges towards me. I instinctively step backwards but he stretches out a hand and grabs mine and our hands are pumping up and down like we were are sharing a Wii controller.

"Mr. Seth Gordon. I welcome you to Korea. I am team manager Soong Kim. Coach Yeong is busy with team."

I shake Mr. Kim's hand. And ask him how Coach Yeong is doing.

He smiles blankly and says, "I am Soong Kim. Team manager. I welcome to Korea."

Then he motions the second, older man over, bowing his head as he does. "This is Mr. Kim, marketing director of special projects, ANC Computers."

I shake his hand, also very enthusiastically. For an oddly long time. I wonder if the Kims are related. He's got a fixed grin on his face that looks like it might be stuck there permanently. The stalemate is broken when the uniformed man at the desk says with a heavy accent, "Passport and card please."

I hand my stuff over and he starts thumbing through my passport as if he can't find a blank spot, then grabs a hand stamp and hammers it onto a page. He holds my passport out for me and I take it with a mumbled thanks.

"Mr. Seth Gordon," the older Kim is saying. "Very nice to meet you and have you in our Korea," he says, in a way that suggests it may be his only phrase in English.

The younger Kim half pulls off my backpack and grabs my big bag, and despite my protest that I can manage, starts dragging it out of the room. I'm surprised how cold it is. People bustling in and out of the terminal in coats and hats, just like back in Kansas. I can tell that Koreans believe in getting their money's worth out of their car horns.

A driver in a black sedan is waiting at the curb. Kim leans forward and mumbles something to the driver and then he plops back in the seat next to me. He reaches into his pocket and pulls out a card and reads.

"We go directly to your new apartment. Put you to sleep. But there is some one thing to see on way. Surprise."

I can see from the dual-language road signs we are headed towards Seoul, which looms hazily in the distance like the Emerald City, except for the coloration, which is a pale shade of yellow.

Kim gives the driver some more directions and I can see we're heading into the towers of downtown, inching towards a section which is glowing like Las Vegas. Store signs are vertical, from street level up several stories. Mostly in Korean, but with a smattering of signs and brands in English: Canon, Coffee, KFC. A light changes and we take a turn to the right and Kim shouts out something in Korean. He's pointing up in the air, at the roof of the car and at first I look there, but then I realize he wants me to look outside. I press my face against the glass and peer up at a wall of neon signs that are each stories high.

One sign is blazing a Starfare logo and an ANC computer logo with a moving scene from a game. I turn to Kim and say, "Very cool," but he is gesturing wildly, so I look again, just as the screen blinks.

"Holy crap," I say. Because there, on a hundred-foot sign, is a picture of me, with a backdrop from one of the Starfare maps. I'm looking towards the map, as if playing. Underneath is a streaming row of Korean characters.

I turn toward Kim and stutter something.

He jabbers something excitedly.

"What the hell does it say?"

The young Kim shakes his head and leans forward and says something to the older Kim, who has been riding quietly up front. They chat for a second.

"Big star," Kim says.

"Me? How can I be a big anything? I haven't done a thing."

Kim looks at me with a proud grin and says again, "Big star!"

All I can think is that I better be getting into training. Immediately.

The car drives another twenty minutes from downtown. When we get into my apartment the doorman sets down the luggage and bows to Kim before leaving. The door snaps shut. Kim reaches past me and flips a switch and I can see the rest of the place. It's a narrow room, with a tiny kitchen to the right and an open floor with a big screen TV on the left. A curtained window at the end.

I hear the door opening and look up and see Coach Yeong, marching straight towards me, his hand held out as stiffly as if he were pointing a gun at me.

"Very nice, no?" Yeong says, grabbing my hand and shaking. "No need to share, like other players. Americans prefer single room, is this not correct?"

He walks all around the little apartment opening cabinets and displaying features like he personally designed the place. Finally he pauses before a pair of narrow doors and, with a flourish, opens them up to two stacked white appliances.

"Washer and dryer!" He says. "Very convenient for younger player!"

I smile like I actually know what he's talking about. Yeong hands me a key card, which is attached to a Starfare key ring.

"I am in apartment 1321," Yeong says. "Not a single." Then he snickers. "I have wife and two children."

"You get rest. Team breakfast in Suite 1201, end of hall. 8 a.m. No worries," he says, one hand on the door. "We take all your cares."

Just like that Yeong and Kim are gone. I flop down on the couch across from the black sheen of the TV screen. Exhausted and a little dizzy. My picture on the huge billboard etched into my mind like a burned LED screen. What was that all about? I knew I was just an experiment, a long shot. A long way, at least a year, maybe two, from playing with the top pros. If ever.

I look at my cell phone. Before I left I checked online and the AT&T site said that the phone would work in Korea. But as far as I could figure it would cost a fortune for local calls, and worse for international. However, the time says 6:20 p.m., so I'm connected. I figure it's 3:20 in the morning back home. The day before. Crap, it's confusing.

Realizing that if I fall asleep now I'll be totally screwed up in local time, I find the remote on the table next to the couch. Whip through about twenty channels when I get to one that is a Star-fare game, with a commentator prattling on in Korean. I watch for a bit and, during a commercial, find a second channel with two Korean guys playing WoW. I run through all the channels, and find two in English before I flip back to the Starfare game. I turn down the Korean commentary and watch the first game. I had heard about the gaming channels, but it's still a bit of shock, actually watching one.

When the first game winds down I check out the refrigerator. It's stocked with what I think is bottled water and some cans that might be some sort of soda or sports drink. One cupboard has some food in it and I take out a couple rice cakes and grab bottle of water. The cakes don't taste like anything and the water has something off about it, but I drink it anyway.

Behind a little desk in the corner I find an Ethernet cable and so I unpack my laptop and plug in. I'm amazed I get online without a hitch. I open my email account and find a bunch of new mail, but nothing from Hannah. Garrett has a short note wishing me luck, Mom has a long one telling me all about a new yoga class she's started. Even Dad has sent me a good luck note. I send out a reply to my family list, letting everyone know I got in safely. Then I decide to send an email to Hannah. I write about twenty different versions and finally send one with a subject line that says, "Hi from Korea" and a message that says, "Korea is amazing. Everyone is my height. Write me back if you want. Would be nice to Skype sometime."

Even though I have a piece of tape over my webcam. Through a webcam I look even dorkier than normal, my face blown up like it's been inflated. I'm staring at my computer screen, thinking about Hannah when an IM pops up. I shake my head in disbelief.

STOMPAZER: HEY PUTZ HEARD UR IN KOREA...GUESS WHO BEAT U HERE...TRYING NOT TO PUKE, SEEING UR POSTERS & ADS NEVER KNEW HOW MUCH U LOOKED LIKE A GRL...BUT THAT'S WHY THEY LOVE U ISNT IT...LET ME NO WHEN UR READY TO GET PWNED

I shut down the IM application. Wondering if he's kidding,

about being here. But then, how would he know about the posters? I decide not to think about it and watch Starfare games until I can't stay awake even though every game is just amazing. When I finally decide to crash I realize there's no bed. I open up a small closet and see a row of about a dozen crinkly red team shirts, just like I wore when I did the photo shoot. Underneath are some rolled up pads, blankets and some pillows that look and feel like they could be used as airline seats. I spread the pads out on the floor and prop my head up on one of the pillows. My head is buzzing. Every time I'm about to fall asleep I think about meeting the rest of the team in the morning and get a rush of nervous, sinking feeling which jars me awake.

And as I lie awake I can't stop thinking about what it must be like back in Kansas. I could tell how many guys at North had become tuned into Hannah. Especially that one guy in the environmental club that I was particularly paranoid about. It would only be a matter of time before one of them clicked.

I'm sure I had just fallen asleep when I hear a doorbell and then knocking on the door.

3.

I throw on a T-shirt and the jeans I wore on the plane. Open the door to a grinning Yeong.

"You sleep good, yes?" And before I can answer he says, "Good, good."

He looks at my chest and frowns.

"You not find team shirts?"

I tell him I did indeed discover the shirts.

"Must wear. Every day. Team Anaconda is very famous here in Korea. Photos all the time. Our great sponsor, ANC Computers, they be very sad if picture printed and no shirt and no ANC logo."

"Right," I say. I wave Yeong into the apartment but he just

stands in the doorway. So I rush back to the closet and slip on the first team shirt. It's just as scratchy as I remember.

"Come, come," Yeong says as I follow him down the hall. He swipes a card across the double doors at the end and pushes one open, holding it for me to enter.

Inside the entire Team Anaconda is sitting at a series of small, low tables, chopsticks in hand. They all turn, simultaneously, and just stare at me, chopsticks pointing at me like accusations. With their identical shirts and similar haircuts I feel like I've been dropped into some sort of clone experiment.

Yeong steps past me and starts babbling in Korean. Then he grabs my arm and walks me around the room, spitting out what I assume is everyone's name, but too fast and too thickly accented for me to follow. No one stands up. No one offers to shake hands.

I recognize two of the players from the Chicago trip and expect them to be more friendly, but they're not.

I figure it must be the Korean way. After we've made the circuit he takes me into the suite's little kitchen and gives me a bowl and while I hold it, scoops a mound of white rice into it. He takes another, smaller bowl and dips a big ladle into a pot as large as a beer keg and as he brings the red stuff towards me my nose burns and my eyes actually start to water.

"Kimchi," he says. "Korean national dish. You try little at first."

I'm thinking my definition of little is none. He dribbles a bit more than a little onto my rice. Then he leads me past a bowl of what looks and smells like some sort of canned fish, which I politely decline. At the end of the counter is at last something that looks familiar, a loaf of odd looking bread. I take a couple slices and Yeong points me back towards the team.

In the far corner there is a table with one player and two empty chairs. I sit down and nod at the player. I glance around the room and the rest of the team all seems to be staring at me. I stare into my rice, push it around with chopsticks. Trying to find some untouched by the pungent kimchi.

I look up when I hear the player across from me say something in almost a whisper. Look at him and shake my head.

"My name Sung Gi Park."

"Sung Gi?" I repeat, my heart lifting. "You speak English?"

"English not very good," he says, looking past me around the room. "But best on team. Maybe someday I go to America university. I try learn. You speak to me? I call you ActionSeth?"

"Just Seth," I say. "Of course I will talk to you." Then I lower my voice. "Sung Gi. Did I say that right?"

"Yes. Very good."

"The rest of these guys," I whisper. "They don't seem so friendly."

Sung Gi takes his time. Maybe because he has to translate what I'm saying. Or it's a hard question.

"They not know you, ActionSeth. But it is hard for new members on Team Anaconda. I am next newest. I sit alone."

"They don't like you either?"

"They like great Starfare champions. I not a great champion. They say you not great player."

"Not yet," I admit.

"You play hard, get good. They like you."

"OK, sounds like a plan."

When I glance around the room I see that the rest of the team has gone back to eating and chatting among themselves. When one of the players from Chicago, Tae-Uk, glances up and sees me looking his way he gives me an evil glare. I grin his way and wave. He shakes his head and mutters something to the guy next to him. I eat the first slice of bread. I can't bring myself to try the reeking rice. So I sit and stir and stare into the pink bowl.

I have about a hundred questions for Sung Gi. But I don't want to annoy the only guy who doesn't seem to already hate me. Plus I can tell it's a stretch for him to communicate beyond the basics in English.

After breakfast I follow the group into a room equipped with rows of back-to-back flat screen monitors and blue-glowing high-performance computers. Bed pads like mine are rolled up in the corners, and I realize that the rest of the team must sleep right here, in front of their monitors. The team lines up and down the center of the room and into the next room equipped the same way. I follow suit and stand at the end of the line. Yeong yells something and they start jumping up and down. After a minute he yells something else and they drop into a sort of push-up position, with their butts stuck up in the air and start pumping up and down. I do my best to follow along, but honestly, I'm not in the greatest shape and I just sort of dog it, doing one or two for every ten of theirs.

After about fifteen minutes everyone breaks to a seat in front of a monitor and they fire up their computers. Just being in the same room with this much Starfare talent, and seeing the screens light up, I get a little dizzy. It's a mixture of excitement and fear and disbelief. I shake my head to clear it. Then find an open spot, but before I can figure how to power up Yeong taps me on the shoulder and says, "Plenty of time to start training. Other things first."

The other things start with some sort of press event downtown. I get stuck in front of this room with about forty folding chairs and while I'm blinded by camera flashes as reporters yell questions in bad English.

I don't get all of them, but they want to know if I have an American girlfriend, what I think of Korean girls, how soon before I make it to a televised match, whether I like Korean food, and if I played Little League baseball. When I say I have—or had—a girlfriend they ask for name and photos. I just shake my head and say no over and over. I honestly have no idea how much I'm communicating, between the overlapping questions and the flash of cameras and the rolling chatter of Korean which sounds like I'm trapped in a flock of thousands of honking geese.

Afterwards Yeong seems very pleased. "You already big star!" he gushes. As we walk out onto the busy sidewalk a dozen people freeze and stare at me. Others come rushing over, pointing. Finally three teenage girls step forward and say something to me.

"They want to pose picture with you," Yeong says. He seems to think this is a great idea and two at a time, they pose, standing on either side of me, grinning and bouncing with excitement, while the third snaps pics with her cell phone.

After the press event Yeong ushers me back into the car and we drive about ten minutes and get dropped off in front of a large office building. A steady stream of dressed-up Koreans is flowing in and out of the glass doors at the front. As we weave through the crowd I wonder if any of these busy people speak English, and if they did, how I would ever know.

We take an elevator to the fourteenth floor and get in line. Turns out it's some government office and we have a bunch of paperwork to go through to get my Work Registration and Korean ID, which only involves standing in six different lines for three hours. Then we stop at a bank called Woori and I sit like an idiot while Yeong gets my account set up. I only figure this out when he hands me a credit card with a Visa logo and says, "Good in any ATM anywhere in world." He also hands me a receipt with what I take to be my balance. It says 3,300,000 won, which is what they call the Korean dollar. I looked up the currency conversion before I left and impressive as the balance looks, it converts to only about $3,000.

"We deposit three million won first of month," Yeong explains, with a proud little grin. He hands me a stack of bills. "This is what I think you call bonus." I thumb through them, and they are five and ten thousand won notes. I don't want to be rude and count them in front of him, but something about those zeros is comforting. For the first time in the day I actually feel like grinning back.

I do a quick calculation and figure that it's about midnight back home. So no wonder I feel as if I've just pulled an all-night Starfare marathon. When we get back to my apartment I lie down on the couch. I take out a folder that I've carefully packed into the center panel of my suitcase. Inside are some photos from Hannah. The framed kissing photo, of course, but another of my favorites. Hannah had taken this self-portrait between two giant mirrors. So that she's sitting in a chair, looking over her shoulder at the camera, and to either side of her are the reflected images, angled so they make a long, infinite hall of Hannah profiles. I prop it up against the back of the couch and I'm counting Hannahs when I pass out.

4.

So naturally, it's still dark when I wake up, having slept about twelve straight hours. Hannah's picture has flipped over during the night and I pack all the photos back into my bag and stash it in the closet. I draw the curtains and look out my window. In the gap between two high-rises the first fuzzy light of dawn.

I tell myself it's time to start honing my game so I fire up my computer. I'm not surprised to see plenty of action on the Korean server, even though it's 5:30 a.m. local time. I get in the queue on the advanced level and within a few seconds my in-game IM screen is lighting up.

At first I think there's a software glitch. The messages are rolling in so fast I can't read them all, like trying to read movie credits on fast forward.

I catch a few of them. "ActionSeth! Really you?" "Send picture please!" "Private chat, Mira1278 please please please." "LOVE U KISS KISS KISS" "U make me a big happiness!"

I flip off the IM screen and in a few minutes get in a game with someone named KKim1994. I reboot the IM screen and mute everyone but KKim. It feels great to be back into the game. We're playing the Neverland map, which is not my favorite, but I've spent significant time on it and feel pretty confident.

KimK and I both are going for early force development over infrastructure and I think we're pretty even, going into the midgame. The action is heated, and we're in one of those fierce battles that is so frantic you start sweating when I realize that I'm grinning. Because Starfare is such an awesome game and nothing is more fun than a close game like this. Then we get into a series of battles with three major fronts. I'm pumping on the mouse and keyboard so hard that I'm actually getting winded and when it's over, it's just barely over. In our final clash I'm left with just enough units to finish him off.

"GG," KimK writes. "You nice to take it easy on beginner."

"You're no beginner," I say.

"I #5," KimK writes.

"#5?"

"I playing team. School team."

"University?" I write.

"No, no. High school team. Inha Academy in Inchon. We becoming good. Finish 2 in district. But I #1 girl on team."

As I sign off I'm trying not to panic, thinking that I just played a very good game, and it was barely enough to beat a girl from a high school team. Then my stomach growls and I look at the clock. It's six-thirty and the sun is glowing through the haze on the horizon. I sign off and after pushing the rice cakes and unknowns around in my cupboard decide to head downstairs. I slip on a sweatshirt and scoot down the hall towards the elevators, looking back as if someone was about to jump out and catch me.

As I step outside our high rise I immediately wish I had taken my coat. It's at least as cold as Kansas, a few snowflakes are drifting down and tiny waves of snow are blowing across the sidewalks. Everyone is wearing ski jackets and scarves and it's odd, because some of the young women are walking with umbrellas open, as if it were pouring rain.

The traffic is already heavy and the chilly air is filled with the smell of bus exhaust and the sound of horns, and a distant siren. Even the siren is different, kind of a *wha, wha, wha* sound. I'm surprised to see so many bundled up business people hustling along the sidewalk. So many people in such a hurry towards a place where they have jobs they know how to do, colleagues they can talk to.

I step into the flow of foot traffic and at the corner there's a little cart, cooking something that smells like real food. I get in line, stomping my feet back and forth to stay warm. When I get to the front the old guy in a greasy coat working the cart looks at me funny but hands me something hot in a paper wrap. I pull out my wallet and hand him a bill. He just stares at me so I hand him a couple of more and he hands one back with a few coins.

When I step to the side and open it up it's still steaming and smells great. It has two pieces of bread with what looks like a scrambled egg inside. The bread is sticky with a coating, like a sugar donut. I open it up and stare at it. While I'm looking a younger guy in a black coat and a red tie stops and says, "Tost-u."

"Tost-u?" I say, stupidly.

He says it again, slowly, like he's talking to a two year old. "Very delicious."

I bite into it and agree. I would have never thought of putting a sugar topping on an egg McMuffin, but I would now. The guy smiles and bows and then walks away. I eat the whole thing on the spot, get back in line and get another one and carry it back upstairs. I'm just relieved, knowing that there is now a distinct possibility that I won't actually starve to death.

5.

I have a little time before eight o'clock team breakfast so I log on and check email. My heart skips, and I blink, before clicking on a message from Hannah.

"Can't believe u r halfway round the world and I'm still stuck here. Sent out my portfolio to the art schools—fingers crossed! Thanks for helping. Hope u r getting used to it and like it there. I know u will do gr8t…gtg"

And that was it. Nothing about how she might feel about me. Nothing about whether she was missing me, or already hooking up with someone new, like that guy from the environmental club. But, I'm thinking, at least she wrote.

I sit and stare at a blank email screen, trying to think of a response. Something that will make her want to write back, and then

I can write again, and pretty soon it will be like we're talking all time. But before I come up with a clever message I see that it's a couple of minutes past eight and I log off and hurry down the hall. I swipe my apartment card and the door clicks and I step inside. Same scene as last time—a buzz of conversation, the team all dressed in the same shirts, working through their food with chopsticks. Only this time they don't stop and stare. I guess they're getting used to me, which is some sort of progress.

I look for Sung Gi, but I don't see him. Although I'm not hungry after the Tost-us I get a little bowl of rice and sit in an empty spot at a table with three of the guys on the team. I actually know most of the names from studying the team before I left Kansas. But I haven't been able to match them up with faces yet.

When I sit down the guys all acknowledge me with a little bow of the head. Then they go right back to their Korean chatter. I play around with my bowl of rice and try to look like I'm deep in thought. Which I am, still trying to figure out what to write back to Hannah.

I jump when the guy across from says, "American girls, is it true…"

I look up and all three of the guys at my table are looking right at me.

"How you say, easy to go to bed?"

I sort of shake my head. First of all, I'm shocked to hear English. But what kind of thing is that to ask, first time you say a word to someone?

So I say, "So you speak English?"

The three of them all laugh.

"Every Korean study English in school," the questioner says. "We just more good studying Starfare, not studying school."

This sparks an animated round of laughing and Korean.

"You have American girlfriend?" he continues.

"I used to."

The three of them lean into the table and talk slowly. Probably trying to interpret what this means.

When they're done the original questioner asks, "So this girl-friend. She do everything?"

I redden a shade.

"Look," I say. "I'm not talking about stuff like that. Not even if we were friends. And to tell you the truth, I'm not even sure what your names are. How about we start there?"

The three of them lean in and chat. One of them points at my bowl of rice, where I've left my chopsticks sticking into the air. "Very bad in Korea. Big…" He looks at the other guys and it seems like he is asking them how to say something. I reach for the chop-sticks with my left hand and as I do all three of the guys start yell-ing at me. "No! No! Bad!"

Finally the guy across from me points at my left hand and says something in Korean. He wrinkles his nose and points at my left hand and says, "Bad. Bad hand." He leans across the table and lays my chopsticks across the bowl.

Then they tell me their names, speaking slowly. I repeat each one and they smile, either because I got it right, or because I botched it in a funny way.

Then Yeong barks out some orders. Everyone puts away their plates and then we line up for exercise. Afterwards I'm relieved when Yeong leads me to a chair in front of a glowing monitor.

He leans over to me and says, "Today we test new map. Beta map. It's called Mordant Isles."

"You get to see maps before they're published?" I never heard of that before. After all, getting a head start on a map before it was issued would be a huge advantage in tournament play.

"All the big teams test maps," Yeong says, as if he were telling me the world was round. "Part of sponsorship. Help pay for won-derful apartment!" He motions around the room and grins.

"We have three groups, work as team," Yeong said. "You start here with Yeun, Choi and Kim. You and Kim partners." Kim is one of the guys from breakfast. "Start game and you see."

A few minutes later I'm live in the new Isles map. I pull back and see that it's a series of islands. It looks like you have to build bridges or boats to navigate from one island to the other.

Before I can even get started I hear team members yelling out stuff. I look over to Kim's monitor next to me and see he's found something on the far side of the starter island. I send some troops to the same spot, but he's already got his men there, mining ore and setting up a refinery.

I decide to see if I can get established on the opposite side of the island and I find these caves, which may have some important resources. I try to tell my partner that we should check them out, but there's so much chatter, much of it in some sort of hybrid, English/Korean script which is inscrutable. About every thirty seconds one of the team members shouts out something in Korean. Probably some new resource or tip which, of course, means nothing to me. I realize I have to develop some firepower fast, but I can't find any energy sources anywhere. I finally find some vortices just off shore and start transferring energy from them into my troops.

I'm still looking when suddenly a whole line of some sort of new fighting ships comes sailing around the corner of the island sending out a cloud of explosives, which destroy the scouts I have checking the caves, and then take my base and troops out too.

A screen automatically pops up and I see that it's some sort of log. My partner is keying something in and I'm pretty sure it's the coordinates of the ore mine. He leans over and asks me something in broken English.

I shake my head and then he motions me to look and he opens up the map and focuses on an area near the caves. I try to tell him about what I saw in the caves and he types something into the log and then I point where the energy vortices were and tell him what the energy flows were. He types in some more coordinates and some numbers which correspond to my energy gains.

Then I see that he's scrolling through the log, probably picking up the tips from all the other teams. I try to keep up, but even though it's written using English letters, he's going way too fast and even if I could stop and study I wouldn't know all the shorthand

and abbreviations and Korean words using English characters.

Then we do it again. In this game the other three players develop power so much faster than I do that even though Kim is doing fine, we're doomed as a team. But they let me live and I do my best to help Kim discover how to develop the bridge-building capability that you need to jump to the next island, and the one after, each one hosting a precious commodity that gives you a huge boost in power. I may be having trouble keeping up, but I keep thinking that the Starfare developers have done it again, because it's an awesome map, with all kinds of new twists coming out of the island geography.

After about three hours of this, we break for another kimchi avoidance exercise. White rice for me. When I'm about to head back to my computer, Yeong puts his hand on my shoulder and leads me the other direction. In the hallway I see the driver from the day before.

Yeong says, "Choi will take you now. You go to see tutor. Learn Korean. She very best in Seoul. Soon you be talking to fans!"

6.

Within a few days I'm into the routine. Breakfast, morning practice, lunch and then I get pulled away for Korean lessons and various meetings. Then back with the team for an evening session where I just struggle to keep up. By the time I get back to my apartment I'm wiped. Still, I always check for messages from Hannah. I've written her three short ones in the last few days, but nothing.

DT is another story. He wants a replay of every minute of every day. He writes at least twice a day about how boring school is and how cool it must be to be able to just game all day with some of the greatest players in the world. I guess it is pretty cool, but somehow it's better in theory than in practice. I mean, it's not like hanging out online with DT and my other Starfare buddies at home. For one thing, I can't even talk with these guys and as far as I can tell, they don't goof or joke around or even go out. They just grind away, hour after hour. And while we get Sunday off, it seems like they all go home to their parents.

The weirdest thing I do in the first week is go on what I finally figure out is a Korean talk show. They put me through the makeup thing and then I get led out onto a set where I sit next to this animated guy in an odd, electric blue suit. Naturally, they provide a translator, but the whole thing is so manic that I'm never quite sure what's going on. Then, in what turns out to be a grand finale, they release about a dozen Korean school girls in uniform and they sort of jump me and knock me to the floor. As I fight to get up I see the cameras teams jockeying around us, trying to get the best angle.

Then an older guy who looks like he's in charge comes running out shouting and seems pretty happy. The school girls disappear and the host shakes my hand and bows and, before I know it, Yeong is leading me out of the studio.

"Very big show," he says. "Very big. Like your Jay Letterman. Sponsors be very very happy."

The sponsors may be happy but I'm not. First of all, Choi shows up at my door that night with a big duffle. As I take it from him I smell something rank.

"What the hell is this?" I ask.

He answers me with a flurry of Korean and I just shake my head. He tries some obscure sign language, but I can't follow. Finally he grabs the bag from me, pushes past me into the apartment and heads over to the small doors. He takes the duffle and upends it on the floor. A big pile of crumpled team shirts and discolored socks and boxer underwear.

He points at me and says, "You." And then he points at the washer and dryer.

Then I remember what Yeong said the day he showed me my apartment. About how the washer and dryer would come in handy for the youngest member of the team. Choi gives me a look like I'm the village idiot and then stomps out.

So I'm up to two in the morning doing laundry. Playing my English lectures from my online course, which are infuriating. They're set up so you can't fast forward. And they have these interactive popups where the lecture stops until you answer some questions. So I have to keep an eye on the screen. Then type in a response to questions like, "Can you think of a modern example of the sort of treatment Hester receives from her pilgrim community?" Just begging for you to type AIDS. So I do.

Then I just daydream as the lecture plays and the dryer spins. Thinking, sure, I can now see how these Korean pros get so good. First of all they're absolutely cranking, four hours in the morning, four in the afternoon, three in the evening. Six days a week. Plus the guys will actually squeeze in extra games online for fun. Instead of one guy working on a map for ten hours a day, you get twelve guys working on the same map, sharing all their discoveries. The problem is that between Korean tutorials and mall appearances I'm missing every afternoon and when I'm on board I can't follow what they're shouting and sharing. I pick up what I can by watching and absorbing what I can from the logs. But at best I'm getting maybe ten percent of the benefit of the team's insights.

After two weeks of frustration, I finally tell Yeong that we need to have a talk. We've had breakfast and exercises and I say, "Mr. Yeong. We need to sit down and discuss a few things."

"Very good," he says. "But not today. Too much things to do."

"Well," I tell him, heading back to the meal room. "I'll just sit and have some tea until you have time."

"Tea?" Yeong says. "You no like tea."

"I'm not drinking it," I explain. "I'm just going to sit in there and stir it until you get a few moments to talk."

A couple of team members who were close enough to hear me are staring at me like I just insulted their ancestors or something. Yeong turns and barks some orders and they scramble to their stations.

"Very well, we have that talk."

The two of us head to the far table in the meal room and I sit down. Yeong stands.

I've got a pretty good idea what I'm going to say. That if my game is going to progress, I need to practice full time with the team. And I'm going to need help understanding what's going on. A translator on site, for at least the time being. And Korean lessons are fine, but they can't take up half my afternoon. I'm going to propose that the tutor come here and we do it during lunch, which I barely touch anyway.

"Mr. Yeong," I begin. But before I can say another word Yeong takes a step toward me and leans in very close, so it seems like he's shouting at me. Even though he's more hissing.

"You are not in America anymore Mr. Seth Gordon! You are here in Korea. Part of the great team Anaconda. My team! I am the coach! I am the leader!" He's got his face about two inches from mine, and even when I lean back he stays right with me. His eyes are bulging and his face is glowing like a stoplight.

I stutter something but he's not about to stop.

"In Korea, no player tells coach what he is to do. No one. Not even the greatest star in Starfare. Not the world champion. And not American teenager. Especially not American player who cannot beat Korean grade girl!"

I want to tell him that I'll never beat anyone if I don't start getting more out of the practices. That going to autograph sessions and making TV appearances don't do anything for my game. But I figure there will be a better time. I let him rant for a while longer and then I stand up and do my best imitation of a Korean bow and say, "I understand Coach Yeong. May I get back to practice now?"

He nods and I scoot out of there as fast as possible. I just tell myself that I'll have to learn to decipher the logs and maybe get Sung Gi to take some time to explain things. I'm sure as hell not going to ask Yeong, who seems to think I don't need any extra coaching now that I'm with the team all day.

7.

That night, after evening practice, I sign back onto the team's intranet in my room. I download the day's log on the new map and I start going over it, line by line, trying to understand it. Some of it is straightforward, when it talks about map coordinates or landmarks, but every so often there's a couple lines that I assume are transliterated Korean. Google translator is as weirded out by this text as I am. I take out my English Korean dictionary and try to sort it out, word by word, but after about a half hour, I'm nowhere.

Without really thinking I just drift over to one of my old favorite Starfare message boards and I start reading a thread about the relative merits of deflector shields versus force fields when countering cruiser attacks.

DTerra: hey, ur a hard guy to reach

I look at the computer clock and calculate back to about 7:50 in the morning in South Dakota.

ActionSeth: u2 isn't this a little early for you?

DTerra: back 2 school u don't remember? School? They herd all the young Terrans into a massive building and make them sit in hard wooden chairs and listen to droning speeches from elders.

ActionSeth: the trick is not 2 listen.

DTerra: Easy for u to say. I have to get decent grades or I'm going to end up stuck in Fargo forever, going to school with your brother at ND State. So how's the training going? When u going to enter ur 1st pro event?

ActionSeth: Soon I hope. Lots of red tape and bs over here. I spend half my day going to meetings and signing autographs and taking Korean lessons. It's driving me crazy because these guys r insane good and if I don't start training like a madman I'll never catch up.

DTerra: Don't worry. UR the best, man. Hey, gtg or I'll be late for 1st period. CU later.

ActionSeth: Right

8.

Next morning after exercises, Yeong unveils a complicated draw sheet. He lectures the team for about five minutes in Korean, followed by a few questions, and then everyone breaks for their machines. I spend another couple minutes studying the draw, where I can see my pairing against Sang-Chul Lee, who is currently the top-ranked member of the team. When we go out as a team, he gets pestered the most, because real fans of Starfare want his photo and autograph. Some of them guys as old as my father, not just the teenie-bopper girls like the ones who pick on me.

Yeong takes me aside for a minute to explain that entries are due the end of the week for the first big national televised tournament on the Mordant Isles map. Each pro team gets to enter three players and we're playing off for those spots.

"Big luck!" Yeong says with a smile that seems to contain less than the best wishes.

"Right," I say, knowing my chances.

And guess whose match finishes first? And I'm pretty sure that Sang-Chul slowed down at the end out of pity. Playing this guy is like a race where you're in the water swimming and your opponent is running alongside on land. When first round matches are done, the draw pits me against another loser and probably because the guy is pissed off about his first round, he takes no mercy on me and pins me in less than twenty minutes. That gives me time to wander around and watch the other matches which are really intense. I can see where I'm failing—these guys know exactly where to go and can manage multiple development sites without any seams. They're all over the map and they're typing out instructions so fast that each of their keyboards sounds like a dozen tap dancers warming up. Back in the U.S. tournaments I was one of the fastest guys around and people would gather around and I could hear them oohing and ahhing as I jumped across the maps and pounded out commands. But here, I could see that it was the difference between the speed of high school and pro football.

It takes most of the day to work though all the round robin matches. Final round I lose to Sung Gi. Which makes me last, and him second to last. Coach Yeong congratulates the top three finishers and everyone gives them a rousing round of applause and many shouted Korean encouragements. The thing is, even though only three players can represent the team, the entire team shares in the winnings. Which makes sense, because the only way the three top players can have a chance is the depth of work that the whole team puts into understanding a map.

Then Yeong has another long address and everyone cheers some more. When we break for dinner I ask Sung Gi what it was about. He says to get food and then he'll explain. I get a big plate of grilled chicken and some rice. We get some sort of grilled meat every night. Mom is always asking about fruit and vegetables and they sometimes have little oranges or these pale round things that Mom thinks are Asian pears. They're actually delicious.

But when we sit down Sung Gi has trouble explaining. In the end I get the impression the rest of the team gets to play too. Finally I corner Yeong and he says that a great honor has been granted Team Anaconda. We've been picked to play a televised exhibition match prior to the big Mordant Isles pro tournament. Against the national high school championship team.

"First television match!" he exclaims. "Very big audience. Very big."

Very big, all right. Very big chance for embarrassment.

9.

That night I knock out a five paragraph essay on what I think are the lingering effects of Puritanism in American society for my English class. Writing it, I think of Hannah's angel picture, which would make a great illustration. If English papers had illustrations.

When I finally get to sleep I dream about Starfare again. This time I'm playing in front of these giant TV cameras and my opponent is a little toddler. I just can't seem to get my game rolling and I look down and instead of holding a mouse with my right hand I'm holding chopsticks. Weird thing is, if I squeeze them just right, the cursor moves, but it's like trying to play pick-up sticks with your toes. Then I realize I'm starving and I call out for food and Coach Yeong puts a big steaming bowl of kimchi right on top of my keyboard and of course there's a live audience and they're laughing like it's not Starfare but *Saturday Night Live.*

I wake up earlier than usual. I decide to slip on my headset and Skype Hannah on her cell. It only costs a few cents a minute and I have to start thinking like a working guy instead of a broke student. I'm hoping I can improvise something clever for her voicemail and when I hear her say hello I'm just thinking it's her recorded message. But then she says it again, "Hello, who is this?" and I realize she's live.

"Seth. It's Seth," I blurt out, because if I don't say something really quick she'll think it's some sort of bot call and hang up.

"Where are you?" she says.

"In my apartment."

"In Korea?" Like she was hoping I was back in Kansas and she could run right over and give me a hug.

"K-O-R-E-A," I spell. "What time is it there?"

"It's three-thirty. I'm just leaving school. But how…how did you know to call?" And even all these miles, I can picture her from her voice. It's her sad voice, and her sad face means she's looking at the ground, pulling her fingers through her shoulder-length hair like she's trying to sift out the troubles.

"What's wrong?"

Silence. Maybe some sniffling, but I can't tell.

"Hannah? Hannah?"

"I'm fine."

The way she said it, meant she wasn't.

"Hannah? I know something's wrong."

Like I could do something, five thousand miles away.

"It's no big deal. It's just…"

"Just what?"

"Well, you know how my father took this job with the company in Leawood?"

I did, sort of. She had told me all about it, but I had been distracted. Biomedicine start-up blah blah. Looking at her eyes, probably, thinking about touching her.

"Well, it looks like something is going on. Some sort of buyout and Dad may be out of his job and he's been talking to the people back at Squibb. They want him back. Which means he'll be moving back to New Jersey."

"And you?"

"I've already told them. I'm not moving again. It would just be impossible. But Dad, he doesn't want to split up the family. Our old house is still on the market in Princeton. He keeps telling me I could pick up just where we left off, but I know that's not the way it works. Things change. Things are always changing."

Tell me about it.

"Anyway, I did get some good news too. The Savannah School of Fine Arts? I told you I sent them the portfolio?"

"Sure."

"Well, they loved it. The head of the photography department called me last Thursday personally and told me that I was being offered this big scholarship. And then he talked to Dad and I think he was really convincing because afterward, Dad's not saying I can go. But he's not saying no either."

I tell her congratulations, which is what I think I'm supposed to say. I mean, what difference does it make? Kansas, some school out East. I'm still halfway around the world.

"So if your family goes and you stay, where are you going to stay?" Wondering if I should offer her my empty room at Dad's. Which seems pretty unlikely on all accounts.

"I don't know. Really. I'll come up with something, I guess."

And then we just sort of are both breathing into the phone.

Until finally she does that thing, when she clears her throat before saying something important.

"So, Seth. What's it like there?"

"It's OK. I've got my own apartment. Hardly a minute to myself. These guys train like maniacs."

"But you like it? You're happy?"

"Sure. I guess. I'm going to be on TV. Next week."

"That's amazing. I told you you were going to be famous."

"Famous for losing, maybe," I say.

"Stop it. You'll do fine. Anyway, I've got to go. But call me again, when you get the chance."

When I shut down Skype I feel this weight, like gravity had just doubled. It makes me want to just lie down and go back to sleep. Instead, I check the time, put on my regular T-shirt instead of that itchy team one, my winter coat, and trudge downstairs for my breakfast Tost-us.

10.

Just when I'm at peak anxiety about the televised match Yeong comes up to me at breakfast and tells me to come with him. I follow him out into the hallway where Choi is standing.

"Today big day for ActionSeth," Yeong says, grinning like a fool. "You tape first big commercial for soda. Very special soda. Named for you!"

I shake my head. This sounds completely crazy. Even Michael Jordon doesn't have a soda. So I think maybe I heard him wrong as I follow the two of them to the elevators and down to the parking garage.

But an hour later I'm in makeup. The rest of the day they have me pose in front of this green background, while I hold a bottle of orange soda. It says ActionOrange. I have to hold it a bunch of ways. First with my right hand. Then my left. Saying, "ActionOrange. Let it power *your* game!"

The director of the commercial is shouting at me in Korean and pidgin English. "Orange soda!" he says, over and over. "Very American! Very American! Say again! 'ActionOrange. Let it power your game!'"

Like all we do is hang around the soda counter at the local drug store, sitting on round stools, drinking orange soda. Because it energizes us. I'm pretty sure it's the longest day of my life. I'm so exhausted when we get back I skip dinner and just lie on the couch with my laptop, getting through the lectures on *Silas Marner*. I type in some nonsense when I have to answer questions like my thoughts on the nature of guilt.

The next day I feel like I'm hopelessly behind. The team is working the Mordant Isles map like crazy. I'd be shocked if there are any big surprises left on any of the islands. We're still trying to get a handle on all the underwater resources, because you have to build special equipment and train your troops before they can start exploring.

Maybe because I'm still lagging the rest of the team, I try some odd stuff. A couple of days before the big event, while the rest of the team is exploring the edges of the map, I decide to see if there's anything we missed back near the home bases. I gear up my underwater abilities and start working my scuba troops and aquabots through every underwater crack and crevice. That's how I stumble onto this little undersea hatch which surprises the hell out me. My troops can't open it at first but when I blow the door up to maximum magnification I see a kind of lock which I manage to cut by transferring a laser bazooka from one of my ground forces to an aquatrooper. The door opens into a tunnel with three passages. I send scouts down each of them and discover that they hyperjump to outer islands that would otherwise take half a game to reach.

I type this up on the log and within thirty seconds the entire team is gathered around my monitor and I backtrack and show them the door and how I cut it open. They all immediately break into chatter and Sang-Chul, our star player, pushes me aside and sits down. He repeats my exploration and then jumps up, says something that sounds like a compliment and pounds me on the back.

Then they're all patting me on the back and laughing and for the first time in the month I've been here I feel like I actually might belong.

11.

The day before the televised tournament I have my weekly call with Mom. Back in Kansas this was not exactly the highlight of the week, but maybe because I just don't have anyone to talk to over here I'm actually looking forward to it.

I have to do the call after our evening practice, so I can catch Mom at the Institute's office. Which is, weirdly, the morning before.

"Seth!" Mom says, "Is that you?"

I never know what to say to that. So I say, "No, it's an imposter."

"Oh Seth, don't be like that. I've been so worried about you."

"Mom, no need to worry. It's like going to summer camp. They keep an eye on me 24/7."

"I know, Seth. But it's just that you are so far away. If anything were to happen…"

"Nothing's going to happen, Mom. I'm telling you. They even make us exercise every day."

"Well…that's nice."

The thing is, it's hard to find stuff to talk about with Mom. She doesn't have a clue about Starfare. I don't have a clue about Zen meditation. So we talk about the weather. And then she tells me about her studies and how she feels like she's reaching new levels.

We hit a sort of gap in the conversation. So I talk about food. Mom's always interested in what I'm eating, so I tell her how disgusting kimchi is and about these delicious Tost-us which she likes because they're pretty much vegetarian. And healthy, compared to hamburger and fries, which, I don't tell her, I really miss. But not as much as pizza.

When I hang up I check out Hannah's Facebook page, which she hasn't updated in a long time. Still that weird picture of her in a costume. And I like to look through her portfolio. Because each of her photos is like a puzzle. I think that if I stare at them long enough they'll reveal something, some secret part of Hannah that I've never known. So I stare for a long time.

12.

So the next evening when the team packs up and heads out in a big van, I'm a mess. I'm honestly scared to death about this exhibition and failing epically to some high school kid in front of a huge TV audience. I ride in the very back of a large van. Sitting next to Sung Gi. He doesn't seem too upbeat either. So we don't talk much. I stare out the window. Looking at all the parts of Seoul I probably will never see again.

After about forty-five minutes we pull up to a large building with a milling crowd out front. My face is pressed to the van window, thinking there must be thousands. Huge cloth banners hang from the second story, with Starfare logos and "Mordant Isles" in some sort of old style script, with pirate flags and pirate vessels in the background. I know that the Mordant Isles release hit the Isles public just two days ago. I read online that they've already shipped six million copies worldwide. Of course, we've been working the map for almost a month straight, but that doesn't seem to be public knowledge.

The van lets us off at the curb and about forty policemen in riot gear, including plastic face shields, are keeping open a path to the main doors. Kids are screaming at us from behind the police line and holding out autograph books and trying to take pictures of us. The other Team Anaconda players seem in no hurry, stopping to sign the occasional book and giving out high fives to fans.

"Seth, Seth, Seth." I can't believe that they're actually chanting my name. I can see the other guys on the team glancing over at me and I know I'm blushing. I try to imitate the other players. Make a foray to the police line to greet some fans, but as soon as I get close I feel someone grabbing my shirt and someone else actually pulling on my hair as if they wanted scalp-deep souvenirs. I karate chop the hand on my head and jerk away from whoever has my shirt and sprint up the stairs and through the doors, breathing like I just ran a quarter mile in gym. I look down at my shirt to see if it's ripped and suddenly realize the utility of that rough fabric. It must be woven out of Kevlar, the bullet proof vest stuff.

I follow the rest of the team through some corridors and into a back room where they have the standard makeup mirrors. Everyone takes a seat and a dozen makeup girls appear out of nowhere and start slapping on the powder and combing hair. I seem to be getting more than my fair share of attention and chatter, which I suppose is because they don't get to work on Westerners with blond hair very often.

Whenever someone comes through the door I can hear the buzzing sounds of a large crowd. After what seems like an hour they get tired of messing with my hair. The other guys are all talking Korean, probably strategy points that I could really use. I decide to sneak out and check out the scene. I follow the noise up some narrow stairs and down another corridor and realize I'm backstage. The curtain is down and the stage is set up with about a dozen gaming stations. Hanging overhead are four giant screens like they have at rock concerts. Still curious, I scoot around the edge of the curtain and work my way to where it meets the side of the stage, crack it just enough to get a thin glimpse of the auditorium. It only takes a glance to see that's it huge—a fan of seating rising from the stage level and at least two balconies above. Holy crap, I'm thinking. I'm playing in front of thousands of live fans. If Hannah was here she'd flip out.

Of course, then I'm thinking about Hannah. I look at the time and count back fifteen hours. Three o'clock in the morning back home. So I retreat to a back room where it's relatively quiet and try to text Hannah on my Korean cell, but either I don't have the right international codes or the phone is set up to block international calls. I'm trying for about the twelfth time when I hear someone yelling my name and I stick my head out the room.

Yeong is there, looking at me like I've lost my mind.

"You hiding?"

"No, I had to make a phone call."

He looks as his watch, which is one of those big gold ones that old rich guys wear back home. "Two minutes. We have introductions in two minutes. And you go hide to make call."

"I wasn't hiding," I say again.

"Come, come," he shouts, like I've been a bad dog.

He leads me to the side of the stage where all the Anaconda players are queued up. We can see the stage, but not the audience. After a couple of minutes the crowd starts screaming and the curtain must be rising because colored spotlights are strafing the stage, making the computer equipment and silver scaffolding and monitors shine like fireworks.

Then an announcer quiets the crowd and they start introducing the team. One at a time, the guys run out onto the stage to huge cheers and then stand at attention at the front of the stage. When there are only four of us left the announcer takes a lot more time and then each of top three players is introduced. The screaming is thunderous, so loud I actually hold my hands over my ears. I'm absolutely relieved that they've left me out because I really don't deserve to be playing with these guys. So I'm sort of breathing easy when I hear the announcer say something that sounds familiar, but I can't quite make it out because the screaming is doing what I thought impossible—hitting a new level of volume. Then I hear it again, and someone is physically pushing me on stage where I'm stumbling, blinded by the spots. I can't see a single thing past the edge of the stage, it's like looking into the sun. The noise hits me front-on like a fire hose on full blast and I must freeze, before Sung Gi takes pity and jogs over and leads me to the line, where the guys are standing and smiling and waving. I look at them and finally raise my hand and wave and it's like I'm an orchestra conductor signaling a fortissimo finale.

Finally the spotlights are off us and they introduce, much more quickly, a group of boys in red and white team shirts. I try to figure out which one will be my opponent. Within a few minutes they have us sorted into pairs and I'm sitting in front of a monitor, across from a kid who looks about twelve. Then the monitor in front of me flashes to life and begins a countdown from twenty, each number has a different Mordant Isles theme. The crowd is yelling out each number, and I actually recognize the words when they get to ten. My wonderful Korean tutor taught me how to count to ten at one of our first sessions.

At zero the screen lights up with the Mordant Isles starter map and I start with a standard troop development, trying to remember all the shortcuts that the team has discovered. My opponent seems a bit slow and lost. But then, I have to appreciate where I'd be if I had only two days to work the map, probably solo, instead of close to thirty with twelve pros. Even as bad as I am compared to my teammates, it's no contest, and I have to work hard not to close him down in ten minutes. I glance right and left and see that the other pros are dogging it too. At around the twenty-minute mark I hear an announcement and a loud cheer, which I take to be the first declared victory. The rest of us finish sometime over the next ten minutes. I'm close to the last when I finish off his last troops. The two of us stand and he bows and I try the same, trying to remember what my Korean teacher told me about how low to bow when someone is younger and you've just trounced him in front of thousands.

The Korean fans are cheering my name like I just won the World Series and I turn and wave a couple times before jogging off stage.

Yeong is there, greeting each of us as we step out of the lights, patting each of us on the back. But me, he pulls me aside.

"You see, ActionSeth. How much they love you already. You are big star!"

I thank him and tell him I'm not feeling well and better lie down and rest. Could I go back to my apartment? He waves over a guy I don't recognize who leads me down a maze of halls and out a backdoor into the chilly Korean air, lit with yellowish streetlights and hundreds of headlights. He waves a cab down, tells him my address, and a half hour later I'm back in the apartment, watching our three best players on Sky Game TV playing in the tournament.

I glance up at the TV to the sound of some very familiar, awful pop music and see the hideous sight of me fake-smiling while tipping back a can of that lame orange-flavored Korean soda. We spent two entire days getting that stupid shot just right. I jump up and turn off the TV. It's around noon back in Kansas and I Skype dial Hannah's cell a half-dozen times before realizing that it's still Friday back there and she's probably in the middle of school. I leave a text message. I don't know who else to call. I Google her name, to see if anything pops up. Then I check her Facebook page and she's added some information about the Savannah School for the Arts. It links to their website. The school looks like something out of *Gone with the Wind*. Lots of that stuff that hangs from trees. I Google "stuff that hangs from trees in Savannah." Spanish moss.

So I just sort of stare at the Skype screen for a long while, waiting for a pop-up message that never appears.

13.

I continue to Skype Hannah's cell every half hour or so, wondering what she'll think, when she sees all these missed calls. I flip the TV on to see how our guys are doing. Tae-Uk loses first round to the number one player from the Pusan Raiders. Our top two players make the final eight, which is a very good showing, guaranteeing that the team will get a decent payout. I get caught up in Sang-Chul's quarterfinal match, which has an amazing frantic

ending with the Korean announcer screaming like it's a photo finish at the Kentucky Derby. I find myself standing up and cheering
as he finishes off the last of his opponent's ships. He's our last hope
in the semis, but can't quite pull it off. When they show a close-up
of him after the match his face is glistening with sweat and he
looks exhausted.

When I try Hannah's number again after the match she picks
up on the first ring.

I tell her it's getting late, Saturday night.

"So how's it going?"

I want to tell her how frustrating it is. That I have no idea what
the guys on my team are talking about. That it's like a dream where
you go onto the field to play soccer and when the whistle blows
you realize it's not soccer, but some weird sport like rugby and
you've got the ball and a dozen giant guys are converging on you
to squish you like a bug.

"Pretty good," I lie. "I played on TV earlier this evening. In
front of a live audience of about five thousand. Probably a couple
million on TV."

"Wow, so how did you do?"

"I just played one match, but I won," I say, skipping over the
part about my opponent being a twelve year old kid who had no
clue how to play the map.

"Wow. I Googled you and found this big ad with all this Korean writing and your picture. I think it was like for some sort of
soft drink."

"Yeah," I said. "ActionOrange. It's my first big endorsement
deal."

"Endorsement? Wow. I can't believe I know someone famous."

*Hannah, I miss you, I hate it here. What do you say I come home
and the two of us, we can pick off where we were* I'm thinking.

Instead I say, "Yeah, all the Korean girls go nuts over me. It's
like I'm in a chart-topping boy band or something."

"I'm jealous," Hannah says. "Although I can always say I knew
you when."

"Yeah, you can always say that," I say, but thinking, she said "jealous." Then wondering if any of the guys on the team actually get within ten feet of a girl outside of the occasional autograph and snapshot. I can't imagine when. They're either programmed every waking hour or off with their families on Sundays.

14.

On Sunday I sleep until it's time for my call with Mom. At first she was leery of the whole Skype chat thing, but it only took a couple of calls to get her acclimated.

"I hope you haven't lost weight," is the first thing she says. "Are you getting enough to eat?" I get the fruits and vegetables lecture.

Mom is pretty good at seeing through me, so she asks six variations of "what's wrong?"

I don't give her the whole story, but I do say that it's hard, being so far away without anyone who speaks English.

"Maybe we should talk more often. I could ask Steve here to set me up on Thursday nights. That would be, what, Friday mornings for you?"

I explain that they keep me way too busy for that—that Sundays are my only day off.

To fill the gap she tells me all about Martin and how far his yoga has progressed and I listen, because it's nice to hear her voice, even though I couldn't care less about Martin's plow execution. Mom always seems almost on the verge of tears when it's time to disconnect and it ends up me consoling her, instead of the other way around.

Afterwards I resist the urge to call Hannah, even though it's a good time to connect, since it's early evening back home. It's great when we're talking, but afterwards, the hollow feeling is so awful.

I do get DTerra online and we have a pretty good conversation.

I'm upfront about the suckiness of my situation. He thinks I'm exaggerating. Still prefers to think of it as a dream come true, but after I bitch for about a half hour he's finally getting a sense of the downside.

ActionSeth: I'll never catch up with these guys. Not speaking Korean. It's just 2 hard.

DTerra: You've got to give it a shot. I know how good u r.

ActionSeth: U don't know how good everyone is here. Even the little kids, they could kill in a US tournament. I can barely make a high school team here.

DTerra: That's bogus. U hang in there and in a few months you'll be owning them all.

ActionSeth: Right.

DT has to do something with his family so after he signs off I clean up my email and visit a bunch of my favorite message boards.

I'm so bored after a couple of hours that I'm actually kind of pleased when I see an old, familiar name slipping through my IM filter.

Stompazer2: HEY PUTZ I SAW U OWNING SOME GRADE SCHOOL KID ON SKY TV NICE JOB.

I don't give him the pleasure of a response, but I'm curious. If he was kidding about being in Korea then he wouldn't have seen that show on TV. But if he wasn't, then why I hadn't heard a thing about him?

Stompazer2: Got some news for u. We just got accepted into the Prozone League.

Prozone is the premiere Starfare league, where Team Anaconda plays.

Stompazer2: Yeah, u heard it here 1st. It will be announced on Monday. One of 2 new expansion teams.

Stompazer2: hey, u there.

ActionSeth: yes?

Stompazer2: We're set 2 go. Xerus International. Remember that name, noob. We got the best guys from Europe, South America. You know most of them. Bendo, from Germany. TheBorg, from Sweden. Me. Of course.

ActionSeth: So?

Stompazer2: So we got 1 requirement. English. We train in English.

ActionSeth: So?

Stompazer2: So I happen 2 know from my contacts that ur getting nowhere fast. Not the 1ˢᵗ time. These Koreans can b real dicks. That's why it's so easy to get the best European guys. They love it. Joining forces to beat those asswipes. We're going to do it our way. None of this bs indentured servitude and ass-kissing coaches. Want to hop into the sack with a pair of Korean twin teens, we're all for it. Private rooms, state of the art training facilities, plenty of seed money.

Stompazer2: Of course, u got a no-compete clause built in to your contract, so ur stuck with those Korean snakes for 2 years unless u can get fired. By then, we'll b tops in the world. 2 bad u will miss out. Besides, ur 2 much of a noob for r standards.

ActionSeth: Up yours.

Stompazer2: U would b expert in that department—what with all those Anacondas porking u daily. we've got 1 Korean player committed to the team—Doo-Ri Song. Or Song Doo-Ri as these ass-backwards tards say. You never heard of him? He's young and good and hungry. Maybe the other guys mentioned him?

Stompazer2: didn't think so. He's the guy they kicked off to make room for the blond bombshell.

I just stare at the screen dumbly.

Stompazer2: How come u live every day with these guys and I know more about that team than u? The only guy on your team who speaks fluent English and they kick him off. He's hilarious. he'll be doing standup after he retires from E-games. And the guys on the team, they loved him. Treated him like a little bro. Makes u wonder how they feel about the American blondie who got him fired.

As much as I want to disbelieve anything Stomp says, it all makes such good sense.

Stompazer2: And by the way, that orange soda tastes like ass.

15.

Back when I was in Kansas I'd dream of having a whole day to myself with nothing but broadband and Starfare. No one bugging me. But by evening I'm going stir crazy. I know the team has all these rules about where you can go when and always signing out with the coach, but honestly, what's that about anyway? Say I want to step outside, get a snack. You think the coach wants me to wake him up and get his OK?

I get out the phrase book from my Korean teacher and look up "nightclub." I say it to myself about a hundred times while I get dressed in my regular clothes instead of that annoying team shirt that I've worn over a hundred days in a row.

When I get down on the street I hail a cab which is just some little Korean compact painted yellow. I get in and carefully say the words for nightclub. The driver repeats it and I say yeah. Then he opens up with a flurry of Korean, which is probably a list of every nightclub in Seoul. I just say the word for nightclub and I'm guessing he's made a choice because we're off.

It takes about twenty minutes to get to a part of downtown that isn't familiar. The sidewalks are jammed with people, who spill over into the street, slowing traffic to a crawl. Each side of the street is lined with huge vertical neon signs in bright shades of yellow and green and red, crammed with Korean script and the occasional English word.

After about ten minutes of weaving through this district he drops me right in front of a place with a flashing sign that says Helios with a long queue outside. I don't know what it takes to get into this club, but based on who's waiting, it certainly isn't fancy suits or sequined dresses. Although the weather is warmer than when I first arrived in Seoul, about forty beautiful Korean girls look like they're freezing to death, standing in line, knee high boots and bare thighs. Arms wrapped about their short leather jackets. As I dig out my wallet I look down at my T-shirt (it's a black one from last year's nationals) and my worn jeans and al-most bark out one of the only other things I can say in Korean–my address. But I've gone this far, might as well give it a shot.

As soon as I get out of the cab I can hear the dance music seep-ing out of the building the way the smell of grilled meat surrounds a fast food place. I swear everyone waiting is staring at me, prob-ably because I'm the only Westerner. A guy in a suit, who appears to be guarding the door, immediately comes over and bows and gestures for me to follow. And just like that I'm inside the door, the warmth and music and cigarette smoke hitting me with a wave. I pay a girl in a fancy black dress twenty-five thousand won and take a stairway downstairs, with each step the throb of the bass and the dance music and the buzz of the crowd crescendos until I step into an ear-deafening cavernous room which is lit by strobes and spotlights shooting through the smoke. I don't recognize the music, but it could be any one of a thousand of those computer-generated dance tracks.

The floor is packed with young Koreans jumping around in what might be called dancing while shouting and drinking and smoking. The crowd sort of parts as I walk through, heading to-wards what I think is a bar in the back. The drinking age in Korea is eighteen but I've heard it's loosely enforced, if at all. So when I get to the bar I order a beer. I'm not much into drinking, but I always liked the way cold beer looks in all those commercials, with the condensation streaming down the bottle.

Of course, nothing is that easy and the bartender is shouting something, probably twenty different brands of beer. I look around, see a guy standing a few feet away with a bottle that says OB and point at that. Living where you don't speak the language, it's like going back to being two years old, pointing and grunting.

Before the beer arrives I feel a presence behind me and I turn to find about a half-dozen young Korean girls. I don't know what they're saying, but they seem to know my name. So naturally I smile and nod and when one of them finds a pen and paper in her purse I sign my name. Off to the side is another young Korean girl with a red streak in her hair, looking at me with what I take is amusement.

The DJ puts on a new song, this one in English. It even sounds familiar, some sort of hip-hop dance cut with the hook, "You get it on you take it off." Before I can take a sip the girl with the red streak in her hair half drags me onto the floor and starts gyrating so I just sort of join in the fray. Now, my dance moves are so lame that they've never ventured further than my bedroom mirror, but with the strobe lights and the mass of humanity it's pretty easy to just sort of jump around and no one can really tell what you're doing.

Actually, I'm stealing glances at this girl and I like what I see. This girl is looking me right in the eyes, and so I stare right back. She's wearing some sort of multi-layered outfit that seems to expose a couple layers of underwear. She's got that normal black, square cut hair with the red streak dyed down the side and she manages to dance her way in front of me, no matter which way I turn. I'm still holding onto the cold bottle of beer with one hand, and when I stop jumping to take a sip, I'm sort of gagging at the awful taste when she wraps both arms around me and kisses me.

Still holding me, she leans so that her lips are against my ear and she says something that sounds like English. A hot Korean chick who speaks English? I can't believe I didn't find this place sooner. Then she takes my hand, the one without the beer and pulls me across the floor. I don't know where we're going, but I hope it's a dark corner.

Across the dance floor is a spiral staircase and I follow her up and through a double door. When the door shuts the music is still loud, but not abusively so. We go through another door, and enter a large room full of people sitting at round tables. The music is thinner but the smoke thicker.

My new friend continues to lead me across the room to the far wall where there are a series of booths. Deep in the far corner, in a booth which could hold a dozen people, is a startling sight. Six westerners, four guys and two girls, sitting with drinks in their hands and looking at me with puzzlement.

"This is great Starfare player Seth Gordon," says my new friend.

"Haven't I seen you somewhere?" says one of the girls in an accent that could be British or Australian. She is looking at me the way you might eye an odd animal at the zoo.

"I believe that would be on a neon poster, about twenty times life size," says the guy on the far right. He semi-stands and reaches out with a hand. "Guy Hamilton," he says. "Good to meet you, mate."

I shake hands all around and they shift over and I sit down, absolutely ecstatic to be among English speakers again, only then realizing exactly how much I'd been missing it. I set my beer in front of me and realize that I'm grinning like an idiot. A mute one, because I have yet to say a word.

Hamilton says, "I see you've met Sumi. Her hobby is collecting foreigners and then getting them all together in one spot, like a collection of dolls."

Sumi blushes and says, "It is only that I practice my English so I someday study in America."

The Western girl next to me hands me a little cocktail napkin and points to her lips. "It seems Sumi has been practicing a little more than English." No accent at all.

I wipe and see the red smear of lipstick on the napkin.

The American girl says, "You're welcome. And since you looked like you were in a state of shock, I'll repeat the introduction. I'm Sarah. From Hollywood. Florida, that is."

Then I get about six questions at once and for the next half hour explain how a high school kid from the Midwest has ended up, not only in Korea, but unaccompanied at the hottest nightclub in town. Turns out all six of them are teaching English at various Korean schools and from what I gather, none of them is liking it much. They either aren't getting paid as much as they were promised or their students are arrogant and indifferent or their bosses are either trying to get them to go to bed with them or trying to make sure they don't go to bed with anyone at all.

When I finally check the time I'm shocked how late it is.

Everyone at the table seems at least a little drunk, except me. I really didn't like the taste of that beer very much and didn't order anything else. All evening Sumi just kept wiggling closer until now she is sort of draped over me, a position that seemed to amuse but not surprise the other English speakers.

And while I'm not exactly pushing her away, it's so weird touching another girl. And while this Sumi is pretty and seems willing, it just makes me think about Hannah. So I'm stuck with this awful mixed feeling, this excitement of physical contact and wishing it was Hannah instead.

But even with the building guilt, I'm still thinking how I can sneak Sumi back into the apartment. When I announce I have to go, Sumi hands me a slip of paper, which I assume will be her phone number. Instead I unfold it and realize it's a bill. For a lot more than I've spent all night.

The Westerners at the table all have a big laugh at my expense and throw some bills on the table, apparently splitting Sumi's fee.

The Aussie guy says, "It's an old Korean custom. Female companionship, at a price."

I think he sees something in my expression, something hopeful, because he adds, "In case you were wondering, the fees are for public companionship only. And I'm not telling you anything that you probably don't know, but the locals here, they don't abide having their girls mixing it up with foreigners. I had a mate who taught with me, got jumped a few months ago, walking out of club with a Korean girl. Got messed up pretty bad. Threw in the towel and headed back to Sydney. Can't blame him."

I count up the bills and add the difference and give it to Sumi, who now appears to be all business. She takes the money and bows and says "I hope to see you again soon." As I get ready to go Sarah, the girl from Florida, tells me that they try to meet at the club every Sunday night and that I should catch them next week.

Then she pulls me aside and says, "Look, you seem awful young and alone here. If you every need any help…"

And then I connect the dots. I pull out my wallet and find the folded scrap of paper I got when I was in customs. I read the phone number out loud.

Sarah looks at me like I just grew horns.

"Is this some kind of parlor trick?"

"No, no," I protest. "It's just when I was going through customs I met this couple and…"

"Christ," Sarah says, shaking her head. "You met my mother."

"Yeah," I say. "That's what I was trying to tell you."

"Crazy old Mom. She's always adopting every waif within miles. Well, all the more reason to give me a call if you need anything. You know, I've been here a few years. I have the system down pretty well."

I thank her and weave my way out of the club and to the street where the cabs are lined up waiting. Once in a cab I pronounce my address as clearly as I can and it must be good enough because it doesn't take long to get there. I pop the main door of my apartment building with a slide of my card key and head to the elevators. And even as I'm still buzzing from the excitement of meeting all these English speakers and the feel and smell of Sumi hanging onto me, I realize I'm just as alone and lonely as ever. Upstairs I can't even stand to look at Hannah's pictures or open up Facebook. It's better to just head into the welcome unconscious of sleep.

16.

I don't drop off until 2 a.m. and it feels so good to sleep in, taking advantage of our Monday morning break. I can't remember if we're supposed to be back to practice at twelve or one, so I pick one. When I catch up with the team they've already done their exercises and are deep into practice. I figure I'm going to hear about being late from Yeong and sure enough, I'm barely inside the door when I hear him.

"Seth Gordon!" he yells. "Come with me!"

I can tell by the way he struts into the breakfast room that he's hot. He slams the door behind us and I start to apologize for being late.

"You not say anything!" he shouts. He reaches into his pocket and unfolds a newspaper. It's one of the tabloids that I see every day at newsstands. They always have huge black headlines like war has just been declared.

Yeong unfolds the newspaper on the table and I hear myself croaking something that sounds like the noise you might make if someone unexpected drilled a fist into your stomach. I lean over the wrinkled newspaper and stare at the large picture. It's me all right, with the Korean girl, Sumi, both hands over my neck, looking like she's expected a long, romantic kiss.

"Seth Gordon!" Yeong is shouting. "You know the call I received this morning, from our great sponsors, ANC Computers? You know how I shout at you. Now think twice as loud from a man who is my superior who pays for this apartment and your food and your salary. And he pay for me also."

I'm wondering what the caption says. But think better of asking.

"It was nothing," I say.

"SHUT UP THE MOUTH," Yeong is now about two inches from my face. "It is everything. Everything! How you get to this club and find this person," pointing at Sumi, "this girl of bad morals? How you find a way to embarrass whole team?"

He crumbles up the newspaper and throws it against the wall.

"You go back to room. Now! I cannot stand to look your way. Go!"

I slink out the door and go back to my room. Sit for about an hour, wondering if I'm going to be sent back home. Surprised that I'm actually feeling OK with that. And then just thinking about how hungry I am and how I better sneak out now, while the Tost-u cart is still doing business. I slip on my coat and stick my head out the door, see no one and sprint around the corner to the elevator. When I step out of the building a little gust of wind blows scraps of paper into a little tornado and I can feel the chill cutting through my pant legs.

The street is still busy with traffic but the sidewalks are no longer congested. Like every day I've been in Seoul, the sky, where you can see it between the buildings, is gray, rather than blue. The air smells of car exhaust and some sort of spicy cooking, as if the entire city is permeated with kimchi. I look up and down the street, thinking of the thousands of people who drive by or walk by this spot every day. And I don't know one of them.

Five minutes later I'm taking a bite out of the hot, steaming egg sandwich. Thinking that here's the one thing I'll miss the most if I get sent home. But I'd be happy to trade the best Tost-u for a twelve-inch pie of good old authentic American pizza.

17.

The next morning I'm not sure whether to just hang out in my apartment and wait to hear from the Coach or write some sort of Korean-style letter of apology or just show up like nothing happened. At first I just hang out, doodling around the Internet. I check Hannah's Facebook but nothing new and then I Google my name and get a screenshot of that billboard I saw the night I landed. The one introducing me as the newest member of Team Anaconda. I cut the Korean copy and paste it into Google Translator.

"New Team Anaconda. Very best of American E-gamer is blond sexy. He is very happy of Korean girls to meet them soon."

I swear under my breath and then decide, what the hell, to just go for the "show-up and see what happens" option. As I walk towards the training rooms I just keep seeing that translation "blond sexy" in front of my eyes. I can't believe how slow I've been in figuring out just what the "great team Anaconda" sees in me.

When I walk into the breakfast room there's a moment when everyone looks up and then the conversation starts buzzing again. I get a little bowl of rice and find a place to sit, at a table with

Sang-Chul (who, of course, did best in the big release tournament) and two others.

Coach Yeong is stalking around the room, giving what looks like pep talks to each of the tables, but he skips over ours and heads out the door into the practice rooms. Sang-Chul looks over at the other two players and then he sticks his hand up in the air. I don't recognize this as any Korean gesture I've yet seen so I shrug my shoulders, hoping that a shoulder shrug isn't some sort of insult.

"High five!" he says, only it sounds to me like "Hig I've."

Still, I get the drift and give him a resounding slap. The rest of the guys on the team swarm over and are patting me on the back and saying stuff in Korean and broken English.

Sang-Chul raises his hand and everyone is quiet.

"You very just-do-it American," he says and from the buzz that follows it seems the rest concur. "Korean player, he be good-bye."

I smile and say, "Well, sometimes you have to say, what the hell, and just go for it."

They take a minute to do a communal translation and they seem to like the sentiment. Then Sang-Chul whispers, "So you do something with this Korean girl?"

I shake my head. I want to explain that I paid for the attention, but have no idea how to communicate this subtlety.

Then Yeong comes back through the door, gives a sour look at the gathering around my table and shouts something that gets everyone scrambling to line up for morning exercises. It seems like we do a lot more than usual, but it's no sweat for me. I actually think I might be getting into decent shape.

18.

Things settle down into the old routine for a few weeks. Morning practice, Korean lessons in the afternoon. I still can only say a few dozen lines, but that's because we spend a lot of time doing stupid stuff like practicing bowing. One bow for someone your age, another if you are a bit older, another if you are a little younger. My Korean teacher gets completely flustered when I don't even see the differences. It's like this guy I used to know in grade school who was really into comic books. He could glance at an old Superman book and instantly tell if it was in fine, very fine, or just very good condition, while they all looked the same to me, even if I paged through them for minutes.

Mom and I continue to have our Sunday morning chats, and the longer I'm here, the more I seem to be looking forward to them. She keeps me up to date on Garrett's basketball. The thing is, after we disconnect I always feel worse than I did before the call.

So after the call where Mom tells me how glad Garrett is to be done with basketball season I call his cell.

"Good God," he shouts, when I get him online. "What the hell time is it over there?"

I tell him it's Sunday morning and that I just talked to Mom.

"She worries a lot about you," Garrett says. "It was the same when I went away to college."

Which is just the opening I need, because I have a serious question for him and I was afraid I wasn't going to be able to ask.

"When you left for college," I say. "I mean, it wasn't like a surprise or anything. But when you got there, were you ever, you know, sad or whatever?"

"You mean homesick?"

"Yeah, I guess."

"Hell yes. You remember that girl I was going out with the summer after senior year?"

"Kimberly?"

There's a pause and he says, "Seth, I know you're smart, but how the hell did you remember that? I don't think you ever met her."

I don't say a thing.

"Anyway I was totally crazy about her. We were going to call each other every day and we had plans to set up visits, but then, just before I go, her parents convince her to break up with me. I was, like, just blown away.

"So anyway, there I am, up in Fargo in this athlete-only dorm, every night, just pining for Kimberly and missing everyone and feeling all sorry for myself and wondering if I made the right decision. I really thought about quitting."

"Yeah?"

"But then, just like that, I go to this fraternity party and I'm sitting kind of alone in a corner and this beautiful girl plops down on the couch next to me. Like she was dropped from heaven. Seth, you should have seen her. She looked like she came off the cover of *Maxim*. So we start to chat, turns out she's a huge basketball fan, and before long we're hitting if off like we'd been going out for a year. So man, if you're homesick, just get laid."

"Great," I say. I could always count on Garrett for good practical advice.

Meanwhile, Coach Yeong hasn't spoken a word to me since the day the picture appeared in the paper. So I'm a little unnerved when he taps my shoulder while I'm deep into a practice round with one of the lower-ranked guys on my team. And actually holding my own.

"Mr. Seth Gordon," Yeong says. I'm loath to look up from the game, but after a few dozen quick clicks, turn in my chair.

"We have entered you in very large tournament. It is National seventeen-and-under championships. You only pro. I believe you have chance."

"Great," I say, wondering how long I was going to be just a patsy for the guys on my team. "I'm getting my game in pretty good shape."

Yeong shakes his head. "Not so good yet, but it important for our promotions to get you TV. You win three rounds to get to TV round. Not easy. Not for American."

"How long do I have to gear up?"

"Tournament tomorrow."

"Tomorrow. Thanks for the warning."

Yeong scowls. "You not like my coaching strategy? You like to worry, worry and not sleep and train right? No, this is the best."

I stand up and try a bow and say my Korean words for "thank you very much." The bow for someone who is older and more powerful and who has just done you a big favor. I think I nail it, but how will I ever know?

When I glance up, Yeong at least seems pleased by the effort.

19.

Yeong got one thing right. I didn't sleep too well that night. Thinking about the tournament. I kept coming back to that game I played when I first got to Korea. Against that girl who was number five on her high school team. Who thought I was sandbagging, to make the game close. And when I can't sleep, I always seem to end up wondering what it must be like back in Kansas. I imagine Hannah at her environmental club meeting, getting everyone fired up about eliminating plastic bags on campus or something. The tall guy, the one I'm sure is only in the club to bag Hannah, pretending he's fascinated with her every word. I drift off to sleep. Wake up thankful I can't remember any dreams.

At breakfast Yeong leads me to the front of the room and gives a little speech. All the guys applaud politely and then the two of us head out. I was wondering if anyone else on the team would be competing, but I know I'm the youngest. The guys on the team remind me every day. They're real hung up on age in Korea. If you're one day older than someone they have to give you the bow used for an elder. I may be the only one seventeen or under, which is actually sixteen or under the way we count years. My tutor tried to explain—what I got is that they start counting age from conception, rather than birth. They do a lot of weird things in Korea.

Yeong and I sit silently in the back seat of the team car and get dropped off at the rear of a large building. It turns out the tournament is in an auditorium that's at least as big as the one for the pro event and from the sound of things, the crowd is even younger and louder.

Only eight featured matches are on stage, the rest of the games are played in a big barn-like center which is down a long corridor. Somehow I'm not surprised when my first match gets announced as a feature. I try to remember his name which I hear as Lim Jin-Ho. He's small, even for a young Korean, and his baggy team shirt hangs halfway down his arms.

An official in a shirt striped like a NFL referee leads us down the corridor and onto the front of the stage where an announcer broadcasts our names. When mine is said, I'm immediately blinded by hundreds of camera flashes and deafened by the screams of thousands of girls. I glance at Jin-Ho and he looks like he might be sick any second.

I never really thought much about it from the other point of view—the view the player I was facing. When I saw his frightened look I realized, in a flash, what a huge psychological advantage I had. Just being on a top pro team would scare the daylights out of any normal kid, and on top of that being foreign and somewhat famous. I'm guessing he had never played in front of large crowd, let alone one that seemed to be entirely against him.

The other thing I realize as I win my first two rounds easily is that even though I'm not getting in the kind of training time my teammates are, pounding on a map for eight hours a day was way more than any school kid was getting. Plus every day I was fighting to keep up with players who were among the top hundred in the world. So even if I'm still a little behind the top hundred, I'm now way ahead of where I had been when I first arrived. And the Mordant Isles map is as familiar to me now as the keyboard itself. I can simply flow into the game and for twenty straight minutes pound out as many keystrokes as is possible for me to make— which is more than another person could make just typing nonsense for the same amount of time.

So I relax and find myself on TV for the final eight, which clearly makes Yeong one happy coach. He tells me that my next round is against a young player with a great future who should be on a pro team as soon as he graduates from high school.

We battle evenly for close to forty minutes when I noticed one slip from him, a slight misplay on the fourth isle, which hampers his development of an important late-game weapon system. Once I see this gaff it's just like being a piece up in a chess game. It's just a matter of trading down until my troops are the only ones left standing.

With this win, my confidence is at new heights and the last two rounds turn out to be against lesser opponents, and just like that, Korea had its first ever foreign-born seventeen-and-under Starfare champ.

Yeong is beside himself and the next day comes to breakfast with an array of newspapers and tabloids, all opened to pictures of me competing or accepting the large glass trophy (which now belongs to Team Anaconda, of course).

"So what do they say?" I ask.

"Much controversy. They say, no foreigners in national junior tournament again. Next year, no pros allowed. It is all good."

Yeong points to a picture and the prominent ANC logo on my shirt. "Great sponsor very happy. Very happy."

I'm thinking I must have made up for the nightclub publicity, when Yeong, like he's reading my mind says, "One bad picture, now good pictures. You back to even."

So, back to even. Better than being in the hole.

20.

If I was expecting any new cred from my Anaconda teammates, I soon get over that expectation. I suppose they look at the national junior title as kids' play, and perhaps it is. So on Friday night, the bags of laundry are back at my door. One good thing—those scratchy shirts we all have to wear dry quickly and seem impossible to wrinkle.

I'm up late, as usual, doing the laundry and getting frustrated that none of my stateside friends are online. Of course, when it's evening for me, they're either still at school or, for the college guys, either in class or sleeping. In a couple of months they'll be out for summer break and online all day. So I put out a couple text messages, linking them to some of the Korean gaming e-zines that have pictures of me at the junior championships.

As I sit in front of my laptop, the hum of the washer and dryer in the background, I do a Google image search on some of my old haunts. I actually find a picture of the KenTacoHut in Overland Park where I used to go all the time. That makes me think of old times and old obsessions. So I hit Brit's Facebook page. She's featuring a set of snapshots with some guy I don't recognize and it's been so long, and feels so far away that it's like looking at a family scrapbook of pictures taken before you were born.

Then I look up more Kansas pictures. After the congestion of the Korean streets, the wide open streets of Overland Park make it look like a ghost town. I blow up the few pictures that have people in them, and then stare at them for a while, looking, pathetically I know, for Hannah.

On Saturday morning Yeong breaks routine after breakfast and leads us all downstairs to a lounge on the first floor where a big screen is set up in front of a couple of rows of tables. In the back of the room are four round tables, covered with white tablecloths. Two guys in suits, both looking to be in their twenties, are sitting at a table in front of the room. They fire up a projector and start a lecture which has a ton of charts and equations. Now charts and equations are good news for me, because I have a fighting chance of following these, even in Korean. Interspersed are screenshots of various Starfare situations.

All the guys in the room are taking notes on the little pads like the one in front of me. Except me—I'm just fighting to get the drift, which is clearly the application of some mathematically based strategies, which strikes me as very cool, even though I'm missing too much from their lecture to really follow along.

After a few hours lunch is wheeled in on carts. Large tureens of soup and bowls of kimchi. I've figured out which soups are least offensive and get a bowl and sit down at one of the round lunch tables at the back of the room. I'm surprised when the older of the two speakers pulls up a chair next to me.

"Michael Kim," he says, in accentless English, extending a hand out Western style. I shake his hand and tell him my name.

"Of course," he says. "You're famous, you know."

"Not exactly," I protest. "And certainly not for anything deserved."

"Well," Kim says. "We could discuss whether or not there is a quantifiable metric that links merit and celebrity. Sort of thing we would bat around all night when I was at MIT."

"You were at MIT?"

"Undergrad and grad school. PhD in economics. All morning, I'm thinking about my freshman lectures at MIT and how lost I felt. How much of what we covered did you follow?"

"Not much," I admit. Kim asks about my math background and I tell him about my AP courses and the class at UMKC.

"Very impressive," he says, even though I know enough about Korean math prodigies to know that whatever I've done is modest. "You are eighteen?"

"Sixteen," I correct. He arches his eyebrows and says, "Very impressive. Let me give you the ten minute version in English," he says. And even in English it's a bit of a strain, but I pick up that Team Anaconda has hired him and a graduate assistant to apply some cutting edge game theory mathematics to determine what is the best course of action when balancing decisions about how to decide which resources to develop in relation to your opponent's decisions.

"It's actually a very interesting problem," Kim says. "Very similar to some of the real world policy decisions that game theory addresses regarding nuclear armament, the positioning of offensive forces on national frontiers, that sort of thing. Clearly there are some optimum strategies in Starfare that are not always intuitive."

I ask him a bunch of questions that must be totally noobie, but he doesn't seem to mind trying to answer.

Then he sort of screws up his face, leans closer and in a softer voice asks, "So you have any family in Korea?"

I shake my head.

"Friends?"

"Not really."

"Well, do you at least have people to speak English with?"

I hesitate, thinking of the people at the bar, and then just say, "Coach Yeong."

"Yeong?" he says, looking around to find him at the back of the room. He laughs. "I've tried English with him." He gives me a look. Concern? Sympathy?

"Look," he says. "You need to get away from this scene a bit. See another side of Korea. Have a chance to relax. Chat in English. We'll have you over to our place. It's not that far."

I begin to demur, but he interrupts. "No discussion. I'll talk to Yeong. He'll see the benefits. Trust me."

Then he gets a wave from Yeong to start up the second part of the session and he excuses himself.

Before he walks away I blurt out one quick question: "What would you recommend, if someone wanted to know about this stuff?"

As he stands he says, "I'll send over a couple of books that might do the trick." Then he smiles and adds, "Don't worry. They're in English."

21.

Sunday morning I sleep late and when I log on I curse out loud when I find a series of missed Skype calls from Hannah. An email from Mom congratulating me on my tournament win, news of which has taken days to filter all the way back to her at the Institute. I hold the best for last. After deleting all the junk mail I open a voice message from Hannah.

"Seth—this is unbelievable, but today I heard from RISD! *I got in!* And the scholarship is terrific. We'd be paying less than a state school! It's like you getting the call from the Korean team…call me when you can and I'll give you details."

So Hannah will be off to the East coast. When? In five months? I try to picture her at college. Studying art. I imagine a big studio with easels and dozens of students standing around with brushes, looking at a naked model. Then in my mind the model turns for a different pose and it's that tall guy from the environmental club. Hannah is now snapping pictures like crazy from just a few feet away, getting him from every angle, smiling and enjoying every moment.

That night after surfing the net for hours, I just lie on my pads, staring at the ceiling. I'm waiting for Hannah to wake up back in Kansas so I can catch her before school.

I brush past Hannah when she opens the door. She's wearing a swimsuit top, ragged cutoffs, and she has her hair tied back, the way she does when she goes running. Her eyes are wide, startled.

"Won another world title this week," I say when I'm in the entryway. "So I hired a private jet. Flew right into the downtown Kansas City airport."

I gesture towards the door.

"My limo is outside waiting. I came all this way to say one thing."

Hannah's upper lip is trembling. She's about to say something.

I silence her with a wave of my hand. "I love you."

Now Hannah is crying. She takes a step towards me, tentatively. Then she's throwing herself into my arms and I'm holding her so tightly I can feel her breasts flattening against my chest.

"Oh, Seth," she says. "I didn't know how much I missed you. Not until just now."

Then she takes me by the hand. And leads us up the stairs. And this time we take a left at the top of the stairs. Towards her room.

Finally at ten o'clock I go back to the computer and Skype her cell. She picks up on the third ring.

"Seth? Why are you calling so early?

"Well, I'm about ready to go to bed."

"Omigod, I'm so sorry, I just can't seem to figure this time change thing out. And I don't mean to sound so bitchy. I mean, it's great to hear from you. It's just so hectic here in the morning. Hang on."

In the background I can hear a muffled, "Zeb, don't you dare go in the bathroom again. I swear I will…" I hear a door slam.

"What a brat! I swear I'm going to kill that boy…Sorry, so how are you? How's the job?"

"It's OK."

"Just OK? This is not sounding like the job of your dreams."

"Anyway, the only reason I'm calling is that you left a message about getting into a college last night. So congrats."

"Oh it's amazing, and not just getting in, but the financial aid. You know when you keep telling yourself, don't get excited. Don't get your hopes up. There's nothing wrong with going to your second choice or even one of the safeties. And then, all of a sudden, everything just falls into place?"

Like going to Korea and staying up to midnight doing team laundry?

"Anyway, I still have to choose between the offers. But I've been telling everyone it's really a no-brainer for me… Zeb! I need to get in there!" Then to me she says, "Hang on. Here comes Mom."

I can hear Hannah, muffled as she covers the cell's mic, telling her mom to tell Zeb to get out of the bathroom. Then her mom yelling something.

"Seth, I'm really, really happy to hear from you, but I'm going to have to go. Call me later, OK?"

Then I go lie down and it's very, very quiet. I can still hear Hannah's voice echoing in my ears. I hear her say she's happy to hear from me. I hear her saying *call me*. I'm sure I will be able to hear her voice saying these things for a long, long time.

22.

On Wednesday I get a note in my mailbox and I get Sung Gi to translate. It takes a few tries, but finally I understand that there's a package for me at the front desk. Professor Kim has sent me two game theory books and a card: "Will pick you outside the lobby at 5 p.m. on Sunday for dinner. Yeong thinks it's a capital idea." That night I begin reading the one that looks easiest and it's almost 2 a.m. when I finally fall asleep.

During practice I find myself thinking about some of the ideas in the book instead of concentrating on Starfare and Yeong comes by about a dozen times, clucking his tongue and looking over my shoulder with what I can tell is disgust.

But somehow my mind is stuck on this tangent. I start thinking about the mathematics of other parts of the game. That maybe there could be a way to quantify some of the strategic decisions. So I grab a pad and a pencil and jot this down: "Assuming your opponent maintains perfect macro during a harass, how many spybots should you attempt to kill in order to end up ahead considering you are seeking an attrition drop rather than fast expansion?"

I look at this for a minute and I'm pretty sure that I could come up with an algorithm that could provide the answer. And this is just one little piece of the puzzle. What if you could find the equations for all kinds of moves? Wouldn't it be possible to find the absolute efficiency mathematically, rather than by the kind of trial and error and intuition that I see the Team Anaconda pros using?

I fold the paper and stuff it in my pocket.

That night, after our evening practice, I take the note out of my pocket and grab a notebook from my desk. Start working out some of the formulas. When I look up it's after midnight. Two hours just gone. I've got about ten sheets of notes and I've simplified it all down to about three lines of calculus.

I fall asleep instantly. In the morning I tear out the page with the final calculations and take them to breakfast. Get a bowl of rice and sit down at a table with three of the guys. Take the calculations out of my pocket and unfold them. The guys each take a look, shake their heads and pass it along. The last guy, Tae-Uk, stares at the paper for a minute and then yells something out.

Sang-Chul comes over. Grabs the paper out of Tae-Uk's hands and stands there for minute. Then barks out something in Korean. The three guys at the table point at me.

Sang Hoon looks at me, with what I take to be skepticism. He starts babbling at me in Korean. The other guys start talking at the same time. Sang Hoon shakes his head and laughs, crumples the paper and throws it on the table. Walks away. The guys at the table look at me sheepishly as I unwad the paper, fold it up and put it back in my pocket.

I should have figured that these guys were too busy playing Starfare to keep up with their math. Screw them. It just makes me more determined to come up with something on my own.

That night I attack another problem. I know that the guys on the team have figured out what they consider to be the optimum ratio between mineral production and spybot development. But when I think about it, I realize that it's a pretty crude approximation. I think it could be solved exactly using some basic calc. So I work on that for the next couple of nights.

Sunday I sleep in, chat with Mom, then get on the computer and waste the afternoon. I catch DT and tell him about the math stuff. He seems optimistic about it. But when I send him the actual formulas he claims it's beyond him. I forget he hasn't started calc yet.

So a little before five I'm in the lobby, waiting for Professor Kim. Watching all the weird little cars zip by. Wondering why half the people in Korea seem to have the same last name.

A few minutes after five a small blue sedan pulls up in front of the building. I start for the door as the driver leans across and rolls down the window. Kim is waving at me as I step through the apartment building's door. The air is still crisp but over the last few weeks it seems the worst of winter is fading.

Kim pops the door and I slide in. I look at the car—think it's a Hyundai. Either that or a Kia—guess one of these two and you'd be right about seventy-five percent of the time.

He reaches out and I shake his hand.

"Good to see you, Seth," he says. And my heart actually leaps at the sound of good English.

"Me too," I say. "I sometimes wonder if I'm going to forget how to speak. That I'll get home and sound just like Coach Yeong."

Kim laughs. "Not much of a chance of that."

As we head down the road Kim says that his family is really looking forward to meeting me.

"My wife's name is Annie," he says. "And we have one son. Alexander. Alex, for short. He can't be believe his old man not only knows the great Starfare warrior Seth Gordon, but is bringing him home."

I wish he had told me. I'd have brought something for him. A Team Anaconda T-shirt, or something.

For some reason I pictured Kim living in a suburban neighborhood like Overland Park, but we stay right in the city. Take so many turns that I'm completely lost. Drive down another canyon of buildings not unlike the one I live in and turn into an underground garage.

"Home sweet home," Kim says as he pulls into a narrow parking spot next to a pole. I'm pretty sure I won't be able to get out the door. But there's just enough room. I'm thinking, no wonder everyone drives tiny cars.

Elevator up to the sixth floor and down the hall. Kim swipes a key and we step into a brightly lit apartment. It smells wonderful, a bit like the restaurant in Westport.

I blink twice when Kim's wife comes around the corner, wiping her hands on an apron. She's tall and blond.

She marches right up to me and offers me her hand.

"I'm Annie," she says. She frowns at Kim. "I suppose he didn't mention that his wife is half Swedish, half Dutch and grew up in Providence?"

I shake my head. I'm thinking Providence is somewhere out East but I can't quite remember where.

"That's so like him. The absent-minded professor. Come on into the playroom. Alex is a little shy."

I follow her and Kim through a small living room and around the corner into an even smaller room. The room has one wall of shelves crammed with toys and there are Legos all over the floor. Alex is sitting among them, a controller in his hand, but he's staring at the door and us. The screen is frozen on the beginning of a Mario Kart race.

"Alex," Kim says, "Where are your manners?"

He stands up, but doesn't move.

"Alex, this is Seth."

"I know," Alex says, almost in a whisper. "I know who it is."

Alex is looking at the ground, shuffling. He's got straight, light brown hair. At first I don't see the Korean side of him, but when he looks up, it's there, in his dark eyes.

"Hope you like lasagna," Annie is saying. "I have to have half the ingredients shipped, so it's a special meal for us too."

I nod, and say I used to work in an Italian restaurant, back in Kansas.

"Alex is a little shy," Annie continues. "We speak English at home, but he goes to a Korean school. So he doesn't get to meet a lot of other native English speakers."

Alex continues to fidget.

"I know he'd like to play a game or two with you," she says. "Would you be willing?"

I look at Annie and then Kim. "Mario Kart? I used to kick… butt on that game."

They smile at each other while Alex scrambles to find the second controller. He holds it out to me.

"We'll be ready to eat in about fifteen minutes. Alex?"

He's jumping up and down like he has to go the bathroom.

"Alex?"

"Fifteen! I heard you!"

I sit on the floor next to him and try to get accustomed to the controller and the unfamiliar course. We do a couple of practice rounds. Alex giving me commentary and tips. He beats me the first two games but then I get back in the groove and whip around the course without an error.

"Wow," Alex says, staring at the screen. "1:24.25? That is so fast." He looks at me with abject worship in his eyes. "I've never heard of anyone doing it that fast."

"Well," I say. "I used to practice a lot."

"I saw you win that tournament," Alex says. "On TV."

"Well, yeah. That was something." Beating up on high school kids.

"Duk-Ho doesn't believe I'm meeting you."

"Duk-Ho?"

"Yeah. My friend at school."

"What will you tell him?"

"I'll tell him 1:24.25."

Then Annie is in the doorway, saying that dinner is ready.

Which is delicious. The only thing keeping me from making a pig of myself is all of Annie's questions. Answer one between each bite. She can't believe that I came all this way, at my age, all alone.

"I don't know," I say. "I'd probably be going away to college pretty soon anyway."

"Yes," Annie concedes. "But you're so young. And college. You're with all those kids in the same situation. I hear you don't even have anyone to speak with."

Mouthful, I nod.

"That's just awful," she says.

Swallow and say, "But I Skype my mom once a week and get lots of email and text messages from my friends."

"Your mom," Annie says. "She must be worried sick. I want you to give me her email before you go. I'll tell her that we're going to make sure you get a decent American meal at least once a week."

I look over at Kim who is nodding and see that Alex is grinning.

"Can I bring Duk-Ho?" Alex says.

"We'll see," his mom says. "If you eat your salad."

Alex winkles up his nose, but doesn't say anything.

After dinner Alex wants to play some more but his parents shush him away. Kim and I sit in the living room and I ask him a few questions about the book he gave me.

"You read the whole thing?" he says. "I didn't think they gave you ten minutes a day to yourself."

"It's not that bad," I say. Then I remember the notes that I stuffed into my pocket. I pull them out and hand them over to Kim. Who looks at them with a serious expression.

"I've been working on a bunch of these," I say. "It's just that I can't keep up with these Korean players. They work so well together and so fast and I'm just left behind."

Kim is clearly interested. So I continue.

"So after your lecture. And reading that book. I start thinking that so many aspects of Starfare are mathematical, when you think about it. But as far as I know, no one has tried to figure it out. So maybe that's the way I get an edge. I do the math."

Kim looks again at the page of equations.

"Look," he says. "I'm an economist. Who studied a lot of math, true. But this stuff…how much more of this do you have?"

"I don't know. About five pages of decent stuff. I've only been working on it for a week or so."

Kim looks up at me and I think maybe he's impressed.

"Can I borrow this?" he says. I say of course.

"I've got a young colleague at the University. He just finished his doctorate in applied math from Brown and this is right up his alley. Let me share this with him. I'm betting he'll be interested in getting together."

Annie comes in and the three of us sit around and talk about all kinds of stuff. Mostly things we miss. Our old favorite TV shows and fast food places and movies.

When Alex comes in wearing his pajamas to say goodnight I suggest it's time to go.

Kim and I head back to the car. On the way home he says he's really happy that I'm interested in the books he sent over. Asks me to tell him when I get through the second one. Drops me off at the door and says, "Same time, next week?"

And I'm happy to say that'll be great.

When I get back to the apartment I check for messages from Hannah but there's nothing. So I leave her a text, telling her about my new friends.

I don't hear back from her that night but when I get up on Monday I find a short text.

"New friends?" she writes. Then she has a link. When I pop it open it leads to a picture from the tabloid of me and Sumi draped over my shoulders. I swear and then write her a long note about how it was just another crazy fan and that there was nothing to it. Because I don't want her thinking I've got anything in common with that creep she used to go out with in New Jersey.

23.

Coach Yeong has a team meeting on Monday. I sneak in a minute late and sit in the back and imagine what he's talking about. What I know is what you know about every coach of every pro team when the season is about to start. He's worried about his job.

The pro season starts with a series of dual matches—team against team. The top seven players are randomly paired against each other. What has me most interested is our first pairing— against one of the two new teams. Stomp's Xerus International.

I can feel the intensity at practices increasing day by day. But I'm not even close to being in the top seven, so I don't get too worked up.

On Wednesday I get an email from Professor Kim. He's invited his math prof friend Song to join us for dinner on Sunday. So that gets me motivated and I work up a couple more problems that I think could be attacked mathematically. Although I have some ideas and make some progress, I'm finding it harder than I thought.

So on Sunday evening I have a little bag with my math notebook and other stuff and I'm standing outside. There's a strip outside my building where the sun is finding its way to the pavement. I stand in the sunbeam. Wearing just a hoodie, but not cold at all. Watching the cars zip by, seeing if I've gotten any better at telling a Daewoo from a Hyundai.

When Professor Kim pulls up I hop right in.

"Hey, Tiger," he says. "How's your game?"

"Pretty good." But I'm really wondering about this math professor and what he'll think of my project. Probably laugh.

Alex is at the front door when we arrive, standing with a shorter Korean boy.

I say hello to Alex, who gives his friend an "I told you so" look. Inside, the smell of cooking. Something different. Baking, I think.

"You must be Duk-Ho," I say.

The boy nods.

"You two ready for a quick game of Mario Kart?"

I don't have to ask them twice. Before we start Annie comes into the playroom and I thank her for having me over.

"It's our pleasure. Right Alex?"

Alex is trying to unscramble the cords for a third controller. Annie shakes her head.

"That's all he could talk about all week. Seth coming over for dinner again."

I almost say I was the same way, but I'm too embarrassed.

"And I exchanged a couple of emails with your mother. She sounds wonderful."

"She's great," I say. "And really flexible."

Annie looks at me oddly.

"From all that yoga. She can bend like a pretzel."

"Well," Annie says. "We didn't discuss that. We talked about you. She didn't seem to understand that you're something of a celebrity over here."

"No? I mean, I'm not really. Except maybe for that orange soda.

ActionOrange. Sounds like a stain remover."

Alex, Duk-Ho and I get in a couple of rounds before the doorbell rings. Before I go to meet Professor Song I give Alex and Duk-Ho two black Team Anaconda T-shirts. As I hand them over, the two of them are besides themselves, grinning back and forth while holding the too-large shirts against their chests.

In the living room I step over to Professor Song and start to bow, but he offers me a hand instead.

"Just call me Song," he says. "That's what they called me back at Brown." I'm relieved because I'd probably mangle his full Korean name, Kyung Chan.

He has a bit of an accent, but not heavy.

"You know, I think of the Kims like an unofficial American Embassy. A little island of the States in the middle of Seoul. So we do with handshakes rather than bows." Song is young, maybe late twenties.

Kim comes back and the three of us sit down and chat for a while. Kim takes his time, but eventually gets around to my mathematical work on Starfare.

Song asks to see it, and when I ask him if he's played Starfare he says yes.

"When I was younger. A bit. Not seriously."

So I explain the first problem. About trying to quantify the best yield between mineral harvesting and spybot production. As I do, Kim gets up, excuses himself to help with dinner.

Song looks at my notes. Makes a face. I'm actually flushing, thinking I've just made a fool of myself.

He thumbs to the next page and I try to explain what I was doing there, but he raises his hand.

After another few minutes he looks up at me and says, "Interesting. Very interesting. You know, in applied mathematics, we're always looking for real-life examples. What makes this especially intriguing is that it all a construct. It all starts off with someone sitting down and typing binary code. So that it might be revealed in mathematical terms is initially surprising, but on second thought, quite predictable."

I nod.

"So tell me about your background in mathematics."

I give him the quick summary.

"What I see here—and keep in mind that this is just a quick glance—what I see is an impressive integration of some very fundamental principles. It shows a very deep understanding of the basics. I can also see where you're running into some walls. But on first glance I imagine they are not insurmountable. Maybe some more advanced techniques."

I'm just so relieved he wasn't dismissing it as trash that I'm only catching parts of what he's saying. Then Annie and Kim come in, call out to the boys that dinner is ready.

Fried chicken, mashed potatoes and what Annie calls Rhode Island cinnamon rolls. I stuff myself.

After dinner Song and I sit in the living room. He points at my math notebook on the table in front of us. "Would you be interested in working on this together?" he says. "I can't promise anything, but it could lead to something interesting."

Of course I'm all over it.

"The only problem," I say, "is time. We don't get a lot of free time."

We talk some more about some of the individual problems I've identified and Song mentions a couple more. I'm thinking maybe he played more Starfare than he let on.

When Kim and Annie join us, Song explains my concerns about time. Kim is nodding. "I think Yeong might make an exception for this. If I convince him it could help the team."

So we leave it at that.

24.

Yeong has this thing about lineups. He wants everyone on the team working as hard as possible, so he doesn't announce the lineup until an hour before our first dual.

The venue is this big auditorium downtown. We have a team meeting back stage and Yeong pulls a slip of paper out of his pocket. Gathers us all around. I sort of hang in the back, half paying attention as he reads the names.

At first I think I'm imagining it, when he says something that sounds distinctly like "ActionSeth." But then I see the entire team has turned and is staring at me. Not nice looks.

My first instinct is to protest, but if I've learned one thing since I got on the team, it's to keep my mouth shut in situations like this.

The team breaks up into small groups. Lots of buzzing discussions. All about my being named to the lineup, I would bet.

I find a folding chair off to the side and sit down. Try to get my head in the right place to play. I don't even notice Yeong coming up, carrying a chair. He sits down, puts his head right next to mine.

"You wonder, Mr. Seth Gordon?"

I just look at him, blank.

"I know you like to question Coach Yeong. So I tell you. You not top seven."

I raise my eyebrows, about to say, then why am I playing, but Yeong cuts me off.

"It is for team, ActionSeth. It is always for team. This is business. Sponsors. They want you on TV. So we play this new team with Americans, Xerus International. Not so good. We win all seven. So instead we win, maybe six? Maybe seven. You play American, you can win, no?"

I shrug. Maybe. I'm certainly playing tons better than when I got to the final eight at Nationals. If Stomp is in the top seven, I'd be more confident.

"OK, OK," Yeong says. "We have understanding?"

I nod.

"You play hard, and when you are done, win, lose, you smile at camera. You think about all your fans. They love ActionSeth. They love drink ActionOrange!"

So I'm a nervous wreck even before we step onto the stage for the introductions. The crowd is a howl in the background, behind the blinding lights. I see Stomp on the other side of the stage, in the middle of his team. I have to admit their team shirts are pretty cool. Some sort of electronic graphic on a blue background. Blue metallic accents that glow in the spotlights.

Unbelievable as it seems, it looks like Stomp has gained weight. He must love Korean food. His shirt looks more like a cape. I recognize some of the other guys from the U.S. tournaments. Including the older guy who I split with, MilesBlue. The Swedish champ, TheBorg, I recognize from pictures.

Then one-by-one, the pairings are announced. I'm in a daze as the first six are announced, not keeping track. But I'm staring across the stage and Stomp is grinning like a fool before the last pairing is announced. I should have guessed.

We take our places behind each of the pairs of keyboards. Stand and then, along with my teammates, we bow in unison. I notice that the guys on Xerus International don't bow. The crowd starts booing at this and yelling stuff.

As I sit down, I shake my head. Look over the top of my monitor to Stomp who is still standing. Maybe that's their strategy. Piss the Koreans off. Be like one of those professional wrestlers who makes his living dressing up as a devil, or mullah or whatever rednecks are into hating this year.

Stomp leans around his monitor and hisses, "Hey, noob. Looks like you're getting good at kissing Korean ass. Now get ready to get *your* ass kicked."

I don't even bother with a response.

Then the game starts and I'm too busy to think. Playing at this level, it's like running six speed-chess matches simultaneously. I've got to keep track of dozens of activities at once while trying to figure out what tactics Stomp is employing. The crowd noise fades to nothing and my mind is inside the monitor, beyond the monitor, flashing across this world which is no longer flat and one-dimensional, but as textured and complex as the vertical face of a mountain is to a freestyle climber.

Although the clock is spinning at the bottom right hand corner of the screen, there is another time that subsumes this monitor of reality. Because despite the frantic action of my hands and the flashing armies and battles on the screen, game time is infinitely slower than real time.

The thing is, without even knowing it, I've slowly adjusted to the pace of game played by my Korean teammates. It's like when you were twelve and would go to the doctor and he'd say you had grown two inches. You don't notice it, you don't feel it.

And Stomp, he might have gotten better, but I know he wasn't training like the Koreans train. And I can guarantee that he wasn't getting regular matches with guys ranked in the top ten of the world.

Small advantages get magnified over the course of a game. By endgame it's clear that Stomp is not even close to winning. I can hear him huffing and swearing and can see the mass of him not hidden by the monitors between us shifting, the chair under him creaking with the weight. By the final minutes I'm relaxing. Thinking it would be very cool if his chair broke.

Then the game is over and I can hear the crowd chanting. They're chanting my name.

As the monitor goes back to the Starfare logo I stand, as is Korean tradition. Both players stand and bow. I stand, and so does Stomp, knocking his chair to the ground. Storming off the stage, mumbling obscenities.

So instead I turn to the crowd and bow to them.

The cheers are deafening. I wave and back slowly off the stage. Two of our games are still in progress. We've won all of the first five.

Yeong is waiting backstage. Slaps me on the back.

"Good job, Mr. Seth Gordon. Very, very good job. You beat enormous American and fans love you more!"

We split the last two matches, with the Swede winning a close one. Yeong asks us to hang around for the second dual, to scout the other teams. But to tell you the truth, I don't absorb a single thing. All I can think about is getting home and Skyping DT. He's going to go crazy when he finds out who I drew in my first pro dual.

25.

When I get home I try to Skype DT and send out an email message to my family contacts. Telling them about my first big pro event. Then I spend about an hour trying to write something to Hannah. Finally I just boil it down to the facts. I played that obnoxious American guy, won. Hope everything is OK. Please don't make more of that tabloid story than you should.

I'm looking at Hannah's Facebook page when I get a message from Yeong. It says that instead of language lessons on Tuesday and Thursday afternoons I'm going to be meeting with Song.

"Maybe this mathematics help team," Yeong writes. I hope so too.

I'm trying to figure out what kind of algorithm might explain the growth curve of a Surrakan army's power when I hear a Skype beep on my computer.

I pop open the window and just about have a heart attack.

Because there's Hannah. In the little Skype window, grinning and moving in that sort of herky-jerky way you get from webcams.

"Hey," she says. "I got a new laptop for college. High end webcam!"

"So I see."

"Very funny. How do I look?"

I don't know what to say. Like Hannah? Like home? Like an angel?

"That bad, huh?"

"No, no. You look awesome. It's just…I don't know. I'm just surprised."

"So how come I can't see you? So I can make fun of the way you look too."

"I'm not making fun…"

"And I'm just kidding. But am I doing something wrong?"

"No," I say, and peel back the tape and stare at the little glowing light. "Here I am!"

"Ohh. You look so…I don't know. Korean?"

I push my bangs back. It's that stupid Korean gamer cut.

"So tell me, how's life in the Far East?" When she looks up from the keyboard my heart just melts. But I figure she's really asking about me and the picture with Sumi.

"Far out," I say, automatically. Then add, "Actually, it's not all good. Not all bad, either. I've made a few new friends. Found some people who I can speak English with."

"Well that's encouraging. Any more action with those hot Korean girls?" Normally I love the way she looks at me when she's teasing like that, but I'm not sure she's teasing.

"As you know, they love having their picture taken with me…"

"Well, as a photographer, I can say the pose is everything."

"We're talking snapshots on the sidewalk. Nothing like one of your photos."

I wiggle uncomfortably, even knowing it will look goofy through the webcam. "Well, you can't blame a girl for imagining. I get the feeling you're not telling me everything. I mean, you're like some sort of celebrity right? And everything I know about celebrities says that means plenty of action."

I shake my head.

"It's not like that over here."

"So let me tell you how I got the laptop. The deal to sell Dad's company fell through, so he's still got a job and we're not moving. The same week we got a firm offer on our old house in Princeton. He's so pumped that he goes out and gets Zeb a new fifty-two-inch screen. Mom gets to renovate the kitchen. Barkley got a new chew toy. And I got a new Dell laptop! It's like Christmas in April!"

I ask her how school is going. She starts talking about the yearbook and how totally changed it's going to be. And how behind they are on it. And how her environmental club has convinced the school board to take out the vending machines from the school cafeteria. I tell her she's amazing and not to worry. That she'll figure out a way to get everything done on time.

Hannah smiles. "That's so sweet. You know, that's why I miss you so much."

When she says that I'm really tempted to put the tape back over the camera. Because it just makes me want to cry. Then I hear someone talking in the background. Hannah steps away from the screen and I want to yell out, "Come back! Come back!"

Then she ducks her head in from the side.

"Sorry Seth, but I got to go. But now that we can see each other."

I feel myself blushing. "Yeah, we'll do it again. Soon."

We sign off and I look at my watch. It's late. I walk over to the mirror and muss my Korean-cut hair. As if a haircut will make me a true member of Team Anaconda.

26.

On Tuesday I have my first math meeting with Song. He's got an office at the University, which is about a fifteen-minute drive from our apartment. Choi drops me off at a modern, four-story building that says Seoul University Department of Mathematics.

Song's office is on the fourth floor. He's waiting for me, papers strewn across a table next to his desk.

"Sit down, sit down," he says.

I start to say something but he waves his hand. "Just a second. I've almost got this worked out."

I sit for a few minutes, watching his pencil fly across the page. Then he slides it across to me. I spin it around, see it is one of the pages from my notebook. Which looks like it had been attacked by a dozen mathematical graffiti artists.

"This is really coming together," Song says.

Maybe for him. It makes no sense to me. I look up from the paper and he can see I'm lost.

"OK, I know it's a mess right now. But trust me. You were absolutely right to tackle this problem the way you did."

He stands up, and grabs a piece of chalk and begins writing it out. "Let me break it down for you."

I have to ask questions now and then, but it starts to make sense. At one point he does a series of steps and I have to stop him.

"You haven't studied Bayesian Analysis?" He looks at me like he was saying, "Never had pizza?"

I shake my head. Song clears a section of the blackboard and begins to explain. I just nod or say OK when I get it and he goes through it in about ten minutes. It reminds me of basic algebra. I remember thinking I could learn the entire semester in about two weeks if I had had a private tutor and could just say, "got it," whenever I had absorbed a topic and move on to the next. Instead the teacher would go on and on about some obvious point. Followed by an entire week of doing dozens of problems which were just variants on the same principle.

So we buzz through it and continue with Song's notes. At one point I ask what I think is a dumb question, but Song stops and thinks. Then goes back to the page he was working on and adds some notes.

"Excellent point," he said. "I think that would be a much more streamlined way to approach this."

We're scheduled for an hour and a half and I can't believe it when Song says, "Well, that's as far as we can take it today."

He reaches up behind him, takes out a thin text and hands it to me. *Algebraic Complexity Theorems.*

"On Thursday I'll show you how we can use this to get into that problem you outlined about the ratio of minerals to spybot development. Just go through the first three chapters. That will give you everything you need."

IN REAL LIFE

27.

That night I draw Sung Gi for our evening round-robins and we play a quick game. I can tell he's not into it. After I finish him off Yeong wanders out of the room. Sung Gi leans across the table and whispers.

"This is secret, but I leaving team."

"Quitting?"

"Yes. I have long talk with father this weekend. I go to school. Study engineer."

I'm thinking, it's that easy?

"Is that what you want?"

"Oh yes," he says. "I am very tired of playing many hours of Starfare. And I tell father that I never get so good as Sang-Chul or even Tae-Uk. Maybe you not know. My father is senior vice president with ANC. He put me on team. It is father's dream that I be great champion. Not my dream."

"But who will I talk with?"

"You will be good. No worry. I think you are getting better and better. And maybe new player will speak English with you like I do."

"Maybe."

"Anyway. My father will speak to Coach Yeong soon. Say that I will be going back to school."

"OK, man. Good luck. I'm actually sort of jealous."

"Jealous?"

"You know. Like I wish I could do what you are doing."

"You want engineer too?"

I shake my head. "No, not really. Just that you've decided exactly what you want to do. And I'm still not sure."

Then Yeong comes back and yells something and we switch partners and I get Tae-Uk. He grins as he sits down in front of the monitor across from me. I can tell he's going to be all business. These guys seem to really get a kick out of beating me.

250

It doesn't help that I keep getting distracted. I start my mining operation in the standard Team Anaconda spiral style. I remember that it was one of the first things Yeong taught me. But then I start wondering about whether any spiral is as good as the next, and whether it could be determined mathematically. I remember studying logarithmic spirals as some sort of digression in pre-calc. I jot down the formula.

$$r = e^{\,a\phi}$$

When I look up from my notepad I see that Tae-Uk is looking around his monitor at me, puzzled. And when I look at my monitor I can see why. I've done absolutely nothing for the last fifteen seconds or so. I'm even more hopelessly behind than usual.

So I start punching up my development and I hear Tae-Uk sort of chuckle as he steps back into the game and begins the process of throttling whatever I try.

I'm OK with that, because I'm looking forward to meeting with Professor Song on Thursday and asking him about the spiral thing.

28.

I'm just a few minutes late to breakfast Friday morning, but when I get there everyone is looking at me like I just lost the deciding match in a team event against a kindergartner. I head to my regular table, in the corner, where Sung Gi is sitting alone. After everyone has their food, Sung Gi whispers that I should come with him. We both pick up our plates and head back to the kitchen.

Sung Gi glances back at the closed door and then leans in close. "I tell you important thing."

I nod.

"Last night team have big meeting with Coach Yeong. They not happy. Not happy that Yeong has you play against American team."

I start to say something, but he interrupts. "Yes, you won. They worry Yeong play you. When we play best Korean teams."

I nod, about to say that I'm worried too.

"You know. Team pay is better when team wins. Korean players worry you lose, they lose."

I wait for Sung Gi to continue.

"Yeong very, very mad. This not happen before. Korean players and coach, you understand?"

"That players try to tell the coach what to do?"

"Yes. But more. Players angry that you do not train like them. Go away for many hours."

"Hey, that's not my choice…"

We hear something from the breakfast room and Sung Gi looks nervously at the door.

"Not important. Players want you off team. They say you join American team. You be happy. Team Anaconda be happy."

I have no idea how to explain the complications here.

"OK, thanks for the info."

"This last week."

"For me?" I say.

"No, no. For me. I start tutor program to get ready for university tests."

"Oh. So soon."

Because that leaves me with no one to sit with at meals. Or to explain stuff that I miss. Like the team lobbying to get rid of me.

"I like you ActionSeth," Sung Gi says. "Yeong likes you. Sponsors like you. More important than players like you."

"Right," I say, thinking, that's easy for you to say. You won't have to live with these guys from dawn to dusk, day after day. "Thanks for telling me."

Then we hear one of the players leaning into the door to the kitchen and we step apart. Pretend to be trying to make a decision. More kimchi or salted fish?

29.

That morning at my gaming station I realize something. It's not that my place in the world has suddenly changed. It's just that I suddenly see it clearly. It's like trying to figure out when, between the ages of eleven and thirteen, girls had shifted from being simply otherly to objects of obsession. At some point, who cares, bring on the girls.

For a long time, probably months, the hours of playing Starfare have begun to shift from something that was totally fun back in Kansas to something else entirely. I'm putting in my hours, at least as many as my schedule allows. But I can scarcely remember the excitement I used to have, sneaking out of school early, racing back to Dad's place to fire up my computer. Playing Starfare used to take me to this other place. Like those researchers at the Institute talked about. Transcendence. Now it's mostly about stress.

My mind is wandering as I wait for a practice game to start. I'm thinking about what Hannah is doing back in Kansas. Wondering what time it is at the Institute in California. If Dad is already at the airport. If Garrett is depressed, now that his college basketball career is over and graduation is coming up. He texted he doesn't even want to go to the ceremony but Mom and Dad are making him. I don't know. I bet he'll get a huge cheer from all the basketball fans. Mom will probably give him something stupid for graduation, like a yoga mat. Dad will probably give him his old golf clubs or something. I know it can take forever to ship stuff from Korea so I make a note to wrap up one of my Anaconda shirts and send it to him. I think he'll get a kick out of it.

Then I start thinking about the last meeting I had with Song. It was really amazing the way we could get into a problem and bounce ideas back and forth. We'd be scribbling notes and formulas as fast as we could write. And the feeling. The feeling is entirely familiar. It's the way I used to feel at the start of a Starfare game.

So I get through the morning and skip the team lunch. Go

back to my room. I've accumulated some snack food and have Cokes in the refrigerator. I grab a bag of Korean pretzels and a Coke. When I sit down at my laptop I see that there's a missed Skype call from Hannah. My pulse races as I call her back, first on her computer. No response. And then on her cell.

"Hannah?"

"Oh Seth! I just had to tell you!"

I wait for her to tell me about her new boyfriend. Eloping with the environmentally friendly tall guy.

"Remember the Nelson-Atkins Museum?"

I almost say, "Remember afterwards?" But instead just say sure.

"Well, they have this exhibit every spring. They select art done by high school students from all over the city? And I got three photos in the show! One of them is the sailor kiss. So you're going to be in an art museum!"

I tell her congratulations. But it's not me that will be in the museum. It'll be her.

"You deserve it, Hannah. Your stuff is great."

"I don't know about that. But thanks. At least someone liked them enough to put them into the show. I really, really wish you could be here for the opening. At the end of the month."

"Me too," I say. But it's not the exhibit I wish I could see. And touch. "Hey, do you have time to switch to your computer?"

I cut the call and reconnect to her computer. She picks up after about fifteen seconds. The first thing I see is her broad smile.

"Hey," she says. "Are you getting blonder?!"

"Maybe. The put this stinky stuff in my hair. But the hair guy, he doesn't speak a word of English."

I knew she was going to say something about my hair. Koreans have some weird thing for blonds. I had tried to protest, but Yeong stepped in and told me to shut up.

Hannah made a face. "Maybe it's just the lighting. But it looks really, really blond."

My red face probably made it look worse. "No. You're seeing right. Blond hair is really a big thing over here. Any Western celebrity, they get double visibility if they're blond. And you should see these pop stars with bleached hair. It's just wrong."

"Well, I think it looks fine. I'm just happy to be able to see you at all! Even if you kind of look like you're moving like a puppet."

I try to sit really still.

"So how's it going?" Hannah asks. "Have you won any more tournaments?"

"Not likely. But I did get some interesting news today."

"Yeah?"

"Well, I just heard that every other player on the team petitioned the coach to get rid of me."

Silence. Then, "You're kidding, right?"

"No. Serious. They hate me. I get all the attention. Get to play in matches when better players have to sit out. Make more money from endorsements. I'd hate me too."

"But, Seth. That's awful. None of that is your fault. They should hate the coach or whoever is making those decisions. Not you."

"They want me to transfer over to the new English-speaking team."

"That makes sense, doesn't it?"

"Not if you know who's running that team. Remember that guy who was always harassing me back home, Stomp? He's in charge. And he hates me worse than the Koreans. I am so totally screwed."

"Oh. That sucks. I mean, really sucks."

No argument from me.

"So what are you going to do?"

"I don't know, Hannah. I just don't know. But that's great news about the museum thing. I really wish I could be there."

"Me too. They have this big exhibition party. String quartet. Fancy food. I'm really looking forward to seeing what the other students have done."

"Yeah," I say. "That should be great."

"Hey one more thing," I add. "I just heard from my English e-course. I got a B on the final paper. That means I'll be graduating with you. I got this form letter from the school district. They want to know how I want my name to read in the graduation booklet. So look for me when it comes out, OK?"

We chat for a few more minutes but I know it's late back home and we only get a half-hour break for lunch. Then I have an hour of practice before I break for my now weekly Korean lesson. Which are still pretty awful, but I'm actually starting to look forward to them. Just getting away from the computer screen and the other guys. It's actually not so bad.

30.

Usually on Friday Choi brings me the team laundry. But that night, after practice, someone knocks on the door. When I open it no one is there. But the big duffle of laundry is there. It seems extra heavy as I drag it in and as soon as I get it inside the door I realize that something is wrong. I gingerly pull the ties at the top and as I do an awful odor rises. I snap my head back and notice that the bottom third of the bag is wet.

The whole team must have pissed in it.

No wonder Sunday is turning out to be the best day of the week by far. No practice. Plus, I really enjoy visiting the Kims. Goofing around with little Alex, playing some stupid video game, just for fun. And the food is always great.

The previous Sunday Annie had actually made pizza from scratch. And while it wasn't quite Westport, or even Saviano's, it was the most delicious meal I'd had in months.

So on Saturday when I get a call from Kim asking if I could come over early, spend the afternoon, I say sure. He says that Song is going to be there too. Has some stuff to discuss.

"Pick you up at noon?" he asks.

While I'm waiting to get picked up I'm debating with myself whether I should tell Kim and Annie about what's going on with the team. With me. Normally I never talk about stuff like that. I just figure I can work it out myself.

Kim pulls up just on time, like always. As I step outside I realize that I don't even need a hoodie. It must be the warmest day since I've arrived.

"Hop in," he says. And just hearing a stupid expression like that makes me instantly happy.

"We're going to take a little detour," Kim announces. I ask what for, but he says it's a surprise. All I can think of is that they've put another giant poster of me up downtown. I'm praying it's something else.

My prayers are answered when Kim scoots around a corner and suddenly we're driving down a street that's a tunnel of white flowers.

"This is a very famous street," Kim explains. "Yunjung-ro. See, at the end, that large building? That's our National Assembly."

"Wow," I say, as we cruise down the street, surrounded by white blossoms. Off to the right is a river, with more trees in blossom. Hundreds of Koreans are walking along a path under the trees.

"Fourteen hundred cherry trees on this street alone," Kim says. "It's my favorite time of the year here in Seoul."

When we get back to Kim's place I get a hug from Annie and Alex grabs my hand and drags me towards his playroom.

"Honey," Annie says. "You're going to dislocate his arm! He's not going anywhere—right Seth?"

"Actually, I'm going to take on Korea's number one eight year old Mario Karter."

Annie laughs and tells Alex that he can only have me for a bit, since Professor Song is coming over to talk.

"Then we have to hurry," Alex says, and I let him drag me toward the waiting controllers.

"Something to drink?" Annie calls out.

"Nothing for me," I say.

"Can I have a Coke?" Alex replies.

"No you can't have a Coke," Annie says. "You know that."

"But this is special," Alex pleads as we head down the hall. "ActionSeth is here!"

I see Annie smiling and shaking her head as we duck through the doorway.

Alex groans when Annie steps in to say that Professor Song has arrived. But I promise him that we can get in another game after dinner. That seems to satisfy him.

When I step into the living room Song is sitting on the couch, with a manila folder in his lap. He jumps up, beaming, and bounds across the room to shake my hand.

"Come. Sit down, sit down," he says. "I have something very exciting to show you."

I follow him back to the couch and he opens up the folder so we can both read what's inside.

It's a stapled paper. The title reads "Algorithmic Solutions to Optimizing Strategic Decisions in Starfare Cyber Games." After this are two names in bold, Kyung Chan Song and Seth Armstrong Gordon.

"How'd you know my middle name?" is the first idiotic thing I say.

Song thankfully ignores me and says, "You must forgive me, because the deadline was last week, and I needed to get a draft submitted. We can still change anything. Anything."

I pick up the paper and begin the thumb through it. It's a compilation of the problems that we've been working on. All neatly laid out and full of academic jargon.

"Wow," I say. "This looks like a lot of work."

"The hard work was already done. Once you've done a few of these papers, the layout is simple."

"OK," I say, not believing a word of it. The paper is about fourteen pages long. It would take me months to do anything close to this.

"So anyway," Song is saying. "I've sent it in for peer review for presentation to the annual meeting of the Southeast Asian Mathematical Society at the end of June in Bangkok. I'm very optimistic that it will be accepted. If so, we must arrange for you to help present."

"I don't know," I say, thinking that Song had written the entire thing.

"Yes, yes. I insist. I am very optimistic. This is very interesting work. And it is yours."

"Not mine," I protest, glancing through the paper. Reading some of the formulas. "I mean, I might have gotten started on some of these. But…"

"Nonsense. Perfect example of collaboration. And I'm also going to send it to a few journals. After you've looked it over. It would be very prestigious for a young mathematician like you to get published. Very prestigious."

I'm thinking, mathematician? I'm the pitchman for a crappy orange soda. A mediocre Starfare pro. The Korean national seventeen-and-under champ. But mathematician?

Kim and Annie enter the room, like they had been prompted. Kim shakes my hand and says he is very proud of my work. Annie is beaming like I'm related.

And here I was going to get them all together and tell them that my life was falling apart. Which when I think about it, it still is. Some obscure math paper is not going to change that.

I'm sure they're all wondering why I'm so somber during dinner. Afterwards I just say that I'm not feeling that well and ask if it's OK for Kim to take me home early. Alex is crestfallen but I really need some time alone.

When I get back to my apartment, I look at my IMs and messages. Check my phone for texts. Flip through the Korean TV channels and then say, the hell with it. Grab a sweatshirt and head downstairs and onto the street, waving for a cab.

When a taxi finally pulls over I try "naiteu keuleob"—nightclub. Then, "Helios." He seems to understand.

31.

I must be early because there's no line outside. But I still have to pay a cover charge. And the music is just as loud, even though the dance floor is mostly empty. I scoot around the edge of the room to the bar and get a Coke. Try to remember where the stairs are to the upstairs lounge. Keeping an eye out for the girl with the red streak. Sumi. I would really prefer not to see her.

I find the stairs, make my way through the doors. The music dimming behind me. At first I think the booth in the back is empty but when I get close I see two people sitting with drinks. The Australian guy and Sarah, the girl whose parents I met in customs.

"Well, look who's here," the Aussie says. "It's Gamer Boy. Come on, lots of room, mate."

As I sit down he says, "Guy Hamilton. In case you forgot. And this is…"

"Sarah," I interrupt.

"Hello, Seth," she says. "We've been wondering if you would make it back."

Guy points at my drink. "You got some ActionOrange there?"

I shake my head. "Have you tried that slop? Tastes like poison, like Agent Orange, if you ask me."

Maybe they've been drinking for a while, because they both seem to think this is hilarious.

I slide into the booth on Sarah's side.

"So, we spent a whole Sunday talking about you," Sarah says. "You know, after that picture showed up in the tabloids. We figured you got a little heat over that."

"More like a lot," I said. "I was really worried that I'd see that girl again."

"Don't worry," Guy says. "We'll protect you. Right, Sarah?"

"Like a mother bear protects her cubs."

I ask them how things are going at their jobs and they both groan.

"We come here to forget that stuff," Guy says. "So how about you? Haven't seen you on TV lately. Other than that commercial."

"Don't remind me," I say. I try to make light of it all, but Sarah is immediately on to me. She keeps saying that something must be wrong. That she can tell. And between the two of them they sort of squeeze it out of me. How the team has rejected me. How I've lost the spark. That the only good stuff has nothing to do with Team Anaconda. And I tell them about the work I've been doing with the math professor.

After I've told them I feel a little better. But lame too, for pouring all this personal stuff on people I hardly know. I almost mention Hannah seeing that picture of Sumi, but that would mean explaining me and Hannah. And how can I explain something I don't even really understand?

But Sarah seems really interested. And disturbed.

"So what are you going to do?" she says. "You know this is never going to work, right? They're not interested in you. And I don't mean just helping you become the best player you could be. They're just using you to help with the ratings, to sell soda."

I don't know what to say. Because hearing it like that, I know it's true. I'll never overcome the language barrier. The players are never going to accept me. I could stay with Team Anaconda for years and still be a second-tier player.

"You've got family at home   right?" Sarah asks.

"Sort of," I say. And tell them about how my mom has joined some sort of cult. And my dad, always on the road. "Personally, I've been trying to figure out how I could wrap things up and start college."

"So you could get a degree, come back and teach English like us, right?" Guy says, with a sad smile.

"But I don't know," I said. "I think I screwed that up too. It's so late. Kids are already getting acceptance letters."

"You taken your boards?" Sarah asks.

I give her a lost look.

"You know, like SATs."

"Oh, of course," I say. "Well, sort of. I took them in eighth grade."

"People take SATs in eighth grade?" Sarah asks.

"It was some sort of talent identification program thing," I said. "You take the SATs and then a bunch of colleges try to get you come for these really expensive summer programs."

"So what did you get?" Guy says.

"Get?"

"You know. On the test."

"Oh, I don't remember exactly," I say. "I know I made this stupid mistake on one of the math questions. So I got a 760 there. And on the English. I'm not that good. I think I just barely got 700. We didn't have to do the essay."

"Christ, that would be 1460," Sarah says. "And you were, what? Fourteen?"

"Thirteen," I say. "I sort of skipped a grade somewhere in there."

Sarah and Guy exchange glances.

"You should take it again," Sarah says. "It's not too late. I've got a couple of kids taking it again in three weeks. You've got a couple days before the deadline. Sign up."

"I don't know," I say. "It's complicated. I'd have to get permission. Figure out where it is. How to get there."

"Bullshit," Sarah says. Pulls out her cell and makes me give her my number. "I'll text you the URL and you sign up. You do have a credit card?"

I nod.

"Ok, now give me your address." She keys that in too. "You sign up and I'll pick you up. It's given on Sundays here. That's your day off?"

I nod again.

"Fine. I'll pick you up and take you to the test. Least I can do."

And when I cab home a few hours later, I go online and sign up for the SATs. I just hope they don't have any questions on the last half of *The Scarlet Letter*.

32.

So three weeks later, I'm sitting at dinner with Kim and Annie and say, "Guess what I did this morning?"

The two of them look at each other and shrug.

"Beat the world record for Mario Kart?" Alex guesses.

"Not quite," I say. "I took the SATs."

Kim and Annie exchange another sort of look.

"I'm thinking of winding down my Starfare career." And realize that it's the first time I've actually said it out loud. It feels surprisingly good.

"But you just started," Alex squeals. "You haven't won the World Championship yet."

"Well, that's true," I admit as Annie gently tries to shush Alex.

"Why don't we talk about this after dinner?" Annie says, shooting at glance at Alex. I nod and turn to him and say, "So what's this I hear about a school trip to the natural history museum?"

"They've got a huge shark!" Alex says. "His teeth are this tall!" He holds his hands as far apart as possible. "I mean it's not a live shark. It's shark bones. But it's huge!"

We let Alex finish his tour of the museum. And then Annie sends him to play some games. And I tell them about the problems with the team. I leave out the pissing in the laundry thing.

"It's just not working," I say.

Annie looks so sad I think she's going to cry.

"Oh Seth," she finally says. "We had no idea. We were like Alex. We thought you were living a dream."

"Oh I am," I said. "This was exactly what I wanted. It's just that I had no way of knowing…"

"No, you couldn't have," said Kim. "But you are so young. And have so many options."

I nod. Wondering if it's true.

"Anyway," I say. "I was thinking of talking to Song. About studying math in the U.S. You know, where I might go. How I might get in. Pay for it."

"Yeah, you definitely need to talk to Song," Kim says. "If fact, let me give him a call. He lives only five minutes away."

When Song arrives I give him a shorter version of my sad story. But he doesn't think it is sad. He keeps saying things like, "Very good," and "All for the best."

"And you just took the SAT test today?" he asks.

I nod. Kim and Annie and Song are all sitting in a circle with me, leaning towards me and speaking softly, as if Alex might be around the corner, trying to listen.

"And how did it go?"

I tell him that I thought I got all the math right. Unless I did something really stupid. And the English wasn't as hard as I remember. And I thought I did OK on the essay. I chose the topic about whether or not the grading system in high schools should be revised. I did this essay on why it should be because it didn't reflect the real world.

"Think about it," I say. "Let's say you study three hours a day and get an A in math. And someone else gets an A without studying at all. If you have a job and it takes you ten times as long to do something, even if you do it just as well, you're not nearly as valuable to the company. So I wrote about the need to add an effort component."

They all look a little puzzled.

"Hey, it was just a stupid essay. Don't worry. I made my case. I even made up a study to support my argument that I said was done at Yale. Who's going to take the time to check it out…"

They laugh at this.

"So you are committed to this course," Song says. "You are going to leave all this behind? I mean, you're the only person I know who has been on the Tommy Min show."

"Or has his own soda," Annie adds.

And I realize, in a flash, that I must look to them so different than I look to myself. Like some sort of success prodigy. The amazing sixteen year old celebrity.

"I've got a few ideas for you. Brown might be a really good

match," Song finally says. "Let me do a little work and I'll bring you up to date in a few days."

"And no matter what you decide," Annie says, "you know you are always welcome here, in this house. If it gets too bad for you downtown, with the team. You call. We'll put up a cot in the play-room and you can stay with us."

"Absolutely," says Kim. "It would be our great pleasure."

33.

I'm ready to face Yeong the next day. But think better of it. I want to get things worked out first. Make sure I have an alternative. Access to the money in my account. Which is somewhere around $30,000 now, depending on the exchange rate.

So I do my best to put up a good face. Smile at the guys at break-fast. Try to concentrate during the practice sessions.

At the end of the week I get a call from Song. He says that he's got some information for me. That we can go over it at Kim's on Sunday.

That takes the bite out of any initiative I have left. Yeong stops by and watches over my shoulder at morning practice, sniffing and grunting as I try to ramp it up under his eyes. He watches for about ten minutes and then walks away, not saying a thing.

We have another dual match on Saturday and it's against the Analogs, one of Anaconda's biggest rivals. I'm praying Yeong comes to his senses and leaves me out of the lineup.

So Saturday afternoon it's the familiar scene. The team gath-ered back stage around Coach Yeong. The sound of the crowd in the background, fast-paced Korean pop music over the PA system. The team all dressed in our green snake shirts, shifting nervously. The outcome of these duals determines who makes the playoffs, and the bonus pool for the teams that make it is a big deal. A team can double their annual salaries by making it to the finals.

Yeong calls out the names, one at a time. The tops dogs, Sang-Chul and Tae-Uk, and then another four names, all expected. Then coach looks directly at me and my heart falls.

"ActionSeth," he says.

Immediately the other guys start moaning and shouting stuff out in Korean at Yeong. He waves his hand and puts on his best scowl. Then he begins berating the team in Korean, no translation necessary. And of course, we all know it has nothing to do with winning. It goes directly to the sponsors and endorsement deals. Which Yeong must get a huge cut on.

Then before the players can say another word the PA system switches from music to voice and I know from the routine that the player introductions are about to begin.

As the team heads toward the stage I get jostled from one side, then the other. One of the guys, I can't even tell who in the scrum, leans in and grunts, "You win. Or else." It's amazing how much English these guys have when they need it.

As the pairings are announced I have one hope. The Analog's top player, Jun Hwa Jung, is the hottest guy on the circuit. The only guy on the team who has a chance against him is Sang-Chul, and I bet the coach would not like to see that matchup. Because Sang-Chul is automatic against anyone else on the Analogs. So if I draw Jun Hwa and lose, it really won't hurt the team.

But as the lineups are announced Jun Hwa draws our number four player and I get a matchup against one of Analog's rookie pros. A match the team could expect to win.

As the match slowly gets away from me I feel myself starting to sweat out my shirt. It's not just losing. I'm furious at Yeong for putting me in this spot when he knows I'm not ready. I can already feel the heat from the other guys too. God knows what they're going to do to me. Especially if the team loses.

My loss is the first match done. I have to sit on the sidelines and watch the excruciating process as we win one, lose one, win one. And then drop the deciding match to lose 4-3. The van ride back is silent. I'm wondering if the guys are looking for an opportunity to jump me. I bet at least half of them studied martial arts. I can see them kicking the shit of me in some dark corner.

So I'm the first one out of the van and I scramble up to my room, lock the door. I sit back on the couch with a sigh of relief. When my breathing gets back to normal I decide to do a little research on Brown. The home page has a video and it opens with these cool-looking buildings and then some dancers, backlit and in silhouette this one dancer looks just like Hannah and my heart just leaps. I check out the math department and the courses and only when I dig a little deeper do I realize the school's right in the middle of Providence, Rhode Island. It's a long way from Kansas, but a lot closer than Seoul. Then I remember Annie is from Providence. I make a mental note to ask her about what it's like, living there.

34.

On Sunday Song is waiting for me when we get to the Kims'. He seems as pleased to see me as Alex, who must have been briefed on my availability. Alex runs up, gives me a big hug and then runs back to his playroom.

"OK, OK," Song says. "Sit down. I've got stuff for you."

He's got a big folder and he motions me to sit next to him on the couch. He thumbs through it and shows me a couple printouts of forms.

"I've talked to a few of my old colleagues in the Brown math department," he says. "They say they'd be very interested in hearing from you. So here's what you have to do."

He pulls out a page.

"This is just the first page of the online application. You have to fill this out when you get home."

Attached is a checklist of things I need to do. Email North and get my high school transcript sent. I mentally add the same for UMKC. For letters of recommendations I've got Song. I have to get hold of my prof from UMKC and get him to write me a second one. Get Mom and Dad to fill out this complicated-looking form for financial aid. Make sure that Brown gets my SAT scores.

"This is also online," Song says. Handing me another printout. It's titled, Hershman Fellowships for Undergraduates. "Brown got his huge gift a few years ago. It provides for full scholarships, merit based. Make sure you fill it out carefully."

Then he shows me a handful of copies of the math paper.

"This is your trump card," he said. "I've already forwarded copies to the math department and I've emailed you an e-copy. You're going to need to attach that to your Hershman application."

I just nod as he goes through it all. I mean, I still don't know much about Brown. Kim said that they were known for their applied mathematics. They have a nice website. That's about it.

But I've got this feeling. Like a warm spot inside my chest that's slowly expanding. A feeling that maybe things might work out after all. That I could go back home, see Hannah, go to college like a normal kid. Study stuff I liked and was good at. And throw the Team Anaconda laundry back in their faces. Or maybe just throw it out. Just to spite them. After I get my money out of the bank, of course.

When I get back to my apartment I sit down at my laptop to find out more about Brown. But there's a Skype message from Hannah. I call her on her computer, but she's not online. So then I have to add some money to my account so I can call her cell.

"Hey," she says, picking up after the first ring. "When you didn't answer? I was worried. Thought maybe you got strangled by those Anacondas."

"Funny," I say.

"So are you getting along better?"

"Worse," I say. "I dropped a match last week and the team lost 3-4."

"Doesn't that mean that three other guys lost too?"

"Sure, but that's not the way they see it."

"No offense," Hannah says. "But it sounds like those Koreans are really messed up."

"It doesn't matter," I say. And I mean it.

"No?"

I want to tell her about the latest development. But it's all so iffy. I can tell her when I know more for sure.

"Anyway," Hannah says. "I've got more good news!"

"Yeah?"

"You know we had the opening at the museum last week? It was so great. I got to meet the other kids. They had such amazing work. There's one kid, from this magnet school in downtown Kansas City. He does these charcoal drawings that are so…"

And in an instance I see what's happened. Hannah and this artsy boy from the inner city. Hitting it off immediately. Soul mates. Sneaking off to some dark corner of the museum. And then, after the reception…

"Sorry. I mean, you'd have to see his work to understand. Anyway, getting back to the good news. At the reception I met this really cool lady who runs a gallery. It's in the Plaza. Right down the street from FAO Schwartz. I bet you've walked by it a million times."

"I can picture it," I say. Although I can only really picture the toy store with its giant stuffed animals.

"So she sees my photos and tracks me down. We chat about this and that. She asks if I have more work. So yesterday I take my whole portfolio to her gallery and I just about died. She says she's interested in representing me. Picks out six photos. I have to get them printed up in a limited edition. She's going to try to sell them for $400 each! I get $300 for each one she sells!"

"That's a lot of hours at Saviano's," I say.

"No kidding. Plus she wants to see my new work as I do it. So who knows…I mean, Seth, I don't know if you understand this. But to get represented at a gallery like this. It's so unbelievable. I mean, there's plenty of artists who've been studying and working for years. People with MFAs, who do really great work, who would kill to be in this spot. It's just so unbelievable."

"I told you you were good," I say.

"Well, yeah you did. So maybe you do have a future as an art critic. In case this gaming thing doesn't work out."

I'm thinking that it's going to work itself out all right. And soon, if I have anything to do with it.

"And I've got to email you this form. It's a model release. For the kiss photo. Maybe you could print and sign it and scan it back?"

"It's going to cost you," I say. "After all, I already have one big endorsement deal."

"How about I give you a percentage. If I ever sell one."

"How about we get together and practice making another one," I blurt out. As soon as I say it, I'm sure I've crossed some line.

And sure enough, there's a silence.

"Seth?" she finally says.

"Yeah. I'm sorry…"

"No. It's just that it's not the same. Here. With you away. I don't know."

"What if I told you I was coming back?"

"For a visit?"

"For good."

"Seth, are you joking around?" I can't tell if she's excited or worried.

"I'm serious. I'm not sure I can take it here much longer," I say. "And I do have a return ticket."

I've had that ticket in my hand a few times over the past weeks. Sitting there in my apartment. Holding it and thinking about how easy it would be to call a cab and just head out to the airport. Without even a goodbye to my dear teammates.

"If it's as bad as you say, then you ought to just do it."

I'm thinking, that's me. The just-do-it American.

"But, Seth. It's not going to be the same."

I'm not sure what she means. But I'm thinking it has to do with that tall guy in the environment club. Or the guy with the charcoal drawings.

"OK," I say. "I know…I've been gone a long time. And I know there are other guys…"

"It's not like that," she says. "It's just that it's never the same. People go away. They come back. They've changed. Things change."

"I'm pretty sure I haven't changed," I say. "Although I do know how to bow a little."

"OK, wise-ass," Hannah says. "You're blond and have a weird haircut. Case closed."

"I can dye it back."

"Yes you can," Hannah says. "And maybe you should. But in the meantime, just sign that form, will you?"

I promise I will. But what I'm thinking is, be prepared. I might just deliver it in person.

After she hangs up I get online, see what I can figure out about what courses I could be taking in the fall if this Brown thing works out.

35.

I have to get up on Monday for team breakfast. As soon as the alarm goes off I'm thinking about what I read the night before. About how little I know about colleges. For instance, Brown is in the Ivy League. Like Harvard and Yale. That's how bad I'd fail a test on American universities. And then I'm thinking about my slack-off semesters at North. Why would a school like that be interested in me? Plus it costs like $60,000 a year, which is going to give Dad a heart attack if he finds out.

He'd just remind me how Garrett got a free ride and graduated on time on top of it. Mom and Dad were so grateful they both showed up. Mom sent a bunch of blurry photos of the ceremony and Garrett in his graduation costume. Naturally, not a single photo of the three of them together.

So I think about my salary and the bonus I might get if I hang in there the whole season. I keep swinging back and forth. Work my ass off and show these guys that I deserve to be on the team. Or just screw it and do as little as possible. See how long they'll keep me.

After breakfast Yeong pulls me aside.

"No more Korean lessons. Not during season. You stay, work hard."

"Yes Coach," I say. But what I'm thinking is, up yours. Even though the "best teacher in Seoul" is a fraud, it was better than hanging here all day.

But, like always when we do afternoon practice matches, I don't have to fake it. I've always hated losing. I take two of the lower guys on the team into the third game in best of threes and probably should have won both of them.

You know, it's kind of the same thing Garrett told me once. He was out in the driveway, shooting free throws. I stood out on front stoop and watched him for a while. Two bounces, spin the ball, shoot. Retrieve the ball, do it again.

"How can you stand to do that over and over," I finally said. "For hours. It looks totally boring."

Garrett turned and looked at me. That look of total condescension.

"You get better whether you're bored or not."

I'm also finding out it takes forever to get all these forms completed and transcripts and scores sent. I go online every day and check out my admissions status. So far all they have is my electronic application. Meanwhile I imagine the number of openings dropping on a daily basis.

I call Song up.

"Don't worry," he says. "You're in a special situation. They don't get many prospective students who are gamer pros who have co-authored a paper accepted for the Southeast Asian Mathematics Society annual meeting in June."

"They took it?"

"Of course," Song is saying. I can picture him grinning. "You did very good work."

"You did the work," I insist, and I congratulate him. He says that I should plan on coming with him to present. That I would enjoy seeing Bangkok before I returned to the United States to start my promising career in mathematics.

But it seems clear to me that I'm going to be around for a while. The pro league season goes all summer, with the playoffs in the fall. After the loss to the Analogs we've been picking up win after win. It looks like we'll be in the playoffs for sure. And that could mean big bonuses.

So I've got that working for me.

36.

I get emails from both Mom and Dad. They're both freaked out about the FAFSA forms for college aid.

Mom, I talk through. They've got a high school at the Institute. So they've got counselors who can answer the questions. Help her fill it out. I know she's making just enough to pay her expenses, so that's good for my prospects.

Dad, on the other hand, is paranoid. He thinks I'm going to hit him up with some enormous college bill.

"Just so you know," he writes. "With the divorce and the problems at work and the economy. I wish it wasn't so. But I don't have anything saved for college. And this year was probably my worst in a decade."

I try to calm him down. Explain that I'm not asking for money. Tell him that I'm saving some money. And I still have my account in Kansas City, with the $2,000 from Nationals. That he just needs to fill out the forms. I even give him the name of my old counselor at North, in case he has questions.

So that night I complete Hannah's model release. Scan it on the team's copier and email it back. Think about the picture of the two of us. Hanging in some fancy gallery in the Plaza. How totally weird it would be to walk in there and see it. Me and Hannah.

Wondering if that's what we are. A photo in an album. A little snippet of ancient history. Hannah thumbing though her work years from now. The tall guy from the environmental club sitting next to her, arm around her. I imagine him going bald.

"And who's that in the picture?" he will ask.

"Just a guy I knew for a while when I first moved to Kansas. We worked together in that pizza place that used to be in the strip mall. Around the corner from KenTacoHut."

And then they turn the page.

37.

As we get into summer Yeong seems to be getting better at how to use me. I sit out the close ones, play when we win 6-1 or 5-2. If I had any time outside I'd probably admit that I like Korea better in the summer than the winter. It was certainly more pleasant to run out for Tost-us. When I can, I sneak outside during breaks. I like to look at the Korean girls. As the weather warmed they shifted to short skirts, leather boots. Sometimes a small group of them will stop and cover their mouths and laugh in my direction. I've never said a word to any of them.

If I forget to put something over my Anaconda team shirt, everyone seems to recognize me. Take pictures with their cell phones. Occasionally ask for an autograph. Young guys in business suits will try to corner me to practice their English. It's actually pretty annoying.

By the end of June Anaconda is right at the top of the standings and the players are basically leaving me alone. Over the past few weeks I actually had won a few matches, surprising everyone. But even when I lost it wasn't affecting the outcome. So I guess they were resigned to putting up with me.

We're about two thirds of the way through the season when Choi hands me a package at breakfast. It's a big white envelope with Brown University stamped on the top. I don't want to open it there, so I slip out and take it back to my room.

My heart's racing as I rip it open.

I read the first line, "We are pleased…" and then skim, looking for anything on the scholarship. Because getting in was not the same as going. Not at $60k a year.

It's in the second paragraph. "The Hershman Fellowship is intended to cover all of your tuition, living and academic costs for your entire undergraduate program, assuming that you maintain the standards itemized in the attached…"

I have to shake my head and read it again. Which I do. And then I just have to tell someone.

So I sit down at the laptop and send off IMs to DT and Garrett. Write a quick email to Mom and Dad. Send a text to Hannah. Then I send a note to Song, thanking him for all the help and the recommendation. And one to Annie and Kim, telling them the news.

Then I open the drawer with the airline ticket. Go to the American Airlines site and begin looking at schedules. I'm deep into this when someone bangs at the door.

"Not feeling well," I yell.

They bang again.

"I'm sick. Leave me alone."

That seems to do it.

So I book a flight out Monday morning. Send out my itinerary to everyone back in the States. Then I sneak out of my apartment and take the elevator to the lowest level. Walk out the back through the loading dock so the doorman doesn't see me.

I know there's a Woori Bank branch down the street. I go in, cash out my entire account in won. Take it down another block to a Citigroup branch. Just in case Yeong or someone tries to muck with my earnings. Sit for about ten minutes until an English-speaking banker is available. Set up a new account, which I'm told I can wire out to a bank back home without any complications.

I hold out enough money to cover a few special expenses. From the lobby I call Sarah and we have lunch.

When I show her the letter from Brown, she says, "Omigod. This is fantastic!"

I nod. Thank her for the help. When I walk her back to work we stop in front. She reaches out with both hands and holds my face and plants a sharp kiss on my lips.

"You are just so adorable," still holding me. "And smart too. I wish they made you in my age!" We say goodbye and she makes me promise to write.

When I get back to my apartment I check my messages. Kim and Annie and Song have sent notes of congrats. I'll have one more Sunday dinner with them and Song will come too. My emails arrived late back in the U.S. and I'm betting no one has picked them up.

I hang around until team lunch. This will be the fun part.

38.

When I walk into lunch no one pays any attention. Most of the guys have their trays of food. They don't even look up. When Yeong sees me he walks over.

"You feel better?"

"I'm OK," I say. Now that I'm getting ready to announce my resignation, it no longer feels like such a great moment.

"Look," I say. "I'm not very good at these things. So I'll just tell you straight out."

Yeong is looking at me in the eyes, puzzled.

"I need to resign from the team."

Yeong shakes his head. "No, this is not possible," he says. I imagine he's thinking about the endorsements and the publicity I've been getting the team.

"I have a flight out on Monday," I say. "It's been a great experience. But it's not going to work out."

"Yes, yes. We are working out good!" Yeong seems totally unwound. "Season playoffs soon. Players get big bonus. No one leaves teams now. No one." His voice is raised and the players are now looking up from their food. Trying to follow the English.

"Well, I am. I'm starting school at the end of August. I've got to get back home and get prepared. I think I should say something to the other players."

Then I walk up to the front of the room.

"Can I have your attention please!" I say loudly. "I just want to tell all of you that I am leaving the team. As of today."

There is an immediate buzz as the players collectively try to translate. I look over to Yeong, to see if he is going to translate. But he looks stricken. I try to keep it simple.

"So this is goodbye. I learned a lot from you. Thank you for putting up with me. Good luck with the rest of the season. I know you will do well."

Then I turn and walk out the door, into the hall. As I head to my room I feel so much lighter that its like floating.

39.

The next few days are a whirlwind. I spend Saturday morning with the crowds in the Myeong-dong shopping district. Wearing a baseball hat and sunglasses, which seems like a pretty lame disguise. But I'm amazed that it seems to work—no one bothers me. I'm trying to find presents for people back home. But mostly something for Hannah. You would think that with hundreds of shops it would be easy, but it's just about impossible.

Finally I decide I need help and I call Annie and Kim's home number. Annie picks up. I explain that I've trying to find presents for my mom and dad and brother. And this special girl from back home. Who I haven't seen in more than six months.

"Hang on," Annie says. I wait for a couple of minutes.

"You say you're in Myeong-dong? Kim's got Alex for a few hours. I can meet you at one o'clock."

I protest. Say that I was just looking for a couple of ideas.

"Are you kidding?" Annie says. "I love to shop. Especially in Myeong-dong. And I'm very good at it, thank you."

She tells me to meet her in the coffee shop at the Ibis Hotel. "It's right in the center of the district. If you need help finding it, just ask anyone."

I figure I've got well over an hour. That gives me time to get something for the Kims and Song. I still beat Annie to the hotel, sit at a booth and order a Coke.

After about ten minutes Annie bustles in. Just about everyone in the café turns to look at her and I realize that I've only seen her at her apartment. I can see why they're staring. Not just because she's tall and blond. But I've never really thought about how pretty she is.

She sits down and starts talking a mile a minute. Pulls out a little notebook and starts asking me questions about everyone on my gift list.

A couple hours later I'm carrying about twenty pounds of gifts in a half-dozen shopping bags. Shopping with Annie was like watching Anaconda's top player in a Starfare groove. We share a cab back and she gets dropped first. She makes me promise to come over early Sunday afternoon. For Alex's sake.

When I get back I throw the shopping bags on the couch and get on the computer. Everyone has gotten back to me. Mom wants me to book a trip to California "for at least three weeks." Garrett says he's working basketball camps for the summer while he's waiting to hear from the European teams. Dad says he'll stock the refrigerator but that he's going to be at a show all week and can't get out of it. So I'll have to take a cab from the airport. Hannah has left me this message, "Congrats on Brown! Call me when you get back!"

So she can tell me about her new boyfriend? An environmental artist who just won a MacArthur genius award for his multimedia performance art?

After starting and stopping about ten times I finally send a short message, asking if she'd consider picking me up at the KC airport. I get in at 9 p.m. local time. Hoping she comes alone.

I bought some wrapping paper before Annie arrived and I fold up one of my ActionSeth team shirts, wrap it up and write "Alex" on it. For the Kims I wrap up Hannah's sailor photo. And a really cool small framed oil painting of the cherry blossom street I found in a gallery. For Song I wrap a small, polished box made of black stone filled with spiral-shaped fossils. I think it will make him think of the Bernoulli spirals we calculated for the optimal Starfare mineral harvests.

For Garrett Annie suggested a goofy K-pop outfit, so he could dress up like Psy. When I cab over to Kim's house on Sunday, the whole way I'm trying to figure out what to tell them. Like how much I appreciated Annie's shopping help. I have this whole little speech worked out but when I get there and begin she just laughs it off. I have my presents in my backpack, for later.

I hang out, play some games with Alex. When Song arrives we all head to the parking garage and cram into Kim's car. I'm relieved when we end up at a place that serves Korean-style barbeque. Kimchi optional. I fill up on these sticks of meat which are spicy but not so hot that they make you choke, like some Korean food.

Back at Kim's I explain I have to head back to pack. I'm really bad at these kinds of things. I never know what to say and whether to hug people or shake hands. But I do try to tell them all how much they helped me. And how much I'll miss them. I get out my presents and everyone opens them. At first the Kims seems kind of puzzled by Hannah's photo, so I have to give them the background. And they seem to like the cherry blossom painting. Song smiles as he holds up the spiral-encrusted box and I know he gets it. Everyone is kind of emotional but when Alex pulls out his shirt and starts crying it somehow breaks the ice. We all hug again. Kim insists on driving me home, but we don't say much.

Back at my apartment I pick up a message from Hannah.

Saying she'd be able to get the van and pick me up at the airport. Not that's she excited or delighted to pick me up. Just that she will. I'm thinking she'll want that nice, quiet, forty-minute drive to explain where things stood.

Still, I'm not without hope. So I Skype a call to Garrett, who thankfully picks right up.

"Christ," he says. "What the hell time is it over there?"

I tell him it's 9 p.m. on Sunday.

"Sunday? This is frickin' confusing as hell. Anyway. Sorry to hear your pro career is coming to a premature end."

"Yeah. No tears. I gave it an honest shot. How 'bout you?"

"I've got a maybe offer from a Greek team. Pay is OK. I just don't know if I want to play overseas."

"Yeah, I can relate to that."

"So are you going to come up and visit me when you get home?"

"Sure," I say. "Why not? Unless you've still got snow on the ground."

"Up yours, it's summer here."

We chat for a bit more before I drop my real reason for calling. I explain the situation with Hannah. How I'm pretty sure she's in some sort of relationship.

"But you're still hot on her right?"

I sort of mumble something, and he says, "I'm taking that as a yes. And you want to know what you should do."

"Sort of," I admit.

"Sort of my ass," he says. "OK, here's my advice. Do not, whatever you do. Do not give her any indication of your interest."

"Huh?"

"You get off that plane and say you've been pining over her for months you're just going to look pathetic."

"But I thought girls like that romantic stuff."

"Are you looking for advice or do you want to just totally fail?"

I say advice.

"Then trust me. If you come on like a love-lost puppy you're going to panic this girl. You're not just some dorky kid who she used to neck with. You're a celebrity. You've been worshipped abroad. You're now a man of the world. You have no interest in juvenile romances from your past."

"Yeah?"

"Yeah. And if she wants to confess that she's fallen in love with some college guy, she'll tell you. At least you'll know where you stand."

"OK," I say, even though I'm skeptical. "Thanks for the tip."

He makes me promise again to fly up to Fargo. That Dad has plenty of mileage points.

But even though I left the Kims' promptly I'm still up at 1 a.m. getting everything crammed into my suitcase. I leave behind a couple of beat-up T-shirts and all but one Team Anaconda shirt.

Who knows, I might go to a costume party some day.

40.

I don't realize how exhausting the whole process has been until I finally settle into my Korean Air seat. I feel like I'm sinking into the softest sofa in the world. I have some vague sense of a flight attendant making her rounds. When I wake up for a moment, groggy, we're already in the air and there is a pillow and blanket in my lap.

So the first ten hours of the trip is just a thankful blur. I finally wake up to activity in the cabin and get to the bathroom before the meal arrives. It's breakfast, I think, although the time is so screwed up who knows for sure.

When I stumble out of the plane in Los Angeles I feel like a zombie. But even zombies can walk and I find my way through customs and to the connecting flight. Watch an animated movie with hot-air balloons and talking dogs. Think about meeting Hannah at the airport. And what Garrett said.

The last leg of the trip is endless.

We're only a half-hour late arriving and I see her as soon as a crowd of us walk past the security gate. She's standing off to the side. Hasn't spotted me yet. Which is good. Because I'm literally short of breath, seeing her. She's cut her hair. Looks worried, kind of shifting from foot to foot. Like maybe I'm not on the flight? Or that maybe I am? I try to pull myself together. Step out from the crowd and she sees me. I head right towards her, drop my carry-on bag just short of her toes. I was thinking a Korean bow would impress her, but I just wrap my arms around her and give her a deep hug. Her hair smells like flowers, like cherry blossoms.

I step back, her hands still on my shoulders.

"Oh my God," she says. "I can't believe it!"

"Me either," I say. Thinking how I could have forgotten how amazing her eyes are, deep amber in this light. Wondering if she means, "thank God you're back" or "was I ever an idiot to agree to do this" or "Oh my God he looks like he's just spent the better part of a day crammed into an airline seat."

She's staring at me so hard that I want to turn away.

"I think you got taller," she says.

"Korean food," I say. "It's very nutritious."

We just look at either for another moment before she says, "So, how does it feel to be back in the U.S.?"

"Han gaji jim mun mot hae," I say, and then bend over to pick up my backpack. It's one of the totally useless phrases my Korean teacher had me memorize. Translation: "one language is never enough."

"Wow," says Hannah. "What does that mean?"

"It means, 'there's no place like home.'"

"Well, that may be true. But you're not in Kansas."

"Missouri," I say. "Close enough. Come on, let's get my bag and get out of here. The farther I get from airports, the better I'll feel."

"Can you say that in Korean?"

I think for a second and say, "Geu."

"You can get the entire sentence into one word?"

276

"Actually it's a common article in Korean, similar to our word 'that.'"

She blinks for a second and then smiles. "So you can say 'that' in Korean!"

"Exactly."

As we wait for the luggage carousel to start I ask about her photos and the gallery. She says that she's just started showing, but nothing has sold so far.

"I have a confession," I say, as we stare towards the stationary carousel.

"You don't have to tell me about all those Korean girls," she says. I look over at that familiar, sly smile. "That would be too much information."

"I'm sworn to secrecy about that," I say. "Actually, it's about your photo."

I tell her about the Kims and how nice they were to me. That I gave them the kissing photo. That I had shopped for hours but had found nothing nearly as good.

She doesn't seem upset. "I'll print you another one," she says as the carousel starts beeping and then turning.

A few minutes later I'm wrestling my bag off the belt and we're off for the parking lot.

As we cruise out of the airport Hannah glances over at me. "You must be exhausted."

"That obvious?"

"That obvious."

We drive in silence for a bit.

"I brought you something back from Korea."

"You brought yourself. That was enough."

I may be exhausted, but I'm alert enough to wonder if she's just saying that. Or if it means something.

Then she asks when I start school.

"Freshman orientation is August twenty-ninth. How about you?"

"After Labor Day weekend."

So we have almost five weeks. If we are we.

At my place I punch in the code for the garage and am thankful that it opens. I still have a key, but where I don't remember.

Hannah insists on helping me carry in.

When I flip on the light I see everything just the way I left it. The velour couch across from the flat screen TV. Hannah's favorite seascape over the larger couch.

"Now this is home sweet home," Hannah says.

"Just a second," I say as I bend over and unzip the big suitcase. I dig around a bit and come out with a white box.

"I would have wrapped it," I say. "But they tell you not to wrap presents that are going on planes."

Hannah looks uncomfortable as I hand it to her.

"Go ahead," I say. She backs over to the couch, sets the box down and opens it with a gasp. Pulls out the present that Annie helped me pick out and holds it up.

"Oh my God," Hannah says. She lifts the bright red, silk Korean dress head high. The gold highlights sparkle, even in the uneven light of our living room. I told Annie that I wanted to get something really special. That cost wasn't an issue. She took me at my word. It was one of the most expensive hanboks in the shop.

"I don't know," I say. "I thought maybe you could use it in one of your photos."

Hannah is sort of dancing forward with the hanbok stretched out.

"I bet you stole this from one of your Korean girls."

"Actually," I say. "It was a princess. We're secretly engaged. She's got dozens of these. Won't ever miss it."

"A princess? They have princesses in Korea?"

"Of course."

"And when is this betrothal date?"

"Open ended," I say. "Unless she finds out about the dress. Then it's off."

"Can I try it on?"

"Sure." And then I just about faint when she peels off her T-shirt.

"A blue T-shirt would spoil the effect," she explains, as I stare at her black bra.

She looks up at me as she lifts up the dress. "I'm not making you uncomfortable, am I?"

"Uh, no, of course not."

Then she has the dress over her head.

"Help me with this belt or sash or whatever," she says. And I help her wrap it around and she ties in front. Skips across the carpet into the downstairs bathroom. The tail of the dress behind like a shadow. Looking like the real princess.

"Wow," she is saying. I can see her turning and twisting over her shoulder to see that back. "So what kind of photo were you thinking?"

"Your department," I say. "I'm just in costumes. And by the way, there's something else in the box."

"Oh Jesus, Seth," she says. "This is too much." But she glides back across the room to the dress box and finds the smaller one. Opens it and shakes her head. Holds the gold earrings up to the light. Each is a series of gold loops which highlight the gold patterns in the dress. She takes out a stud from each ear and back in the bathroom puts on the earrings.

"OK, Mr. Gamer Boy," she says as she comes out of the bathroom. "What is this all about?"

I shrug. Tell her it's not about anything. Other than coming home. That I bought gifts for my mom and dad and brother too.

"After all," I say. "It's the first time in my life I've had the cash to do anything like this."

"And it doesn't have anything to do with you picking Brown?" She's giving me a hard look now, like I had pulled some sort of major cheat or something.

I'm shaking my head and if I look honestly puzzled it's because I am.

"You know I accepted the RISD offer?"

I shake my head, trying to remember what RISD stood for. "I don't know…"

"I told everyone. Are you telling me I forgot you?"

I really don't remember and I say so.

"And you picked Brown because?"

"I didn't really pick it," I say. "It was where my friend Professor Song went." I try to explain the circumstances. But Hannah interrupts me.

"You must think I'm really slow," Hannah says.

Now I'm really at a loss. I shake my head.

"OK, let me spell it out," she says. "I tell everyone I'm going to RISD. And then a couple of months later you tell everyone where you're going."

"And…"

"And where is Brown?"

"Providence," I say. "It's in Providence." But the fact is, from Korea it all seemed like Never-Neverland. I still wasn't thinking of Brown as a place. More like an act of God.

"And what state is Providence in?

"Rhode Island?" I answer.

"And what does the RI is RISD stand for?" Hannah has one hand on her silk-clad hip and is looking at me with what I take is total disdain.

"Rhode Island?" I say, and actually feel my heart rise. We're going to be going to college in the same state!

"And how far apart are Brown and RISD?"

"I don't know," I admit, and add lamely, "It's a big state?"

"Right. You honestly don't know? I find that hard to believe."

Now I'm thinking if Hannah had told me where she had decided to go to college I would have remembered. I'm almost sure I would have remembered.

"I could Google it," I say.

"I'm sure you could," Hannah is saying as she carefully removes one earring, then the other. Then steps out of the dress and drops it back in the box. Pulls her T-shirt over her head.

Then she steps right up to me, face to face, inches. Looking deeply into my eyes.

"How can I believe someone as smart as you could be so stupid?"

"Because you know me?" I say.

"You almost have me believing you," she says. Then her eyes soften as she leans forward gives me a kiss. On the lips. Not like the sailor kiss, but it has the same effect. It lights up my travel-weary body like an injection. The urge to grab her and pull her close is overwhelming. But I remember Garrett's advice.

She steps back. "The dress and the earrings…beautiful."

She leans over and packs the dress and the earrings up, holds the box in her crossed arms. Backs towards the door.

"You need to get some rest," she says. "And I need to do some thinking."

"OK, great," I say. Step over and open the door for her. Watch her walk onto the landing and turn back towards me. In the dark I can't tell if her eyes are sparkling or full of tears.

"And just so you don't have to bother Googling," she says. "They're five blocks apart."

I watch her turn. Watch her step down the stoop and walk down to the street all the way to the van. Put the box on the passenger's seat and then walk around the van, disappearing. Never once looking back up to the doorway where I'm still standing. The van pulls slowly away.

Five blocks? Five stinking blocks? Wondering if those five blocks just ruined my next five weeks or whether they might, just possibly, make the year to come.

The Tuttle Story

"Books to Span
the East and West"

Many people are surprised to learn that the world's largest publisher of books on Asia had its humble beginnings in the tiny American state of Vermont. The company's founder, Charles E. Tuttle, belonged to a New England family steeped in publishing.

Tuttle's father was a noted antiquarian dealer in Rutland, Vermont. Young Charles honed his knowledge of the trade working in the family bookstore, and later in the rare books section of Columbia University Library. His passion for beautiful books—old and new—never wavered throughout his long career as a bookseller and publisher.

After graduating from Harvard, Tuttle enlisted in the military and in 1945 was sent to Tokyo to work on General Douglas MacArthur's staff. He was tasked with helping to revive the Japanese publishing industry, which had been utterly devastated by the war. After his tour of duty was completed, he left the military, married a talented and beautiful singer, Reiko Chiba, and in 1948 began several successful business ventures.

To his astonishment, Tuttle discovered that postwar Tokyo was actually a book-lover's paradise. He befriended dealers in the Kanda district and began supplying rare Japanese editions to American libraries. He also imported American books to sell to the thousands of GIs stationed in Japan. By 1949, Tuttle's business was thriving, and he opened Tokyo's very first English-language bookstore in the Takashimaya Department Store in Ginza, to great success. Two years later, he began publishing books to fulfill the growing interest of foreigners in all things Asian.

Though a westerner, Tuttle was hugely instrumental in bringing a knowledge of Japan and Asia to a world hungry for information about the East. By the time of his death in 1993, he had published over 6,000 books on Asian culture, history and art—a legacy honored by Emperor Hirohito in 1983 with the "Order of the Sacred Treasure," the highest honor Japan can bestow upon a non-Japanese.

The Tuttle company today maintains an active backlist of some 1,500 titles, many of which have been continuously in print since the 1950s and 1960s—a great testament to Charles Tuttle's skill as a publisher. More than 60 years after its founding, Tuttle Publishing is more active today than at any time in its history, still inspired by Charles Tuttle's core mission—to publish fine books to span the East and West and provide a greater understanding of each.